At first Alexander thought he'd only imagined the faint knock on his door because he wanted her to come to him. It was only when he heard a second, louder knock that he responded.

"Come in," he called, his heart pounding a little faster.

His door opened and in the faint moonlight casting in through his windows he could see her silhouette in the doorway. "Did I wake you?" she asked.

"No, I'm not even close to being asleep," he replied. "Did you need something?" His voice sounded slightly hoarse to his own ears as blood rushed through his body.

"I need you."

Her voice sounded stark and his heart pressed painfully tight against his chest. "You've got me, Georgina. Whenever you need me, you've always had me."

She remained standing, as if weighing her options. "It's just for tonight, Alex. I'm using you. I'm only inviting myself into your bed for tonight, not back into your life in any meaningful way."

"So, you j_____ __ ____ advantage of me for a single night

"That's ab

"Then wh

SCENE OF
THE CRIME:
BATON ROUGE

BY
CARLA CASSIDY

Published in Great Britain 2014 ✳
by Mills & Boon, an imprint of Harlequin (UK) Limited,
Eton House, 18-24 Paradise Road, Richmond, Surrey, TW9 1SR

© 2014 Carla Bracale

ISBN: 978-0-263-91372-9

46-1014

Harlequin (UK) Limited's policy is to use papers that are natural, renewable and recyclable products and made from wood grown in sustainable forests. The logging and manufacturing processes conform to the legal environmental regulations of the country of origin.

Printed and bound in Spain
by Blackprint CPI, Barcelona

New York Times bestselling author **Carla Cassidy** is an award-winning author who has written more than fifty novels for Mills & Boon. In 1995, she won an award from *RT Book Reviews* for *Anything for Danny*. In 1998, she also won a Career Achievement Award for Best Innovative Series from *RT Book Reviews*.

Carla believes the only thing better than curling up with a good book to read is sitting down at the computer with a good story to write. She's looking forward to writing many more books and bringing hours of pleasure to readers.

Chapter One

His heart jumped just a little when he saw her. Alexander Harkins wasn't really surprised. His heart had jumped the very first time that he'd met her, and now even two years after their divorce, it was as if it was an involuntary response that he had a feeling he would never be able to control.

Special Agent Georgina Beaumont might wear her rich dark hair boyishly short, but there was nothing remotely boyish about her large green eyes fringed with long dark lashes or her classically beautiful features.

There was definitely nothing faintly masculine about her full breasts, tiny waist and long slender legs. Even in a short-sleeved white blouse and neatly tailored black slacks, she managed to look effortlessly feminine and ridiculously hot.

He was seated on the other side of the large conference room when she entered and struck up a conversation with two other FBI agents who stood near the doorway.

Since their divorce, they'd worked out of this same building but hadn't been assigned a case to work together and had only run into each other occasionally.

The fact that they were both in this same room indicated that was about to change.

A knot tightened in Alexander's chest as he speculated on what they were all about to be handed. It didn't really take much thought on the matter. He knew the people in this room had been called together to form a task force to handle the issue of missing FBI agents and their loved ones.

He was more than happy to be part of the team because the last agent who had disappeared was a close friend of his.

Jackson Revannaugh had gone to Kansas City to work a case and had returned two weeks ago with a fellow FBI agent named Marjorie who had obviously won his heart. Three days ago Marjorie and Jackson had gone missing from Jackson's lavish apartment… just like an agent and her husband in Kansas City and another agent and his wife from the nearby small town of Bachelor Moon.

Two nights before their disappearance, Alexander had met Jackson and Marjorie for dinner at a restaurant known for its creole cuisine. He'd been charmed by Marjorie, who talked as if she intended to transfer from the Kansas City bureau to Baton Rouge in order to continue the relationship with Jackson. He'd never seen his friend, famous for being an unashamed ladies' man, so taken by a woman. Alexander had definitely heard the peal of wedding bells in the not-too-distant future for the two. And now they were gone, apparently taken from their bed in the middle of a Tuesday night.

There were eight agents in the room when Director Jason Miller entered. The tall, gray-haired man would be an imposing figure under any circumstances, but at the moment, with his strong jawline throbbing with tension and his blue eyes sharp and narrowed, he looked ready to breathe fire. The agents quickly found chairs at the long conference table and fell silent.

Alexander found himself seated across from Georgina. She cast him a quick smile and then directed her focus on her boss. That little smile of hers evoked old memories that he shouldn't have retained, that should have been erased the minute he'd signed the divorce papers two years before.

He quickly turned his attention to Director Miller, already dreading the job he feared was ahead of them all. On the wall behind Miller was a whiteboard / bulletin board that at the moment was covered with a large sheet of blank white paper.

The silence in the room shattered as Miller turned to the board and ripped off that paper. The whiteboard side was pristine, ready for dry-erase markers to get to work, but the bulletin board was papered with perfectly aligned photos of the missing people.

Alexander's heart squeezed tight as he looked at the photo of seven-year-old Macy Connelly and then moved to a picture of his dark-haired, handsome friend, Jackson. There were a total of seven pictures of people who had seemingly vanished from the face of the earth over the past couple of months.

These weren't ordinary people, four of them were seasoned FBI agents, one a respected sheriff, one a beloved wife and one a precious little girl. There was circumstantial evidence that they'd all been taken unwillingly from their homes.

"We have a problem," Miller said, his voice booming in the room. "We have seven missing people, no bodies, no ransom notes and you all are going to find out what has happened to these people. Officially, you are now a task force working solely on this case."

"Why here and not in Kansas City?" Alexander asked, knowing that two of the people had disappeared from the small town of Mystic Lake, just outside of Kansas City.

"Because this morning we believe we received communication from the perp." Miller moved to the board and tapped what was obviously a copy of a note that was pinned there. "For those of you who can't see from where you're seated, it reads, 'Right under your nose I work my plan, to become the best killer in the land. I've collected my research subjects two by two, and the world will shudder when I'm through.' It's signed by the FBI-trained serial killer." Miller looked disgusted.

Several of the other men muttered curses beneath their breaths and shifted in their seats. *Right under your nose*—that implied the perp was somewhere here in the Baton Rouge area. Alexander's stomach muscles knotted. *Research subjects*—that sounded like some crazy mad scientist who was taking apart the brains of his victims, he thought grimly.

As he listened to Miller give the condensed version of each of the crimes, he focused intently and tried to keep his gaze from the woman across the table.

He knew these particular crimes had stymied the law enforcement officials in Bachelor Moon, a small town not too far from Baton Rouge, and in Mystic Lake, Missouri. There had been no clues, no forensic evidence, nothing to indicate whether the vanished were dead or alive. The note, if it could be believed, at least indicated that the person responsible was someplace in this area... right under their noses.

Already adrenaline surged through him, the eagerness for the hunt and the anticipation of the chase. As one of the agents passed around thick folders to each of the people in the room, Alexander glanced up and his gaze met Georgina's.

Her green eyes appeared electrified and he knew she felt the same flood of energy, the readiness to get to work, that he did. He tried not to remember that her eyes had also lit up like that when they were making love.

They had been married for two years and the amount of information he knew about his ex-wife could be written on a small cocktail napkin.

He frowned and focused on the contents of the folder he'd been given. It was filled with the details and reports of the FBI agents who had originally investigated each event.

"Harkins," Miller said, the stern voice pulling Alexander from his reading.

"Sir?" he replied.

"I'm appointing you lead on this. Every agent will report to you, and you will report to me."

Dread mingled with the faint tease of potential redemption. The last time he'd taken lead on an important case, a young woman had been murdered a single minute before his team had arrived, and soon after that debacle, his marriage had failed.

He'd been plunged into a depression that had lasted for weeks, haunted by the face of the murdered woman and later enduring the pain on Georgina's face as she'd told him she needed out.

He knew he was a good agent, one of the best, and he also understood that his director was showing his complete faith in him by giving him the lead in a case of such importance.

"Thank you, sir," he replied. He stared down at the reports in front of him. Although he didn't have a marriage to lose this time around, he was intensely aware that seven people were depending on him doing the best job he possibly could to lead this task force to save them.

GEORGINA WAS ACUTELY AWARE of Alexander's presence from the moment she'd entered the conference room. He was a force of nature, emanating energy as his blue eyes focused on his surroundings.

Miller had left the room and Alexander had moved to take his place at the head of the conference table. He looked confident and at ease, but she knew him well enough to recognize how important this case was to him.

It was important to her as well. It was the biggest case she'd ever worked and, as the only woman in a roomful of men, she was desperate to prove that she was more than up to everyone's standards.

She'd spent her five-year career with the FBI trying to raise herself from being a good agent to a great one and this was the kind of case that could make that happen for her.

"We'll spend our first couple of hours here going over the contents of the folders and getting familiar with what's already happened and where we are now," Alexander said. "We'll start with what happened in Bachelor Moon."

She listened to his deep rich voice detail the fact that former FBI agent Sam Connelly, his wife Daniella and Daniella's seven-year-old daughter had disappeared during what had appeared to be a late-night snack session in their kitchen. Cookies and milk had been half consumed and a chair had been overturned, indicating that something untoward had occurred.

Although he looked calm and focused, she knew the torture he'd suffered the last time he'd been lead on a case that had gone bad. It had been a torment that had highlighted all her failings as a wife—as a person—and had ultimately forced her to make the decision that he was better off without her.

But that was then and this was now, she reminded herself. She couldn't dwell on the past, she needed to get her mind in this game, to prove she was as good as, if not better than, every other agent in the room.

"The second disappearance occurred in Mystic Lake, Missouri," Alexander continued. "Amberly Caldwell, an FBI agent, and her husband, Cole, the local sheriff disappeared from Cole's home. Our own Jackson Revannaugh was sent to Kansas City to help in that particular investigation. And then, as you all should know by now, three nights ago Jackson and his girlfriend, an FBI agent from Kansas City, went missing."

"How do we know that Jackson just didn't take his honey off somewhere for a few days?" Agent Nicholas Cutter asked. "He was on vacation for another week or so, wasn't he?"

"Yes, but according to the agents who investigated Jackson's house last night, all their identifications, their weapons and personal items were still in the bedroom where we assume they were sleeping," Alexander replied.

Georgina shot a glance at Nicholas. He was relatively new to the bureau and already had a reputation for being a hotshot wanting to make a name for himself. While she shared the same desire, she was a team player and she wasn't sure that Nicholas cared about any team.

She rarely made snap judgments about anyone, but the first time she'd met Nicholas Cutter, she hadn't particularly liked him. Still, she was a professional and never, ever let her personal feelings show. In her job this ability was a blessing. In her personal life it had been a curse.

"I want you all to take some time now and read through all the reports, look at all the photos that are included in your folders and familiarize yourself with everything that's been done so far with all the different law enforcement agencies that have been involved," Alexander said.

He returned to his seat across from her and the room fell silent except for the turning of pages as each of the agents began to learn the details of what had been accomplished through the different investigations and what was ahead of them.

Despite the fact that September had arrived on Wednesday, two days before, brilliant warm sunshine drifted into the windows and dust motes floated in the air.

Georgina was a fast reader and easily retained what

she read. She was finished long before the others and leaned back in her chair, hoping to escape the faint scent of Alexander that drifted across the table.

He wore the same spicy cologne he'd worn when they had been married. The scent of it stirred not only memories of being held in his arms, of making love, but also a depth of failure she had tried for two years to put behind her.

She looked back down at the folder and opened it to the photos of the victims. Failure was not an option now. She might not make friends easily, she might be incapable of any real intimacy with anyone, but she was going to work her butt off to find out what happened to these people.

"I think they're still alive," she said, breaking the silence that had filled the room. "We have no bodies, and the note, if it's really from the perp, implies he's keeping them as some sort of scientific study."

"I agree," Agent Tim Gardier replied. He was the youngest agent in the room. Painfully thin, with glasses and a head full of red hair that had probably not seen a barbershop in the last five years, he was also a genius computer geek and a genuinely nice guy.

"I don't know, maybe we just haven't stumbled on their bodies yet," Nicholas said.

Georgina mentally groaned. Just what they all needed, negativity at the very beginning of an investigation.

"It would be quite a challenge to house and feed seven captives," Agent Frank Webb added. "Especially if only one person is responsible for all this."

"It's too early in the investigation to make the assessment that we're only hunting one perpetrator," Alexander said. "What I hope is that the note received this morning really is from our man, and I hope it's the beginning of him becoming chatty."

"He hasn't had much to say until now," Nicholas said, a frown cutting across his broad forehead. "We don't even know if he's finished or if he intends to kidnap more people."

"You're right," Alexander said with a touch of impatience in his voice. "We don't know much of anything about this person. We don't know if he has enough 'research subjects.' We don't even know if his plans for more subjects include someone in this room."

These words sobered everyone. Their discussion lasted until one o'clock in the afternoon at which time Alexander called for a lunch break.

"Everyone back here at two o'clock sharp and I'll start breaking this down with assignments," he said.

Alexander was still seated in his chair with his focus on the contents of the folder as Georgina and the rest of the agents left the room.

She had no idea where the others were going, but she found herself walking next to Tim, who was obviously heading in the same direction as she was, to the cafeteria in the basement of the building.

"I have a feeling we'd better fuel up while we can," Tim said as they stepped into the elevator to ride down two floors. "I'm seeing long hours and few breaks in my future."

She gazed up at him, noting that the lights in the elevator turned his red hair into a furry ball of orange. "Have you worked with Alexander before?"

"Never as lead, but he has a reputation for being tough and driven. You should know how he works." The elevator stopped and the doors opened, and together they followed the hallway that would lead them to the cafeteria.

"He's definitely tough and driven," she replied.

Alexander had always been driven, it was part of what had attracted her to him in the first place. She could only imagine since the Gilmer case, which had gone wrong the last time he'd been lead investigator, that his drive for success was even deeper.

She grabbed a salad and Tim took two cheeseburgers and fries and they found a quiet table in the corner that suited them both. She knew Tim was comfortable with her, but like her, he wasn't necessarily a people person.

They ate quickly, not talking about the work ahead of them, but rather Tim explaining about a new computer program he was working on. Georgina found most of his talk gobbledygook, but she apparently nodded and murmured in the right places for he seemed pleased with both her and himself by the time they had finished their meal.

When they returned to the "war" room, Alexander was still in the same place he'd been when they'd left, letting her know he hadn't taken a lunch break.

She wasn't surprised. There had been many times during their marriage when they'd been working separate cases that she'd have to remind him to stop and eat or to fall into bed and catch a couple hours of sleep.

She knew how he worked. Without anyone in his life to tell him to slow down, he'd go until he crashed and burned. But he wasn't her worry anymore, she reminded herself.

She and Tim were followed into the room by most of the rest of the team. Nobody wanted to be the last one back from lunch.

The minute everyone was seated, Alexander once again went to the head of the table. "Right now we're all going to function on the supposition that the note we received is real, that our perp is holding these people and he's from the Baton Rouge area," he began. "I'm assigning Tim and Jeff to work on getting locations of all abandoned buildings and warehouses on the outskirts of town. If this person is holding seven people captive, then it would be in a place where nobody would see his activity and nobody could hear our victims scream." His jaw tightened.

Georgina's stomach clenched as she thought of seven people, including a little girl, yelling for help or shrieking with pain, from a place where nobody could hear them. Her determination to hunt and find, to capture and end this case, filled every cell in her body.

It was a familiar, welcome emotion, one where she dwelled most of the time. Work was her life…despite the dangers of being an FBI agent, it felt safer to her than personal relationships or friendships. She knew her failings and she did neither of those well.

"I want Nicholas and Frank to work on finding some sort of connection between all these missing people, besides the obvious that four of them were FBI agents," Alexander continued.

"Isn't that enough of a connection?" Frank asked as he raked a hand through his thinning gray hair.

"I don't think so. If that was the case, why would our perp go all the way to Mystic Lake? Why take somebody from Bachelor Moon? If all he wanted was random FBI agents, then he could have taken his pick from people who work right here. There has to be more of a connection. It feels to me like these people were specifically targeted, and we need to find out why."

"We'll get on it," Nicholas replied with a firm nod of his head.

Alexander looked at the last two male agents in the room. Terry Connors and Matt Campbell, both seasoned agents who were known for their attention to detail.

"I want you two to go over all the information we have from both the Bachelor Moon and the Mystic Lake disappearances and maybe your fresh eyes can see some detail, something that so far has been missed. You can travel to Bachelor Moon, but at this point, will interact with Mystic Lake authorities by phone or whatever. As we go along, if you need to travel there, we'll make arrangements."

Georgina tensed as she realized she was the only person in the room who hadn't been handed a specific assignment. Alexander's blue gaze met hers.

"Georgina, you'll be working with me, and we're going to start at Jackson Revannaugh's apartment and continue the investigation into his and Marjorie's disappearance."

She made sure her face revealed no emotion other than compliance, although she'd rather work with anyone on the team other than Alexander.

In the past two years they had managed to have very little interaction with each other and that had suited her just fine. Apparently he intended the two of them to work as partners within the task force.

I can do this, she told herself. She could remain professional and not tap into any memories that belonged to the two of them alone, memories that served only to remind her of what a pathetic life partner she had been.

There would always be a piece of her heart that would carry the Alexander brand, but it had nearly been buried now, and there was no digging it up, not that she thought he might want to.

All she wanted to do was find the bad guy and rescue the people who needed them. If working closely with Alexander helped her achieve that goal, then she was more than prepared for the challenge.

Chapter Two

It was nearly four o'clock when Georgina got into the passenger side of Alexander's company car. She buckled in as he slid behind the steering wheel, his energy a fierce entity that instantly filled the interior of the car.

He'd pulled on a lightweight black suit jacket that hid his shoulder holster and gun, but he still was a commanding presence without the show of firepower. She preferred a belt holster that she'd pulled on before they left.

"How have you been? I haven't seen you around for a couple of weeks," he said as he started the engine and then headed for the parking lot exit.

"Busy. I was working on the Browning fraud case. We managed to tie things up yesterday. Mr. Browning should be spending quite some time in prison."

"Chalk up another one for the good guys," he replied.

Georgina tried to relax against the seat, but it was difficult to find any relaxation at the moment. Her heart beat with a quickened rhythm. She assumed it was caused by the knowledge of the case she was now working and not how Alexander's familiar cologne filled the air.

"You met Jackson's new girlfriend?" she asked.

"I had dinner with the two of them last Sunday night, and then we were supposed to meet for drinks on Tuesday evening. When they didn't show and I still couldn't get hold of Jackson all day Wednesday, I knew in my gut that something was wrong. Last night, at my urging, Miller sent a couple of agents over to check on Jackson, and that's when they discovered they were gone, but all of their personal items were still there."

She saw the tightening of his fingers around the steering wheel and knew he had to be worried sick about Jackson's well-being. "What was she like? The woman from Kansas City?"

"She's Special Agent Marjorie Clinton." A hint of a smile curved his lips. "She's everything that Jackson isn't…she likes healthy food, she thinks he's full of baloney most of the time and it's obvious they are crazy in love."

"Jackson needs a good woman in his life," she replied.

"It appears he's found her." He frowned. "Now all we have to do is find them."

"It isn't possible they flew back to Kansas City if their identifications were left behind," she said, thinking out loud.

"They wouldn't have gone anywhere without his wallet and her purse, both of which were left at Jackson's place. And they definitely wouldn't have gone anyplace without their weapons."

"Any sign of a struggle in the bedroom?"

He shook his head, the late-afternoon sun gleaming on his black hair. "I haven't been to the scene, but according to the two agents who checked it out last night there were some bedcovers rustled, but no real sign of a violent struggle and, trust me, Jackson would have put up quite a fight. I'm hoping maybe you and I can find or see something they missed that might give us a clue."

"There weren't any clues found in Bachelor Moon or Mystic Lake," she replied.

A new knot of tension formed in his jaw. "Don't remind me." He pulled into the driveway of the luxury apartment complex where Jackson lived.

The Wingate apartments were set up more like condo units and definitely were for the wealthy who didn't want the responsibility that came with owning a home.

Jackson's unit was on the end of the last building in the complex, bumping up against a heavily wooded area and attached by a common courtyard entrance to the unit next door.

"Any sign of forced entry?" she asked as the car came to a halt.

"Not according to the initial walk-through." He cut the engine and turned to look at her, his blue eyes like hard-edged sapphires. "We either have a perp who is an expert at picking locks or, knowing Jackson, it's possible he went to bed without checking that all the doors were locked. He always thought he was invincible." Frustration deepened the tone of his voice.

"Then let's just hope that whatever has happened to him, he remains invincible," she replied.

He cast her a quicksilver smile that lingered only for a moment, just long enough to whisper heat through her. "Let's get inside and see what we can find." He opened his car door and was halfway to the courtyard entry as she hurried to catch up to him.

They had just reached the fence that led to the courtyard when a figure stepped out of the woods. Alexander filled his hand with his gun in the blink of an eye and then muttered a curse and jammed it back into his shoulder holster.

"Jeez, Joe, do you want to get yourself shot?"

FBI agent Joe Markum stepped closer to them with a wry grin. "Jeez, Harkins, are you trying to give me a heart attack?"

"You know my motto…shoot first and ask questions later," Alexander replied. "What are you doing out here?"

"I was assigned late last night to sit on the place to make sure nobody except appropriate officials gained access. Somebody should be arriving soon to take my place, but I'm assuming it isn't you two." He nodded to Georgina with a friendly smile.

"We're here to investigate," she said. "Miller formed a task force this morning and Alexander is leading it."

"And we're hoping to find something that was missed last night," Alexander said.

"Knock yourselves out." Joe gestured toward the front door. "It's unlocked and there's protective gear in boxes on the porch."

"Thanks," Alexander said and together he and Georgina walked through the gate and to the front door where a box of booties and latex gloves awaited whomever might venture into the house.

Georgina pulled on the protective gear and once again her heart began to beat faster. She'd never been in Jackson's home before, but it was the fact that she was about to enter what they'd already determined to be a crime scene that had her adrenaline flooding through her.

As she followed Alexander into the house, she tried not to notice how his lightweight suit jacket pulled over his broad shoulders, how his black slacks fit perfectly around his slim waist and down his long legs.

She tried not to remember what it had felt like to dance her fingers over his naked muscled chest, how her legs had often twined with his when they'd made love.

They had been great in the bedroom. It had only been when they got out of bed that she hadn't been able to get the relationship right. She firmly shoved these thoughts out of her mind as they entered Jackson's living room.

Jackson was the epitome of a Southern man and his furnishings reflected the style of warmth and invitation that would have done any Southerner proud.

The oversize sofa was a rich burgundy and gold print, flanked by burgundy wing-backed chairs. The coffee table was a large square of wood that held a gorgeous floral arrangement. The room was beautiful, but obviously rarely used and not the center of the home.

"Nothing looks like it's been touched in here," Alexander said as he moved into the next room, a large great room more casually decorated and obviously the space where Jackson spent much of his time.

A huge flat-screen television hung over a stone fireplace and two leather recliners provided the perfect places to sit and watch a movie or dancing flames. Again, it appeared as if nothing untoward had occurred in this room. There was no sign of a struggle or anything amiss.

Neither of them spoke as they entered the kitchen with its large table and variety of pots and pans hanging from a baker's rack on the wall. Everything was neat and tidy and she watched as Alexander dragged a hand through his dark hair.

"I guess the report we got that they were taken from their bed is true. Nothing seems to be out of place down here. We should head upstairs."

She nodded and once again found herself following him up the stairs that led to three bedrooms and two baths. The first two bedrooms and the hallway bathroom showed nothing untoward.

She felt her entire body tense as they approached the master bedroom. She stepped into the room just behind her partner. The king-size bed was unmade. The sheets trailed off to the floor on the closest side of the bed to the door.

"That bedding doesn't look normal to me," Alexander said as he stood still as a statue, his gaze lingering on the bed.

"By the way the sheets are hanging off, it looks like somebody was dragged from the bed," Georgina observed.

"I agree." The knot in his jaw throbbed as he pointed to the farthest nightstand. "But, how could anyone drag them out of bed when Jackson had his gun right next to him."

The gun was on the nightstand next to a silver-and-black lamp, an easy reach even in the darkness of night. "Maybe he drugged them? Drugged the food they ate before they came to bed? Slipped something in their drinks?" Her mind raced to make sense of the scene.

"I'll have the crime scene guys come back and check everything that's in the refrigerator to see if they find anything tainted by drugs."

He remained standing at the foot of the bed, staring at the room as if in a trance. Georgina did nothing to break his focus. She knew this was part of his process, this concentration that he used in an effort to see the crime as it happened, to understand any clues that might have been left behind.

She wondered if he still had nightmares. If somebody was seeing to it that he ate right. She'd heard no rumors that he was dating anyone, but that didn't mean he wasn't. He'd had two years to move on, and two years was a long time for a man to be alone, especially a man as vital, as alive as Alexander.

"Were the lights on or off?" He finally broke his trance and turned to look at her. "Do you remember from the report if the lights in here were off or on when the first agents arrived on scene?"

She frowned thoughtfully, trying to picture the initial report. "Off," she finally replied. "Jackson is a big man. If they were both somehow drugged, then how did our perp move their unconscious bodies from here to a waiting vehicle down the stairs and outside?"

Alexander looked closely at the carpeting around the bed where the covers trailed to the floor and then stepped out of the room and stared down the long hallway toward the staircase.

He turned back to Georgina, a deep frown cutting across his forehead. "I don't know."

"Maybe they weren't drugged at all," she said thoughtfully. "Maybe the perp just got the drop on them, appeared in the doorway with a gun pointed at Marjorie, making it impossible for Jackson to take a chance at grabbing his own gun."

"Maybe," he replied absently. "Let me take a look in the master bath to see if there's anything there and then let's get out of here."

He disappeared into the bathroom and Georgina felt his pain, his worry for his friend resonating in her heart. He'd been given a huge job, made all the more important because his good friend was now one of the missing.

The Gilmer case had given him nightmares and thrown him into a black hole that she feared he would never climb out of. If he was unsuccessful on this case, she feared it would completely and utterly destroy him.

"It's six-thirty, you want to stop by Nettie's and grab something to eat and talk about all the things we don't know about this case?" he asked Georgina when they were back in the car and headed away from Jackson's place. "I don't know about you, but I haven't eaten anything today except a bagel early this morning."

She hesitated only a moment before replying. "Sure, Nettie's sounds like a plan. Besides, if I say no, you probably won't eat anything tonight."

He smiled tightly. "I always did hate to eat alone."

The restaurant was a favorite place for the FBI agents to grab meals as it was only a block away from the building where they all worked. The prices were reasonable, the portions generous and the food was delicious.

He tried to fight against the discouragement that attempted to work its way into his psyche. He'd hoped to find something at Jackson's place, but given the fact that the other two crime scenes had yielded nothing in the way of clues, he shouldn't be surprised that nothing had been found there, either.

Reminding himself that he'd had the case less than twenty-four hours, he wanted to eat and then take the files he had on the previous cases home to study them all again.

Before they'd all left the office, he'd told the team to be in the war room at seven the next morning, even though it was Saturday. Weekends and holidays would have no meaning at all until this case was solved.

The fact that nobody from the team had contacted him while he and Georgina had been gone meant none of them had anything to report. Hopefully by morning that would change.

They remained silent on the rest of the drive to the restaurant. He knew it was probably a mistake partnering himself with Georgina, given their history. He also knew how bright, how dedicated she was to the job, and that because of her knowledge of him and his habits, she'd make the perfect partner.

He pulled into the crowded parking lot. Nettie's on a Friday night was busy, but he hoped that he and Georgina could grab a booth in the back where they could talk in relative privacy.

Nettie's had an identity issue. While the food was more along the lines of home cooking, the interior was dim, with candles lit at each table as if it was pretending to be a fine-dining place.

Nettie greeted them at the door with a wide smile.

"Two of my favorite agents," she said. She was a testament to the good food she served. Short and wide with brassy red hair, it was rumored that she'd once scared away a young would-be thief by wielding a large wooden spoon and threatening to spank his ass clean off his body with it.

As Alexander had hoped, she led them to a booth in the back of the restaurant where the noise of the other diners was less audible and he and Georgina would be able to talk without shouting.

The moment they slid into the booth across from each other with the candlelight glowing on Georgina's face, a sense of déjà vu struck him and brought with it a sense of loss he'd never quite recovered from.

They'd eaten out often during the early days of their marriage in places where candlelight had bathed her beauty in a golden glow. At those times her eyes had glimmered with a love that had showered him with warmth.

Now that glimmer was gone and in its place was the pleasant but focused gaze of professionalism. *As it should be,* he reminded himself.

The waitress arrived with menus and to take drink orders. Georgina went with a Cobb salad while he ordered a steak and baked potato. They each ordered a glass of wine.

"This is going to be a tough one," Georgina said. "FBI agents in two different locations haven't come up with any clues to help apprehend or identify a suspect."

"True, but we possibly have something they didn't have," he replied.

"The note."

"Exactly. If it's the real deal, then we have the first communication from the unsub and I'm hoping it won't be the last."

She unfurled the cloth napkin to reveal her silverware and placed the napkin in her lap as the waitress arrived with their wine. "I don't want to be negative, but you know it's possible that note is from some crackpot, or that single note will be all we get from him," she replied once the waitress had left the table.

"I know, but I've got a gut feeling that this guy is the real deal and at a place where he wants to crow about his victories."

She smiled. "Rumor has it that your gut is rarely wrong. It will be interesting to see if he makes any more contact with us."

They sipped their wine, falling into a silence that he'd often experienced when married to Georgina. She'd never been good at small talk, as if afraid she might somehow give away a piece of herself she could never get back.

"How's life treating you?" he asked, perversely forcing the small talk issue while they waited for their meals to be delivered.

"Fine. I spend most of my time at work, which is how I like it."

"Are you seeing anyone?"

She raised one of her dark eyebrows wryly. "I don't have time to see anyone, and in any case I'm not looking for a relationship. What about you?"

He shook his head. "There's nobody in my life. Like you, I work so much it's hard to even think about starting a relationship with anyone."

He didn't say it aloud, but the truth was that the woman across the table from him had burned him so badly he had no interest in getting close to the fire ever again.

"I have a feeling we're all going to be putting in a lot of hours with this one," she said, deftly turning the subject back to work issues.

"I can't help but think that somehow there's a connection between the victims…the FBI agents who were taken. It has to be a connection beyond the fact that they were FBI agents—perhaps their specific expertise—otherwise why take Sam Connelly from Bachelor Moon? Why go all the way to Missouri to snatch Agent Amberly Caldwell and then come back here to take Jackson?"

"So, you believe the people who were taken with the agents weren't just collateral damage?" she asked.

The conversation halted as the waitress appeared with their dinners. Alexander waited until she'd moved away once again and then replied, "They could be some sort of leverage. There's no better way to get a man to talk than to threaten his wife or his child."

"But, Sam was a retired agent. He hadn't worked actively as an agent for some time," Georgina reminded him.

"True, but he left the agency with the reputation of being one of the best profilers in the country."

Georgina took a bite of her salad, a tiny frown of concentration dancing across her forehead. "Is it possible that somehow Sam, Jackson and Amberly all worked a case together?"

"Sam and Jackson might have worked together in

the past, but I can't imagine how Amberly figures in. She wouldn't have been a part of any investigations that Sam and Jackson might have worked here in Louisiana."

"Even peripherally?"

He gazed at her thoughtfully. "I don't know. That's definitely something we should check out. We need to find out about any cases Sam and Jackson might have worked together and how, if at all, Amberly might figure in."

"Maybe Nicholas and Frank will have something for us tomorrow morning," she said.

"The sooner the better," he replied.

They fell quiet as they focused on their meals. Alexander found himself remembering all the silences that had filled the two years of their marriage.

For the first six months or so, Alexander hadn't noticed it. Captivated by her passion, eager to share who he was as a man, what he wanted for their future, he'd talked enough for both of them. He'd been crazy in love with her and thought she'd felt the same.

It was only after she'd left that he realized the marriage had been a one-sided disaster. They were great in bed, they could talk late into the night about the cases they were working on, but when the conversation turned personal she grew silent.

He knew her parents were alive and that she had two older sisters, but she was estranged from all of them. She never told him what had caused the estrangement, in fact had told him she rarely thought about her family.

She knew everything about his childhood, but he knew nothing about hers. She'd been adept at changing the subject when the conversation got too personal and he'd been too crazy about her to mind.

When he'd decided to partner with her on this case, he'd thought he was choosing her because he knew her work ethic matched his own and he believed she was one of the brightest agents on the team.

Now, as he gazed at her across the candlelit table, he wondered if there wasn't more to his decision. Perhaps he not only wanted her by his side to help in the investigation, but maybe he was also hoping that by spending more time with her, he would finally unlock the mystery of Georgina.

Chapter Three

Georgina awoke the next morning just after five-thirty, her mind already whirling with the horror of the night-mare that had plagued her for years.

The dream was always the same. She was in a dark, small space, her stomach growling with hunger as the scent of food drifted in the air. No matter how hard she tried, she couldn't escape the dark place except by awakening.

Never one to linger in bed, by the time six o'clock arrived she was showered and dressed and in the kitchen waiting for the coffee to quit brewing.

She had thirty minutes to relax until she'd have to leave to get to the FBI offices by seven. Minutes later she sat at her table with a cup of the fresh brew in hand. As she played over the events of the day before, the last thing she could find was any kind of relaxation.

Already she felt tension riding her shoulders, a knot of anxiety in the pit of her stomach. It was bad enough that they had a complicated case where they didn't even know if the kidnapped victims were dead or alive.

As the only woman on the task force, she felt extreme pressure to overachieve, to prove herself to be the best that she could be.

It didn't help that Alexander had chosen to partner up with her. He reminded her of her biggest failure, not as an agent, but as a woman. She couldn't imagine why he would make the choice he did when he could have partnered her with any other member of the task force.

She sipped her coffee and stared out the window to the tiny fenced-in backyard. She had bought this small house three months after her divorce. It had been a bargain buy, as the place had been on the market for two years.

The Realtor who had sold it to her had explained that the small size of the two-bedroom house made it unappealing to any couple planning for a family or any family looking for a home.

It was perfect for Georgina, who knew there would never be a man in her life again, who knew there would never be any children. The spare bedroom was now an office, and she'd done little to decorate other than buying utilitarian furniture and hanging a couple of cheap landscape pictures on the walls.

She took another drink of her coffee and thought of the seven missing people and the note that had been sent to headquarters. If it was real, then it held a hint of crowing, of an ego that needed to be heard.

She could only hope that the ego needed constant feeding and the perp would maintain contact. It was often through some sort of communication that they got clues and found leads to follow in difficult cases.

At exactly six-thirty she left her small house and headed into work. Although it was only a fifteen-minute drive, she'd rather be a little early than late.

As she drove, she carefully kept her thoughts away

from Alex. She had no idea how the past two years might have changed him and didn't want to remember the man he'd been when she'd walked out on him.

She'd have to walk a fine line to remain strictly on a partner level and not allow herself to fall into anything personal. She couldn't emotionally afford to make a second mistake where he was concerned.

The Baton Rouge FBI field office was located in an unassuming two-story building nestled between a dry cleaning store and a bank. She drove around to the back of the building where there was a large parking lot and pulled into one of the empty spaces. She grabbed the file folder that had kept her up reading reports and looking at photos far too late the night before, and then left her car.

The sultry morning air pressed oppressively against her chest. Or was it just the anxiety of the case and the uncertainty of working closely with her ex-husband?

The bottom floor of the building was dedicated to computer rooms and bookkeeping; the basement held storage and a cafeteria. It was on the second floor that agents actively worked at their own desks.

This morning she passed by her neat and tidy desk to head down the hallway to the conference room that now housed the task force. The scent of fresh coffee greeted her as she stepped into the room, finding Alex and Nicholas Cutter already there.

A large coffeepot had been set up on a side table, along with several boxes of doughnuts. The cliché of law enforcement at all levels. But Georgina knew as well as anyone that the sugar rush of a doughnut and the caffeine of a hot cup of coffee often provided the energy needed to get through long hours.

She smiled at the two men as she entered and sat in the same chair she'd sat in the day before. While Nicholas looked energized and eager, Alex's face wore the faint lines of fatigue. Like her, he'd probably been up most of the night going over the files of the previous kidnappings.

Before either of the two men had a chance to greet her, other members of the team began to arrive and soon the room was full. Once they'd all found seats, Alex eyed them with a weary resignation. "How many of you saw the news this morning that broke the story that a seven-man, one-woman task force had been formed to investigate the disappearances of FBI agents?"

"I saw it and I'd like to know who leaked it," Frank said irritably. "We hadn't had much publicity about these disappearances until now."

"At least it didn't list our names," Jeff said.

"You know any reporter worth his salt will have our names by the end of the day," Nicholas added.

"If I find out anyone in this room leaked anything to the press, I'll have your job." Alex's voice didn't hold a threat, but rather held a determined promise. "Now, let's get to the updates."

The first came from Tim and Jeff, who had spent the day before with both paper maps and working on the internet to locate vacant buildings that were isolated enough for seven people to be held captive.

"There's dozens of places," Tim said. "There are abandoned warehouses and old factories all over the surrounding areas and within the city."

"We're making a list of addresses and working through city records to find out owner names," Jeff said. "But it's going to take at least a week or two for us to get them all and even then there might be some places that slip through the cracks."

"I'll check with Director Miller and see if we can get some help from the local authorities to physically check out the places on the list you're compiling," Alexander said.

It wasn't unusual for the FBI to occasionally work with the Baton Rouge Police Department when it came to a job too big for the agents to handle alone. The police would be able to cruise by the buildings and check them out in person, lightening the manpower needed for the actual footwork of the investigative end of things for the FBI.

Despite the tired lines that creased his forehead and made the small wrinkles around his eyes look deeper, Georgina couldn't help but notice that Alex hadn't changed much in the two years they'd been apart. His shoulders were just as broad, his stomach as flat and the air of command that emanated from him came naturally.

He was born to lead, and if it hadn't been for the Gilmer case, he would have led most of the difficult investigations that had come along in the past couple of years. She knew he'd been asked to be lead in other cases but had declined, indicating a lack of faith in himself. She was glad he'd finally decided to step up once again.

There was no question that if she allowed it, she would be attracted to him again. All the qualities that she'd fallen in love with in the first place he still possessed. But she couldn't allow it and besides, he'd given no indication that he wanted it.

Although there had been little change in him physically in the last two years, she had no idea what changes had occurred on the inside. The one thing she knew for sure was that nothing had changed her. She'd been wrong for him then and she'd be wrong for him again.

She tightened her fingers around the pen she held, telling herself it was vital she maintain her objectivity where he was concerned. Alex was nothing more than her partner, her immediate boss, and that's the way it would stay for as long as they knew each other.

When Jeff and Tim had finished their report, Alex moved on to Nicholas and Frank. "We've got nothing," Frank said, his brown eyes dark with frustration. "We went through social media, used Google on all the names of the missing people, used Google on the FBI agents, and nothing popped up to tie them together other than the fact that they are all agents."

"Actually, I found something," Nicholas said, a touch of smugness in his voice as his partner looked at him in obvious surprise. "There's an author who has a new book out and the book includes sections about Sam Connelly, Amberly Caldwell and Jackson."

A touch of new disdain swept through Georgina. It was obvious Nicholas had blindsided his partner, kept the information to himself so that he would get all the glory of the find. Nicholas Cutter was definitely not a team player and that was a big strike against him as far as Georgina was concerned.

"Continue," Alexander's voice was like a gunshot in the room.

"The author's name is Michelle Davison and the book is titled *Heinous Crimes / Men of Honor*." Nicholas sat up straighter in his chair, obviously pleased to be the center of attention. "She has a section about Sam Connelly, who was head investigator when four children were kidnapped and he successfully recovered them. Amberly Caldwell is showcased for her work on what was called the Dream Catcher murders in Mystic Lake. She also has the details of the case Jackson worked a year ago…the Twilight Killer."

As much as Georgina hated Nicholas's showboating, his information sent a rush of excitement through her. This was the first definitive tie they'd found among the three.

"Do we have an address for Michelle Davison?" Alexander asked.

"She lives in New Orleans, but I spoke to her literary agent last night and Michelle is set up to have a book signing right here at the Baton Rouge College bookstore at seven tonight," Nicholas said.

"Georgina and I will attend the book signing and do an initial interview with her," Alexander said, ignoring how Nicholas's smile fell into a pouty frown. He'd obviously hoped to do the interview himself.

One of the agents had moved a box of doughnuts into the center of the table and Frank reached for one. "I don't see how a woman writer could have anything to do with kidnapping seven people. There's no way I believe we're dealing with a female perp." He took a bite of his doughnut and grabbed a napkin as raspberry filling fell down his chin.

"We all have to keep an open mind," Nicholas said.

"At this point we can't know if the perp is male or female or even a team. We just don't have enough information to make that call."

"That's right," Alex answered. "Matt and Terry, anything new on your end?"

"Not yet," Matt replied. "But we're digging for anything we can find."

As he continued to reaffirm assignments for the day, Georgina was already eager for the night to come. This was their first real lead and she couldn't wait for them to follow it.

"Nicholas, get me everything you can on Michelle Davison by noon. Frank, continue to look for other connections between the missing people. Georgina, you and I are going to get the files of the cases that this author showcased in her book and see if we can figure out exactly why she chose these particular cases, these particular agents to write about."

Georgina nodded. Catching a killer was rarely like it was shown on television, with high-speed chases and shoot-outs in dark alleys.

So much of the work to catch a killer took place in chairs, researching the victims' lives, going through reports until you were nearly blind, searching the web for something, anything, that might burp up a clue.

Granted, they didn't know if this particular unsub was a killer or not, but he or she was definitely a serial kidnapper and these cases would be investigated as if they were chasing a killer.

Her gaze drifted up to the bulletin board where the victims' photos remained. Her focus was drawn to the little girl who had vanished with her parents.

Of all the people showcased on the board, Macy Connelly would be the most expendable. The seven-year-old would be of no use to the kidnapper, especially a kidnapper who claimed to be an FBI-trained serial killer.

Georgina had always loved children, but even when she'd been married she had never envisioned having any of her own. She knew what she was capable of giving and it had never been enough to be a mother.

Still, there was something that haunted her about Macy Connelly, an emotion that skewered deep into her soul. It was as if Macy might have been the daughter she and Alex would have had if Georgina had been different, if she had been whole.

She could only hope and pray that they could solve this case before something tragic happened to the agents and their spouses, before something tragic happened to the blond-haired, blue-eyed little angel who appeared to be personally pleading with Georgina for help.

THAT EVENING AT SIX-THIRTY when Alexander pulled into Georgina's driveway and she stepped out on the porch, he was immediately sorry that he'd told her not to dress like an FBI agent, but rather as a woman attending a social function.

She walked toward the car clad in a short, green dress that he recognized as the dress she'd worn on their second date. The only difference was that she'd added a gold belt around the fitted waist.

Didn't she buy new clothes? Did she even remember that the green dress had been one of his favorites? Probably not. Georgina wasn't particularly sentimental. She was pragmatic and dealt only in the present.

In the brief time he'd been her husband he'd realized she didn't dwell on the past and she rarely looked to the future. She was always in the here and now, and there had been times during their marriage it had made him slightly crazy.

She opened the passenger door and slid in, gold hoop earrings dancing on her ears as the familiar scent of her perfume filled the air. She exuded a thrumming energy as she greeted him and then buckled her seat belt.

"You look nice," he said as he backed out of her driveway.

"Thanks, so do you."

He didn't look all that different from what he looked like every day. The only difference was his black slacks were paired with a black-and-blue pin-striped shirt instead of the regular white dress shirt. His blazer was the same one that had been slung across the back of a chair for most of the day.

"I'm so excited," she continued. "We've only been at it for a day and already a lead has come to light."

"We don't know how good this lead might be," he replied in an attempt to temper her enthusiasm. "The odds that we're going to solve these crimes tonight by attending a college bookstore autographing session are pretty minimal."

"True, but at least it's a place to start." She shifted positions to face him more fully. "We'll solve this one, Alex. We'll solve it and save every single one of those people."

The diminutive use of his name felt both familiar and intimate and he shoved away the wave of warmth that suffused him as he heard it. She was the only person in his life who had called him Alex. Both professionally and personally he'd always been Alexander.

"We're a long way from a solve, but I hope your optimism plays out," he said gruffly.

Damn her green dress and her use of Alex. The last thing he needed was to get lost in memories, in questions from the past that would splinter his attention. He needed to remain focused on the case and nothing else.

The Baton Rouge College campus was both huge and beautiful. Stately stone buildings were linked together by tree-lined sidewalks, and courtyards with benches invited students to gather for impromptu study sessions or social activities.

The bookstore was along a side street, and Alexander was surprised to discover the parking lot next to it full. He found an open curbside space about a block away and he and Georgina got out of the car to walk in the sultry evening air. "Feels more like early August than September," Alexander said.

"It is warm. Looks like she's drawn quite a crowd," Georgina said.

"Murder and mayhem always sell well," Alexander replied with a touch of disgust.

Georgina shot him a quick smile. "You can't blame people for being interested in the same things we are. If the readers who buy these kinds of books are freaks, then that makes you and me super freaks."

Alexander laughed, knowing that she was right. Neither of them would be where they were if they weren't drawn to the dark side of humanity.

He fought the impulse to place his hand at the center of her back as they walked side by side, as he used to do. It had always been a proprietary touch and he hadn't had that right for two years.

Focus, he thought as they entered the door to the busy bookstore. This job was his chance to stanch the nightmares of failure that played over and over again in his head. He was haunted by a single dead young woman; he couldn't imagine seven people haunting him if he didn't get this job done right.

Alexander estimated Michelle Davison to be in her mid-thirties. She was an attractive blonde with blue eyes and appeared to be greeting her fans with genuine warmth and friendliness.

There was a long line before her, and as he and Georgina fell into the line, he also noted the man who stood just behind the table where Michelle sat.

Tall and muscular, although he was neatly dressed in slacks and a short-sleeved white shirt, he looked like a thug. A tattoo rode the side of his neck and others crept up his muscled arms. Boyfriend? Bodyguard? Partner in crime?

Alexander couldn't help the suppositions that raced through his mind. His plan was to buy a book, chat like a customer and then once the signing was over have a more in-depth discussion with the author.

"I didn't expect this kind of crowd," he said, leaning closer to Georgina.

"I checked her out before you picked me up. This is her fifth crime book and she's grown quite popular," Georgina replied. "You think the guy behind her is her agent?" she asked dryly.

Alexander flashed a tight smile. "I've heard that

literary agents are tough, especially those from New York City."

A small laugh escaped Georgina and the sound pooled warmth in the pit of his stomach. It had been over two years since he'd heard the sound of her husky laugh.

He averted his gaze from her and instead focused on the other people inside the store. It was possible the very man they sought was right here in the room, eager to buy a book about the people he'd kidnapped.

Or perhaps Michelle took her research to a whole new level and she and the mountain man behind her were responsible for the disappearances of the FBI agents. It would make one hell of a publicity stunt.

His stomach knotted. Could that be what this was all about? Surely not. He hadn't seen any publicity concerning the missing FBI agents and the book that was being sold. The various departments involved had been playing the details of each case close to their vests.

As far as Alexander knew, no reporter had tied them all together to come up with a serial kidnapper at work. Until this morning, when it was reported that a task force had been formed. He'd like to get his hands around the neck of whoever had leaked that information.

He glanced at Georgina and noticed that she was perusing the crowd with narrowed eyes. She was probably thinking the same thing he was, that the perp might very well be right here in this room, eager to buy a book about the people he held captive. Hopefully the author they were about to meet would have some answers.

He breathed a sigh of relief as finally there was only one person in line before they'd be at the author's table.

"Professor Tanner," Michelle greeted the man in front of them warmly. "I can't believe you're here."

"Now, how could I miss such a special event for one of my best students?" the tall, well-built man replied.

"You're part of the reason I'm where I am," Michelle said as she signed a book for him. "Your classes were always so fascinating."

"Thank you. Let's hope there continue to be plenty of students who enjoy my classes." He took the book she'd signed for him and then Alexander and Georgina stood before the author's table.

"Hello, would one or both of you like a book autographed?" Michelle asked with a bright smile.

"I'd like one," Georgina said. "You can just sign it to Georgina."

"And we'd both like to have a little chat with you when this is all over this evening." Alexander pulled his official identification from his pocket and placed it on the table. *To hell with the idea of pretending to be a fan,* he thought. He just wanted to cut to the chase.

Michelle looked at it and then at him with a faint alarm on her pretty features. Alexander quickly tucked his identification away.

"Can we talk someplace other than here?" she asked. "I'd rather not have any of my readers know that the FBI is questioning me about anything."

"There's a coffee shop about three blocks from here at the corner of Magnolia and Mission Road," he said.

She nodded. "I know the place." She glanced at her wristwatch. "I'll be here for another half an hour or so. Shall we meet there in about an hour?"

She appeared curious and a bit apprehensive, but not

particularly scared or guilty. Alexander was eager to question her and find out what, if any, role she might have played in the crimes. "Make sure you're there. Otherwise we'll find you someplace where it might be less private."

"I'll be there," she replied, her lips morphing into a thin line as she turned her attention to Georgina. "Did you really want a book?"

"Yes."

Michelle quickly signed the book and handed it to Georgina. "I hope you enjoy it," she said as if by rote.

The two of them left the table, paid for the book and then exited the still-busy bookstore. It wasn't until they were back in Alexander's car and headed to the coffee shop that Georgina spoke.

"So, thoughts?" she asked.

"I have several. My first thought is what a great publicity stunt it would be for the three agents she wrote about in her book to suddenly go missing."

He felt Georgina's gaze lingering on him, could almost hear the wheels churning in her head. "It would be a great publicity stunt, but there's been nothing in the news until this morning to let people know that we've determined that the missing FBI agents are tied together."

"Odd, though, that the news broke on the morning of her book signing." He glanced over to her, noting how pretty she looked in the faint glow of the dashboard lights.

"Odd, or coincidental," she agreed. "Nobody in the crowd caught my eye as looking particularly suspicious. Even Michelle didn't look overly worried or guilty when you showed her your identification and said we needed to talk to her."

"I guess we'll have a better feel for her after questioning her," he replied as they pulled up in front of the coffee shop.

They grabbed one of the tall tables in the back where they would have a little more privacy, although there were few people in the place. Most of the college students would frequent the coffee shop throughout the day, but on a Saturday night they would all have better places to be.

"Sit tight. I'll go get us some coffee," he said. She sat on one of the tall stools and opened the book she'd bought as he headed for the counter.

"I'd like a medium black coffee and a medium caffe mocha, hold the whipped cream." He was vaguely surprised that what had been Georgina's favorite drink rolled effortlessly off his tongue after all this time. He wasn't even sure if she still drank what he'd just ordered for her.

He paid for the drinks and grabbed them, and as he turned to face her, he immediately knew something was horribly wrong. She had her cell phone at her ear.

Her face was the pale shade of death, but her eyes were huge and darted at him frantically. He raced to the table at the same time she set her cell phone down with a hand that visibly shook.

"Georgina, what happened? Who was on the phone?" He set the cups down and reached for her hand. Her icy-cold fingers grabbed onto his and held tight.

"It was him." Her voice whispered from her. "He said he was the person we were hunting." She drew a deep breath, some of the color returning to her cheeks as she disengaged her hand from his and instead curled her fingers around the warm cup in front of her.

"Are you sure it wasn't some sort of a prank phone call?" he asked.

Her green eyes held a faint tinge of fear as she slowly shook her head. "He said he'd be in touch again and that Macy told me to get a good night's sleep, that I was going to need my rest if I was going to save her."

Myriad emotions rose up inside Alexander, questions about if the call had really come from the man they sought and when he might make contact again. More importantly, why out of all the task force members had he connected with Georgina? His stomach clenched tight.

Did this mean that Georgina was in danger?

Chapter Four

Georgina took a drink in an effort to warm the cold that had gripped her insides the minute she'd heard "his" voice on the phone.

"Are you sure you're okay?" Alex asked, his handsome features fraught with concern.

"I'm fine. It was just such a shock." She took another drink of her coffee, subconsciously noting that Alex had ordered her favorite. But even the comfort of the familiar drink couldn't chase away the horror that still held her in its grip.

"What did his voice sound like? Young? Old? Any accent that you could discern?" Alex asked. He leaned toward her, as if he wanted to wrap her in his arms, and for just a brief moment she wished he would.

She remembered far too well how it had felt to be cradled in Alex's arms…the sense of safety, of security she had found there.

Instead she stared down into her cup and then looked back at him. "It wasn't his real voice. He obviously was using some kind of voice-altering equipment. Still, I know it sounds crazy, but I feel like I've been touched by pure evil."

She straightened her shoulders and drew a deep, steadying breath. She couldn't allow herself to get spooked by a single phone call—Alex would pull her off the case if she appeared that weak.

"What did your caller identification show?" Alex asked. She was pleased his voice held no sympathy, no coddling tone.

"Unknown caller," she replied, also glad that her voice held no sense of the cold turmoil inside her. "He probably made the call from a throwaway phone. He's too smart to allow himself to be traced." She paused a moment. "If it really was him, then why me?"

"I don't know. Maybe because you're the only woman on the team?"

"How would he even know that I'm on the team? The article this morning didn't mention any names."

"I don't have any answers for you right now," Alex replied, his voice deep and his eyes fierce as he held her gaze. "But I promise you that by tomorrow we'll have some. If there's a leak in the department, I'll get to the bottom of it."

She saw the depth of anger simmering in his beautiful eyes and would hate to be the person on the receiving end of that ire.

"We can't know for sure that it was really the perp who made the call," he said thoughtfully. He took a drink of his coffee and set the cup back down. "There were plenty of news reports out of Bachelor Moon when Sam and his wife and little Macy went missing. The call could have just come from some creep."

"Creeps don't generally know my phone number," she replied dryly.

"We'll figure it all out," he said in an obvious effort to soothe, but she knew it was more likely than not that they wouldn't learn how he had gotten her phone number.

They fell silent for the next few minutes. She sipped her drink while Alex slugged down his coffee and got up to order himself another one. She had a feeling it would be a sleepless night for him as well as for her.

Macy. Why had the caller mentioned the little girl who had already found purchase in Georgina's heart? Perhaps he had just reasoned that since she was a woman, the child would be the best way to get to her. What a calculating creep.

By the time Alex returned to the table, Michelle and the man who had stood behind her at the autographing table walked through the door.

The big bruiser had his arm around Michelle and a scowl on his face that indicated he was definitely not pleased to be here. "Why would the FBI want to talk to Michelle?" he asked as the two of them reached the table where Georgina and Alex were seated.

"Maybe you're the one we need to talk to," Alex countered as he stood.

Georgina released a sigh. She'd already had enough drama for one night. She didn't need a macho showdown between the two men. "Why don't we all sit down and we'll explain exactly what brought Michelle to our attention."

Michelle took the stool next to Georgina. "I already know why you want to talk to me. This overly protective brute is my boyfriend, Jax White. Sit down, Jax, and let them ask their questions."

Jax took a seat as Alex returned to his. "I know the people I wrote about in my book are missing," Michelle said. "But that's all I know about the situation."

"So the kidnapping of these agents isn't part of a publicity stunt to sell more books?" Alex asked.

Michelle shot him a derisive look. "I don't subscribe to the 'Any publicity is good publicity' theory."

As Alex questioned Michelle further, Georgina tried to put the phone call out of her head and instead get a read on the woman and man seated at the table with them.

"I have some contacts in the agency," Michelle said, "and they pointed me to Sam Connelly, Amberly Caldwell and Jackson Revannaugh as three of the best profilers who had all recently solved fairly high-profile cases. I decided to showcase them in the book as some of the best of the best when it comes to catching killers."

"And exactly how did you do your research?" Georgina asked.

"She sure as hell didn't kidnap the agents," Jax exclaimed in obvious irritation.

Michelle ignored his outburst. "Unfortunately none of the agents would grant me interviews, so I did my research the hard way—by getting files on the cases they'd worked, by reading every article and news item I could find. I traveled to Mystic Lake and here to Baton Rouge to talk to some of the people who were involved with the crimes. I talked to the people in the towns, friends of the missing people. I also tried to talk to friends of the FBI agents. Unfortunately they all refused to talk to me."

Her chin rose defensively. "I worked hard to write

the stories of heroes and the criminals that they caught. I saw in the paper this morning that a task force had been formed to deal with the case of the missing FBI agents. I knew you'd be coming to question me, but I can't help you. I don't know what happened to them. I can't help you in any way in your investigation."

Jax stood and placed an arm around Michelle's shoulder. "Are we through here?"

"One more question…where were the two of you four nights ago?" Alex asked.

"At my home in New Orleans," Michelle answered without hesitation. She exchanged a glance with Jax.

"Do the two of you live together?" Georgina asked.

Michelle hesitated a beat before replying. "No, but Jax spends most nights at my place. I'm sure he was with me four nights ago."

Jax squeezed her shoulder. "And now I think we're through here." Michelle rose as if his hand on her shoulder was a magical wand that lifted her off the stool.

"Where can we reach you if we need to ask you more questions?" Alex asked.

"I'm leaving tomorrow on a book tour. If you'll give me your email or fax number I'll have my agent send you my itinerary," Michelle said.

Alex pulled a card from his pocket. "My cell phone and email is there. If I don't get that itinerary from your agent by noon tomorrow, then we're going to have problems."

Michelle nodded and the two of them left the coffee shop.

"Want another coffee?" Alex asked.

"No thanks. I think I'm ready to call it a day." She

knew they'd talk about this little interview in the car, but once the author and her boyfriend had disappeared from sight, the phone call Georgina had received filled her head once again.

Minutes later they were in Alex's car and headed toward her house. "I feel inclined to do a little background check on Mr. Jax White," Alex said.

"Probably wouldn't hurt," she agreed. "There was just a moment when Michelle said that Jax was with her on the night that Jackson and Marjorie disappeared that I didn't quite believe her."

"Maybe he decided to help his lover get a little extra publicity with her book," Alex said. "He's big enough to carry bodies over his shoulders and he looks like a man who might have a record."

"And he knew I was an FBI agent and had time before they met us here to make that phone call." Her stomach ached as she thought of the call.

They spoke no more until he pulled into her driveway. He cut the engine, turned out the car lights and then looked at her, his features visible in the streetlight next to her driveway.

"You want me to take your cell phone?" he asked.

She frowned at him in surprise. "Why would I want you to do that?"

"In case he calls again…so you don't have to deal with it."

"If he calls again it's because for some reason he wants to talk to me. You can't protect me, Alex. I can handle this. I'm fine."

She saw the frown that shot across his brow. "You're

always so damn strong, Georgina. You never need anyone."

She drew in a breath. "Are we talking about a phone call or are we discussing personal history?"

Leaning his head back, he raked a hand through his thick dark hair. "I don't know, maybe a little of both," he admitted.

"I won't discuss history," she replied. "What's done is done. All I'm interested in is catching this guy and saving not only our fellow agents but precious little Macy. I'll keep my phone and if he calls again I'll record the call and you'll be the first to know."

She opened the car door in an effort to stanch any further conversation that might turn to old heartaches and failures. "I can do my job, Alex. I don't need you to do anything but watch my back as a good partner would."

She got out of the car and shut the door and hurried toward her house. It was only when she was inside that she saw the lights on Alex's car beam on and then he pulled out of the driveway.

She locked her door and then went into her living room where she placed her gun, her official identification and her cell phone on the coffee table. She didn't want to admit that the phone call had completely creeped her out. The fact that the person on the other end of the line had called her by name had ignited a fear in her that she hadn't felt for a very long time.

Had the call really come from the man who held little Macy and the others captive? And why had he focused his attention on her when there were seven other members of the task force?

Maybe it was just some jerk who had managed to get her phone number and make the call. Crimes often brought out the mentally ill and the pranksters to play in the game.

Still, she couldn't discount the sharp intuition that told her he'd been the real deal.

She got up from the sofa and moved to the window to peer outside into the night. Her front yard held trees and bushes, hiding places for somebody who might be watching her.

Was he out there right now?

Watching her?

For the first time since her divorce she wished Alex were here with her, to assure her that the boogeyman wasn't after her, to hold her in his big strong arms and make her feel safe.

She'd told him she was fine, that she didn't need anyone. The truth was she was afraid to tap into any need she might possess.

Needing anyone, loving anyone made you vulnerable, made you appear weak. And Georgina knew better than anyone that weakness could set the predators circling overhead. And they would circle until you were too weak to fight them off when they attacked.

ALEXANDER DROVE AIMLESSLY after leaving Georgina's house. He often did his best thinking while in a car cruising without any specific direction, and at this moment he had a lot on his mind.

He wasn't particularly satisfied that Michelle and Jax hadn't pulled off a world-class publicity stunt. The two had set off tiny alarm bells in his head, but it was too early for the alarms to be a signal that they were guilty.

It would be interesting to see how this case played out as Michelle went on her book tour, if the kidnappings became a tool for garnering her publicity.

His bigger concern was the call Georgina had received, a call she was certain was from the man they hunted. He'd expected the perp to make contact again, but he'd assumed it would be by another note sent to headquarters. He hadn't expected the "reach out and touch someone" approach.

He definitely hadn't expected Georgina to be the one touched so personally by the perp. If it had really been him…if it hadn't been some kind of sick prank phone call, he reminded himself.

He knew he'd gone against protocol by not taking her phone away from her and carrying it immediately to one of the tech men to see if they could identify the location from where the call had come.

Turning down a dark side street, he knew he was betting on three things…that the call had probably come from a phone they wouldn't be able to trace, that the call itself hadn't lasted long enough for any kind of a trace, and finally that the potential perp would call her again.

Tightening his fingers on the steering wheel, he thought of that instant when he'd seen fear in the depths of her beautiful green eyes, when he'd seen the faint tremor of her hand as she'd placed her cell phone on the table. She'd recovered quickly, as she always did… as she always had.

As much as he'd loved her, that was the part of her that had frustrated him to distraction during their marriage. She gave him all the passion she had in her heart, in her soul, when they made love, but she never gave him her hopes, her fears or her dreams.

She'd given freely of her body, but had offered him no intimacy of her heart or soul, had shared nothing of her past to allow him to see what kind of influences had made her into the woman she'd become.

As he turned the car to head home, he told himself the last thing he should be doing was thinking about the days and nights he'd spent with Georgina, the love for her that still simmered in the very depths of his heart despite the fact that she'd walked away from their marriage seemingly without a backward glance.

He had a case to solve, seven people who were depending on him to find them. What he'd like to know was how the perp had focused in on Georgina? Had he read the paper that morning and managed to dig up the names of the people on the task force? Had he zeroed in on Georgina because she was the only woman on the team?

There was no doubt that there was a snitch someplace in the office. There was always a snitch willing to sell out names of agents and/or details of ongoing cases. There was always a bad apple somewhere. Alexander just wished he could be certain that the bad apple wasn't on his task force.

He would watch them all closely, and if he discovered that one of his men had given up Georgina's name to a reporter or anyone else, he'd see that the man no longer had a job, and no longer had a full set of teeth.

Pulling into the driveway of the house he'd once shared with Georgina, a deep weariness tugged at him.

He'd barely slept the night before and hoped tonight he would sleep without dreams.

He needed to be fresh and alert to begin a new day. He parked and got out of the car and entered the house that hadn't felt like home since the day Georgina had left.

Minutes later he stood in the master bath shower, allowing hot pellets of water to pummel his body. Once the tension of the day had eased away, he shut off the water and stepped out of the stall.

A large towel awaited him, along with a clean pair of boxers that served as his nightwear. He wasn't going to spend a single minute looking at files tonight. He just wanted to get into bed and sleep without dreams until dawn.

The bed seemed to embrace him as he fell supine and pulled the sheet up around his shoulders. He forced himself to empty his mind as he stared up at the patterns the moon made on the ceiling as the faint lunar light drifted through his curtains.

He must have fallen asleep immediately for the nightmare unfolded in horrifying, familiar detail. He drove the car at breakneck speed, knowing the killer held Kelly Gilmer in the old warehouse on Walker Street.

The killer was on his phone talking to Alexander, taunting him, unaware that Alexander was closing in. Through the line in the background he could hear Kelly begging for her life.

"Just let her go," Alexander said. "Daniel, if you walk away now we can work things out."

"I've killed three other women. How you going to work that out?" Daniel had screamed. "She's a faithless slut, just like the others before her and she deserves to die."

Alexander pulled to a halt in front of the warehouse, his heart beating so fast he feared he'd drop dead before he got inside where Kelly needed a hero. He desperately needed to be that hero.

He left the phone in the car with Daniel ranting and raving and stealthily made his way to the warehouse door. He opened it, his gun leading the way, as he slid through and looked around the dim building to get his bearings.

Daniel and Kelly's voices came from a room just ahead. Alexander crept forward, energized by the fact that Kelly was still well enough to plead for her life.

He stepped into the room, and instantly saw Daniel straddling Kelly, a wicked big knife in his hands. "Freeze!" Alexander screamed.

Daniel Bowie, a man who had kept the FBI busy by killing three other women, smiled at Alexander and then plunged the knife downward. Alexander fired his gun, shooting the young man in his chest.

As Daniel crumpled over, Alexander rushed to Kelly, already knowing it was too late, that she was dead. As he reached her, he looked down and instead of seeing Kelly's unseeing blue eyes, it was Georgina staring up at him with sightless green eyes.

He awoke, heart pounding and automatically reached to the other side of the bed. In his sleep-groggy mind, with the horror of the dream playing inside his head, it was only when he touched the cold empty sheets next to him that he remembered Georgina wasn't there. She hadn't been there for a very long time.

Dawn light crept through the windows and the sound of birds beginning to sing their morning songs pulled him out of bed. The dream was a familiar one since Kelly Gilmer's death, although Georgina had never made an appearance in his nightscape before now.

By the time he was dressed and drinking a cup of coffee in the large airy kitchen, he knew that the phone call she'd received bothered him more than he realized.

Although she was a seasoned agent and well trained in self-defense, fear for her knotted in the pit of his stomach. She would hate him for being afraid for her. She would hate him feeling anything for her.

But he couldn't help it. He felt as if she'd been personally touched by a malevolent force and he could only pray that the man who had called her had either been a fake or had no plans to touch her again.

Chapter Five

It had been a quiet day, with agents drifting in and out of the war room and everyone busy with their own particular task. First thing that morning Alex had asked Georgina to dig up everything she could on Michelle Davison and her boyfriend, Jax.

Since it was Sunday, Alex had given Nicholas, Matt and Jeff the day off. The rest of the team continued to work as if it were any other day of the week.

Georgina had spent the morning gathering information from traditional sources, checking out police records, news articles and whatever else she could find. Her cell phone sat on the table in front of her. Thankfully it had remained silent.

After a quick lunch, Alexander had left to go speak to the director, and Tim had gone on some mission of his own, leaving his partner, Jeff, to keep working on potential locations.

Georgina had finally moved on to social media sites, her eyes starting to glaze over as she read posts and looked at photos.

"I can't believe what people post on these public sites," she said as she found a photo of Jax half-naked and with a half-crazy look in his eyes. The caption read: The Exterminator, Got a Problem? I Can Handle It. And then it went on to say that he was a professional bodyguard/bouncer.

Frank, who was seated next to her, leaned over and looked at her computer screen, then shook his head. "I keep telling my daughters that what they put out there is out there forever," he said. "But in a house full of females, my voice is rarely heard," he said jokingly.

Georgina smiled. Frank not only had a beautiful, strong wife, but he also had four girls between the ages of eleven and seventeen. Her smile faded, she looked pointedly at Nicholas's empty chair and leaned closer so that only Frank would hear her. "It seems like your partner isn't listening to your voice very well, either."

Frank gave her a look of disgust. "He's a showboat. I keep telling myself he's young and trying to make his mark, but a task force isn't the time or place to play by your own rules. I'm glad he's off today. It's bad enough I'll have to deal with him again tomorrow."

He kept his voice low as well and Georgina knew he would say nothing to anyone else. As a team player, Frank wouldn't want to bring dissension among the group.

As Frank got back to work, Georgina rubbed her eyes and got up to get herself a cup of coffee. All the members of the task force had been told about the phone call she'd received the night before.

Tim was at this moment working with her cell phone company in an effort to get the record of the call, and then triangulate pings off cell phone towers to get a location from where the call had come. He would also work with them in an effort to identify the specific phone number of the caller and then would begin to search for serial numbers and stores where the phone might have been bought.

She didn't expect him to have any real information for a week or two. He might know a general area where the call had come from any time, but it would take much longer to learn more facts about the phone used to make the call to her.

With her coffee cup in hand, she returned to her seat at the table. She knew when Alex returned to the room he'd expect updates from the agents working.

She had a ton of information about Michelle Davison and her brute boyfriend. What she didn't have was any evidence that might point to them as persons of interest other than the book Michelle had written.

Tim had returned to the room and he and Terry had their heads together working off a single computer screen that had Google Earth up to focus on the Baton Rouge area.

They were all looking for a needle in a haystack… a location where seven people could be held, a man or men who had managed to kidnap those people without being seen, without leaving behind a single clue.

She stared at her phone, almost willing it to ring, almost wanting to get another call. While the idea of having any kind of personal interaction with a self-pronounced potential serial killer chilled her, she also knew that if he connected with her, he might make a mistake.

He could unconsciously give her a piece of information that might make it easier to identify him. There might be background noises on the call that could be magnified by tech workers to focus a search on a particular area of town.

She'd just gotten back to work when Alex came into the room. She glanced at her watch, surprised to realize it was after four. Surfing the internet had made the hours of the day melt away.

"I don't sense much excitement in here," he said as he went to the head of the table.

Frank shrugged. "Not much exciting to relate.

"I just finished speaking to Director Miller and Lieutenant Craig Burnett from the police department. He's agreed to have ten officers be our feet on the ground in checking out abandoned warehouses and factories and whatever building might be a potential hiding place for a kidnapper with seven hostages."

Alex turned to look at the two agents at the opposite end of the table from Georgina. "Any addresses you two get together on a list, give them to Lieutenant Burnett. He'll be checking in here every morning and working as a liaison between us and the police."

He moved his gaze to Frank. "I want you to get photos of all the victims made into posters and distributed all around town."

"We're officially taking this public?" Frank asked.

Alex nodded. "Miller is holding a news conference first thing in the morning. We're all to be press-ready by nine. We're setting up a TIPS line and hoping that by blanketing the city with posters, somebody saw something that might break the investigation wide open."

He turned to face Georgina and at that moment her cell phone rang. She immediately knew it was *him*. She didn't need to see the unknown number that her caller identification displayed.

The war room was completely silent and all the men stared at her as she picked up the phone and hit Speaker and Record as she answered. "Agent Beaumont," she said, aware of Alex moving closer.

"Such formality. May I call you Georgina?" It was the same deep voice, obviously computer-altered. "I thought we were going to be friends."

"You can call me Georgina." Her mouth was achingly dry. "And what should I call you?"

Before there could be a reply Alex grabbed the phone from her. "This is Special Agent Alexander Harkins. I'm the lead investigator on this case. I think I'm the one you want to talk to."

"If I'd wanted to talk to you, I would have called your phone, Agent Alexander Harkins." There was an audible click, letting everyone in the room know that the caller had hung up.

Georgina snatched her phone away from Alex, angry that he'd interfered and screwed up what might have been a call that contained a clue, concerned that he'd done so in an effort to protect her.

Before she could voice her outrage over his action, her phone rang again. She glared at Alex, daring him to pull another stunt, and then once again hit Speaker and Record and answered the call.

"Don't let that happen again." It was obvious the man on the phone had been angered.

"It won't," Georgina replied with another glare at Alex. Even though her heart was beating way too fast, despite the fact that the cold chill of evil had crept from the cell phone to take over every part of her body, she knew this connection was their best chance to catch the man.

"You never told me what I should call you," she said.

"FBI-trained serial killer is a mouthful, isn't it? Why don't you call me Bob?"

"Okay, Bob." It didn't seem right that evil should go by the name of Bob, but she was playing his game. "Is there a reason you want to talk to me, Bob?" She kept her gaze focused on the phone that was on the table in front of her and refused to look at any of the men in the room.

"I know you and your team are working very hard to try to find me, but in the meantime I've done a little research of my own…some research on you."

Georgina couldn't imagine that her blood could get any colder, but his words shot a new icy chill through her veins. "You must have been bored to death," she replied, glad that her voice didn't betray any of the emotions roaring through her.

"On the contrary, I think you and I have a lot of things in common."

Revulsion rose at his words. She couldn't imagine what she could possibly have in common with this man. "How do I know that you're really the person who kidnapped the FBI agents and their loved ones?" she asked, deciding to ignore his previous words.

"If you'd like me to I could send you Sam Connelly's ear in the mail. Or perhaps you would prefer a finger from Amberly Caldwell."

Georgina flinched. "That isn't necessary. Just let me speak to one of them."

"I might be able to arrange that, but first I want to talk to you about your childhood."

Georgina's throat closed off as a flash of old memories torched through her brain. She was grateful the phone was on the table for she would have probably dropped it as her hands began to tremble uncontrollably.

She quickly clenched them together and moved them to her lap beneath the table where nobody would be able to see them. "What about my childhood?"

"Was it good or bad?"

She thought about lying, she considered not allowing him to get any real piece of her, but she was also afraid that if he already knew the answer and she lied, she'd break trust with him and he'd stop calling and this chance for clues would be lost forever.

She was more than aware that building trust with him through the phone calls might be the only way they'd get any clues as to his identity. She desperately needed to build some mutual trust with him.

"It was bad," she finally replied. She looked up and found herself staring into the blue depths of Alex's eyes. How many times had he asked her about her childhood and she'd always deflected the conversation, had refused to give him any hint of the hell she'd endured.

It was a time of her life she refused to revisit except in the form of torturous nightmares and she would do it only now to hopefully save the lives of the people he held captive.

"Your mother and father, did you ever dream of killing them?"

"I already answered one of your questions. Now you need to let me talk to one of your captives before I answer any more." She broke eye contact with Alex and held her breath, hoping for honor from a creep.

"Who do you want to hear from?"

"Jackson," Alex whispered.

"Macy," Georgina replied.

There was a long moment of silence. Georgina held her breath, knowing it was possible she would face Alex's wrath once the call eventually ended.

"Hello?"

The childish voice squeezed Georgina's heart painfully tight. "Macy? My name is Georgina."

"Are you going to come and get us?"

"Who is with you?"

"There's Daddy Sam and my mom and Ms. Amberly and Mr. Caldwell and Mr. Revannaugh and Ms. Clinton. We're all waiting for you to come and find us. We all just want to go home." A small sob choked from her.

"Where are you, honey?"

"We're in cages," she replied.

Georgina frowned. "Cages?"

"You talked to the little girl, now it's my turn again," Bob said. "Now, answer my question. Did you ever dream of killing your mother and father?"

"Never," she replied and then couldn't help but add, "I sometimes wished them dead, but I never entertained the idea of actually killing them myself."

Pressure filled her chest, making it difficult for her to breathe as emotions untapped for nearly a lifetime rushed in. She hated Bob for making her remember, for making her feel those emotions she'd tried so hard to put behind her.

"For years I dreamed of killing my mother and father, and then one day when I was twenty-five years old, I went back to the old homestead and I did it. I killed them. They were my first victims," he said. The line went dead.

THE SILENCE IN the room was deafening. Thoughts thundered through Alexander's head as he stared at the woman he'd once been married to, a woman who had just given more information about her past to a killer than she'd ever shared with him.

She raised her head to meet his gaze, her green eyes hard and impossible to read. "I'm sorry. I probably should have asked to speak to one of the men, but in my mind Macy was…is the most expendable and I needed to make sure she was still alive."

"It's fine," Alexander replied. He tried to ignore the paleness of her cheeks, the obvious toll the phone call had taken on her.

"So, if Bob is to be believed, he murdered his parents," Frank said. "Even though he'd altered his voice, he didn't sound that old…maybe early- to mid-thirties."

"Then the murder of his parents would have happened within the past ten years or so," Terry said.

"And if he killed his parents, then why isn't he in prison?" Tim asked.

Alexander's attention was split between the conversation going on among the team and Georgina, who seemed to have disappeared into herself. Her shoulders were slumped and her gaze remained focused on the cell phone on the table in front of her.

He told himself it wasn't just because he'd been her husband and that it wasn't because on some deep level he still loved her that he was concerned. He would be concerned about any of the team members who had shared a rather intimate conversation with a self-professed killer.

Tim took her phone and downloaded the message into his computer. As a techie, he could work on the recording to see if there were any background noises that could be amplified. He'd also try to chase down the number the call had come from.

Georgina remained quiet until they called it a day. As the men left the room, Alexander caught hold of her arm so he could talk to her alone.

"Are you all right?" he asked softly.

"I'm fine." Her shoulders stiffened in a familiar posture of defensiveness. Her eyes were a dark green that he'd never seen before, filled with shadows he could never breach, he would never fully understand.

"Want to grab coffee at Cup of Joe's before heading home?" He kept his tone light, knowing that if she sensed any concern for her in his voice she'd decline.

"Okay," she surprised him by saying.

Together they left the room and headed to the elevator. "At least we got a little more information," she said as they rode down to the first floor. "We know that right now they are all alive."

"And I'm adding to Terry and Matt's workload by having them check every case of any couple murdered in their homes or under suspicious circumstances in the past fifteen years in the state," he replied.

"That could take months of work," she said as they left the elevator and headed for the front door of the building.

Cup of Joe's was a small hole-in-the-wall coffee shop three buildings down from the FBI building. It was a popular place for tired agents to fuel up or wind down.

Joe's menu offered no fancy froufrou drinks, nothing but coffee and a variety of muffins, cookies and little cakes. As Georgina took a seat at one of the narrow booths against the wall, Alexander ordered two cups of coffee, one black and one with cream and sugar.

When he joined her with the drinks, she was curled into the corner between the back of the booth and the wall. She looked more fragile than he'd ever seen her. As he sat down, she quickly straightened, her eyes overly bright as if she were working too hard to keep it together.

He slid her coffee halfway across the table, but when she went to reach for it, he grabbed her hand in his. He held tight even as she tried to pull away.

"Just sit for a minute and let me hold your hand," he said softly.

"I don't need hand-holding," she protested, but she didn't attempt to pull her hand away again.

"You were amazing," he said. "You kept your cool and played your own game with him. You forced him into letting us hear from one of the victims."

"It didn't feel amazing. It was terrifying," she admitted. "I was so afraid that if I said something wrong there would be terrible consequences."

This time when she pulled her hand back, he released it and watched as she wrapped both her slightly trembling hands around the hot foam cup of coffee.

Alexander picked up his own cup and leaned back against the booth. "For some reason or another it's obvious that he's decided he wants a relationship with you."

Her eyes widened but quickly resumed their normal shape. "If that's what it takes to solve this, then I'll be his best phone buddy."

Protests rose to his throat, but he swallowed them. The need to protect her from having any contact with this man was overwhelming, but he had to think of what was in the best interest of solving the crime. She was a member of the task force. It was her job to do whatever she could to help catch the creep.

He couldn't think like a man who needed to protect his woman. She hadn't been his woman in a very long time. When he looked back on their marriage, he sometimes wondered if she'd ever really been his woman.

They sat in silence, sipping their hot coffee. The silence wasn't uncomfortable. He was accustomed to her being a woman of few words.

It was finally she who broke the silence. "If what he said about his parents is true, then he's already killed and won't hesitate to kill again." She took another sip of her drink and then continued. "You know he won't let them live. Once he's gotten whatever he thinks he needs from them, he'll kill them all."

Her eyes held a hollowness, as if she were already grieving for their loss. He didn't try to tell her differently. He knew what she said was true. "All the more reason we've got to work every angle to find him before that can happen."

"He'll keep calling me." She said it as a statement, not as a question.

Alexander nodded. "Yes, I think he will. He's connected with you and I think he'll want to maintain that connection until the end, whatever the end looks like." He took another drink of his coffee and then leaned forward. "What you said, about your childhood being bad. Was that true?"

She released a sigh, as if she'd known he'd ask and yet had hoped he wouldn't. "Yes, it's true, I had a difficult childhood, but it's not something I want to talk about." Her chin lifted a bit, as if daring him to pursue the topic.

It had always been that way with her. When he'd attempted to dig too deep, he'd been met with resistance. He'd quickly learned not to try to get into anything about her past. He'd just been happy to have her in his life. But apparently he hadn't been enough for her.

"Maybe the tech department and Tim will be able to enhance any background noise on the recording or they'll be able to get a handle on his speech pattern and give us some ideas about education or where he might be from if he isn't a native," he said.

"Hopefully, when he calls again, I'll be able to get more from him. More about the murder of his parents, more of his background information or something else important," she said. "We need to find them." Her eyes took on a haunted look. "Macy will be the first one he'll kill. Even though she's with her mother and father, she has to be so afraid. No child should ever be that afraid."

He had to fight his instinct to once again reach out and grab her hand, to get up and move to sit beside her and pull her into his arms. He had a feeling she knew that kind of fear, the kind no child should ever know. She had lived it in her "bad" childhood.

"You know how dangerous it is for you to lose your objectivity," he said softly. "You know that it's not good to identify too closely with any victim or the perp. Trust me, I lived it. Get too emotionally involved with a victim and it will destroy you if things go bad."

She took a drink of her coffee, her gaze locked with his. "Do you still have nightmares?"

"Only when I sleep," he said in an effort to lighten the mood. "What about you?"

"Occasionally I have bad dreams, but not as often as I used to. I work so hard I usually fall into bed too exhausted to dream."

"That's good, and I hope it stays that way."

She smiled at him. "Was this a mental-wellness-check cup of coffee?"

He returned her smile. "Maybe a little bit. It would shake up any seasoned agent to be receiving phone calls from a perp. I should have known you'd be strong enough to handle it."

"If it's a chance to get those people home safely, then I can handle anything." She finished her coffee and grabbed her purse. "I need to get home."

"Wait a minute. I'll walk you to your car since we're parked in the same lot." He got up and threw their disposable coffee cups into a trash bin and then they stepped out into the September night air.

"It's odd, he called me both times at about the same time of the day," she said as they headed back down the sidewalk toward the parking lot behind the FBI building. "Around four o'clock."

"Maybe he works a job and that's his break time?" Alexander speculated.

"It's Sunday, you would think he wouldn't be at work at all today."

"We'll have to wait and see if the pattern continues. That could be another potential clue in this mess we have."

"Terry and Matt said the investigations that took place in Bachelor Moon and in Mystic Lake look pretty solid, so they probably aren't going to find anything there to help us."

"How about we end the night by not talking about the crimes," he said.

She cast him a sideways glance. "Then what do you want to talk about?"

"I don't know...the weather, the latest movie you've seen, what you're reading?"

She grinned at him, that impish grin that always managed to stir a wealth of emotion inside him. "The weather is sultry, I can't remember the last movie I saw and I'm reading Michelle Davison's book."

"And that begs the questions that lead right back to talking about the case," he replied with an answering grin. "So, learning anything new about the missing agents?"

"Actually, I didn't know that Jackson's father was a criminal," she replied.

A shaft of pain shot through him at thoughts of his friend. "It was Jackson's biggest shame. His father was a con man who married wealthy older women and then drained their savings and divorced them or arranged for accidents to happen to them. Jackson helped put his father in prison, but when he got out, he wanted Jackson to pay. When Jackson was in Kansas City, he had a showdown with his father, who was shot to death by another agent."

"That part of it wasn't in the book," she said as they reached her car.

"It only happened a couple of days before Jackson came back here. Michelle wouldn't have known about it when she wrote the book. She was focused solely on Jackson's role in the Twilight Killer case."

"Well, I guess I'll see you at seven in the morning," she said as she clicked her key fob to unlock her doors.

He grabbed her arm and turned her back to face him before she could open her car door. She looked up at him curiously. "Georgina, I just want to warn you not to let him get inside your head."

Unable to help himself, he reached up and stroked two fingers down her delicate jawline, stopping when he reached her chin. It was an old habit, one that had always ended before with him tipping her head back so he could take total possession of her lips.

He wanted to kiss her, he desperately wanted to wrap his arms around her and kiss her until her head spun and her brain was filled with nothing but him.

To his surprise, without him urging her chin upward, she dropped her head back slightly, as if inviting him to finish the old routine.

He didn't hesitate. He lowered his mouth to hers, tentatively at first and when she didn't protest he wrapped his arms around her, pulled her close and deepened the kiss.

She tasted like coffee and heat. The kiss evoked old memories. She tasted like home. He wanted to kiss her forever, but before he could make a fool of himself, he reluctantly ended the kiss and released her from his arms.

She stared at him for a long moment and raised a finger to rub across her full lower lip. "You know we can't go back, Alex," she said softly.

"I know," he replied. "But if that creep starts to mess with your mind, if he gets too far into your head, I want you to think about me, about kissing me and hopefully that will keep you grounded."

"You have a lot of confidence in the power of your kiss," she said with a wry smile.

He laughed. "You used to tell me that when I kissed you, you couldn't think about anything else. Maybe some of that old magic still exists…at least enough to keep you mentally stable against a killer."

"We'll see," she replied and then got into her car. With a wave of her hand, she started the engine and pulled out.

He watched her taillights until they disappeared from view and only then did he walk to his own car. He sat behind the steering wheel and leaned his head back.

The truth was that he wanted to go back in time. He wanted a do-over with Georgina. He'd never understood why she'd walked out on him in the first place.

She'd been by his side when he'd gone through the worst of his depression, and when things seemed to finally be back on track, when he'd eventually gotten his head back on straight, she'd decided she needed out and he had been left with questions that had never been answered.

He hoped by the time they solved this crime he'd have some of those questions answered and maybe, just maybe, he and Georgina would be back together where he believed they belonged.

Chapter Six

That kiss.

That damnable kiss.

It had kept her tossing and turning all night, fighting against the old feelings the kiss had evoked. When she'd finally fallen asleep, she had dreamed of the two of them together in the bed in their master suite making love.

Alex had been a passionate man and he'd stirred a want, a desire inside her she'd never known before him. He was like an intoxicant to her and she to him. She'd wanted him the first time she'd met him and she'd wanted him the day she walked away from him.

The kiss and the memories of those dreams had remained in her head the next day when she arrived at work. She'd timed her arrival to be right at seven, knowing that most of the team would already be present and there would be no time for any personal talk between her and Alex.

She had to keep things strictly professional between them, and last night she'd allowed a slip that couldn't be repeated. She couldn't be pulled back into Alex's life in any meaningful way. He deserved a better woman than she would ever be.

"Let's get updates," Alex said as Georgina slid into her chair at the conference table.

"Georgina, you've been researching Michelle Davison and Jax White. Anything earth-shattering come from your work so far?"

"Michelle was born and raised here in Baton Rouge. She attended the Baton Rouge College, and soon after graduating with a degree in journalism, she published her first book, an in-depth look at the Baxter kidnapping case. For those of you who don't know, Kimberly Baxter was kidnapped at the age of sixteen and held captive for two years at which time she managed to escape. The book got rave reviews and Michelle has written three more books since then, the latest the one that brought her to our attention."

Part of her information she'd gained the day before, but much of what she had learned had occurred last night when Alex's kiss had burned her lips and made sleep impossible.

"She's never been arrested, hasn't even had a traffic ticket and seems to be squeaky clean," she continued. "But that's not the case with her boyfriend. Before he hooked up with Michelle three years ago, he was in and out of jail for assault, public drunkenness and a variety of misdemeanors. The most important point of interest I found out late last night is that Jax's parents died in a fire in their home nine years ago while Jax was away on a floating trip with some buddies. I'm waiting to get a file on the case to look further into their deaths."

"So the author and her boyfriend don't fall off our persons-of-interest list," Frank said.

Alex turned to the whiteboard where both Michelle's

and Jax's names were written in bold red marker. "They'll stay right there until we can clear them of any culpability."

"Too bad they're up there all alone," Terry said.

"I might be able to add a name to that short list," Frank said. "I was surfing the internet late last night and discovered some kook who runs his own 'news' show. His name is Roger Cambridge and he's been following these cases since the family disappeared from Bachelor Moon. Last night he talked about the task force. He had all of our names listed and when I checked his previous posts, he had photos taken in Bachelor Moon and Mystic Lake during the investigations."

Georgina saw the light that shone from Alex's eyes, the shine of a predator scenting prey. She'd seen that same light in his eyes just before he'd taken her to bed. "Did you get an address?"

Frank nodded. "He lives in unit 215 at the Beacon Apartments just off Beacon Street, across from the college campus. He's twenty-eight years old, and according to the stats I checked he has a growing fan base. He does his news show three times a week, on Sunday, Tuesday and Thursday nights."

Georgina knew the apartment complex. It catered to college students who preferred parties to class work, and she knew that the local cops were regulars there on the weekends, busting up fights or arresting underage drinkers.

"We've handed addresses of over forty empty buildings that are surrounded by more than three acres of land to the cops," Tim said. "They're in the process of checking out those locations while Jeff and I continue to compile addresses."

Alex nodded and then turned his gaze to Nicholas, who had looked surprised by Frank's new information. "Looks like your partner just evened the score for your showboating yesterday," he said. "Both of you continue to work together to get me more connections, no matter how tenuous between these people." He directed his gaze at Nicholas. "Team players, that's what I want from everyone."

Nicholas gave a curt nod of his head, but Georgina had a feeling this little dressing down wouldn't affect the eager agent's desire to lone-wolf it and save the day.

"You all have your work," Alex continued. "Georgina and I are taking off to check out Roger Cambridge. If anything breaks here, call me."

Georgina stood as Alex left the head of the table. Despite the fact that it was obvious they would once again be spending time alone, she was determined that their conversation would remain strictly professional.

He was worried about their killer getting into her head, but she was equally concerned about Alex getting into her head. She couldn't allow either man in.

"Sleep well?" he asked as they exited the building and headed toward his car.

"Like a baby," she replied. Was he wondering if the kiss had shaken her up? Was he hoping that it had disturbed her, forced her to remember how it had once been between them?

The physical side of their marriage had never been at issue. They had both been passionate and giving and each time they'd made love it had been beyond magical.

"How did you sleep?" she asked and then instantly regretted the question as his eyes deepened and a familiar slow grin curled his lips.

"Do you want me to tell you about my dreams?" he asked.

"Not unless you thought of something to help solve the case," she replied. She opened the passenger door and got into the car, wondering if he'd had the same kind of erotic dreams she'd had of them together.

Damn that kiss anyway.

"Thank God I talked Miller into doing the press interview this morning without our attendance," he said as he made the turn to take them toward the college campus.

"I always hate being in a press conference," she replied. "We all stand behind Miller looking like trained monkeys ready for action."

Alexander laughed. "I never really thought about it that way before." They were silent for a few miles and then he spoke again, knowing he was navigating dangerous topics.

"Do you ever think about it? About our marriage? About our time together?" he asked.

"Sometimes," she admitted after a long hesitation.

"We had some good times." He shot her a surreptitious glance. She remained staring straight ahead out the window and she was just as beautiful in profile as she was straight-on.

"We did," she agreed, not looking at him. "But that was then and this is now. Every time we're alone together, you can't talk about the past. It's over, Alex, and we're here to do a job."

She didn't turn to look at him and for that reason an edge of frustration rippled through him. "I was happy with you." He pulled into a parking spot in front of the Beacon Apartments. He cut the engine but remained buckled in the seat. He stared at her until she sighed and turned to look at him. "I just want to know what happened, what I did to make you leave. Was it because I fell apart after the Gilmer case?" He'd always wondered if the weakness he'd shown after that case had somehow turned her off, had made her see him as less of a man.

"Oh, Alex, no. It had nothing to do with you." Her eyes shimmered in the morning light, like green leaves on a newly budded tree. "I just wasn't happy. I realized that I wasn't meant to be in a relationship."

Her eyes darkened with an uncharacteristic plea. "You have to leave it alone. Please don't pick at old scabs. Otherwise I'll have to request that I be taken off the task force and that will hurt my career."

Alexander suddenly felt small, and recognized in some part of his brain that he was trying to force something from Georgina that she couldn't or wouldn't give to him. He had to let it go. He had to let her go and stay with the unanswered questions that would always plague him where she was concerned.

"I'm sorry. I've been completely unprofessional where you're concerned and it won't happen again," he said sincerely.

"I just need you to treat me as part of the team," she said. "Nothing more and nothing less."

"Done," he said and unbuckled his seat belt. "Now, let's go in and see what the deal is with this hotshot internet reporter."

He heard her sigh of relief as she got out of the passenger door and he mentally kicked himself for being a fool. He hadn't realized until now that he'd been holding onto the thought of them somehow, someway getting back together again since the moment she'd left him.

He had to keep his head in the game of this case. It was time to let go of foolish fantasies that would never be. Georgina was gone to him as the seven missing people were gone to the world. He would do everything in his power to find those seven people, but he had to let Georgina go.

Minutes later they stood in front of unit 215. The hallway stank of stale smoke and food, with an underlay of urine and vomit…definitely a party floor. The apartments were quiet. The students who lived here either were still sleeping or had already left for early morning classes.

As they approached unit 215, he couldn't help but notice that Georgina appeared more relaxed than she'd been since the first time she'd walked into the conference room that morning and saw him there.

He knocked on the door where Roger Cambridge resided. There was no reply. He knocked again, this time harder. "Hang on, wait a damn minute," a deep male voice called from inside.

The door finally opened to reveal a big guy clad in an undershirt and boxers. His hair was light brown and definitely sporting the bed-head look. "What the hell?" he demanded. "Everyone knows I work nights and sleep late in the mornings."

"Sorry to interrupt your beauty sleep," Georgina said and gazed pointedly at his hair. "It's obvious your hair hasn't had enough." She flipped out her identification as Alexander showed his.

"We have some questions to ask you," Alexander said. "You want to do it out in the hallway or are you going to invite us in?"

Roger raked a hand through his unruly hair and then opened his door. "Come on in. Do you mind if I at least pull some pants on?"

"Go ahead," Alexander said as they stepped into the small living room that had the feel of a very low budget television studio. Several computers sat on a desk, along with a couple of high-powered lights on stands. A large bulletin board appeared to serve as a backdrop and held a map of the United States, photos of the missing FBI agents and photos of the crime scenes.

Alexander exchanged a glance with Georgina, who shrugged and sat on a sofa shoved against one wall. *Freaky fan, or just a freak making news so he can report it?* Alexander wondered.

Roger returned to the room, now clad in a pair of worn jeans and with his hair damp and combed. "I assume you're here to ask me questions about my part in the missing FBI agents case," he said. He picked up his cell phone from the desk. "Mind if I videotape this interview?"

"The only person doing any kind of taping is going to be me," Alex replied and pulled a small tape recorder from his pocket.

"Put your phone down," Georgina said in a stern voice.

He placed his phone back on the desk and then slumped down into the desk chair. "I can tell by your tones that there's no good cop / bad cop thing that's going to happen. You're both bad cops, right?"

"You've been watching too much television," Alexander replied dryly. "We just want to ask you some questions...like how you have photos of crimes scenes that haven't been released to the public."

He was particularly interested in the picture that depicted Sam and Daniella's kitchen, with the milk and cookies on the table and a chair overturned. That was the only scene where it was obvious something wrong had happened.

"I follow crime for my show." Roger leaned forward, his round face animated. "The Roger Dodger Crime Scene Show. Have either of you ever caught it on the internet?" He gave them no time to reply. "Well, I guess one of you did. Otherwise, you wouldn't be here."

"Actually it was a colleague of ours who caught your show last night," Alexander said. "And I'd like to know how you got that photo of the Connellys' kitchen. It was obviously taken during the crime scene investigation."

Roger beamed proudly. "Unfortunately, I can't divulge my sources. It's one of those amendment rights. But I'm very good at my job, and my job is to get as close to the investigation as possible, to make my viewers feel as if they know everything that's happening with these cases."

"Why these particular cases?" Georgina asked. "There's all kind of crimes happening all around the country."

"When I first heard that a former FBI agent, his wife and their kid had disappeared from Bachelor Moon, it felt like a story that might be big, so I immediately headed down to Bachelor Moon and started doing news-casts about that case."

"And how did you hear about the Mystic Lake case?" Alexander asked, at the same time trying not to be distracted by the scent of Georgina so close to him.

"I check all the major news sources all the time. I caught wind of that one from a Kansas City source and left here by plane. I rented a car in Kansas City and then drove to Mystic Lake and started on-location podcasts."

For the next hour Alexander and Georgina grilled the baby-face Roger Dodger, who appeared open and eager to help them in any way possible. Unfortunately, nothing he had to offer was any help.

By the time they left his apartment Alexander's head was jumbled with thoughts. Neither of them spoke until they were back in his car.

"I've heard of perps insinuating themselves into some element of the investigation," he said thoughtfully. "I don't know if that's the case with Roger or not."

"He's physically fit enough to be able to move the bodies if they were unconscious," Georgina replied. "And he definitely simmered with excitement while he talked about the case."

"Yeah, simmered with a little too much excitement in my mind. Something about him left a bad taste in my mouth." He started the car and pulled out of the apartment parking lot.

"So, he goes up on our whiteboard and we do more digging into who he really is and what, exactly, he's up to," he added. What little background information they had gotten from Roger would have to be vetted.

"That still makes our person of interest list pathetically short," Georgina replied.

"We're only a couple of days into this, Georgina. It's going to take time."

"I know. I just hope…" her voice trailed off as she turned to look out the passenger window.

She didn't have to finish her sentence; he knew exactly what she was going to say. She just hoped the seven people they sought had enough time to be found alive.

JACKSON REVANNAUGH HAD BEEN ANGRY ever since he'd awakened on a top bunk in a jail-like cell with Marjorie unconscious on the bunk below him. The last thing he'd remembered before arriving in the cell was making love to Marjorie and then falling asleep.

He'd gone to bed wearing boxers and when he'd become conscious he'd found a pair of his jeans and a T-shirt in the cell. There had also been clothes for Marjorie, who had been taken from the bed in her nightgown.

It had been six days since then, and in those days Jackson had come to know the others who shared the same fate. On one hand he was relieved to know that they were all alive; on the other hand he knew they were all in big trouble.

The only ray of sunshine was little Macy, who sang songs and made up stories about princesses being rescued by handsome princes. The sound of her sweet little voice coming from the cell on the other side of Amberly and Cole's broke his heart. No kid should be here. Nobody living and breathing should be here. Hell, he didn't even know where *here* was.

He'd already learned the daily routine. The creep who had taken them showed up each morning wearing a ski mask and bearing breakfast sandwiches and cups of coffee or juice. The trays were slid through a slot, just as prisoners were served in jail cells.

There was rarely any lunch, and then dinner was served the same way. There was just enough food to keep them alive, but not quite enough to allow them to thrive.

When their captor delivered the food, he never spoke, although Jackson had learned from the others that he'd interrogated Sam, Amberly and Cole several times.

Jackson now sat on the lower bunk, Marjorie curled up against him. Guilt weighed heavily on him. She shouldn't have been here. He'd encouraged her to leave Kansas City and come to Baton Rouge to continue the relationship they'd formed while he was working the case of the missing Amberly and Cole.

If he hadn't encouraged her, if he'd just walked away from her, then she wouldn't be sitting in this hellhole with him. She'd be safe at home.

He tightened his arm around her and she raised her head and looked at him, love shining from her eyes and pulling a lump into his throat. "I'm so sorry, Maggie," he said softly. "I should have just walked away from you and left you in Kansas City."

"I didn't want to stay in Kansas City. I wanted to be with you," she replied, keeping her voice low so that the others couldn't hear their conversation.

"And now here you are," he replied with a trace of bitterness.

"In your arms, exactly where I want to be," she said. "Jackson, I love you, and no matter what happens here, I will always love you."

His heart filled with his love for her. "And I will always love you." He lowered his lips and gave her a gentle kiss and at that moment the far door in the distance swung open and their captor walked in.

He grabbed a folding chair and positioned it in front of Jackson and Marjorie's cell. "I think it's time we have a little chat, Agent Revannaugh." He sat down.

"I can't imagine what we'd have to chat about," Jackson returned, aware of the silence from the other two cells.

"On the contrary, you have a wealth of information I need."

Marjorie threw herself against the bars. "Why don't you take off that stupid ski mask and face us? Why don't you just go to hell?"

The captor pulled a gun from his pocket and pointed it at Marjorie. "Agent Revannaugh, I suggest you get control of your woman or I'll take care of her and you can spend the rest of your time here with her rotting corpse."

Jackson instantly grabbed Marjorie and threw her behind him. "She won't be a problem. What kind of information do you want from me?" His chest was tight, but it eased slightly as Marjorie curled up on the bottom bunk and the man shoved his gun into his waistband.

"When you were chasing the Twilight Killer, what kind of mistakes did he make that eventually led to his arrest? He killed five women with baseball bats before you finally caught him."

What the hell? Jackson thought. That particular case was a little over two years old, and for a two-month period the women in Baton Rouge had been afraid to leave their homes at the time between day and night.

"He got sloppy," Jackson finally answered. "They always get sloppy and make mistakes."

"Like what?" The captor leaned forward as if eager to hear any information Jackson could impart.

"In that particular case we found the bat he'd used on his last victim in a storm drain. He'd gotten careless and hadn't bothered to wear gloves. We got a couple of good prints off it and the man was already in the system because of an arrest for domestic abuse."

"In your personal experience what other mistakes do killers make to get caught?"

Jackson frowned. This was all so bizarre. Who was this man who'd managed to get seven people in his lair? And where was this place where he kept them?

The question-and-answer period lasted for about twenty minutes. The man was totally focused on how criminals got caught, on what mistakes they made.

Jackson didn't pretend not to cooperate. The price was too high if he didn't. Besides, most of the information he had to impart could be found by studying any criminology book or the dozens of tomes written on profiling.

With a glance at his watch and appearing to be satisfied with the conversation, the man got up. He folded his chair and carried it to the wall.

"You're a mean Mr. Poopy Head," Macy said.

It was as if time stood still. Everyone froze as Macy's words hung in the air. The man pointed his fingers like a gun at her.

"Bang," he said and then left by the door he'd entered.

Chapter Seven

The next couple of days went by in agonizing slow ticks of the hands on the clocks. Georgina's phone had remained silent, and that worried her. She had hoped that the perp would continue to call at regular intervals. She had hoped that somehow the calls would give up some clues as to the identity of the man they sought. Each morning when she arrived, she set the phone in front of her on the table, just in case a call came in.

She was also frustrated by Alex, who had done nothing at all but what she'd asked, treated her as part of the team and nothing more.

It was exactly what she'd wanted and yet now that he appeared distant and completely professional, she realized she missed the way he'd looked at her before, as if he'd never really stopped loving her. She missed the private conversations that had gone beyond the case, even though most of them had made her uncomfortable.

She glanced up from her laptop to see him at the end of the conference table, immersed in paperwork. As usual he wore black slacks, but today he'd paired them with an ice-blue shirt that made his eyes appear a glacier-blue. His dark hair was slightly rumpled, only adding to his overall hotness.

She focused back on her computer, wondering if there would ever come a time when she didn't find him attractive, when she didn't look at him and remember what it had felt like to be naked with him, to feel his warm flesh against her own?

The case, she told herself. *Work on the case and stop thinking about Alex.* She'd been tasked with finding out everything she could about the hotshot self-proclaimed newsman, Roger Cambridge.

All the members of the team were in the room except Nicholas, who had left earlier to get some lunch. A cloud of frustration hung heavy in the air. Everyone felt the lack of forward motion, the stagnant condition of the case, despite the short length of time they'd been working it.

The press conference had gone off, posters of Jackson and Marjorie had been plastered all around town and the TIPS lines that had been set up in another conference room, manned by trained volunteers, were receiving dozens of calls.

The volunteers would be able to determine if the calls were the usual crazies or something that needed to be checked out. So far the TIPS line had yielded nothing worthwhile.

It was just after two and Georgina was fighting against an afternoon drain in energy. She got up from her chair and walked over to the coffeemaker and poured herself a cup. Before carrying it back to her chair, she stretched and tried to shove away the weariness of inactivity.

She was halfway back to her chair with the coffee when her cell phone rang. The coffee sloshed over the rim as she hurried to her seat, conscious of everyone's gaze focused on her.

Her insides trembled as she placed her cup on the table and then answered the phone, as usual punching speaker and record at the same time. "Agent Beaumont," she said.

"Ah, Georgina, have you missed me?" Bob asked.

"Actually I have," she replied. "I thought maybe you didn't want to be my friend anymore."

"You're my closest friend, Georgina, and I want to continue the discussion we were having the other day about family."

Georgina closed her eyes, a familiar pressure of pain filling her chest as she thought about her family. "I'll tell you what, why don't you let Macy go? Just drop her off at some mall or in the middle of a park and drive away and then we'll talk about my family."

"Georgina, are you trying to call the shots here?" Bob laughed, the sound a sinister one that crawled up her spine. "How about we talk about you first and then I'll consider your request to release the little princess."

A reckless hope buoyed up inside her as she kept her focus on the face of the cell phone. "Ask your questions, Bob, and then we'll see if you're a man of your word when it comes to reciprocating."

She felt Alex's presence right behind her, smelled the familiar scent of his cologne and a sense of calm, of security swept through her.

"Do you have siblings, Georgina?"

"Two older sisters," she replied.

"Do you have a good relationship with them?"

"I don't have any relationship with them."

"Why is that?"

Once again Georgina closed her eyes as ancient memories cascaded through her…bad memories…horrendous ones. "I don't have anything to do with any of my family because they were verbally, physically and emotionally abusive to me," she replied, despite the ever-stronger constriction in her chest.

"Why was that, Georgina?" Bob asked. "Were you a bad little girl?"

Alex's hand fell to her shoulder and even though she'd told him she wanted him to treat her only as a professional, she was grateful for the touch that kept her connected to the here and now as she darted down the rabbit hole where all her monsters lived.

"No, I wasn't a bad little girl. My problem was that I was born a girl. My sisters are four and five years older than me. When my mother got pregnant again my father was certain she was going to deliver him the son he desperately wanted. Instead he got me. He called me the abortion that should have happened."

She was vaguely aware of Alex's fingers tightening on her shoulder as she fought the demons of her past. The last thing she wanted to do was bare her skeletons in front of the team, in front of Alex, but she would do it if it helped further the investigation. She would give to Bob what she'd never been able to give to Alex or anyone else on the face of the earth.

She'd give him her nightmares.

It was as if Bob had poked a hole in a dam and now the flood of evil spilled from her in an emotional burst.

"Yeah, Bob, I had a crappy childhood. My father hated me and insisted that my mother and sisters have nothing to do with me. I was kicked and beaten by all of them when I wasn't locked in a closet for days at a time."

"I hear your pain, Georgina. I feel your pain," Bob said. "My old man was a mean drunk and he was drunk most of the time. I was beaten nearly every day of my life and my dear mother did nothing to stop it."

"Tell me, Bob, how did you manage to get the people you kidnapped?" Georgina asked. Despite the turmoil and chaos the discussion about her past had stirred up in her head, she hadn't lost track of her main goal—to get any information she could from him. "Did you take them alone or do you have a partner?"

Bob snorted. "I work alone. Partners only screw things up."

"So did you just surprise them and force them at gunpoint to go with you?" she asked.

"How pedestrian," he replied dryly. "Actually, the one thing my daddy taught me was how to blow poison darts. From our saggy little porch I could shoot a gator in the eye from ten feet out. Of course I didn't use poison for my victims. I used just enough tranquilizer to knock them out long enough for me to move them into their new homes. The drug has the aftereffect of loss of memory for several days, but that worked in my favor. Amberly and Cole were the most difficult because I had to keep them continuously drugged throughout the long road trip home."

Tim gave a thumbs-up, indicating that he'd managed to get the phone number and triangulate the call and had a location where it was coming from. Alex raced over to his computer, took a look and then headed for the door with a nod to Frank and Matt to go with him.

Georgina picked her phone up from the table and hurried after them. "How are you keeping all those people?" she asked, still connected to the call and knowing she needed to keep him talking for as long as possible.

"Very carefully," he said and then laughed, the sound shivering through her already fragile state.

"Let Macy go," she said, aware of the emotion that filled her throat, nearly stifled her voice. "I told you about my childhood. I did what you asked. Now you do something for me. Let her go."

"I've thought about it and I'm pleased that you shared so much with me, but I'm not ready to give up little Macy yet," he replied.

"Please let her go." She drew a deep breath in an effort to keep her emotions in check. "Let them all go."

"I think we've talked long enough for one day," Bob replied. "We'll talk again, sweet Georgina." He clicked off just as the four of them burst out of the building's back door.

As Frank and Matt raced toward Matt's car, Georgina hurried after Alexander toward his. "He hung up," she said unnecessarily as she slid into the passenger seat.

"The call came from the college campus. Let's hope he decides to linger for a while." Alex started the engine and squealed out of the parking lot and onto the street. He hit the button to start his flashing lights, zooming through the light traffic with Matt and Frank close behind.

She was grateful that Alexander didn't talk. She was

in a dark place that she hadn't visited for a very long time. Bob had managed to wrench memories from her she'd thought were long forgotten. He'd reminded her of what it had been like to be unwanted, unloved and unworthy.

It had only been when she'd joined the police force and then later the FBI that she'd found her worth, some form of self-respect and dignity, and the desire to be the very best that she could be at her job.

"The signal appeared to be coming from the bench area in front of the gym," Alex said as he braked to a halt at the curb by the college. Almost before the engine was completely off, he was out of the door and running.

Matt and Frank parked and ran after him while Georgina hurried out of the car and headed in the same direction. She hoped he was still there. She hoped and prayed that this was it, that they'd get him in custody and he'd tell them where he had his captives.

She picked up her pace, running after the men as her stomach rolled with the need to throw up and her brain continued to fire memories of her childhood through her head.

The men reached the area first, where four students were hanging out, two seated on the concrete bench and two standing.

"FBI. All of you put your hands up where we can see them," Alex said as he approached the group with his gun drawn.

The two young men who had been seated jumped to their feet and all of them raised their hands over their heads. "Wha...what's going on?" one of them asked.

Frank and Matt also had their guns drawn and the four were now circled by the agents.

"Very carefully, very easy, all of you get your cell phones out and set them on the bench," Alex instructed.

"This is about a cell phone?" A tall, dark-haired young man asked. "I've got it. It was sitting on the bench when we came out of the gym. I was going to turn it in to lost and found."

He reached into his shirt pocket and plucked out a cell phone and set it on the bench, then quickly raised his hand once again.

"How do we know that isn't your cell phone?" Georgina asked.

The young man gazed at the phone with scorn. "Look at it. It's a cheap piece of crap. It doesn't even have internet capabilities. I've got my own phone right here." He reached into the pocket of a duffel bag next to him and pulled out an expensive phone with all the bells and whistles.

He was here and now he was gone. The sick roll of Georgina's stomach intensified. As Alex questioned the young men, Matt pulled on latex gloves and put the phone in a plastic evidence bag he pulled from his pocket.

They would find nothing on the phone, she thought. Bob was far too smart to leave a phone for them to find unless he knew they'd glean nothing from it. It was a cheap throwaway and she knew he'd left it behind just to taunt them.

Before the men even finished speaking to the students, she turned and headed back to the car, her legs unsteady and a bitter taste in the back of her throat.

She got into the car, and a few minutes later Alex joined her. "Are you okay?" he asked.

"No. I think I need you to take me home. I'm requesting the rest of the day off." Her voice sounded tinny and as if it came from someplace far away.

Alex asked no questions. He started the car and headed in the direction of her house. He apparently sensed that she was in a place where she didn't want to talk, didn't want to listen, for he didn't speak until he pulled up into her driveway. He obviously knew that she'd be no good to anyone for the rest of the day.

"Are you sure you're going to be all right?"

She unbuckled her seat belt and opened the door. "I'll be fine by tomorrow morning. I just need some time alone right now." She got out of the car and shut the door, grateful that she could enter a code that would open the garage door and grant her entry into the house since she'd left her purse in the war room.

She didn't look back. As the garage door rose, she ducked under it and hurried to the door that would take her into her kitchen. She punched the button to close the garage door and then headed for the bathroom where she fell to the floor in front of the toilet and threw up.

She felt as if she was purging all the rage and grief that had been buried inside her for so long. Tears blurred her vision as she continued to be sick.

She hated Bob, not just for the crimes he'd committed but for what he'd done to her. He'd forced her back into a darkness she'd thought she'd escaped long ago. More than anything, she hated him for making her appear weak in front of her team.

When she was finally finished being sick, she pulled

herself to her feet, brushed her teeth and then went back into the living room and curled up on the sofa with the television on.

Tomorrow she'd be strong. Tomorrow she would be the kind of agent she needed to be, but right now she needed to deal with the fact that despite Alex's warnings to her, Bob had gotten into her head and brought up memories she needed to banish from her mind forever.

THE AFTERNOON CREPT BY slowly with Alexander's thoughts split between the case and the broken woman he'd dropped off earlier. He'd never seen Georgina so shattered and he worried that the conversation with their perp had pushed her over an edge he hadn't realized existed inside her.

He now knew why Georgina had never wanted to share anything of her past with him. He now recognized that she had demons inside her he couldn't begin to understand.

"Kind of a coincidence that the phone was found not far from where our kooky reporter lives," Matt said, pulling Alex back to the work at hand.

"He admitted freely that he'd been to all the crime scenes," Frank added. "Maybe he's our perp hiding in plain sight."

"Maybe," Alex replied absently. "Two things I think we can agree that we learned from the conversation Georgina had with Bob. The first is that he probably grew up in the swamps. He talked about blowing darts at gators when he was young. The second thing is that I think he's probably well educated."

"*Pedestrian* isn't a word that normally flows from

a thug's mouth," Terry replied. "Hell, I went to college and I've never used that word in a conversation in my life."

Nicholas walked through the door and Alexander suddenly realized the man had been missing for several hours. "Where in the hell have you been?" he demanded.

"I told everyone I was going to lunch," Nicholas replied defensively.

Alexander looked at his watch and then back at the dark-haired agent. "Since when do we get four-hour lunches around here?"

Nicholas's complexion took on a red cast. "I was only at lunch for half an hour. Then I got a call from a snitch who thought he had some information for us about this case, so I agreed to meet with him."

"And?"

"And the little jerk didn't have anything for me, he just wanted to see if I'd flip him a twenty. It was a waste of my time. What did I miss here?"

"Frank, fill him in," Alexander said and headed for the door. He walked down the hallway to the bathroom and once inside he sluiced cold water on his face and then dried off with a paper towel.

For just a moment as he'd faced Nicholas, he was too angry for words. He knew the younger agent had a reputation as being a lone wolf and had a desire to make a name for himself amid the ranks.

But Alexander had little use for somebody like that on this case. The task force was a unit that would function best as a single entity, with everyone knowing what everyone else was doing and learning.

He frowned at his reflection in the mirror. Had Nicholas ever been present when Georgina had received a call from Bob? No, Nicholas had always been absent when the calls came in.

Crazy. The thoughts that whirled through his mind were crazy. There was no way Nicholas could be responsible for the phone calls to Georgina. Alexander was definitely entertaining crazy thoughts.

He tossed the towel into the trash and then left the bathroom and returned to the war room, his anger back under control.

"Just a word to all of you," he said, although his focus was on Nicholas. "We are a team here and we work together as a team. I've assigned you all a partner and anything you're doing your partner should know about. No exceptions, got it?"

The men all murmured their assent and everyone got back to their assigned jobs. Alexander sat down and opened the folder he carried everywhere with him. It contained all the reports and photos from the previous disappearances and everything that the task force had done in this investigation.

He'd gotten word from the lab that none of the food that had been in Jackson's refrigerator had been tainted by anything, a point that didn't matter now that Bob had confessed how he'd taken his victims. Tranquilizer darts—it made sense given the fact that none of the victims had appeared to have had an opportunity to fight back.

"Tim and Jeff, focus in on all buildings that are near the swamps in the area. My gut says this guy will stay where things are familiar to him. Nicholas and Frank, focus in on any murders that occurred within the last ten years or so around the swamp areas. If he killed his parents at the old homestead, then I have a feeling that homestead is swampland."

"You know it's possible their murder was never reported," Jeff said. "Those swamp people are a tight-knit group that have little to do with law enforcement. Our perp might have killed his parents and fed their bodies to the gators."

"At this point anything is possible. Check missing persons reports during that time period. Surely somebody would notice if two people just went missing," Alex said.

Once again the room grew silent except for the clicking of computer keys. Alex stared down at the folder open in front of him. The photo that stared back at him was Macy's.

There was no question in his mind that Georgina had put herself through a terrible hell in an effort to please Bob enough that he would agree to release the little girl.

The bastard. His chest filled with pain as he thought of what Georgina had shared, as he realized how difficult it must have been for her to go back to such a horrendous time in her life, to dredge up memories that should have stayed buried deep in her mind.

Secrets. He'd always known she had secrets. He just hadn't realized they involved childhood abuse and neglect. There was no question that it bothered him more than a little bit that she would give that piece of herself to a killer, but had never shared any of it with him throughout their marriage.

He wondered how she was doing. He'd never seen

her so pale, so sickly looking in all the time he'd known her. He reached a hand to his pocket for his phone and then dismissed the idea of calling her.

She'd made it clear what she needed from him, and a check-in call wouldn't be considered appropriate under her conditions. Still, he couldn't help the worry that weighed on him as he thought of her at home all alone with only her demons as company.

"I've been checking Roger Cambridge and Michelle Davison since they've both been around the college in the last week," Frank said. "And I found a connection between the two of them that probably means nothing."

"What kind of connection?" Alexander asked, grateful for anything that would keep his mind focused on work and not on Georgina.

"It's weak, but they both took the same class in college, a class called Inside the Killer's Mind: Aberrant Behavior through Case Studies. It's taught by Professor Jacob Tanner."

"He was in front of Georgina and me in line at the book signing for Michelle," Alexander said and then frowned. "But I didn't pay much attention to him." Unfortunately he'd been far more focused on the author and her boyfriend than the man in line in front of him.

"I'll check in with Professor Tanner tomorrow. Maybe he can give me some insight into his former students," Alexander said.

"If Georgina isn't available to tag along with you tomorrow, I'd be happy to," Nicholas said.

"I'll decide who is going where in the morning," Alexander replied. He hoped that Georgina would be back, that today hadn't completely shattered her not only personally but professionally as well.

It was just after eight when he finally dismissed the team. After the room had emptied, Alexander remained, his mind trying to process everything that had occurred in the past eight hours.

Maybe Professor Tanner would be able to give them some insight into Michelle and Roger Dodger, the wonder reporter, some insight that might indicate whether either of them had the potential to be a killer.

It would be nice if Professor Tanner could provide an easy solve to this complicated case, but Alexander didn't hold out much hope for that.

The swamp reference had definitely been a lead to follow, but there were plenty of swamps in and around Baton Rouge. It could take weeks…months to check every building for the missing people.

And he wasn't sure he wanted Georgina taking any more of the creep's phone calls. It had gotten to her today. She'd given up too much of herself, sacrificed a piece of her soul in an effort to negotiate with Bob.

He had no idea if she'd be any use to the team now or not, but what concerned him more was her emotional well-being. He had a feeling she'd only shared a taste from the plate of horror that had been her childhood. How much more she must have gnawing holes deep inside her soul.

It was after nine when he finally left the FBI building with the need to drive around for a while and process everything the day had brought.

At least Georgina hadn't sacrificed herself for nothing. They now believed the man had been born and raised around the swamps and that somehow, some way, he'd become educated beyond what would be expected from a spawn of the swamp.

Either he was a self-educated person or he'd had some schooling additional to high school. Words were Michelle Davison's business. Roger appeared to be a fairly well-educated man. So neither of them could be taken off their list of suspects. He just had a feeling that neither of them were guilty of these crimes.

Of course, he knew Michelle hadn't physically carried out the kidnappings, but her boyfriend, Jax, would have been able to commit the crimes at her bidding or even unbeknownst to her.

He drove for about half an hour and was somehow unsurprised when he found himself pulling into Georgina's street. Darkness had fallen and he told himself he had no intention of stopping in to see her. He just needed to drive by her house and make himself feel better.

As he approached her house, his headlights fell on her front lawn where two people appeared to be fighting. He stopped his car, pulled his gun and got out. "Halt!" he yelled.

One of the figures froze, while the other fell to the ground. The one standing turned and ran and Alexander raced forward. From a nearby streetlight, he saw that it was Georgina on the ground.

"Go," she gasped. "I'm fine, just go catch him."

Alexander hesitated only a moment and then ran in the direction her attacker had gone. His heart beat frantically as a dog barked in the distance. He couldn't think about what might have happened had he not arrived at the scene when he did. He couldn't think about anything but catching whoever had attacked Georgina.

Still, what he wanted and reality were two different things. The darkness of the night played in the attacker's favor and the attacker had enough of a head start on Alexander that by the time he reached the next corner, he didn't know which way to go.

He stopped and listened. The only sound he heard was the frantic beat of his own heart. No footfalls, no crackling of brush or any new barks to indicate which direction the man had run.

He was gone, swallowed up by the night. With both frustration and worry boiling inside him, Alexander turned and hurried back down the sidewalk toward Georgina's house.

When he got there, she was no place to be seen and he breathed a sigh of relief as he realized she'd probably gone inside and locked the doors behind her.

He went up to the door and softly knocked. "Georgina, it's me."

She opened the door and before he could take a step inside she fell into his arms, sobbing and shaking. "It was him," she finally managed to gasp into the front of Alexander's shirt. "It was Bob. He wanted to add me to his collection."

Alexander tightened his arms around her and moved them both deeper into the living room, stunned by two things. He was surprised that Bob had confronted Georgina in a way that was not his normal mode of attack.

But equally as surprising was the fact that in all the years he'd known her, he had never seen Georgina cry.

Bob had gotten pieces of her past and now he'd gotten her tears. For those facts alone, if Alexander ever got the chance, he'd kill the man.

Chapter Eight

Georgina finally moved out of Alex's arms, deep sobs slowing as she sank down on the sofa. She raised her hands to her face and angrily swiped away the tears. She'd not only been terrified, she'd been stupid and the result had nearly been devastating.

She was aware of Alex sinking down next to her, his body warmth radiating out as the scent of his familiar cologne began to slowly calm her.

Dropping her hands to her lap, she turned to face him. "I was so stupid," she said angrily. "I fell for a ruse and I should have known better."

"Tell me what happened." His voice was soft and when he reached for one of her hands, she allowed the contact, needing the warmth of his touch.

"I was asleep on the sofa and I woke up and heard a baby crying. It was such a plaintive wail and it sounded like it was coming from just outside my front door. I was still half asleep, but I decided I needed to check it out. I opened the door, stepped out on the porch and that's when he grabbed me." A new sob escaped her as she thought of that moment when strong arms had wrapped around her and a voice had whispered in her ear.

"The minute he grabbed me, he whispered that I would be the queen of his collection." She shuddered and Alexander squeezed her hand more tightly.

"Were you able to get any kind of description of him?"

She shook her head. "He had on a ski mask so I couldn't make out any facial features, but he was tall and very strong. If you hadn't come along when you did, he would have had me. I fought against him, but eventually he would have won the fight."

Alex frowned. "I wonder why he didn't take you like the others? With some sort of tranquilizer?"

"He said I was special, that I deserved special treatment because we'd shared so much." Once again a shiver rippled through her as she thought of how close she'd been to disappearing, of becoming the eighth person in his den.

"Dammit, we should have seen this coming," Alex said. "I should have known he'd come after you."

She disengaged her hand from his and gazed at him curiously. "Why are you here? Did you have any idea that I might be in trouble?"

"No, I was just driving around for a while before going home and you were on my mind so I decided to drive by your house."

"Your timing was impeccable," she replied and then released a tremulous sigh. "I've been through a lot of things in my life, but I don't think I've ever been as scared as when he grabbed me."

Alex stood and gazed down at her. "Pack your bags. You're coming home with me."

"Okay," she replied, obviously surprising him if the

look on his face was any indication. She stood. "I might be hardheaded, Alex, but I'm no fool. I feel the target on my head and I'm not about to make it easy for him by staying here all alone. I'll be right back with my bags."

She left the living room and went into her bedroom, where she pulled a suitcase from the closet and began to fill it with enough clothing to last a week or so. After that time they'd have to figure out what to do next where she was concerned.

She didn't particularly like the idea of spending time with Alex in the house they had once called home together, but she liked the alternative less.

She didn't have a security system here. She would be vulnerable to another attack if she stayed, and the next time she might not be so lucky.

As she left the bedroom and went into the bathroom to gather up toiletries, she told herself she would rather put up with the memories that being in that house with Alex would evoke than be Bob's next victim.

Within twenty minutes Alex was carrying the big suitcase out her front door and she followed behind with a smaller overnight bag.

She didn't feel completely safe until she was in his car and he was behind the wheel and pulling away from the curb. Over and over again, Bob's voice played in her head. "He spoke to me, but his voice was more a guttural growl than a real voice. I'm not sure I'd recognize it again if I heard him speaking normally."

"I hope you never get close enough to him to hear his voice again unless he's in handcuffs," Alex replied, his voice bearing the deep rumble of a papa bear protecting a cub. "I don't want you talking to him anymore."

She stared at him in surprise. His chiseled features were taut with tension in the glow from the dashboard. "Don't be silly. Of course I intend to talk to him again."

"Georgina, he got to you today. He got deep into your head." Alex didn't try to mask the deep worry in his voice.

"I know. You're right," she replied, knowing that to try to lie to him would be foolish, given what he'd heard on the phone conversation and her reaction afterward.

"I was afraid I'd lost you, that he'd pushed you too far over the edge."

She frowned and stared out the passenger window, remembering the traumatic conversation with Bob. "For a minute he did, he cast me back to a place I never wanted to revisit. But I just needed some time away from it all. I would have been fine by morning."

He didn't say anything and she had a feeling he didn't quite believe her. But she would have been fine. She would have been ready to face her job once again. After all, the job was the only thing she'd ever really trusted.

For the remainder of the drive, they were silent. She had no idea what was going on in Alex's head, but her head was filled with the feel of those strong arms around her, the low hiss of words meant to terrify and the scent of evil that had swelled in the air.

She'd fought him. She'd fought hard, but he'd been so much stronger, and if he'd had only another minute or two, he would have overwhelmed her and carried her away.

God, would she ever be warm again? The intimate contact with the killer and imagining what might have happened had Alex not come along had iced her insides to arctic levels.

A new tension, along with gratitude, filled her as they reached the house and Alex punched the button to raise the garage door.

She was walking back into her past by coming here. It was a past that had been filled with happiness, passion and ultimately the pain of self-realization. Still, she knew she'd be safe here. The house had a security system and an armed and dangerous Alex, who would never let danger come close to her again.

"I'll just put your bags in the guest room," he said as they walked out of the garage and into the kitchen. Georgina followed behind him, stunned to see that the kitchen looked exactly the same way it had on the day she'd walked away.

Nothing had changed and as she walked into the living room she realized nothing had changed there either. He hadn't redone the decor or bought new furniture. He hadn't even taken down their wedding picture that sat on the bookcase next to his criminal investigation books.

She followed him down the hallway to the second bedroom where he placed her suitcase and smaller bag on the floor. "You know where everything is and if you can't find something just let me know. How about I put on some coffee?"

"Actually, what I'd like most right now is a long hot bath and then sleep." She didn't want to sit at the table and rehash the night's events. She just wanted to get warm and feel safe.

She wanted to sleep without dreams, suffer no nightmares of Bob or her childhood and wake up ready to tackle the job once again. The job would keep her sane.

"Why don't we just say goodnight now," she continued. "It's already getting late and we can talk in the morning on the way to work."

He hesitated a moment and then nodded. "Okay, then I guess I'll just tell you good-night now and see you in the morning."

"Good night, Alex. And thanks for being at the right place at the right time."

"My pleasure," he replied with a smile.

She closed the bedroom door, as if to ward off the way his smile made her feel just a little shaky, just a little more vulnerable than she already felt.

She pulled her suitcase up on the bed and opened it, quickly hanging what needed to be hung and then throwing her underwear into one of the empty drawers in the dresser.

Don't think, she commanded herself. *Don't think about what might have happened if Alex hadn't appeared in the night. Don't think about the distant past and all the pain. Just breathe and keep your head empty of all thoughts.*

She grabbed her nightshirt, a pair of panties and her toiletry bag and went across the hall into the guest bathroom. There was another full bath in the master suite so she knew there was no reason for Alex to interrupt her.

She started the water in the tub and then began to undress, eager to get off the blouse and slacks that *he'd* touched. She wanted to scrub away any skin that had touched his. She felt him everywhere on her and she just wanted to scrub him off.

With the tub filled, she turned off the water and stepped into the heated depths. She sank down so that the hot water surrounded her to the shoulders, hoping to heat the inner core of ice that remained inside her.

Closing her eyes, she willed herself to relax, but her thoughts worked against her. How had he found out where she lived? Probably the same way he'd found out her cell phone number. There had to be a mole somewhere in the department. But it was difficult to believe that anyone in the agency would want to see the kidnapping or death of another agent.

As far as she knew she'd made no enemies in her five years as an FBI agent. Granted, she wasn't close to anyone, but she'd always gone out of her way to be pleasant to everyone she worked with.

Don't think, she told herself once again. She wouldn't be worth anything in the morning if she didn't relax and get a good night's sleep. And she wanted to be on her game the next day for she was certain that Bob would contact her again. He'd revel in the fact that he had gotten so close to her.

She shivered and realized the hot water wasn't working, that the core of ice inside her remained. It took only a few minutes for her to use the minty scented soap and scrub herself clean. She sank completely under and then rose up and stepped out of the tub and grabbed a fluffy towel from the cabinet.

When dried, she pulled on her nightgown and panties, finger-combed her damp hair and then left the bathroom and scurried back across the hall. The house was silent and dark, letting her know that Alex had already gone to bed.

It felt strange to be getting into the bed in the guest room. She'd never slept in here before. She'd decorated the room in deep rich browns and tans and had thought it looked quite inviting at the time. But at this moment she only felt cold, afraid and lonely.

"Don't even think about it," she muttered to herself as she punched her pillow. She shouldn't even think about the fact that Alex was just down the hall, that he'd been the one person who had always been able to warm her and make her feel safe and secure.

Going to him now would be one of the biggest mistakes she would ever make in her life. It would definitely give him the wrong impression.

Of course, she could make sure he didn't get the wrong impression. She could tell him that she just needed him for one night, wanted him to hold her and make love to her to banish everything else from her mind.

She would be using him for this night to drive from her mind everything that had happened in the last twelve hours, but as long as she was up front with him about it, then surely he couldn't hold it against her.

She knew she was making a mistake when she got out of the bed. She knew it was a mistake as she made her way down the darkened hallway.

She hesitated in front of his closed bedroom door, knowing that if she knocked there would be no going back. While she could justify this night in her mind, she would never be able to take it back.

Once she knocked on the door, she knew he'd invite her into his bed and she knew they would make love. But before that happened she had to let him know that it was just tonight, not a new beginning for them, not a second chance, just a single moment of need that would never again be repeated.

She raised her hand and, drawing a deep breath, she knocked on the door.

AT FIRST ALEXANDER THOUGHT he'd only imagined the faint knock on his door because he wanted her to come to him. It was only when he heard a second, louder knock that he responded. "Come in," he called, his heart pounding a little faster.

His door opened, and in the faint moonlight casting in through his windows he could see her silhouette in the doorway. "Did I wake you?" she asked.

"No, I'm not even close to being asleep," he replied. "Did you need something?" His voice sounded slightly hoarse to his own ears as his blood rushed through his body.

"I need you."

Her voice sounded stark and his heart pressed painfully tight against his chest. "You've got me, Georgina. Whenever you need me, you've always had me."

She remained standing, as if weighing her options. "It's just for tonight, Alex. I'm using you. I'm only inviting myself into your bed for tonight, not back into your life in any meaningful way."

Although it wasn't what he wanted to hear, he wanted her badly enough to agree to any terms she'd set into place. "So you just want to take advantage of me for a single night," he said with a forced lightness.

"That's about the size of it," she replied.

"Then what are you waiting for?"

She flew across the room and landed on top of him like a long-legged nymph seeking home. Despite everything that had happened through the long day, he laughed with the sheer joy of holding her in his arms once again.

As she crawled beneath the sheets to join him, it was as if the past two years without her had only been a bad dream and now she was back where she belonged.

They lay side by side, facing each other and in the moonlight her eyes glowed with the fire of want, of need.

He reached for her and she filled his arms as their lips met in a fiery kiss. Alexander had two years of desire built up inside him and he gave her that emotion by delving his tongue to dance with hers.

She wrapped her arms around his neck and pulled herself half on his chest as their mouths remained melded together. Someplace in the back of his mind he knew she was giving him no more than her body. She'd always been generous with that, but she'd never been able to achieve any real intimacy with him outside of the bedroom. He would never really have her heart. She kept that so closely guarded.

He shoved this thought away as he focused on the here and now. These moments of this night were all he had and he wanted to savor each and every one.

She slid her hands up and down his naked chest and pulled her mouth from his to nuzzle into the hollow of his throat. His hands glided down her back to the edge of her nightshirt. He was already fully erect, ready to tear her nightshirt over her head, pull her panties off and take her as he'd never taken her before.

But he didn't do any of those things. He knew it was important that he let her set the pace, nonverbally telling him what she needed and when. It was a lack of control that had driven her to his bed. He knew instinctively that he needed to allow her to be in total control now.

She sat up and pulled her nightshirt over her head and tossed it to the floor, then straddled him and leaned forward to kiss him again, her bare breasts against his bare chest.

The contact was immensely pleasurable as she plied his mouth with heat and hunger and her nipples pebbled hard against his skin.

The only thing keeping them from complete intimate contact was his boxers and her panties, but she seemed in no hurry to take them off as her lips once again trailed from his mouth, down his jawline and then over his chest.

He was in a dream that he hoped would never end, a dream he'd had a thousand times since the day she'd left him. She sat up and he reached to cup her breasts, paying special attention to her hard nipples, and was rewarded by a low, deep moan that escaped her lips.

He wanted her moaning. He wanted to make it impossible for her to ever want another man. She was all he'd ever wanted, all he'd ever needed and he loved her as he would never love another woman.

She rolled off him just long enough for her to remove her panties and at the same time he quickly shimmied down his boxers and kicked them off.

When she straddled him once again, all he could think about was burying himself in her, possessing her completely for the length of time he could control him-self, for the length of time she'd allow him.

As if reading his thoughts, she grasped his hard length and then guided him into her. As she sank down, she once again moaned with pleasure.

He tensed, trying to maintain control as her tight moistness surrounded him. She looked beautiful in the moonlight and he had to close his eyes to focus on not letting go too soon.

"Now I feel warm and safe," she whispered.

Whatever words he might have said in response van-ished as she began to rock her hips back and forth. The friction of her movements shot blood through his veins, stole every other thought from his mind.

She gasped and began to move faster and he knew she was on the verge of a climax. He thrust upward, wanting her there before he lost all semblance of con-trol.

And then she was there, shuddering uncontrollably as she half laughed, half cried out his name. His own control snapped and wave after wave of pleasure jolted through him as he found his own release.

She collapsed on his chest, utterly boneless against him as their breathing found a more normal rhythm. She finally raised her head to look at him. "I'm not sure I have the energy to move."

"Then stay right where you are." He stroked his hands down her slender bare back and wished they never had to move again.

"Do you mind if I sleep in here with you?" she asked. "Just this one night," she added as if wanting to remind him that this was a one-shot deal.

"Do you really think I'm going to tell you no?" he replied wryly.

"I'll be right back." She slid off the bed and disappeared down the hallway to the bathroom. He got up and went into the master bath and then found his boxers on the floor and pulled them back on.

He was back in the bed when she returned to his room. She pulled her nightshirt over her head and then got beneath the sheets and snuggled against him.

He stroked her short, silky hair and closed his eyes, wishing the night would never end. Unfortunately, as far as he was concerned, the night was far too short. He awakened just before five to a dark room and the other side of the bed empty.

He pulled on a white robe that he'd gotten when he and Georgina had taken a cruise for their honeymoon and followed the scent of freshly brewed coffee down the hallway.

She sat in the chair at the table where she'd always sat in the mornings when she'd lived here. She was still clad in her nightshirt, her hair a spiky mess that only made her more beautiful to him.

She smiled at him. "You're up early."

"You're up earlier." He got a cup of coffee and joined her at the table. There was a sense of déjà vu about the scene. They had always begun their mornings with coffee at this table, with her in her nightshirt and him in his robe. "Bad dreams?"

She shook her head. "No, I just woke up and couldn't go back to sleep. Instead of fighting it, I decided to go ahead and get up." She frowned. "Did I wake you up?"

"No, I woke up on my own." He curled his fingers

around his coffee mug, unsure where to take the conversation next. He knew she certainly didn't want any morning-after chatter.

"We need to check everyone's alibi for last night," she said, letting him know she'd been thinking about the case. "I know the person who tried to grab me was a man, so Michelle doesn't need an alibi, but her boyfriend does."

"I'll get everyone on the alibi situation as soon as we get to work. In the meantime, yesterday evening we decided it might be a good idea to talk to Professor Jacob Tanner."

"Why does that name sound familiar?" she asked.

"He was in line in front of us at Michelle's book signing," Alexander replied.

"That's right. I remember Michelle greeting him." She paused and took a sip of her coffee. "So, why are we interested in talking to him?"

"We found out that he taught both Michelle and Roger in a class about killers and aberrant behavior. We thought maybe he might be able to give us some insight into the two."

"You mean you want to ask him if either one of them were bed-wetters, fire-starters or into torturing small animals?" she asked teasingly.

He grinned, knowing she'd just named what were supposed to be three precursors to becoming a serial killer. In his years of chasing killers, he had yet to find a bed-wetter among the group. "You never know what he might remember about those two, and right now he's just a straw for us to grasp in hopes that something fresh will come out of it."

For the next thirty minutes he caught her up on everything that had occurred the day before after she'd left. The fact that there was so little to tell her cast a pall of frustration through him.

Even more frustrating was the fact that the perp had come so close to grabbing Georgina last night. Thank God he hadn't succeeded, but Alexander should have managed to catch him. He could have ended it all last night if he'd just run a little faster, if he'd just tried a little harder.

He stared at Georgina, now cast in the glow of the morning sunrise. A fist of tension balled up in his chest. "After what nearly happened last night, we're going to be stuck together like glue."

"I know I'm a target now," she said. "But, what happened after what nearly happened last night isn't going to happen again."

Her sentence would have been quite confusing to anyone else, but he knew she was telling him that she wouldn't be sharing his bed again. When she'd said one night only, she'd meant it.

He would have to live with that. What he couldn't live with was somehow screwing up and causing danger to grab Georgina. He couldn't go through another Kelly Gilmer failure, especially with the woman he loved as yet another victim.

Chapter Nine

"Last night our perp tried to grab Georgina," Alexander said.

It was seven o'clock in the morning and everyone was in the war room. When Alexander made his first announcement to the group, everyone turned to look at Georgina.

"I just happened to be driving by her place and saw her grappling with Bob in her front yard. He ran when I pulled up and I tried to follow, but lost him in the darkness. What I want everyone focused on today is getting alibis as to where Jax, Michelle and Roger were last night between the hours of nine and ten. I want the alibis checked and rechecked."

"Aren't Michelle and Jax on some book tour?" Nicholas asked.

"Yes, and according to the itinerary I got from Michelle's agent, they were supposed to be in New Orleans all day yesterday and until tomorrow. She has a signing there tonight."

"It's only about an hour and a half drive from New Orleans to here. They could have driven back here, attacked Georgina and been back at their hotel by midnight."

"And Roger doesn't do his news show on Wednesday nights so he could have been anywhere last night," Terry said.

"I want to know where *anywhere* was," Alexander replied. "Right now Roger and Jax are the only halfway viable suspects we have. I particularly want to know Jax's whereabouts last night since we now know his parents died in a house fire about ten years ago. Do we have any more information about that fire?"

"I checked all the records from the investigation and it was definitely arson. Jax was at the top of the suspect list but was a hundred miles away when the fire occurred and the authorities could never make anything stick. The case remains open, but hasn't been worked in years," Matt said.

"It still just could be a coincidence that Bob told Georgina he killed his parents and Jax's parents died in an arson fire," Nicholas said. "Or Bob could have been lying about everything he told Georgina."

"He wasn't lying," she replied. Despite everything she had endured the day before, this morning she looked cool and confident.

"How can you be so sure?" Nicholas asked.

"Trust me, I know he was telling the truth. We're looking for somebody who grew up with abuse and trauma in his childhood. He's filled with rage and, according to his own words, has visions of becoming the greatest serial killer of all time. But he's also tightly controlled, a planner and a very organized kidnapper/killer and that will make him even more difficult to find."

She drew a deep breath and glanced around with a

faint blush. "Sorry, I didn't mean to go into a long, boring monologue."

Alexander smiled at her. "Not boring, definitely things we all need to keep in mind." His smile fell as he glanced around at the members of the team. "We also think he's well educated, probably has a good job and may even be married and have a family."

"This isn't your ordinary thug," Frank added. "He's managed to remain elusive in two different cities, at two different crime scenes."

"Right now my money is on Roger Cambridge," Nicholas replied. "He has photos and reports about each crime that he shouldn't have. He's admitted to being in both Mystic Lake and Bachelor Moon."

"I just want to know where he was last night when Georgina was attacked, and I don't want you all making phone calls to the persons of interest," Alexander said. "Frank, Matt and Nicholas, I want the three of you to take off for New Orleans. Check and double-check on Michelle and Jax. If they said they ate at a particular restaurant, then you go to the restaurant and confirm it."

He turned his gaze toward Terry. "I want you to rattle Roger's cage, and Jeff and Tim, you continue to work on potential locations in and around swamp areas." He paused and then sat down. "What are you all waiting for?"

It took only minutes for the room to clear out, leaving behind only Alexander, Georgina, Tim and Jeff. "Grab some coffee and relax, it's too early for us to head over to the college campus," he said to Georgina.

"I'm coffeed out," she replied. "Tim, how is the search going of the buildings you've located?"

He frowned. "The locals have checked out about thirty locations and found nothing. They're being very cooperative, but there are also a lot of empty warehouses and buildings in and around the swamplands."

"Eventually you'll stumble on the needle in the haystack," Georgina said with a warm smile to the younger agent.

The tip of Tim's ears turned pink. "Thanks. Let's just hope I find the place before the student decides he's learned all he can from his teacher captives."

Georgina's eyes held the same kind of horror that rippled through Alexander at Tim's words. It struck home again that if the seven kidnapped people were still alive, it was only because Bob allowed them to live.

He had the power to keep them as captives or kill them, and there was no way any of the team could guess when Bob would decide that his captives were more hindrance than help.

Alexander knew he was working against a ticking clock and he had no idea when the clock would strike the time that people would die. And the team had so little to go on in finding those people and the man who would end their lives when he decided.

It was just before nine when Alexander and Georgina parked in one of the college lots behind the Division of Humanities building. In this building, students learned philosophy, psychology and criminal justice. It was also in this building that Dr. Jacob Tanner taught his classes and had his office.

"West wing, second floor," Alexander said as they entered the front door along with several students. While they had waited for it to be late enough to come to the college, he had done some background digging into Jacob Tanner.

The professor was highly esteemed and his classes were the most popular among the students. He was only thirty-two years old but had zoomed through his education and had gotten his job teaching here four years ago. He lived alone in an upscale townhouse near the college and liked to play chess and bridge with fellow teachers.

"I don't know if he'll remember Roger, but we know he definitely has maintained some sort of contact with Michelle," Georgina said as they took the stairs to the second floor. "I wonder if he had any contact at all with Michelle's boyfriend."

"We should have checked records to see if Jax attended college here. To be honest, it didn't occur to me. He doesn't exactly read as a college-educated man."

"Maybe he's fooling us with his brawn act. Maybe Michelle likes a smart man when it comes to mental stimulation, but likes a thug as a bodyguard and in the bedroom," Georgina replied.

"Would you like a thug in the bedroom?" Alexander asked.

She shot him a dirty look. "You know exactly what I like in the bedroom, Alex, and we're not taking this particular conversation any further."

He liked the way her cheeks flamed with color. She might have told him that last night was an anomaly that wouldn't happen again, but she wasn't as immune to him as she wanted him to believe.

They easily found Professor Tanner's office, and Alexander knocked on the door. "Just a minute," a woman's voice drifted through the door. He exchanged a glance with Georgina who shrugged. Maybe the professor was important enough to warrant a secretary.

The door opened to reveal a young woman with wheat-colored hair that was pulled back into a severe bun, and she was clad in tailored slacks and blouse. She looked as if she were desperate to appear older than she was.

"May I help you?" she asked.

"We're looking for Professor Tanner," Alexander said.

"He's not in yet. I'm Megan James, his student assistant. Is there something I can help you with?" Her smile was cool and professional.

"When do you expect Dr. Tanner to be in?" Alexander asked.

"In about fifteen minutes or so. He has a nine-thirty class."

Georgina displayed her badge. "Then we'll just come in and wait for him." She didn't give the young assistant any opportunity to protest, but instead pushed past her and into the room.

Alexander followed as Megan stepped back. Jacob Tanner had a cushy office, with a bank of windows that looked out on trees and green space. There was a small desk, neat and tidy, and a love seat in hunter green.

The walls held wildlife photos, but it was the bookcase behind the desk that drew his attention. Abnormal psychology books lined one shelf, the collection impressive. The other shelves held books on Ted Bundy, John Wayne Gacy, Jeffrey Dahmer and all the notorious serial killers through time. There were even several books about Jack the Ripper.

"Is Professor Tanner in some kind of trouble?" Megan asked worriedly as she gestured for them to sit on the love seat.

"No, nothing like that. We just have a few questions to ask him."

Megan sank down in the chair at the desk. "That's good, because he's the best. All the students love him, and his classes are always the first ones to fill up." It was obvious Megan had a bad case of hero worship going on.

"How is he to work for?" Alexander asked, just passing time.

"Wonderful. He's so patient and kind, and it's been an honor for me to learn from and work for him." She smiled beatifically.

The door opened and the man of the hour walked in. Megan jumped out of his chair behind the desk while Georgina and Alexander rose simultaneously from the love seat.

"What's this? Some kind of a welcoming committee?" Jacob Tanner cast the two agents a pleasant smile. He was tall, medium weight, with dusty-blond hair and blue eyes. He was handsome in a boyish way, which was probably what made him a favorite among the female students on campus.

"They're FBI agents," Megan said. "They want to talk to you."

"Oh, okay." Tanner didn't appear concerned. "Megan, why don't you go on downstairs to the theater and make sure the podium and video equipment is ready to go for today's classes."

Once the young woman had left the room, Tanner

closed the door behind her and walked over to his desk chair. "Please," he said, gesturing them back down on the love seat as he sat. Official introductions were made. "What is it that you think I can help you with?"

"We saw you at Michelle Davison's book signing last week and from what we understand she was a student of yours," Alexander said.

Tanner nodded. "One of the brightest I think I've ever taught. Is she in some kind of trouble?"

"She's a person of interest in a case we're working on. What do you know about her boyfriend, Jax White?" Georgina asked.

Seated so close to her on the love seat, Alexander was surrounded by Georgina's scent and he tried hard to ignore it and focus on Tanner, who had a look on his face as if he'd tasted something unpleasant.

"Jax was also a student of mine. He barely passed my class and I don't think he actually graduated. He was bright enough but unmotivated. Michelle could do much better when it comes to boyfriends."

"What about Roger Cambridge? We understand he also took several of your classes," Alexander stated.

Tanner leaned back in his chair and smiled in open amusement. "Roger Cambridge. He was a good student, he never missed a class, but he also loved to draw attention to himself. He wanted to make sure everyone knew Roger Cambridge. I'm not surprised that he's doing his cheesy internet show. He desperately wants his fifteen minutes of fame."

"Enough to kidnap FBI agents and make the news so that he can report the news?" Georgina asked.

Tanner's brow creased. "Roger was intense. He really

got into the classes, sought extra time with me to discuss various elements of the serial killers we studied in class. Do I think he's capable of committing a crime?" He leaned forward and shrugged. "To be honest, I don't know."

"We understand that your classes are some of the most popular that are offered," Georgina said.

He leaned back again and smiled. "You have to admit there is something fascinating about the criminal mind and what men and women are capable of doing to each other. In the classes, we explore the nature versus nurture theory and we go into details of some of the most infamous serial killers."

"Do you have any students now that ring bells of having the potential to commit crimes?" Georgina asked.

Tanner laughed. "I have to admit that I'm sure there are some maladjusted, troubled young people who are drawn to the class because of their own issues. Can I forecast who of those students will go on to become killers? Absolutely not. It would be nice for everyone if I could easily identify any students who would go on to commit violent crimes."

He looked at his watch and stood. "I'm afraid I need to leave. I've got a class to teach. Is there anything else I can help you with?"

"No, but if we think of something we'll get back in touch with you." Alexander and Georgina stood and together the three of them left the office.

"Good luck to both of you, and I'm sorry I couldn't be more help," Tanner said as they walked down the hallway toward the stairs. "I once considered becoming a police officer, but then I thought of the danger involved and changed my mind. Those who can, do, but those who can't, teach, right?" He gave them another pleasant smile and then hurried ahead of them and disappeared through a doorway.

"Well, that was a big waste of time," Alexander said in frustration as he and Georgina left the building and headed for his car. "He wasn't able to help us at all."

"Maybe not, but I found it interesting that he remembered Roger and Jax. It's obviously been several years since they were in his classes and Tanner has had hundreds of students since then." Georgina stopped talking long enough to get into the passenger seat and then resumed when he was behind the wheel.

"Maybe it's time we dug a little deeper into Roger, maybe put a tail on him. If he's looking for his fifteen minutes of fame, maybe he is our man," she said.

"Maybe," he agreed. "We'll see what the others have as far as alibis for last night on everyone. Roger better hope he has a damn airtight one."

He tightened his hands on the steering wheel. "What really worries me is that we don't even have Bob on our radar, that he's not Roger or Jax, but rather somebody we haven't even come into contact with other than the phone calls to you."

"Those phone calls will be his downfall," she said. "Somehow, someway, I'll get him to give up some useful information that will lead to his arrest."

Alexander frowned. "Not at the price you paid yesterday."

"Whatever it takes for success," she replied. "He won't get into my head again, but I need to keep the conversation with him going. It might be our only chance."

He glanced at her long enough to see the tension that tightened her features and then looked back at the road. "Why didn't you tell me about your childhood?" It had been a question that had plagued him since he'd listened to her talking about it to Bob.

"It was ugliness I hoped I had left in my past. I certainly didn't want to bring it into our marriage," she replied. She looked out the passenger window as if in an attempt to disengage from the conversation.

However, it was a conversation Alexander intended to have. "It was important for me to know about, Georgina. Your childhood is so much a part of what you become as an adult."

"I didn't want you to know that part of me. I just wanted to forget the way I was treated as a child. I left it behind when Child Protective Services took me away from my parents when I was sixteen."

Alexander shot her a look of surprise. "You went into foster care?"

She sighed and turned to look at him. "For two years I lived with a family who taught me what normal life was supposed to be like. They explained to me that what I'd suffered was called scapegoat child abuse. It's over and done with, and I survived and I don't want to talk about it anymore."

I survived. Alexander played her words over and over again in his mind. She said that it was fine, that she'd survived, but had she really?

He thought of all the times in their marriage when she'd been emotionally distant, as if she was afraid to trust him, afraid to love him with all her heart and soul.

If he'd known this information, maybe he would have

been able to figure out exactly what she needed from him. Maybe he would have been able to find the core of pain that must still reside inside her and soothe it, override it with all his love. Maybe if he'd known what she'd been through in her early life, he would have been able to stop her from leaving him.

Too late now, a little voice whispered in the back of his head. He'd obviously let her down, not been enough, and she'd made it clear to him that there were no do-overs where the two of them were concerned.

He'd always believed her to be one of the strongest women he'd ever known. Learning about what she'd endured had only solidified that belief. Still, he knew that everybody had a breaking point. He'd seen Georgina momentarily break yesterday, letting him know that she was vulnerable.

Now not only did he have to worry about catching Bob and finding the missing, he also had to be concerned about Georgina's physical safety and her mental state.

He didn't want the price of cracking this case to be damage to Georgina's fragile state of mind while playing a game with the killer.

Chapter Ten

The afternoon crawled by. Georgina once again found herself going through the files pertaining to the disappearance of Sam, Daniella and little Macy in Bachelor Moon, of Amberly and her husband Cole from Mystic Lake and everything they had about the disappearance of Jackson and Marjorie from Jackson's home.

She flipped the pages, looking for something, anything they might have missed, all the while acutely aware of her cell phone on the table before her.

As the afternoon progressed, the members of the team that Alexander had tasked with checking alibis began to return to report back what they'd found.

Although Michelle lived on the outskirts of New Orleans, she and Jax had spent the night in a hotel not far from the bookstore where she would be signing books tonight. They both had been seen in the New Orleans hotel dining room around seven the night before, but then hadn't been seen by anyone again until this morning. According to them, they had retired to their room and hadn't left, which meant neither of them had been cleared concerning the attack on Georgina.

The report on Roger's whereabouts at the time of

the attempted kidnapping of Georgina was also not a solid alibi. According to Roger, he'd had dinner with a couple of friends at the Pig Roast, a barbecue place near the campus, but they'd parted ways around seven and Roger had gone home, where he said he worked on notes for his next newscast and then went to bed.

The agents had confirmed that Roger did, indeed, meet friends for dinner at the Pig Roast, but couldn't confirm that he was at his apartment for the rest of the night.

So nobody had been cleared and the frustration of the team was evident in the silence that prevailed in the war room. The silence was broken only by the occasional cracking of Matt's knuckles.

"For crying out loud, stop that," Frank finally said when Matt popped his knuckles for the fifth time. "Don't you know that's not healthy."

"It's not hurting me," Matt protested.

"It's hurting me," Frank exclaimed. "It's making me freaking crazy."

"Okay, why don't we call it a day," Alex said. "It's after five, and I'm sure some of you would like to actually eat dinner with your families. We'll meet again at seven in the morning."

There was a stampede to the door as the men took off. It had been a long stretch for all of them without much time off.

"It's a good thing I wasn't standing near the door when I told them to take off for the night," Alex said dryly. "I would have been nothing but roadkill."

Georgina laughed, despite her general feeling of disappointment. She picked up her phone from the table and dropped it into her purse. "I'd hoped to hear from him today."

"You still might," Alex replied.

"I don't know. All the calls have come in during the afternoons." She started for the door, but paused as Alex didn't move.

She looked at him and he raked a hand through his hair and stared at her for a long moment. "Have you noticed that whenever you get a call from Bob, Nicholas is never around?"

She looked at him in stunned surprise. "As much as I dislike Nicholas, surely you aren't suggesting that he has anything to do with all of this."

"Crazy, right? I'm having crazy thoughts." He ushered her out of the room and into the hallway. "Just forget I said anything about it. You want to grab something to eat out or fix something at home?"

"Let's just cobble something together at home," she replied. "I don't really feel like going out. I'm ready for comfy clothes and an early night."

"Sounds good to me."

As they rode the elevator down to the first floor and then left the building and headed for his car, Georgina couldn't forget what Alex had said about Nicholas.

She brewed his words around in her head while they drove home and once there while she changed into a pair of sweatpants and a T-shirt.

She was in the kitchen with the refrigerator door open, trying to decide what to fix to eat when Alex joined her. He'd also pulled on a pair of black sweatpants and a matching T-shirt. He looked more relaxed than he had all day.

"Finding anything worthwhile in there?" he asked.

"We're looking at a soup and sandwich night or omelets with bacon and toast," she replied. She grabbed the bacon package. "And I know your love affair with bacon."

He laughed and grabbed a frying pan from the cabinet and set it on the stovetop. "Remember how we used to wrap bacon around hot dogs, or water chestnuts for a little cocktail snack in the evenings?"

She handed him the package of bacon. "I remember a lot of things we used to do." She consciously willed away the memory of those impromptu cocktail hours that almost always ended with the two of them making love. She didn't want to remember the good times. It hurt. The memories of being with Alex were almost as painful as her childhood memories, although for much different reasons.

She turned back to the refrigerator and pulled out the eggs, milk, cheese, a green pepper and an onion. For the next few minutes the only sound was the sizzling of bacon cooking and her cutting up the vegetables.

She couldn't let Alex get into her head, with memories of happiness and passion, with memories of laughter and love. There was no way she would return to his bed again tonight no matter how hard he subtly worked to turn her resolve into capitulation.

They worked in an easy companionship. Once the bacon was crisply fried, Alex made coffee and then moved to the toaster while she poured the omelet mixture into the waiting skillet.

It wasn't until they were seated across from each other at the kitchen table that she brought up what he'd said to her earlier. "What do we really know about Nicholas's background?"

"Not much," he admitted. "He doesn't talk about his past."

She crunched into a piece of bacon and then followed it with a drink of coffee. "He's very ambitious," she said as she set her cup back down.

Alex raised a dark eyebrow. "Ambitious enough to commit these crimes, then get himself on a task force and then what?"

"I don't know, set somebody else up to take the fall. Be the hero. You're the one who put the idea into my head in the first place."

He grinned. "I know, but I really expected you to tell me I was crazy. I didn't expect you to actually entertain the idea."

She cut into her omelet and then met his gaze once again. "Unfortunately, I don't much like Nicholas and maybe it's my negative feelings toward him coming into play. But, truthfully, I'm not sure I trust him. I'm not sure what he might be capable of in an effort to make a name for himself in the department."

Alex grimaced. "I hate thinking that he could in any way have anything to do with this, but the fact that he's never been with us when you've received a phone call from Bob, the fact that he has a tendency to disappear by himself for long periods of time makes me wonder."

"Maybe you should look at his personnel file, find out what's in his background," she suggested. As somebody who had been so private about her own past, she felt bad even suggesting it.

The grimace turned into a frown. "You know a case is bad when you start looking askew at your own team members."

"You know you won't be satisfied until you check him out," she replied. "You know as well as I do, you never know what package evil comes in. Who is to say it doesn't come in the package of an overly ambitious FBI agent who committed the crime and now is determined to somehow solve the crime on his own, gaining glory and respect among the ranks."

"You're right, I won't be satisfied until he's vetted. I'll check in with Director Miller first thing in the morning and see what I can do without it coming to Nicholas's attention. And now let's talk about something else because otherwise I'm going to lose my appetite before I finish my bacon."

"That will never happen," she said teasingly.

"Probably not," he agreed with a wry grin.

They finished the meal, talking about the weather, which was predicted to cool off a little bit in the next week, and what else Georgina had learned from reading Michelle's book. After cleanup, they each carried a fresh cup of coffee into the living room and the case was once again the topic of conversation.

"It's too bad we couldn't confirm alibis on either Roger or Jax during the time I was fighting with Bob on the front lawn," she said as she eased down on one end of the sofa.

"It's too bad we only have two names on our persons of interest list—three if we count Michelle." Alex sank down on the opposite end of the sofa.

"I feel like we're missing something, but I can't figure out what it might be," she admitted. "I've read over all the files a dozen times and I can't find anything that the initial investigators missed."

"I've seen plenty of terrible things in my job, but I can't wrap my mind around somebody who would kidnap FBI agents in order to pick their brains on how to become the best serial killer in the world."

Alex shook his head and picked up his cup from the coffee table. He held the cup before him as his eyes bored into hers with intensity. "We have to get this guy, Georgina. We have to get him before he kills those people."

She saw the torment in the depths of his blue eyes, knew that he had to be thinking about the loss of Kelly Gilmer under his lead.

"We're going to get him, Alex." She couldn't help herself. She leaned over and placed her hand on his arm in an effort to ease some of his torture. "You have to let her go. You have to know that you did all that was humanly possible to save her."

The haunting in his eyes eased somewhat. "You know, when I have one of my nightmares about her, I still reach out for you in the bed. Even after all this time, in my sleep-muddied mind I'm always surprised to find that space next to me empty."

His words caused an ache in her heart, even as she pulled her hand away from him and moved closer to the edge of the sofa. She couldn't be pulled in by his needs, his wants, because ultimately she'd never live up to his expectations.

"I'm sorry, Alex. I'm sorry you're still having nightmares and that you have to go through them alone.

Maybe you should talk to somebody professionally about that case, somebody who could help you find the closure that you deserve."

"I don't need a damn shrink," he scoffed. He downed his coffee and stood. "I think I'm going to call it a night. I'll make sure the alarm is set. Just turn off the lights when you go to bed."

He didn't even bother to take his cup into the kitchen but rather headed straight down the hallway to his bedroom. She'd made him mad.

She wasn't sure what he had expected of her. If he'd expected her to volunteer to sleep in his bed with him so that she'd always be there when he had one of his nightmares, he was delusional.

As she sipped her coffee, she decided it was good that he was angry with her, that surely the conversation and her lack of a response would solidify the fact that she was not coming back to him.

She was only here now because she knew she was marked by a killer. She was only here because she trusted Alex to do everything in his power to make sure she stayed safe.

She wasn't here to hold him after he suffered from a bad dream. She wasn't here to jump back into his bed for more amazing sex or to become a partner in life once again.

Once this case was over and Bob was behind bars, things would go back to the way they had been for the past two years. She'd see Alex in passing in the building, they might exchange a few words in greeting, but that would be it.

What she didn't understand as she picked up their

cups and carried them into the kitchen was why her heart ached so badly at the thought of leaving him once again.

ALEXANDER WAS IN A FOUL MOOD. He'd been in a foul mood all morning. He'd barely spoken to Georgina as they'd shared coffee and then ridden to work together.

It wasn't so much that he was angry with her. He was angry with himself for wanting her, for needing her when she'd made it clear she was done. And maybe he'd always retained a little bit of anger toward her because she'd walked away from him so easily, without any real explanation.

His mood hadn't improved when they got to work and he'd gone in to Director Miller's office to discuss Nicholas Cutter with him. Miller had been surprised by Alexander's request to see Nicholas's personnel file, but had agreed to provide it to Alexander before the end of the day.

The mood in the war room seemed to reflect Alex's. Everyone appeared to be in a bad mood, sniping at each other when anyone spoke.

He'd finally sent several of the men home for the day, knowing that working seven days a week and the long daily hours were probably part of the problem.

When he was done, it was just himself, Georgina, Nicholas, Tim and Terry left in the room. He'd tried to send Tim home, but the young agent had refused, telling Alex he had nothing waiting for him at home and would much rather keep working on locations to search.

Georgina sat with her laptop open in front of her and her cell phone by its side. When she'd first begun work, she'd gone to Michelle Davison's web page and had discovered that the author was now using the disappearance of the three FBI agents for publicity, a fact that had put a star next to Jax's name on the whiteboard.

She was now surfing the web to find out any minute information about Jax White that she could find, but Alexander noticed how often her gaze fell on her cell phone.

Waiting for a call from Bob—that's what she was hoping for. Alexander's stomach tightened as he thought of how shattered she'd been with the last phone call. Could she handle another one? Was Bob done talking and instead now plotting on a new way to get her in one of his cages?

And what the hell had little Macy meant by saying they were in cages? He got up from his chair and began to pace the length of the room, his thoughts whirling with suppositions.

"Tim, check for old prison or jails," he said to the redheaded agent. "Macy said they were in cages. Maybe that in itself is a clue that they're being held in some old prison facility that was abandoned years ago."

"I'm on it," Tim replied, not looking up from his computer screen.

Alexander continued to pace, trying to separate Georgina's emotional turmoil from the nervous energy that filled him when he focused on the case.

He stood back and stared at the bulletin board with all the photos tacked up and staring back at him. He darted his gaze to the whiteboard, where the names of Michelle, Jax and Roger were written, along with notes about each one.

His eyes felt gritty. Despite storming off to bed fairly early, he'd been awake for most of the night. He'd tossed and turned, stared up at the ceiling and thought about what Georgina had said about him needing to let go of the Gilmer case.

On some level he recognized that he'd done everything humanly possible to save Kelly from the monster that had abducted her and then ultimately killed her. He just wished he'd been one minute sooner arriving at that warehouse, he wished he'd been able to shoot the bastard before he'd plunged that knife downward.

Maybe he did need some therapy. He'd been encouraged to see the agency shrink right after it had all happened, but he'd refused, afraid to show any weakness, afraid to admit how deeply that case had touched him.

He finally found himself back in his chair. Remembering what Georgina had told him about being a scapegoat child, he typed in the term to bring up some sites that had information on the issue.

He'd heard the term before but wasn't sure exactly what it meant. As he read first one article and then another detailing both what a scapegoat child would suffer and the lasting effects that could occur, any anger he might have felt toward Georgina slowly melted away.

If what he'd read was true, then Georgina had spent the first sixteen years of her life being told she was defective, not wanted and not loved. Her mother hadn't rushed to save her, her sisters hadn't tried to protect her; rather, the entire family had deemed her unworthy and punished her for the simple fact that she'd been born a girl.

Was it any wonder she had been guarded throughout

their marriage? Was it any wonder she'd been afraid to share the very core of her being with him? Maybe she needed therapy as much as he did.

It was close to noon when Director Miller came into the room with a file. Alex took it from him and buried it beneath his other files, knowing this one would contain the information he needed to know about Nicholas.

He'd look at it later, at home tonight, when Nicholas wasn't around. "Why don't we break for lunch," he said. "Let's plan to be back here in about an hour."

Terry, Tim and Nicholas were the first out of the room. Georgina stood and started for the door, but he stopped her. "I want to apologize for my crappy mood last night and this morning," he said.

"It's okay," she replied.

"No, it isn't okay." He took two steps closer to her, stepping into the achingly familiar scent that emanated from her. "I'm frustrated with the case, and I took it out on you." While that wasn't the complete truth, it was all he intended to say.

He couldn't tell her that he loved her, that he'd never stopped loving her. He couldn't tell her that she was an ache in his heart that was relentless. He didn't want to burden her with his problem, and it was his problem.

"What did Director Miller give you?"

"Nicholas's personnel file. We can take a look at it tonight when we get back to my place." He intentionally didn't say *home,* for *home* implied a place where they would live together, love each other.

"I still can't imagine…" Whatever else she might have said was cut off by the ring of her cell phone. Her face paled and her eyes darkened as she sat back in her chair and answered.

Alexander moved to stand right behind her as Bob's voice filled the line. "I nearly got you the other night," he said. "I decided to shake things up a bit."

"You definitely shook me up," Georgina replied, her voice strong and showing her control.

Bob laughed, the altered sound a creepy one that Alexander knew would stay in both his and Georgina's heads for a very long time to come. "You're a feisty one, Georgina, but I would have had you if your friend hadn't come along when he did. You are one lucky lady."

"Bob, why don't you end this all now? Nobody is dead and we can work together to get you help. You know we both share a similar background and I understand the rage that is driving you, but this isn't the way to heal from it. You deserve better than this."

"Oh, is this another attempt to bond with me? To find the innocent little child inside me and heal my boo-boos?" Bob's voice held derision. "How have your childhood boo-boos healed, Georgina? Have you found your inner child and fixed what your family did to you?"

Alexander saw the faint tremble of Georgina's hand as she quickly swiped it through her short hair and he knew that she hadn't resolved the issues from her past, that they still haunted her despite the fact that she was now not only an adult, but a well-respected FBI agent as well.

"You're a smart man, Bob. You didn't have to kidnap all those people to learn how to kill. You could have read all the books on crime. You could have researched and gotten the same results."

"I've done extensive research into the subject of serial killers and what drives them. I've studied case histories to understand what mistakes they made that ultimately landed them behind bars. But I also know there is a time when the teacher has to become the student and I could learn all kinds of things that weren't in books by interrogating the men who had been in the trenches."

"Then why do you need me? You have the best of the best at your disposal."

"I don't *need* you, Georgina. I just want you, and I always get what I want." There was a click and the call ended.

"Not this time," Alexander muttered under his breath.

Georgina leaned back in her chair and released a tremulous sigh. "Did you get anything out of that?"

Alexander sat next to her. "Play the recorded version."

He was grateful that she'd stayed strong and Bob hadn't played the mind games with her as he had before.

They listened to the conversation three times. There didn't appear to be any background noise and his voice held no trace of any specific characteristic that would make anything about him easily identifiable.

"There's something he said that shot off a little bell in my head," she said.

"What's that?"

"Something about it being time for the teacher to become the student." She frowned thoughtfully. "The first thing that jumped into my head was Professor Tanner."

Alexander sat back in his chair in surprise. "Professor Tanner?"

She shook her head and released a small laugh. "I know, crazy, right? Why would a highly esteemed college professor be kidnapping FBI agents to become a world-class serial killer?"

"As crazy as suspecting one of my own team having something to do with the kidnappings," he replied.

"Maybe this case has just made us both so desperate that we really are crazy and grasping at very thin straws," she said.

"Let's go down to the cafeteria and talk about what it feels like to be crazy."

"Sounds like a plan," she agreed.

As they headed out of the room, Alexander mulled over her new potential suspect and the fact that once again Nicholas hadn't been around when a call had come in. Was it possible that one of their own was responsible?

Could they really take a single line of conversation and make it point to an entirely new suspect? Or were they both grasping empty air in an effort to stop a madman?

Chapter Eleven

"Baker's Bayou," Tim said, breaking the silence that had prevailed in the war room since they'd all come back from lunch.

"What about it?" Georgina asked before Alex got the chance. The phone call with Bob followed by lunch in the cafeteria had filled her with a restless energy that refused to subside.

"In the early 1950s there was a small women's prison located there." Tim looked up from the computer screen. "It's been abandoned all these years, but it would probably still have jail cells in there."

Alex was up and out of his chair at the same time Georgina stood. "Tim, get me the exact coordinates. Nicholas, get on the phone and have Jesse Calder from Fish and Wildlife meet us there. He knows the swamps as well as anyone.

"Terry, call Matt and Frank and have them meet us at the mouth of Baker's Bayou. Get the directions from Tim and tell them to come in quiet."

Tim printed out a map with directions. Alex grabbed it and the three of them flew out the door. Georgina's heart pounded loudly in her ears as adrenaline pumped through her.

Was it possible this was it? An old abandoned jail in the middle of a swamp would certainly fit the bill for good old Bob. Was it really possible that they'd located his lair?

They didn't bother waiting for the elevator but instead took the stairs two at a time. They burst out of the back door of the building and raced to Alex's car. Terry rode shotgun and Georgina climbed into the backseat. She barely had her door closed when Alex started the car and squealed out of the parking lot.

Terry read the directions that Tim had provided and other than that there was no conversation in the car. The energy level that filled the car made it feel as if there were twenty people in the vehicle.

She didn't know the Baker's Bayou area at all, but she had worked with Jesse Calder on a case once in the past. She swore he was part man, part swamp creature and he could guide them wherever they needed to go through any swamp in the state.

She knew they were headed into danger. Anytime there was a possibility of a hostage situation, everyone's lives were at risk, particularly the hostages themselves.

The best they could all hope for was that when they did their initial preview of the building, Bob wouldn't be there. She didn't believe that Bob spent all of his time with his hostages. He had to have a job; if nothing else he had to make money to feed the people he held captive.

Sam and Daniella and little Macy had been missing for months. If they weren't being fed, they would have already starved to death.

She glanced down at her watch. It was just after four. If they were lucky, they'd have at least four hours of daylight to maneuver and get into the place Tim had found. Darkness came early in the swamp and even with Jesse's guidance, night would complicate the whole operation.

Her adrenaline shot higher when Alex told Terry to contact the rest of the team. He obviously thought that this was the break they'd been waiting for and they were on their way to save the people who had been missing for too long.

If they were really lucky, they could get into the building and wait for Bob to arrive. That way they would not only ensure the safety of the hostages, but get him under arrest at the same time.

She wanted that. She wanted the man who had caused such chaos, such pain, to be behind bars for the rest of his life where he couldn't hurt anyone else ever again.

It felt as if it took forever to reach the location, but finally they were there and Alex parked on the grass near a dirt road that led into what she assumed was Baker's Bayou.

When they got out of the car, the smell of the swamp hung in the air. The odor was fishy and one of stinking stagnant water and thick sucking mud.

The dirt road disappeared into a heavily wooded area, where cypress trees were nearly overwhelmed by Spanish moss, giving the whole area a spooky aura.

Georgina fought back a shiver as she stared into the semidarkness of the marsh. There was haunting beauty there, but there was also danger…and potentially seven people who desperately needed to be rescued.

She touched the butt of her holstered gun that was on

a belt around her waist. She'd never had to kill a man before, but she wouldn't hesitate to put a bullet into Bob's black heart if it became necessary.

Her firm resolve came from the memory of Macy's frightened voice, the little girl's blue eyes that looked at her day after day from her photo in the war room.

The nearby swamp wasn't silent. Mosquitoes buzzed in the air, brush rustled and in the distance a watery slap indicated either a big fish or a gator.

"We'll wait here until Jesse and the others arrive," Alex said, his deep voice filled with tension. "According to this map that Tim printed out, there's only one way in and one way out of Baker's Bayou." He pointed to the dirt road.

"Are there any homes in the area?" Terry asked.

"There might be a couple, but they look like they're pretty close to the mouth. The building we're looking at is toward the back of the cove. I just hope we don't need a boat to get back there."

"Surely Jesse will know, and if we need a boat he'll have one with him," Georgina replied.

They all turned as two cars arrived, one carrying Matt and Frank and the other with Nicholas behind the wheel and Jeff in the passenger seat. The men got out and Alex quickly filled them in.

"When Jesse arrives, Frank, Matt and I will go in with him. Terry, Nicholas, Jeff and Georgina will stand guard here to make sure that nobody comes out this way."

"I'm not staying here," Georgina said firmly. "I'm going in with you."

"Georgina, you're a target. I don't want you anyplace

near this man." Alex's eyes simmered with emotion as he attempted to stare her down.

She stared right back at him, her chin lifted in a show of resolve. She hadn't come this far, suffered this much, to be relegated to the back of the line. She deserved to go in.

"I'm a trained FBI agent and I'm the only person here who has a personal relationship with Bob. I might be your only hope if things go bad. I'm coming with you."

His eyes narrowed to blue slits of displeasure, even as he gave a curt nod of his head. "Okay, but you'll be sandwiched between me and Jesse as we go in."

"Whatever, as long as I go in with you," she replied, pleased that he had listened to her, even though it was obvious he hadn't wanted to.

Nobody was going to keep her out. She wanted to be there when the hostages were freed. She also wanted to be there if things went bad and somebody had to negotiate with Bob.

Jesse pulled up in a black pickup. He got out and strode toward them, looking like he was already part of the swamp. He wore a long-sleeved camouflage shirt and pants that disappeared into hip waders.

His long black hair was tied at the nape of his neck and his dark eyes were as flat as the gators he knew so well. He greeted them all with a raise of his hand and then took the map Matt proffered and studied it.

"I know this place," he said. "Been back there a couple of times over the years. We won't need a boat. There's a narrow muddy path of sorts that we can walk with water on either side. The water is fairly deep and full of gators and snapping turtles and other critters. I suggest you all step where I step if you want to be as safe as possible."

"We want to go in quiet and see if we can get a look inside," Alex replied. "We don't know if the man we're hunting is there or not."

Jesse's eyes gleamed with excitement. "Then let the hunt begin." Without another word he headed toward the dirt road. Georgina hurried after him with Alex and Frank and Matt bringing up the rear.

They walked in single file down the road and within minutes reached an old shanty. Jesse and Georgina stood back as Matt and Alex checked out the place.

"It's obviously been abandoned for years," Alex said as he emerged from the listing structure. He motioned for them to forge ahead.

The road continued for about half a mile and then narrowed to a path and the swamp took over. Tall cypress, oak and elm trees blocked out much of the light of the day, the oaks wearing Spanish moss like delicate hair.

Georgina followed in Jesse's footsteps but began to feel the suck of muck on her feet. The swampy smell was more intense and the bugs thicker and bigger. Pools of water stood on either side of the narrow path. Georgina kept her gaze focused on the path. She didn't want to see what creatures the waters might hold.

If this was the right place, then how on earth had Bob managed to get the hostages through here? "Is there a waterway to the building where we're going?" she asked Jesse, keeping her voice as soft as possible.

"Yeah, you could get there by a pirogue, you'd just have to enter the area north of where we did," Jesse replied.

Georgina knew that a pirogue was a canoe-like boat and she also knew that the boats could be big enough to carry a body or two. Unfortunately, these boats weren't registered through the state so there was no way of finding Bob by his means of transportation through the swampland, if that's the way he traveled.

With each step she took, she felt the muck beneath her feet suck harder, making the simple act of walking difficult. Her shoes and pants would be ruined, but that was a tiny sacrifice to make if they were successful in freeing the victims and catching Bob.

The primal wildness that surrounded her added to the tension of the situation. The deeper they went into the marsh, the faster her heart beat, and a thin layer of perspiration began to coat her forehead.

They'd all pulled their guns when they'd begun the trek, and hers now felt slippery in her hand as the sultry heat made sweat trickle down her back and streak from her hair.

Get Bob. Free the captives. The two sentences became her mantra as they continued to walk for what felt like forever. Get Bob. Free the captives.

Would Bob turn out to be Jax or Roger or would he be somebody they hadn't even met, somebody who hadn't hit their radar?

Just when Georgina thought she couldn't lift her mud-caked feet for another step, Jesse stopped and turned back to face them.

"The building is just ahead. It's on dry ground. I

don't know how you want to handle the approach," he said. "I could go ahead and check it out, see if the people you're looking for are there."

Alex frowned. "I appreciate the offer, but you've done your job by getting us here. I'd like it if you'd wait here to get us back out, but trained agents need to be the ones making contact from here."

Adrenaline flooded through her and she forgot about the muck, the sweat and the bugs as she realized they were within sight of the place that hopefully would end this case once and for all.

"Matt and Frank, you go to the left of the building and Georgina and I will go right. Try to get close enough to look inside without being seen by anyone. We don't want a hostage situation. We go in slow and quiet." Alex's terse voice spoke of the danger in the situation.

"And if they're in there and Bob isn't anywhere to be seen?"

"There has to be a front door of some kind. We'll see what we can see and then if that's the case we'll meet at the front door to go in as a team." He looked at Georgina. "Ready?"

She nodded. She'd never been more ready for anything in her life. Her head filled with the sound of Macy's voice asking for help. "Let's get this done."

The four of them moved ahead where the path widened and although the area was heavily treed, the land rose higher than the swamp waters that surrounded it.

Through the thick stand of trees and brush, she could see the structure, a rather small, concrete-block building. Small windows were set high at regularly spaced intervals, each sporting a rusty-looking set of bars.

The place looked utterly abandoned, as if the swamp and the primordial wilderness had tried to swallow it whole. This was a place where people could scream and nobody would hear. This was a place that only a swamp rat would know about. And they'd already discerned that Bob was probably a spawn of the swamp.

As the two pairs split up, Georgina's heart banged painfully tight against her ribs as the first tinge of hope she'd felt since beginning this case filled her. The emotion pressed tight in her chest, making her feel almost dizzy with anticipation.

They made their way stealthily through the brush and around the trees toward the right side of the building. Hopefully there would be a window somewhere on the side or in the back that would allow them to see inside without actually breaching the building.

Let them be here, Georgina thought as she stayed close to Alex. Bugs bit at her and branches slapped her arms and legs as they worked through the woods and tried to stay covered from view.

Her heartbeat raced even faster as they finally reached the side of the building and saw a door with a window. Alex exchanged glances with her and in his eyes she saw the same hope that jumped inside her very soul.

Seeing nobody around and using the brush and trees to their advantage, they moved forward. Georgina got to the door first and carefully raised her head just enough to peek inside.

Her heart dropped to the muddy ground beneath her. Empty. Abandoned. There was nobody inside to save and it appeared that nobody had been inside the structure for years and years.

Alex muttered a curse as she turned and leaned against him, overwhelmed by the sense of defeat, of knowing that they were no closer to catching Bob and saving the victims than they'd been on the very first day that the task force had been formed.

Wearily she straightened and headed back. Failure. The weight of it was an accustomed one, a reminder that she would never be good enough, had never been good enough for much of anything.

Failure. It was the first thing she'd tasted when she'd been old enough to understand that she wasn't what her family wanted, and she hated that the taste was no different now.

It was after seven when Alexander left the FBI building with Georgina at his side. The disappointment that the entire team had suffered when they'd arrived back at the war room was palpable.

He'd been so sure. He'd been so positive that they'd found the place where the captives were just waiting to be released from their cages.

As he drove home, all he heard was the loud ticking of a clock in his head, an instinctive clock that told him time was quickly running out for Bob's hostages.

Seeing the location of the old jail, recognizing how many other places there could be in the back of any number of swamps, had shot a wave of discouragement through him that he hadn't been able to shake no matter how hard he tried.

He pulled into the driveway and together they got

out of the car and went into the house. "Dinner?" She looked at him in question, her gaze holding a dull light of defeat.

"I'm not really hungry. What I'd like is a nice stiff drink."

"I'm of a mind to join you," she replied as she sat at the kitchen table.

Alexander opened the cabinet that held his small liquor collection. "I've got whiskey, scotch and there might even be a bottle of wine up here."

"To hell with the wine. I'll take scotch on the rocks," she said.

He looked at her with a raised brow. She normally wasn't much of a drinker, other than an occasional glass of wine. *But you don't know what she's done during the past two years,* he reminded himself. Still, she'd always been a lightweight when it came to holding her liquor.

He poured them both scotch on the rocks and then joined her at the table. Dark shadows rode the delicate skin beneath her eyes and her entire body appeared smaller, as if she'd pulled into herself. She wore the defeat of the day on her face and in her posture.

She took a sip of the scotch and made a face. "I've never understood how people drink this stuff. I think it tastes awful."

"You want me to get you something else?"

She shook her head. "No, tonight I need something strong and biting." She released a weary sigh. "I was so sure we were right, Alex. I was so certain that we were at the end of the case and everything was going to be good. We were going to rescue everyone and get the bad guy behind bars."

"I know. I felt the same way. Seeing that empty, abandoned building kicked the stuffing out of my gut." He downed his scotch in two swallows and then got up from the table, grabbed the bottle and returned. He poured himself another two fingers of the amber liquid.

Georgina tipped up her glass and downed her drink, then gestured for him to refill her glass as well. He did so and then leaned back in his chair, a deep weariness settling heavily on his shoulders, into his very soul.

"You have to promise me something, Alex," she said, her green eyes the color of the swamp that had earlier surrounded them.

"Promise what?" he asked.

"Promise me that if this all goes bad, you won't go back to that dark place where you went with the Gilmer case."

He turned his glass around and around between his hands as he stared down into the scotch. "There's only been one thing that took me back to that dark place, one thing that took me even deeper into the darkness, and that was you walking out on me."

He looked up at her, his heart filled with the love he feared he'd always hold where she was concerned. "I thought the Gilmer darkness was bad, but the pit of darkness I fell into when you left me was even worse."

She broke eye contact with him and instead leaned back in her chair and released a deep sigh. "I thought it was the best thing to do for you."

She took another drink and he couldn't help but notice that her cheeks had filled with pink spots of color, a sign that she was feeling the effects of the alcohol.

When they'd been married he'd always known when

she was getting tipsy by the blushing red that saturated her cheeks. Apparently she was still a lightweight when it came to alcohol.

Maybe now was the time to have the conversation they'd never had, the one where she told him exactly what had driven her away from him.

"You know what I hate most about Bob? I hate him because he got pieces of your past, he got your tears, he got from you things I never got from you."

"I told you before, that was something I didn't want to drag into the marriage with you." She took another sip of her scotch despite the fact that her voice already had a small slur. "Things were so good with us, I didn't want you to know the ugliness of my past. I only told Bob about those things in an effort to help the case."

"I did a little research this morning on scapegoat child syndrome," he confessed.

She took another drink and then pushed her glass away. "Then you know the gist of what my childhood was like. Basically it stank." She reached up and stroked her fingers through her short hair and cast him a slightly bitter, rueful smile. "When I was fourteen I had hair down below my shoulders. As a last-ditch effort to be what my father wanted me to be, I cut it all off."

She released a burst of laughter that was laced with pain, the pain she'd never shared with him. The pain he would do anything to assuage if only she'd allow him in. "Of course it didn't work," she continued. "I was the child who should have never been born and my family never let me forget it."

He wanted to hold her. He wanted to cradle her close and tell her how precious she was, what an amazing person she was despite her tragic beginnings, but she sat rigid in her chair, her chin uplifted in a defensive mode that kept him in his seat across from her.

"You understand that it was never about you, that it was your parents who were dysfunctional."

"Thank you, Dr. Harkins," she replied lightly, but with a faint hint of sarcasm. "Rationally I know that now. When I went into foster care I was told that again and again. The scars I carry are deep, but they're old scars."

"I don't think those scars are as healed over as you tell yourself they are," he replied. He also shoved his glass away. He didn't want to be tipsy to have this conversation with her. He wanted to be clearheaded with all his faculties intact when he asked her what had eaten at him for the last two years.

"Why did you leave me, Georgina? Why wasn't I enough for you? What could I have done differently to make you feel safe and secure enough to share it all with me? Why couldn't I make you feel completely loved and not afraid to give love back?"

"Oh, Alex, the problem was never you. It's always been about me. It always will be me." Her eyes grew misty as she held his gaze. "You're right. Some of the scars aren't as healed as I want them to be. I thought I could be normal. When I fell in love with you, I thought I could get married and have children and walk away from my childhood whole. But the truth of the matter is that I'm damaged goods, Alex. You deserve better and far more than what I could ever give to you."

"You're wrong, Georgina. You were always all that I ever wanted, and you didn't give me enough credit if you believed I couldn't handle both the best and the very worst of you." He leaned forward, his heart aching with all the emotions that had assailed him since the moment she'd left their marriage.

She closed her eyes, as if to shut out whatever else he wanted to say. "It was the right thing for me to do," she repeated. "I only wanted what was best for you, and that wasn't me. That could never be me."

"Did you love me when you left me?" His heart hurt so much. "Georgina, open your eyes and look at me. I need to see your beautiful eyes when you answer me," he said.

She opened her eyes and their green depths were filled with such pain. "Yes, I loved you when I left. I left *because* I loved you so much." Once again she threaded her fingers through her rich, dark hair.

"When you were dealing with the aftermath of the Gilmer case, having bad dreams and so obviously in pain, I didn't know what to say to you. I didn't have the words to comfort you." A single tear fell from each of her eyes and splashed down on her pink cheeks. "I knew then that I couldn't be, would never be, enough for you."

Alexander couldn't stand it any longer. He needed to touch her, to hold her. He got up from his chair and walked around the table to where she sat. As he touched her arm, she folded into herself, as if protecting herself from any onslaught that might hurt.

"Georgina," he whispered her name softly. Tears chased faster down her cheeks. "Honey, all you had to do for me was just be there. When I had my nightmares and I turned over in the bed, you were always there to hold me. I didn't need words from you. I just needed to know that you were next to me. That was enough. You were enough."

He pulled on her arm and breathed a ragged sigh of relief when she unfolded, rose and fell into his embrace. She began to cry and he savored each of her tears, knowing they were a form of cathartic release she rarely allowed herself.

She leaned weakly against him as he stroked his hands up and down her back. He relished her weakness as it was a gift she'd never given to him before. It was a sign that she trusted him enough to give him her tears.

He knew it wouldn't last long, that she would quickly pull herself together and be the strong, stubborn, independent woman she'd always been. But for now, he just wanted to hold her while she dealt with her pain.

"I never stopped loving you, Georgina," he said softly. "I tried to stop. I didn't want to keep loving you, but I couldn't help it. I'd see you in the hallway at work and it would be like an arrow piercing through my heart. There hasn't been a day since our divorce that I haven't wanted you back in this house, back in my life."

She'd stopped crying, but she didn't move from his arms. He relished the feel of her so close against him, her heart beating rapidly against his own. This was where she belonged…in his arms forever.

"Come back to me, Georgina. Come back and be my wife, my lover, my life partner. Nothing has been good since you left me." He was baring his very soul to her, feeling more vulnerable than he'd ever felt in his life.

She raised her head to look up at him, her eyes simmering with emotion. "Alex, I…"

Whatever she was about to say was interrupted by

a loud knock on the front door. They both froze and stepped apart.

Alexander looked at his watch. It was almost ten. Who would be at his door at this time of night?

"I'll be right back," he said to her. "We aren't finished here, Georgina."

She released a sigh and nodded.

As he walked to the door, he pulled his gun, unsure what or who to expect. It might be one of the team members dropping by with new information or it could be something else altogether.

He looked out the peephole, and when he saw who was there, a shock of surprise swept through him. He holstered his gun and opened the door. "Hey, what's going on?" He stepped out on the porch.

Before he could speak another word, he felt a sharp sting in his upper back. He reached an arm up and felt the dart that still clung to his body.

At the same time, a weakness attacked his muscles. He tried to remain upright, but his legs had turned to jelly and his brain felt wrapped in cotton.

Trouble. Georgina was in danger.

This was his final thought as he fell to the ground next to the stoop and the last of his consciousness slipped away.

Chapter Twelve

"Alex?" Georgina called from the kitchen when he didn't immediately return. Who could he be talking to for so long and why hadn't they come inside?

"Alex, is everything okay?" She left the kitchen and her breath hitched in her chest as she met a masked man in the living room. Before she could draw her gun, a dart struck her in the chest.

She stared down at it in disbelief at the same time she fumbled to get her gun from the holster. But nothing was working right. Her legs were going out from under her, and even when her hand finally landed on the butt of her gun, she didn't have the strength to pull the weapon.

She tried to speak, but her mouth wouldn't form the words of panic, the scream of terror that was trapped inside her. He merely stood before her, his face hidden but blue eyes gleaming from the holes in the mask.

"Just let go, Georgina. Give in to it. You can't fight the drugs."

His voice sounded vaguely familiar, but her brain refused to recognize it as darkness began to creep into her head, a darkness that finally pulled her under and she knew no more.

She dreamed that she was a child and once again her father had locked her in the closet because she was a bad girl. She wasn't sure what she'd done wrong to receive the punishment. He'd just looked at her and gotten angry.

She never knew how long she'd be locked up and hated the weekends when it was possible she'd spend all of Saturday and Sunday inside the small, dark enclosure. Her sisters knocked on the door and called her names and laughed, deepening the pain of the isolation.

No good, piece of dirt, a waste of space and oxygen, over and over again their voices called to her, telling her just how bad she was and how they wished she'd never been born.

Then she was a grown-up and Alex was by her side. Alex. Someplace in the blackness of her drug-induced sleep, her heart cried out to him.

Was he dead or alive? It was a nebulous question that floated around in her head, but she couldn't hang onto the thought as other visions and nightmares returned to visit her.

She had no idea how long she'd been unconscious when she began to wake up. She was on a thin mattress, but for several minutes she didn't open her eyes; rather, she listened to the sounds around her.

Whispers.

Was she still a little girl? Were the whispers those of her sisters making fun of her again? No, that wasn't right. She wasn't a child anymore, and as she remembered encountering the masked man in Alex's living room, she knew what had happened.

Bob had gotten her into his lair.

She opened her eyes and found herself on a lower bunk bed in a jail-like cell. She didn't move, but rather allowed her gaze to take in all the details of her surroundings.

There was a sink, a toilet and a shower nozzle and a curtain hanging down that could be pulled around the toilet and shower to provide some modicum of privacy.

She closed her eyes once again, her heart pounding with fear and her head aching with the residual effects of whatever drug Bob had shot her with.

Why would Alex open the door to a man wearing a ski mask? And what had happened to Alex? Had he merely been drugged and left behind, or had Bob killed him?

No, Alex couldn't be dead. She absolutely, positively refused to believe that. He had to live and he had to find her. But how could he? How could the task force find her when they had no leads, no clues to follow?

Blue eyes. That's all she remembered. Did Jax White have blue eyes? Did Roger? God help her, she couldn't remember.

"Georgina, are you awake?"

It was Jackson's soft, drawling voice. She turned on her side and opened her eyes once again, now able to see that Jackson and a pretty strawberry-blonde woman were in the next cell. And beyond their cell she could see the others.

"I'm awake, but I have the headache from hell," she replied.

"It's whatever drug he used. It will go away pretty quickly," he replied. "You might have a bit of amnesia, as well. Some of us suffered from a lack of memories concerning our kidnapping for a couple of days. Must be a side effect of the drug."

Georgina nodded, although she didn't think she had any amnesia.

"You must be Marjorie," Georgina said to the woman. "Alex told me all about you."

"So Alexander is working the case?" Jackson asked eagerly.

Georgina pulled herself to a sitting position, careful not to hit her aching head on the top bunk. "There's a task force working on finding you all." She realized everyone in the room was listening to her. "Do you know who your captor is?"

"No, so far he's always worn a ski mask when he comes in here," Jackson replied. "The task force…do they have any clues? Are they getting close to finding us?"

Georgina heard the hope in Jackson's voice and she didn't have the heart to completely crush it. "We had several people of interest we were looking at. I'm sure it won't be too long now before they narrow it down. The police department is also helping to check out old buildings where we hoped to find that you all were being held."

"And yet he managed to get you." Sam Connelly's voice came from the distance, although his "cell" was too far away for her to see him.

"Georgina, I talked to you on the phone. Remember me? I'm Macy." The childish voice sliced through Georgina's heart.

"I remember, honey," she replied. "And it won't be long now before we're all out of here."

Jackson moved closer to the bars that separated them. With effort, Georgina got up from the bed and joined him. He reached his fingers through and she covered them with her own.

"How close are they really to finding us?" he asked, his voice once again a low whisper.

She hesitated and realized he wanted the truth, not some fairy tale to keep everyone filled with false hope. "Not close at all. The task force is working every angle and hopefully they'll figure it all out."

"How did he get to you?"

"I was staying with Alex. There was a knock on the door. Alex answered, and when he didn't come back to the kitchen, I walked into the living room and encountered the perp."

"And he got you with a dart," Jackson said flatly. "That's how he got us all. So exactly what's being done?"

For the next few minutes she filled him in on the task force investigation, the connection they all had with Michelle Davison's book and the fact that Roger had been at all of the crime scenes.

"We know he grew up in the swamp and according to him he killed his mother and father. We believe he has some level of higher education and that he's obsessed with becoming the perfect, unstoppable serial killer."

"I think it's a good sign for us that he hasn't shown us his identity," Jackson said. "Once we see his face, once we all know what he looks like, there's no way he'll allow us to walk out of here free and clear. He carries a gun and eventually he'll use it to kill us. To be honest, I think that time is growing near. Over the last couple of days he seems to have lost interest in whatever he thinks he can learn from us. He feeds us but then leaves, and there's a new restlessness in him that feels dangerous."

Jackson moved away from the bars and placed an arm around Marjorie and they both sat in the bottom bunk as Georgina returned to her own bunk.

Once again she lay down on her back and stared up at the bottom of the upper bunk. Was Alex alive? She could only assume that he'd been hit with a dart. Was he conscious? Were he and the team now hunting, frantic to find them before time ran out? Or had the dart that had pierced him held enough of the drug to be lethal?

One thing was certain. Nobody was going to die until Bob got a chance to talk to her, to crow about the fact that he'd once again managed to kidnap an FBI agent and get her into this hellhole. He'd want to brag about taking her from right under the protection of Alex.

She closed her eyes again, aware of the other couples talking quietly among themselves. A vision of Alex filled her head as she replayed the conversation they'd been having before being interrupted.

She couldn't think about it. She couldn't deal with it right now. She just had to pray that Alex was still alive and the task force was tearing up every street and building in the entire city.

He feeds us but then leaves. Jackson's words reverberated around in her head, along with a horrifying thought. Bob wouldn't have to use his gun or his darts to kill any of them. All he would have to do is stop coming, stop feeding them and they would all die a slow and painful death.

ALEX WOKE UP to the scent of grass and a headache that made his stomach roll with nausea. He remained immobile for several minutes, his brain too fogged to think.

He finally turned over and realized he was outside of his house on the lawn, his front door wide open as if to invite in any nefarious creatures. Snakes could slither in, a wandering gator could go inside, or Bob could make an unexpected appearance.

Bob!

A rush of thoughts frantically worked through his mind as he struggled to get to his feet. Georgina! Her name scalded his brain as he forced his legs into action. Even as he flew through the front door, he knew she wasn't here.

Still, he raced through every room of the house, frantically calling her name, praying that she'd somehow managed to hide from danger. But he knew in his gut, he knew in his soul, she was gone.

Bob had taken her from him, and now Alexander had no idea where she was or what was happening to her. Thick emotion made it nearly impossible for him to breathe as he raced back to the front door and stared out into the night.

A glance at his watch let him know he had been unconscious for well over an hour. Bob could have taken Georgina anywhere in that length of time.

A sob of despair rose up in his throat, but he swallowed hard against it. Now wasn't the time. He needed to get the team together. They had to figure out where Bob was keeping his captives now more than ever, because now Alexander's Georgina was among the victims.

He had to shove his emotions aside. It was time to

get to work, time to figure out what they had missed and find Georgina and all the others.

It took him only minutes to make the calls that would bring the men back to the war room. As Alexander got into his car to head toward headquarters, he saw the file folder that Director Miller had given him, the folder that held Nicholas's personal information.

He took a moment with the car running to turn on the interior light and peruse the information contained in the file. As he read, a burning fire lit in the pit of his stomach.

He slammed the file down into the passenger seat and roared out of his driveway. He schooled his mind to blankness, focusing only on getting to headquarters.

He couldn't think about Georgina or what she might be suffering at this very moment. If he did that, then he'd lose his mind and be no good to anyone and she needed him to be at the top of his game.

The drive to the FBI building normally took about twenty minutes. Tonight Alexander made it in ten. He was the first one in the war room. Although his instincts all screamed for him to get outside, to rip down buildings and yell Georgina's name, he knew that kind of frantic exercise would accomplish nothing.

He made a pot of coffee and then sank down in a chair, trying to remember what exactly had happened before he'd hit the dirt in his yard.

He and Georgina had been having a talk. She'd been crying and he'd held her. He'd been telling her how he'd never stopped loving her and then there had been a knock at the door.

Frowning, he rubbed the center of his forehead. Who

had been at the door? It couldn't have been any of their persons of interest, for he would have greeted them with his gun in his hand.

The dart had struck him in the back, meaning Bob had been behind him. So who had been on his doorstep? It had to have been somebody who caused him no alarm, but he couldn't remember.

He pressed the center of his forehead, trying to retrieve a vision of who had been on his doorstep when he'd peeked outside. Who had been Bob's partner in crime?

The clue to everything was locked in his brain, and the harder he tried to remember, the more nebulous the whole event at his front door seemed.

Drugs. Maybe his missing memory was a residual effect of whatever drug Bob had used on the dart that had knocked him out cold. He looked up as Frank and Matt flew into the room.

"I need one of you to find out where Roger Cambridge has been this evening and I want the other to check on Michelle and Jax." Was it possible he'd looked outside and seen Michelle on the front porch and Jax had been lying in wait for him?

"Done," they both said in unison.

Before they could leave the room, Nicholas walked in, and before he could say a word, Alexander rushed toward him and grabbed him by the front of the shirt.

"Where have you been tonight, swamp rat?" Alexander snarled. "Why didn't you mention that you grew up in Sampson's Swamp? Why have you never been around when Bob calls Georgina?"

"Hey, what's going on?" Matt asked as he tried to get

between the two men, but Alexander wasn't letting go of Nicholas until he got some answers. "Where is she, Nicholas? Where is Georgina?"

"Do you really think I have anything to do with this?" Nicholas looked at Alexander in stunned surprise. "I've been busting my ass to solve this case and the reason I didn't mention my swamp background was because it was nothing to brag about."

Nicholas's cheeks fired a dusty red. "Let go of me. It's not a damn crime to be ashamed of where you came from. I'm not the enemy here. I'm here to help you get her back from whoever has her."

Alexander saw the truth in Nicholas's eyes and he released the man's shirt and backed away. "I read your file and saw that you were from the swamp and my head started whirling with all kinds of possibilities," he said.

Nicholas straightened his shirt and continued to look at Alexander. "I'll admit I haven't exactly been a team player, but I swear I have nothing to do with these crimes and I had nothing to do with Georgina being taken. What we need to do is figure out how to find her and the rest of them now."

Alexander stared at Nicholas hollowly. "I don't know what we need to do in order to achieve that. I'm lost."

"We aren't," Matt said and jostled Frank's shoulder. "We're going to check out where Roger, Michelle and Jax are right now and where they have been for the last couple of hours. We'll get back to you as soon as we have some answers." With that the two men left the room, passing Tim and Terry as they entered.

Alexander slumped down into a chair once again and

buried his face in his hands. He was vaguely aware of Tim firing up his computer as Terry and Nicholas sat on either side of him.

"Tell us exactly what happened," Nicholas said. "How did he get to her?"

The question created a sharp pain that sliced through Alexander. "He got to her by going through me." He raced a hand through his hair in frustration. "Somebody knocked on the door. I looked out and opened the door without my weapon drawn, but I can't remember who was on the front stoop. I stepped out and Bob blew a dart into my back."

"So we know Bob is working with an accomplice," Nicholas said. "Was it possible you'd open your door and feel no danger if you saw Michelle Davison standing there?"

"I don't know...maybe." Alexander looked at the men on either side of him and then stared at the bulletin board where Georgina's picture would soon be added.

Dammit, he felt as if the key was in his head. If he could only remember who had knocked on his door, he would know who was responsible for not just the seven victims' disappearances, but Georgina's as well.

"All I know for sure is that the end is coming fast," he continued. "He wanted Georgina and now he has her. She completes what he wanted and it won't be long before he'll be finished with all of them."

He hoped the overwhelming hopelessness he felt didn't show on his face, didn't radiate from his eyes. He had to think positive. They *would* find Bob before he could hurt any of his victims, before he could hurt Georgina.

He just needed to think and remember. Otherwise he had a feeling there would be no rescue, there would be no more Georgina.

Chapter Thirteen

"Good morning, my dear friends. And a special good morning to my newest guest, sweet Georgina."

Bob's voice was like fingernails on a chalkboard, interrupting the happy dream she'd been having about Alex. She sat up and heard the sound of the others awakening.

Morning? Where had the night gone? The last thing she remembered was staring up at the underside of the top bunk. She'd obviously fallen asleep and the night had passed, without rescue, without hope.

She stood and moved to the front of her cell as a masked Bob pushed a tray containing a breakfast sandwich and a cup of coffee through an opening at the bottom of the bars.

He straightened and his blue eyes gleamed with glee. "I'm so happy to have you here, Georgina. We have so much to talk about and it's much nicer talking in person rather than over the phone."

"I can't imagine anything we have to discuss," she replied. She grabbed the tray and took it to her bunk where she sat down with her back to him.

He laughed, obviously amused by her little show of

defiance. "Unfortunately, I have a busy day today and don't have time to visit with you this morning, but I'll be back later and we're going to have a nice chat together."

He delivered trays to each of the others, and then came back to stand in front of Georgina's cell. "I've wanted you here since the moment I first saw you and I always get what I want. You *will* talk to me later, otherwise I'll start killing the others one by one, and I'll start with the smallest."

He'd kept his voice soft, little more than a whisper, but his words shot chills up Georgina's spine until he finally left the big room.

"Bastard," Jackson hissed.

Georgina turned on her bed, careful not to upend her tray, and looked at him. Jackson had always been an incredibly handsome man, but at the moment he looked haggard, with deep stress lines cutting across his forehead and down the sides of his mouth.

"They'll find us," she said, recognizing that she was trying to reassure herself as much as him. "Alex and his team won't stop until they find us."

"Yeah, but will we all be dead by then?" Jackson asked softly. "I got the feeling from talking to you last night that the task force didn't have many clues."

Georgina took a sip of the bitter, black coffee before replying. There was no way she wanted the people here to know that the task force only had three potential persons of interest and even they were weak suspects at best.

She didn't want to take away the tiny ray of hope that still remained by telling them the team had no idea where they were being held or who was responsible for their kidnappings.

"They had clues. We felt we were getting close." The little white lie fell off her tongue without apology. Nothing could be served here by telling the truth—that the task force had been scrambling without success for answers, that they were no closer to finding out who was responsible or where the victims were than they'd been on the day the task force had been formed.

She took another drink of the coffee and looked around the space. It was a big room made of concrete blocks with the cells running along one side and nothing but a folding chair on the other side.

There were several doorways, which led her to believe there was more than this single room to the building. "Has anyone been able to figure out what this place is?" she asked.

"I think it's an old women's prison," Jackson said. "In the back of Baker's Bayou."

She shook her head. "We checked out that place yesterday." Dear God, had it only been yesterday that they had marched through the swamp, so certain that they were headed for success?

"Then that shoots my theory all to hell. But I do believe we're somewhere in a swamp. I can smell it. I can feel it. Unfortunately, I have no idea what swamp or what kind of place this might have been."

Georgina looked around her cell. "I think he must have somehow built the cells himself. If it was an old prison, there wouldn't be showers in each one or privacy curtains for the occupants. All the prisons I've ever seen have a communal shower room, not individual ones."

"He definitely planned this out for a long time. We're being fed twice a day and he's even brought clean clothes to the others a couple of times since they've been here. The overhead lights are on all the time so the only way we know it's daytime is when he brings us breakfast."

As Georgina ate her breakfast sandwich, Jackson continued to tell her about the conversations Bob had shared with each of the agents, conversations that had revolved around the mistakes serial killers made that got them caught.

Education—that's what Bob was looking for. And who better to learn from than the men and women who chased the monsters? There comes a time when the teacher has to become the student. Bob's words whirled around in her head and again the only name she thought of was Dr. Jacob Tanner, a professor who immersed himself in teaching about serial killers.

Was it possible that he had decided that teaching about them wasn't enough, that he needed action and to become what he taught about?

It didn't matter what she thought. It didn't matter if Bob was really Jacob Tanner. She couldn't give any information to Alex to help him find them. All she could do was wait…and pray that somehow, someway, he'd figure things out.

THE NIGHT HAD BEEN ENDLESS. Alexander now stood at the window, sipping a fresh cup of coffee as he watched the dawn streaking across the sky.

His eyes were gritty from lack of sleep and his heart held a hopelessness that could cast him to his knees if he allowed it. The only thing they'd learned through the night was that Roger, Michelle and Jax all had solid alibis for the time that Georgina had been taken from Alexander's house.

He leaned his head against the window glass and closed his eyes, angry that he couldn't remember who had been on his front porch…who had lured him out enough that Bob could dart him in the back and render him unconscious.

If he could just remember. He tapped the glass with his forehead in an effort to dredge up a name, a face, anything that he could hang onto. He knew that he held the key to finding Georgina and the others, but it was locked inside his brain and at the moment seemed irretrievable.

He finally turned from the window and sat at the table. He and Tim were the only ones in the war room. The others were using the light of day to recheck his house, which was now a crime scene.

They would check to make sure they hadn't missed anything in the dark of night. They also intended to canvass the neighborhood to see if anyone had seen or heard anything at the time that Georgina had been taken and he'd been drugged.

Tim had worked through the night on the computer, trying to find something, anything, that would break the case wide open. He typed with fevered fingers, as if believing that finding the location was the only way to solve the crime.

Georgina. Alexander's heart cried her name, his very soul ached with the need to find her, to save her from whatever fate Bob had in store for her and all the victims of his craziness.

He took another sip of his coffee, feeling utterly helpless, much the way he had felt during most of the Gilmer case when a young woman's fate had hung in the balance.

Now it wasn't a young woman he'd never met. It was his beloved Georgina, and he knew if something happened and she died, he would never get over it. He would crawl into the blackest hole of pain and never, ever be able to climb back out.

Agony. He was in sheer agony. The key to everything was locked in his head and refused to be dislodged. If he could only remember who had been on his front porch. Who he had felt no danger from when he'd opened his front door and had stepped out on the porch. It couldn't have been any of the potential suspects, for he would have pulled his gun before opening the door for any of them.

He closed his eyes and drew a deep sigh. Remember…he had to remember, and instantly a vision filled his head. He and Georgina had been talking about their relationship. He'd told her that he still loved her and she'd been about to reply when the knock on the door had sounded.

Suddenly a vision of the person who had been standing on his porch the night before appeared in his head. His eyes snapped open. What was her name? He not only remembered seeing her on his porch but he remembered where he had seen her before…in Dr. Jacob Tanner's office.

His heart raced as his body filled with a burst of wel-

come adrenaline that had been sadly missing throughout the darkness of the long night.

Megan. Her name was Megan. What was her last
name? He frowned and fought against an edge of excitement that sliced through him. As he replayed the
day that he and Georgina went to speak to Dr. Tanner
about Michelle, he thought about the young woman who
had greeted them.

Megan. Megan James.

"Tim, I need you to find whatever personal information you can dig up on Megan James. She's a student
assistant to Dr. Jacob Tanner at the college. In fact, I
need both her and his addresses as quickly as possible.
I don't care what avenue you need to use to get the information for me, just get it as quickly as possible."

As Tim began to type, Alexander jumped to his feet
and quickly pulled his phone from his pocket. It took
him only minutes to call Matt and Frank and tell them
to get back to the war room immediately.

Although every nerve in his body screamed for action, he knew he needed backup if what he believed was
true. He'd gone off half-cocked in the Gilmer case and
the result had been tragic.

Of course, in that particular case it wouldn't have
mattered if he'd had a dozen or a thousand agents with
him. The simple truth was that they had been too late
to save Kelly. He would not, he *could* not, be too late
to save Georgina.

Throughout the long night, he and Nicholas had
made peace. Nicholas had been appalled by the fact
that Alexander had entertained any doubt about his
commitment to his job, about his loyalty to the team.

He'd told Alexander how his family had spent the first five years of his life living in a shanty in the swamp, and then his father had gotten a job that had allowed them to move into the city. Nicholas had worked hard to overcome his early beginnings.

The young agent was ambitious and bright. All he needed was some seasoning, and Alexander thought he'd already learned some valuable lessons and would eventually be quite successful within the agency.

Right now, Nicholas and lessons were the very last things on Alexander's mind as he paced the floor waiting for Matt and Frank to arrive.

He needed them to get here as quickly as possible. He had no idea what part Megan had played in the crimes, but it was an indisputable fact that she had been the lure that had drawn him out of the house and onto his porch so that Tanner could dart him into unconsciousness.

Tim got the addresses for both Megan James and Jacob Tanner and handed them to Alex at the same time Matt walked in. "What's up?" he asked.

"I think we've got him." As he explained to Matt what he'd remembered, Frank arrived and within minutes the three of them were on their way to Tanner's off-campus town house.

"If he's leading the double life I believe he is, then he should be at home at this hour of the morning." Every nerve in Alexander's body burned, every muscle tensed.

He could be wrong. They'd all been wrong when they'd rushed to the old structure at the back of Baker's Bayou. He'd never considered that Bob might have a partner, but there was no question in his mind now that it had been Megan who had lured him outside.

He now had a perfect memory of looking out of his peephole in the door and seeing Megan James standing there. He'd felt no fear, only curiosity as to what had brought her to his home.

When he remembered meeting the young woman, he had seen the hero worship she had for her boss. It only made sense that if she were a part of this, then Tanner was Bob.

However, there was no way to be absolutely certain. It was possible that Megan was a puppet for some other sick twist…maybe another student who wanted to become infamous.

As Matt drove toward Jacob Tanner's town house, Alexander found himself second-guessing the move. Maybe they should have confronted Megan first. He voiced his concerns aloud, but both of the other men thought his first reaction, to get to Tanner first, was the right one.

"If nothing else we bring him in and get him behind bars. We'll have twelve hours to sort it out before we have to bring some sort of charges against him or release him," Matt said.

"I hope to hell we solve this long before another twelve hours," Alexander replied. He couldn't imagine going another hour without having Georgina back safe and sound, and he knew wherever she was, the other missing people would be there as well.

Jacob Tanner lived in an affluent area within walking distance of the college. The town houses were redbrick with white trim, the lawns neatly manicured and the overall maintenance of the dozen or so town houses fresh.

Teachers and professors mostly lived here, with easy

access to the campus and the respectable address to give them additional status.

Matt parked in front of the curb of the professor's place and the three men quickly exited the car. Alexander pulled his gun as he approached the front door. "Matt, go around to the back door. I don't want him making some kind of escape."

Matt nodded and left the two. When he had disappeared, Alexander nodded to Nicholas, who drew his weapon and held it at the ready. None of them knew if Tanner was dangerous or not.

Alexander intended to take no chances. If Tanner was Bob, then Alexander would not give him an opportunity to take him down again. There would be no darts in the back with this encounter. There would only be a gun to the chest and it would be Alexander's gun doing the pointing.

His watch read exactly seven o'clock when he knocked on the front door. It was early enough that Tanner shouldn't have left for classes yet. "Maybe he's a sound sleeper," Nicholas said after they'd waited several moments.

Alexander knocked again, this time loud enough to awaken the neighbors. He leaned with his ear against the door but could hear nothing that might indicate anyone was inside. He knocked a final time and then turned to Nicholas.

"I don't think he's here. Walk around and check the windows and then get Matt and we'll head over to Megan's place. Maybe she knows where the good professor would be at this time of the morning."

Nicholas nodded and Alexander watched as he, too

disappeared around the side of the town house. There was a front window and he moved to peer inside. He holstered his gun and cupped his hands to allow him to see a neat and tidy living room.

He saw no shadows lurking in the room, nothing to indicate that anyone was inside. The garages for the town houses were completely enclosed and without windows, making it impossible for them to check to see if a car was parked inside.

Matt and Nicholas joined him on the sidewalk. "I didn't see anyone through the back door," Matt said.

"And same with me in the windows I looked in. I'd say he's not here." Nicholas frowned thoughtfully. "I wonder just how close he might be with his assistant? Close enough to spend his nights in her bed?"

"Let's go find out," Alexander said.

Alexander read out Megan's address as Matt pulled away from the curb. "She'll be arrested no matter what," he said. "If nothing else she's an accomplice to Georgina's kidnapping and the attack on me."

"Then it's possible she won't be home, either," Matt said. "Why would she stick around if she knows you can identify her as an accomplice?"

"I don't know. I can't figure out why she would have let herself be seen by me at all," Alexander admitted. It was a puzzle he had yet to put together.

"Maybe she's a victim, too. Maybe Tanner forced her to participate in luring you out and then he kidnapped her as well," Matt suggested.

"That really doesn't fit the profile," Nicholas replied. "But then again, I guess it would be a mistake to discount anything."

"Maybe she's going to try to convince me it wasn't her at the door, but there's no doubt in my mind that it was her." Alexander pulled his cell phone from his pocket and dialed Tim's cell.

"Tim, talk to Judge Warner and get us search warrants for the addresses you gave me earlier. He's a sympathetic judge, but make sure you tell him we believe the two people who reside at the addresses are a killer holding hostages and his accomplice. See if you can get it done in the next thirty minutes and have somebody from the team meet us at Megan's address with the paperwork."

"No fruit of the poisonous tree in this case," Matt observed.

"We play everything by the book," Alexander said. "I don't want us to make a single mistake that might poison the case we have to build to make sure our Bob and anyone else helping him spends the rest of their lives in jail."

As he dropped the phone back into his pocket, his nerves jangled inside him and his heart beat out the cadence of Georgina's name.

Megan James's apartment building was a far cry from Tanner's town house. Although the outside appeared fairly nice, the hallway smelled of sweaty gym clothes, stale smoke and the day after parties.

Once again Alexander pulled his gun and then knocked on the door. Matt and Nicholas stood just behind him. Alexander's stomach clenched as the door opened to reveal a young woman with long red hair and clad in a robe. Her blue eyes nearly popped out of her head as she saw the men with their guns.

"Wha…what's going on?" she asked.

"We're FBI agents. We understood this was Megan James's apartment," Alexander said.

"It is. I'm her roommate." Her eyes were still huge even as Alexander holstered his gun.

"Where is Megan?" he asked.

"She left just a little while ago to head over to the Humanities building. Professor Tanner called her late last night and told her his mother was ill and she should take over teaching his classes for the next week or so."

"Thanks," Alexander replied and turned to leave.

"Is Megan in some kind of trouble?" the woman asked.

"Let's just say I'd be looking for a new roommate if I were you," Matt said as the three of them hurried back to their car.

"This is so bizarre," Nicholas said a few minutes later as they strode toward the Humanities building. "How can she believe she isn't in any trouble? How can she possibly explain being at your house last night?"

"I'd like to know how Tanner is going to explain having a sick mother when his mother died years ago," Alexander said tersely. He was ready for this to end. He made a quick call to Tim to let him know they were headed to the college campus.

When they reached Tanner's office door, Alexander didn't bother to knock. He opened the door to see Megan at the desk. Her eyes widened as the three men came through the doorway.

"Agent Harkins," she said in surprise. "I'm afraid if you're looking for Professor Tanner again, you're going to have a long wait. His mother is ill and he's left town."

Alexander stared at her, wondering if she was completely psychotic. She didn't appear to be concerned that he was here and acted like she hadn't seen him since the last time he and Georgina had been here to speak to Tanner.

"That's funny since his mother died a long time ago. What I'd like to know is what you were doing on my doorstep last night." Had it only been last night that he'd held Georgina in his arms and told her how much he loved her?

Megan frowned. "Me? At your house last night? I don't know what you're talking about." She gave him a confident smile that suddenly boiled his blood. "Surely you're mistaken, Agent Harkins, I don't even know where you live. Did anyone besides you see me there?"

The tension that had coiled inside him snapped. He motioned toward Matt. "Take her into custody."

As Matt moved forward and pulled handcuffs from his pocket, alligator tears began to track down Megan's cheeks. "Please, I don't know what's going on. Why would you think I was at your house? What is it you think I've done wrong?"

Matt cuffed her hands behind her back as she continued to cry. "This is all a mistake. Please, explain to me what's happening. I don't understand."

Alexander motioned for Matt to get her out of the office. Nicholas gazed at Alexander with a wry, tight smile. "So now we know her defense. There were three people at your house last night. One of them isn't talking and her story is she was never there. The word of a drugged-up FBI agent against a sobbing, innocent teacher's aide." He shrugged. "It might work for her. I've seen defense attorneys work with less."

Alexander's phone rang. Terry was downstairs with their search warrants in hand. Alexander and Nicholas took the stairs two at a time down and out of the building where Matt had loaded a still weeping Megan into the back of Terry's car.

"Tanner's place," Alexander said as the three agents once again were in the car. "My gut says we won't find anything of use in Megan's place, but if Tanner is Bob, then he might have something in his house that will confirm not only that fact but might also point to where he is holding the hostages."

Aware of the minutes…hours lost, Alexander wished he could freeze time. It was already nearly ten. Too many hours had passed. They had to find something at Tanner's. He had to pray that the answers were there.

When they reached Tanner's town house, Alexander knocked on the door once and then he and Matt threw their shoulders against it to pop the lock. It took three tries before the door sprang open and they all entered.

With guns drawn, they cleared each room one at a time, then certain that Tanner was no place in the house, they began their search for some sort of evidence.

"Matt, you take the kitchen and dining area. Nicholas, check out the master bedroom. I'm going to go over everything in his office," Alexander said. "Try to do as little damage as possible but don't leave a single place unsearched."

The second bedroom had been turned into a home office and the first thing he did was sit at the desk and begin going methodically through the drawers. He didn't know what exactly he was looking for, but knew he'd recognize it on sight.

The first desk drawer held pens and paper clips and the office materials that were usually in a desk. The side drawer held hanging file folders that contained what appeared to be old lesson plans.

Aware of time ticking by, he quickly searched each and every file. He found nothing in the desk of interest. He opened up the laptop on the desktop and found it password protected. He shut it down, intending to take it to Tim when they left here.

With his heart ticking off the time...precious time that was moving far too fast, he checked the bookcase that held only books from top to bottom.

Hearing nothing from the other agents, he sat back down at the desk and leaned back, a well of grief threatening to pull him in and drown him.

His good friend, Jackson, six other innocent people and Georgina, all gone...vanished as if lifted from the face of the earth. And the only clue they had was that they were certain Bob had sprung from the swamp.

He frowned as he realized he'd been staring at a framed 8 x 10 photo on the wall opposite him. It was a picture of a swamp and what appeared to be an old, crumbling concrete building peeking through the trees.

He jumped up from his chair and grabbed the photo from the wall. "Matt, Nicholas," he called. When the two agents entered the office, he held out the photo. "Either one of you know where this might be?"

"I have no idea," Matt replied.

"Doesn't look familiar to me," Nicholas added.

Alexander set the photo on the edge of the desk and

ripped off the frame and glass. This was it. He knew that this was where Tanner was keeping the captives.

The pit of his stomach burned as he thought of Tanner sitting at his desk and perhaps sipping a fine wine while staring at the place where he'd stashed his victims. He could just imagine the pleasure that swept through the madman when he viewed this photo.

Once the picture was out of the frame, Alexander looked at the back, releasing a small gasp of relief as he saw writing on the bottom.

"Baton Rouge Institute for the Criminally Insane," he read aloud. "Shelter Swamp, Baton Rouge." He looked at the two men. "This is it. Matt, get on the phone to Tim and get us a location for Shelter Swamp."

"Nicholas, call in the troops, have them meet us here." Alexander's hands trembled too much to make the calls. He clutched the photo tightly, knowing in his very gut that this was the place and Tanner was their man.

But it would take them an hour or so to pull everything together and get there, and he had no idea how long Tanner had been gone or if he was with the victims.

They were closing in, but would they be in time?

Chapter Fourteen

One thing Georgina realized while she sat on her bunk and listened to the conversations of the others was that they had formed a bond, a bond that would see them through the rest of their lives…if they got the opportunity to live the rest of their lives.

The second thing she'd realized was that she believed she would die here. She knew the lack of clues the team had, the vast area of swampland they had to explore. The odds of the captives being found were minimal in her mind.

In facing death, she realized how much she wanted to live…to really live, not just go through the motions as she'd been doing for most of her life.

Alex's words of love had done so much to soothe the wounds that her childhood had left behind. She realized she'd been playing a loop in her head for years, telling herself she was a failure, that she was no good to anyone. Words from her past that had made her believe she was not good enough for Alex, that he would be much better off without her.

She had told him that maybe he needed therapy to get over his guilt concerning the Gilmer case, but she was the one who needed therapy to finally heal the inner child inside her who had been abused and abandoned.

Now it was too late for therapy, it was too late to tell Alex just how much she loved him and that she did want a do-over with him. With the self-realizations that had come from this case, she felt better, stronger and was ready to accept Alex's love and build a life with him.

She supposed she should thank Bob for making her immerse herself in her past. She had come out stronger on the other side. Unfortunately, the only way she might thank Bob was if he released everyone and then sacrificed himself by falling into the swamp and drowning.

As if summoned by her very thoughts, the door on the opposite side of the room opened and Bob walked in. As usual his face was covered by a ski mask. He grabbed the folding chair and then carried it over in front of her cell, opened it and sat.

"Hello, Georgina." His voice seemed to hold genuine affection.

"Hello, Bob." Her voice did not.

"I thought we'd have a little chat. I've so enjoyed speaking to you in the past," he said.

"First I'd like you to just answer one question for me. Why? Why are you doing this? Why do you want to be a serial killer?" She needed to know the reason for all of this before she died.

"I not only want to be the best serial killer in the world, but I also want to be the best teacher." He reached up and pulled off his ski mask and she was stunned to see Professor Jacob Tanner's boyish face.

His unmasking of himself also rang a death knell for

them all. There was no way he'd allow any of them to live now that he'd shown them his face.

"I lied to you when I told you I killed my parents," he said. "I've never killed anyone before, but I've dreamed about it, I've obsessed about it since I was a very young boy."

"Then let us all go. Nobody is dead yet and we'll all ask the judge to go easy on you." She got up from her cot and stood in front of him, her hands gripping the iron bars. "You're an esteemed professor, Jacob. You don't have to do this. You don't have to become a killer."

"Oh, but I do." His blue eyes shone with a brilliance that could only be madness. He leaned forward, the intensity of his gaze sickening her. "How can I teach my students about serial killers without creating death myself? How can I tell them about the power you feel when you watch the life drain from a victim's eyes, when you place your hand on their chest and feel their very last breath?"

"You're crazy," Jackson said.

"Shut up," Tanner replied as he pulled a gun from his pocket and pointed it at Jackson. "I'm ready to begin my new life, as a brilliant teacher and as a killer. I was going to give Georgina the honor of being my first victim, but I'm not adverse to changing my mind and picking you."

"Then pick me," Jackson said as he grabbed the bars of his cage and shook them like an enraged gorilla.

"Stop it," Georgina said frantically. "Jackson, don't try to be a hero. Professor Tanner and I have a relationship that none of you have, that none of you could possibly understand."

"That's right." Tanner lowered the gun and smiled at her.

"Did you lie about your childhood, too?" she asked. At least as long as he was talking, he wasn't killing anyone.

His eyes darkened. "No, I didn't lie about that. I grew up in the swamp and my father was a brutal man who drank too much and then beat me and my mother half senseless. I knew early on that the only way I was going to get out of the swamp and escape him—escape them—was through education. I worked hard and got scholarships that saw me through all of my schooling."

"Where are your parents now?" she asked.

"Probably living in the same old shack where I grew up. When I left for college, I never looked back. I never went back there. For all I know, they both could be dead." He straightened tall in the chair with obvious pride. "I was better than that. I was better than both of them."

"You've done so well, Jacob. Why screw it all up now?" she asked.

Once again his eyes glittered with ill-concealed excitement. "I'm not screwing anything up now. I'm just becoming what I was always meant to be. I've learned everything I need to know from these men and women. How can I screw up when I have all I need to know how to kill unmercifully and never be caught?"

"Eventually you will get caught," Georgina replied. "We always catch them. You'll get arrogant and that will lead to you getting sloppy and you'll make a mistake."

"You're wrong. I've been trained by the very best." He gestured down the row of cells. "It was easy for me to pick them out. Michelle sent me her book chapter by chapter long before it was ever published. I used her research for her book to find three sterling examples of profilers to help teach me."

"You must have been quite amused when Agent Harkins and I came to talk to you about Michelle and Roger," she replied.

He laughed, a sound that was jarringly pleasant given the dire circumstances and the surroundings. "I have to admit I was quite amused, although I admired the fact that you'd homed in on Michelle and Roger so quickly."

"Why me? How did you find me? My phone number and address?" The questions had haunted her.

"I saw you that night at Michelle's book signing. I heard you and Agent Harkins introduce yourselves to Michelle. The internet is a wonderful tool if you can pay for certain services. It only took me minutes to have your phone number and address at my disposal."

"Let Macy go," she said softly. "She can't hurt you, Jacob. She's just a little girl. She deserves to have a long and happy life."

"Not all people get happy childhoods—you know that as well as I do," Tanner replied. "From what you told me, you suffered tremendously as a child."

"That's right," she said, owning the truth for what felt like the very first time in her life. "I was physically, mentally and emotionally terrorized from the time I was born until I was sixteen, both by my parents and by my older sisters. But that didn't make me want to kill people. I chose to turn my life around, to make something of myself. And you've done that, Professor. Your students adore you. Your classes are the most popular on campus. Why can't that be enough?"

"Because it's not," he cried in sudden rage. "I have a plan that will cause people to tremble when they think of me, to have nightmares about me. I want to make headlines and I want to kill. I have a bloodlust, Georgina, and finally I'm going to satisfy it. I'm done killing gators in the swamp. I want to kill people."

He stood abruptly and kicked his chair back. He waved his gun in the air and Georgina backed away from the bars. Danger crackled in the air and the only sound was a faint whimper from Macy.

Tanner laughed again, knowing that he was the one in control, knowing that he struck fear in each and every person in the room. His laughter held a sickening glee that Georgina feared would linger in her head even as she died.

"I'm tired of talking," Tanner said. He stalked up the line of cells, pointing his gun into each one, obviously reveling in the fear he struck in each of his captives' hearts.

He finally stopped and stood once again in front of Georgina's cell. "It's time to quit talking and start acting." He raised his gun and pointed it at her.

"Freeze!" The achingly familiar voice came from the doorway at the same time Tanner's gun discharged and a bullet slammed into her chest, throwing her backward to the floor as pain seared through her.

She was vaguely aware of the sound of other shots and then Alex was at her cell door, yelling for somebody to get the key, to get medical help. Frantic, he was so frantic and she wanted to tell him to calm down, that everything was going to be all right.

She knew that something important was happening, but she couldn't remember what. Cold. Why was she so cold? She wanted to tell Alex to hurry, to come and warm her in his big strong arms, but the words refused to form on her lips no matter how hard she tried to speak.

Finally he was there next to her and she was shocked to see tears trekking down his cheeks. "Hang on, baby," he said. "Help is on the way."

She managed to raise her hand and place it on the side of his beautiful, handsome face. "Do-over," she managed to say, her voice coming from very far away as darkness sprang out of nowhere and took possession of her.

Is THIS WHAT DEATH WAS LIKE? Georgina's thoughts raced as she remained unmoving, with her eyes closed, in a soft, comfortable bed. But, surely, death didn't involve the soft steady sound of deep snoring.

Familiar snoring. She opened her eyes and realized she wasn't dead, but rather was in a hospital room. The snoring came from an obviously exhausted Alex, who was slumped in a chair nearby and sleeping deeply.

She closed her eyes once again and thought about what had happened before she'd fallen unconscious. She'd been shot, but Alex had saved her. He'd saved them all.

She remembered the shots that had rung through the structure as she'd fallen to the floor of her cell. There was no doubt in her mind that Professor Jacob Tanner, FBI-trained serial killer, was dead, but little Macy would hopefully live a happy and wonderful life with her parents who so loved her.

Georgina was in pain, but it was manageable. She wondered what medical magic had been done to her in order to keep her here on earth.

She opened her eyes again and turned to look at Alex, his eyes drifted open, going from a sleepy blue to the blue of an electric charge.

"Georgina!" He jumped from the chair and was by her side in two short strides. "Thank God." He grabbed on to her hand and squeezed tight, his eyes moist with unshed tears.

He looked awful. His eyes were red-rimmed and his jaw sported a growth of dark whiskers. Stress lines dug into his skin, making him look half-sick.

She licked her chapped lips and realized her throat was sore. He seemed to know exactly what she needed as he grabbed a glass of water from a nearby tray and gently lifted her head so she could take a little sip of the cool liquid from a thin straw.

"I've got to let the doctor know that you're awake," he said.

"Wait," the word croaked out of her. "How long have I been here?"

"Two long, terrible days."

"You look like crap."

He laughed and some of the tension eased from his face, from his shoulders. "Honey, you should look in a mirror right about now."

A nurse walked in and stopped in surprise. "You're awake. I'll go let the doctor know." As she turned on squeaky heels and left the room, Georgina looked back at Alex.

"What's the damage?" she asked.

"Two broken ribs, one destroyed spleen..."

"And a partridge in a pear tree," she quipped.

He smiled and once again squeezed her hand. "Now I know for sure you're going to be fine." The smile fell as he released a ragged sigh. "I thought I'd lost you, Georgina. I thought I'd lost you forever."

"You can't get rid of me so easily."

"I don't want to get rid of you ever," he replied. "Do you remember what you said to me after you'd been shot?" His beautiful blue eyes gazed at her intently.

She frowned, trying to remember those moments before she'd fallen unconscious. And then she remembered and she grasped the moment in both hands, knowing what she wanted more than anything else in the world.

"Do-over. I told you I wanted a do-over."

He nodded, the tension creeping back across his handsome features as his eyes darkened. "I didn't know exactly what you meant, whether you wanted a do-over of the night you were kidnapped, or if you wanted a do-over with me...with us."

She could tell he was holding his breath, hoping that she answered the way he wanted her to. "I probably need some therapy," she said tentatively.

He nodded. "We can do that. We can do anything together, Georgina. We belong together."

She gazed at him, falling into the love that shone from his eyes, believing in the love that was in her heart for him. She wanted to be the one he turned to in the night when demons chased him in his dreams. And she wanted him to be the one to hold her when her own darkness tried to claim her.

"I'm good enough," she said.

"Damn straight you are. You deserve to be happy, Georgina, and I promise you that I will spend every day for the rest of my life working to keep you happy."

"Alex, I was a fool to walk out on you...on us. I didn't believe I deserved to be happy, but after hearing what Tanner said about his past and seeing what hanging on to that pain created in him, I know I'm better than that. I need to let go of my past to have my future and I want that future to be with you."

He leaned forward and gave her a gentle kiss. "I want to grab you and hug you tight right now, but I don't think that would be a very good idea."

"That is definitely a bad idea," a man who was obviously a doctor said as he walked into the room.

He nodded at Alex and then walked to the side of Georgina's bed. "Georgina, I'm Dr. Mac Evans." He placed a gentle hand on her wrist and checked her pulse, then stood back and smiled. "You gave us all quite a scare for a little while, but it looks like you're going to be just fine."

"Great, when can I get out of here?" she asked.

"We need to keep you for a couple of days, and then, depending on how fast you're healing, we should be able to cut you loose," Dr. Evans replied.

"I'm a very quick healer," she replied and her gaze went to Alex. "Especially when I have something to heal for."

His eyes burned with the fiery light of desire, with the sweet promise of love, and Georgina knew in her heart that their do-over would last forever.

Epilogue

It was utter chaos. Sam Connelly and Jackson Revannaugh stood over the barbecue grill on Alex and Georgina's back deck, arguing over what kind of barbecue rub was best for ribs.

Macy wore a princess crown and plastic high heels, clomping on the wooden deck like a wind-up toy learning to tap dance. Daniella, Amberly and Marjorie were setting the picnic table in the yard with colorful plasticware. Amberly's son Max was throwing a ball up in the air and catching it with a new catcher's mitt that Cole had bought for him.

Georgina mixed the dressing for a salad and watched out the window, reveling in the life that was happening among the people who had been captive for so long.

It had been six weeks since she'd left the hospital, eight weeks since they had all been released and Jacob Tanner had met his death.

This was the first time they had all joined together for a November picnic to celebrate the friendships that had formed through those long days and nights.

She finished with the dressing and moved on to

slicing tomatoes. As she worked, her head filled with thoughts of the past six weeks.

Magical. That was the only way she could describe her do-over with Alex. She'd started going to therapy immediately after getting out of the hospital, and each week with her therapist, she continued to exorcise her demons.

She had finally realized that she could trust Alex with her good and her bad, with her dreams and her heartaches, and in that trust they had found a new intimacy that Georgina had never thought possible, one that she had never experienced before.

The office snitch had been discovered to be a female cop who had leaked information both to the press and to Jacob Tanner. She was now facing charges of her own.

Georgina smiled as strong arms wrapped around her and she felt the solid presence of Alex just behind her. "Why aren't you out there playing with fire with Jackson and Sam?"

"Because I'm in here hugging you," he replied, his breath warm against her ear. He kissed her, nipping her earlobe playfully.

"Hmm, I think you might be playing with fire after all," she said. She pointed the knife she'd been using to slice tomatoes out the window. "I think we need one of those."

He stilled behind her, his arms tightening their embrace. "You mean, a tap-dancing princess?"

"Or a stick horse–riding cowboy." She set the knife down and turned in his arms.

His eyes glowed the impossible blue that always shot a wave of heat through her. "Really, Georgina?"

"Really."

"We have one little issue to take care of first," he said.

"Just tell me when and where, and instead of do-over I'll say I do."

He grabbed her close and took her mouth in a fiery heat of possession. Tears of happiness misted her eyes as she tasted the complete and unconditional love in his kiss.

He finally broke the kiss and gazed at her with a tenderness she felt in her heart. "As soon as possible," he replied. "I want you as my wife again."

"And I want to be your wife again, but first we have a picnic to enjoy with new friends."

"And maybe later tonight we'll start on that little princess or cowboy," he said, and once again he captured her lips in a kiss that told her that this was the man of her heart, the man who would be at her side till the end of time.

* * * * *

She'd been thinking about Brody and suddenly she was seeing him.

And hearing him.

It wasn't possible. She was in shock. And pain. Her shoulder hurt like the devil. That was it.

She flashed the light again, being careful to keep it away from his eyes. The man's body was long and lanky, with narrow hips and a flat stomach. Nice wide shoulders. Strong chin.

Oh, no. She knew that chin.

"Brody?" she said, her voice squeaking.

Said chin jerked up and she caught the full impact of his hazel eyes. He looked her up and down and, even knowing that it was so dark that he couldn't be seeing much, it had her wanting to run and hide. Thirteen years. And it felt as if it were yesterday.

"Evening, Elle," he said, his voice sounding strained. "I guess this just proves that no matter how bad things are, they can always get worse."

TRAPPED

BY
BEVERLY LONG

Published in Great Britain 2014
by Mills & Boon, an imprint of Harlequin (UK) Limited,
Eton House, 18-24 Paradise Road, Richmond, Surrey, TW9 1SR

© 2014 Beverly R. Long

ISBN: 978-0-263-91372-9

46-1014

Printed and bound in Spain
by Blackprint CPI, Barcelona

As a child, **Beverly Long** used to take a flashlight to bed so that she could hide under the covers and read. Once a teenager, more often than not, the books she chose were romance novels. Now she gets to keep the light on as long as she wants, and there's always a romance novel on her nightstand. With both a bachelor's and a master's degree in business and more than twenty years of experience as a human resources director, she now enjoys the opportunity to write her own stories. She considers her books to be a great success if they compel the reader to stay up way past their bedtime.

Beverly loves to hear from readers. Visit www.beverly long.com, or like her at www.facebook.com/beverlylong. romance.

For my father, who was sent to Colorado
before he shipped out for WWII.
He learned to ski and fell in love!

Chapter One

Brody Donovan moved in his seat, trying to discreetly stretch his long legs. The pretty young woman across the aisle smiled at him.

"Long flight, huh?" she said.

Long, late and the last twenty minutes, bumpy as hell. He glanced at his watch, judging the amount of time he'd have between connecting flights. "Yes," he said politely, and promptly closed his eyes.

He didn't want to engage in any conversation. He wanted solitude. For the next ten days, he planned to enjoy the quiet and forget about the bang of roadside bombs, the sting of metal fragments and the despair of the damaged bodies that he'd been patching up for years. He intended to forget about war and to pretend that everybody *could just get along.*

His destination of choice involved a little backtracking, but he was okay with that. A direct flight out of Miami into Brasília, the capital of Brazil, then a smaller plane to take him an hour north to a place where the sand was white, the water blue and the rum cold.

He had a place to stay, courtesy of his friend Mack McCann. Payback, his friend had said for Brody's assistance in saving Hope Minnow's life. After hearing that Brody had a trip to South America in mind with no particular destination, Mack had been quick to call in a few favors and suddenly Brody had a beach house in Brazil waiting for him.

Peace. A brief interlude before the real world and its real-world responsibilities pressed down upon him. It wasn't as if he was dreading the next step. San Diego, with its three hundred days a year of sunshine and mild temperatures, wasn't something to bitch about. And he was joining one of the leading orthopedic practices in the country. It was just that…

Well, it was just that with both of his good friends finding love, it was hard not to feel a little alone. In just a few weeks, they would both be married. Ethan to Chandler, Mack's younger sister. And Mack to Hope Minnow, who he'd been hired to protect and in the process, had lost his heart.

He should just be happy for both Ethan and Mack and stop the damn pity party. It wasn't his style. Marriage simply wasn't in the cards. He'd come close, but Elle… Well, she'd walked away without a backward glance.

Those had been dark days. But he'd managed to go on even though some days he'd barely had the strength to get out of bed.

He would forget the bad stuff about war, too. Given enough time.

And plenty of rum.

Brody woke up when he felt the wheels touch down. The big plane taxied to a gate and the passengers shuffled restlessly, waiting for the doors to open. Once they did, it was straight to Customs. The fine folks there were moving at the pace of a comatose snail, and he checked his watch repeatedly. If he missed his next flight, it would mean a night in the airport.

Once past the Customs agent, he moved fast, looking for signs that would lead him in the right direction. Fortunately, everything was in both Spanish and English. He started running, being careful to dodge around the elderly and the very young. When he got to his gate, he wasn't surprised to see the waiting room was empty. There was a clerk behind the counter, fiddling with his computer. When the young, dark-skinned man saw him, he immediately glanced toward the big windows.

Brody followed his gaze. The small plane was still there, but they were starting to pull the temporary steps back. The propeller on the nose was turning.

The young man spoke into a microphone on his shirt collar. "One more," he said. Then he looked at Brody. "You just made it."

Brody held out his ticket and his passport. The young man hit a few keys. "Thank you, Señor Donovan. There are no assigned seats."

He knew that. It was a small chartered flight. The plane only held a max of eight.

"I'll hang on to the wing if I have to," he said. Warm sand, blue water and cold rum were a hell of an inducement.

The young man smiled. "I do not think that will be necessary." He opened a door and motioned for Brody to pass through. "Have a good trip," he said.

Brody moved quickly through the short hallway and took the steps down to the tarmac fast. He pushed open a big door and was outside. The air felt sticky even though there was a good breeze. It was darker than it should have been, given that it was still an hour shy of sundown.

Everything was gray. Gray cement. Gray plane. Gray sky.

He was pretty confident that the rain was not far off. That didn't worry him. In this part of the country, they had to be used to flying in it.

They didn't call it the rain forest for nothing.

He ran up the metal steps and ducked to enter the plane. Seated in the cockpit was a pilot, a man close to sixty with dark skin and still-thick dark hair, who didn't look up. The copilot, blond, blue-eyed and freckled, probably not yet twenty-five, reached back over his shoulder, grabbed Brody's ticket and then pointed a thumb to a seat in the empty front row. With the same arm, he pulled shut a curtain, separating the cockpit from the rest of the cabin.

Brody swung into the spot, silently celebrating his good luck, not caring that the pilot seemed a little irritated with his late arrival. In another hour, he'd be at his final destination. Mack had gone so far as to hire somebody to stock the house with groceries. All Brody had to do was show up.

The plane taxied out to a runway and within minutes was gathering speed. The nose of the plane lifted and suddenly they were airborne. The small aircraft rocked back and forth, causing Brody, who had been on some pretty rough flights during his years in the air force, to brace one hand on the wall and the other on the plastic armrest between his seat and the empty one next to it.

"I told you it would be bad," a woman said from somewhere behind him. "You never listen to me."

There was a response. From a man. Too low for Brody to distinguish the words.

"This is the dumbest thing we've ever done," she added, evidently not letting it go.

Brody wished he'd remembered earplugs. The plane continued to gain altitude. And the flight didn't get any smoother. He understood. Planes like this flew at lower altitudes where the air was denser and rougher. They probably wouldn't go much higher than three or four thousand feet.

He closed his eyes.

Fifteen minutes later, the plane started to really rock and roll. He opened his eyes just as a bolt of lightning split the darkening sky off to his left.

More lightning followed.

He leaned into the aisle and looked toward the front. The curtain separating the pilots from the rest of the plane had slid partially open, allowing him to see. The older pilot was gesturing to the young copilot, his hands moving fast. It appeared that nerves up front were stretched thin.

He hoped the woman in back didn't have a good view. The man with her would never hear the end of it.

It probably wouldn't do any good to tell her that lightning wasn't going to bring down a plane. Hadn't happened for more than forty years. The skin of a plane was hyper conductive, causing any electrical charges to skate along the exterior of the plane and then to discharge back into the atmosphere.

Nope. Probably wouldn't make her any happier to know that.

He closed his eyes again, hoping they got out of the storm soon. But his eyes opened fast when he felt the plane start to lose altitude. What the hell? They were descending fast. Way too fast.

The young copilot stumbled out of the front. His face was pale and he was sweating. "Captain Ramano says to prepare for a crash landing."

ELLE VOLLMAN WASN'T prone to regrets, but when she realized the plane was going down, a few thoughts flashed through her terrified mind. Mia, sweet Mia. How could the little girl endure another loss? Elle had wanted so desperately to give her the life she deserved.

She would miss Father Taquero, too. He'd first become her friend, then her employer and, most recently, her confidant. Then he'd taken on his most important role—Mia's protector.

And then, of course, there was her biggest regret. Brody Donovan. The only man she'd ever loved. She wished she'd had the chance to tell him. Not that he'd probably have been interested in listening. He had to hate her for what she'd done.

She leaned forward in her seat, crossed her arms in front of her, bent her head and prepared to die. Her ears were roaring, her head was pounding and when the plane skimmed the first tree, she heard branches crack and bust and then the scream of metal tearing. The plane tossed from side to side, then rolled and rolled again.

Something hit her in the head, right above her left eye. She felt her seat belt give and she pitched sideways. Blindly, she reached out and grabbed air. Suddenly the plane came to a bone-jarring stop. She fell forward, catching her shoulder on the seat across from her. She felt it give and a searing pain stab at her.

She lifted her head. She felt sick and disoriented, and

where the hell was the emergency lighting that every airline promised in the event of emergency? It wasn't pitch-black but pretty dark. She couldn't see much of anything.

A horrifying thought struck her. Maybe she was blind. Maybe the knock on her head had taken her sight. She was seconds away from full-blown panic when she remembered that she had a flashlight in her backpack. Keeping her injured arm anchored to her side, she used her other to claw around on the floor, feeling her way, until finally her outstretched fingers snagged a backpack strap. She pulled the heavy bag toward her and unzipped it. She reached in, past the extra clothes and the books that she carried with her.

There it was. She pulled out the light, turned it on and very quickly realized that sight wasn't always a gift.

It was a gruesome scene. The inside of the plane had been torn apart and strips of metal and chunks of glass were everywhere. There was a gaping hole in the roof at the very rear of the plane, less than three feet behind where she'd been sitting.

The elderly woman across the aisle was leaning back in her seat, her eyes closed, and blood was running down her face. Her husband was still bent over, in the crash position, with a section from the roof of the plane, probably four feet long and at least a foot wide, pressing on his back.

They were holding hands. And the man's thumb was stroking the woman's palm and her index finger was gently tapping on his gnarled knuckle.

It was witnessing that small connection that gave Elle the strength to move forward. She was alive. Others were alive. All was not lost.

She fished inside her backpack again and pulled out her cell phone. She turned it on, knowing it was a long shot. Still, when there was no service, she experienced a sharp pang of disappointment. She dropped it back into her backpack.

It felt surreal. Like one of those dumb movies where the world has ended and there's only a few mopes to carry on.

Get a grip, she lectured herself. The world hadn't ended, and she wasn't the only one left alive. She'd been in a plane crash. Nothing more. Nothing less.

And she needed to figure out what to do next.

The elderly couple was likely injured, but before she assisted them, she needed to determine how the rest of the passengers had fared. She flashed her light into the seats directly ahead of her. There had been a woman there. She'd had her face buried in a thick book when Elle boarded.

She was still there, her arms wrapped around her middle, silently rocking back and forth. Her eyes were wide-open. Blank.

"Are you all right?" Elle asked.

The woman slowly nodded. She did not make eye contact with Elle.

"What's your name?" Elle asked.

"Pamela," she said, her voice a mere whisper.

"Okay, Pamela, I'm going to check on the pilots. I'll be right back." Elle flashed the light forward to the front of the plane. In the aisle was someone's overnight bag, several magazines and other papers, a coat and more pieces of the plane's interior wall.

Elle stepped over the debris. When she stopped to yank back the partially closed curtain that separated the cockpit from the cabin, Pamela almost rammed into her back.

Elle understood. The need for human contact, to know that she wasn't alone, was almost overwhelming.

Elle could see that the pilot was still in his seat, slumped over the controls. The copilot had been thrown out of his seat and was awkwardly sprawled in the small space between the two seats. He was moving, thank God, picking himself up. Half-up, he suddenly crumpled on his right side. Arms flailing, he grabbed for his chair and sank down. "Oh, damn, that hurts," he said, reaching for his lower leg.

His hand came away with blood and Elle thought she might be sick. She forced herself to step closer.

The man had pulled up his loose pants, and sticking out of his lower leg was the sharp, ugly end of a bone. There was blood. It wasn't spurting out, like when Father Taquero had cut his hand at the church a month ago, but to her inexperienced eye, there did seem to be a rather lot of it.

"Don't move," she said instinctively.

"Not much chance of that," he said, his jaw tight. He turned his pale face to the man at his side. "Captain Ramano." His voice was a plea.

The older man groaned but didn't push his body back or lift his head.

They were both alive but certainly hurt.

"Can you call for help?" Pamela asked, over her shoulder, evidently not caring about their injuries.

To his credit, the young copilot fiddled with several switches. "No power," he said, his young voice showing the strain. "There's no radio." He pulled a cell phone from his back pocket and pressed a couple keys. "No signal."

"That's okay," Elle said, attempting to stay calm.

"It's not okay," Pamela said, her voice too loud for the small space. "I smell fuel. We're going to blow up. We have to get out. Now!"

Elle turned. She spoke with the authority that had always successfully quieted a room of preteen girls. "We will. Now, you need to stay calm and help me. We have to help the others."

Pamela pressed her lips together. Then she whirled suddenly, her arm flailing to the side. "What about him?" she asked, pointing to the front row. "Can he help?"

Elle had forgotten about the man who had boarded late. She'd been writing in her journal and had looked up just as he swung his body into the seat. She'd caught a glimpse of broad shoulders in a pale green shirt.

She turned back to the young copilot and swallowed hard. "I am going to help you." She wasn't sure how, but she would do something. "But first, I need to see how badly the rest of the passengers are injured. Can you hang on?"

He nodded and closed his eyes.

Elle turned and stepped past Pamela, to the point where she could shine the light on the remaining passenger's seat. Because the man had been in the front row, there hadn't been any seat for him to use to brace himself. It appeared as if his belt had failed, as hers had, and he'd been pitched out of his seat onto the floor. He was under debris from the wall and ceiling. She could see an arm, a leg, a portion of his back.

She let the light rest there. He was breathing.

Alive. He moved his legs, then his arms.

"Be careful," she said. "You've got stuff on your back."

The man stilled.

"We'll try to lift it off," she said. She motioned for Pamela to help her. "I can only use one arm," she said to Pamela. "But between the two of us, we should be able to do it."

But she wasn't going to be able to hang on to her flashlight, and they couldn't work in the dark. She stepped toward the elderly woman. Now her eyes were open. Alert.

"My name is Elle," she said.

"I'm Mrs. Hardy," she said. "Beatrice Hardy. You need to help my husband."

"Go on, Bea," the elderly man said. "I'm not going anywhere."

Sort of what the copilot had said. "I'll help him," Elle promised. "But first we're going to help the man up front. I need you to hold the flashlight for us. Can you do that?"

The woman unbuckled her seat belt, got up and reached for the flashlight. They returned to the front of the plane. Working together, Elle and Pamela dug the man out, tossing the heavy pieces aside. It was wood or fiberglass or some other combination of materials, she wasn't sure. All she knew was that it was heavy and, while she kept her right arm tucked next to her side, it was impossible to keep the right side of her body from moving. Piercing pain traveling through her neck, shoulder and arm was the result. It made her feel sick to her stomach.

Finally, the man was free. She could hear him moving in his seat, but the light was not quite in the right spot. She retrieved the flashlight from Mrs. Hardy, who immediately returned to her husband's side, and aimed it toward the man.

Evidently right in his eyes.

"Hey," he said, protesting, holding his hand in front of his eyes.

She lowered the light fast.

And wondered if she'd been too quick to dismiss her own head injury. She'd been thinking about Brody and, suddenly, she was seeing him.

And hearing him.

It wasn't possible. She was in shock. And pain. Her shoulder hurt like the devil. That was it.

She flashed the light again, being careful to keep it away from his eyes. The man's body was long and lanky, with narrow hips and a flat stomach. Nice wide shoulders. Strong chin.

Oh, no. She knew that chin.

"Brody?" she said, her voice squeaking.

Said chin jerked up and she caught the full impact of his hazel eyes. He looked her up and down and even knowing that it was so dark that he couldn't be seeing much, she wanted to run and hide. Thirteen years. And it felt as if it were yesterday.

"Evening, Elle," he said, his voice sounding strained. "I guess this just proves that no matter how bad things are, they can always get worse."

Chapter Two

The minute he said it, he was sorry. Over the years, Brody had thought of a thousand things that he might say to Elle if their paths ever happened to cross. That had not been one of them.

He felt worse when he heard her quick intake of breath. And he was just about to apologize when she stepped toward him. "This is Pamela. Mr. and Mrs. Hardy, mid-seventies, are in the back row. Total of five passengers. Two crew. Copilot has a bone sticking out of his lower leg and the pilot is barely conscious and bleeding from the head. No working radio."

It was a nice, concise report but did nothing to explain why she was on this plane.

Damn, the side of his head hurt. When the plane was rolling, everything became a projectile and something had knocked into him pretty hard. He was pretty sure he'd lost consciousness briefly. When he was coming to, he'd heard Elle's voice, like so many times in his dreams. Then, when she moved closer to lift the weight off his back, and he'd smelled orange blossoms, he'd been shocked. Never before had Elle's sweet scent been part of his dreams.

Then she'd said his name and he about jumped out of his own skin.

How many times over the years had he heard her say *Brody?* Her tone rich, a little lower than the average woman's. In friendship—that had come first. In passion—it had followed pretty quickly. In joy—he liked to think so. Maybe he'd have heard it in sorrow when she left, but he'd never know. All he'd gotten was a note.

And now didn't exactly seem like the right time to ask for more information. Now was the time to do what he did best.

"Either of you injured?" he asked.

The woman next to Elle stepped forward. "We have to get out. You have to help us."

"Are you injured?" Brody repeated.

"No. I mean, I don't think so. We have to go now. The plane might explode."

Elle had introduced her. What was her name? "Pamela, right?"

"Yes."

"I want you to sit tight for just a minute." He turned his attention to Elle. "I heard you say something about your arm."

"It's fine," she said, dismissing the inquiry. "What about you?"

He rolled his shoulders back and considered his own injuries. He'd been lucky. He was going to have a hell of a lump on his head, but he could get past that. Something from above had hit his back and it was definitely going to be bruised and sore tomorrow, but if the angle of the hit had been a little sharper and a couple inches higher, it likely would have fractured his spine and he would never have walked again.

He stood up, careful not to hit his head on parts of the hanging interior. "I'm good to go. I'll check the crew first," he said.

She moved, shrinking far enough back in the small space to let him pass without touching her. He was grateful for that. His nerves felt pretty raw. When the copilot announced that they should prepare to crash, he'd prepared to die. Had said a quick prayer, said a mental goodbye to his parents and to both Ethan and Mack, the best friends a man could have had. And he'd thought about Elle, whom he'd loved and lost and never known why.

"I'll need some light," he said. She handed him the flashlight. He took it, careful not to brush up against her fingers.

He saw the young copilot sitting in his chair and moved toward him. "My name is Brody Donovan. I'm a doctor," he said.

"Thank God, a doctor," the young man said, his jaw clenched tight. "I hope you don't deliver babies for a living."

"Orthopedic surgeon," Brody said.

"My lucky day," the copilot said.

Brody wasn't so sure of that. He'd seen enough to know that the young man had a compound fracture of the tibia.

"What's your name?" Brody asked.

"Angus Bayfield."

"Angus, I'm going to be able to help you, but for now, I need you to not move that leg." When a bone broke and one end protruded through the skin, that meant that there was another sharp end still inside the leg, able to do all kinds of damage to veins and arteries. The blood loss wasn't bad and he wanted to keep it that way.

"I'm going to quickly assess the others," Brody said. He'd been in a combat zone for a long time. Triage was the name of the game. Assess everyone, identify the wounded, identify those most *critically* wounded that would *benefit* from treatment, and proceed from there. "Are there any other flashlights on board and what about a first-aid kit?"

The man pointed over his shoulder toward a big flashlight that was still miraculously hanging on the wall. Brody reached over and unsnapped the straps that kept it in place and flipped it on. It lit up the whole space, much better than the small flashlight that Elle had given him.

There were sections of the roof of the plane hanging down and exposed wires. The front windshield was shattered, making it difficult to see anything outside.

He heard movement behind him and turned. It was Elle. He handed her back her flashlight.

"I'm going to sit with the Hardys," Elle said.

"Tell them I'll be there in just a minute."

"Sir," Angus said, "there's a first-aid kit under the captain's seat."

Brody fished around and pulled out the rectangular aluminum box. Holding the flashlight in one hand, he used his other to flip open the lid. He made a quick assessment. Basic stuff. Bandages. Gauze. Alcohol sponges. Ibuprofen. Antiseptic wipes. Antibiotic ointment. Adhesive tape. Scissors. Several pairs of gloves.

He turned toward the pilot. The man was still strapped in and he was regaining consciousness. He pushed himself back from the controls, almost to the point where he was sitting up. He looked stunned. There was blood running down the side of his face from a hell of a gash on the side of his head where something had obviously hit him.

"I'm a doctor," Brody said, his voice gentle. "I can help you."

He lifted the man's wrist and took his pulse. Steady. Maybe a little slow but not alarmingly. He needed to get the bleeding stopped. "You've got a head injury. Are you in pain anywhere else?" he asked.

The man shook his head, very slowly. Brody didn't believe him. He wasn't confident the man even realized that he was a pilot and that his plane had just crashed in the Amazon jungle.

"What the hell happened?" Brody asked, turning towards the copilot.

"I'm not sure. There was some kind of malfunction with the electrical system. We lost power. Captain Ramano did a hell of a job keeping us out of a spin."

Captain Ramano didn't add anything to the conversation, confirming for Brody that he was definitely injured.

"The lightning?"

"I don't think so. I've flown through storms before with Captain Ramano and we've never had any trouble."

First time for everything. "Did you get a distress call through?"

"We did. Although I'm not sure how much good it will do. Even using satellite imaging, it's hard to find a plane in the rain forest."

He was probably right. Rain forests were known for

their dense canopy of trees, and that would complicate an air search. But he couldn't focus on that right now.

"I'll be back," Brody said.

Pamela was sitting in the first row, staring at the door, looking as if she intended to make a break for it. He did not relish the idea of chasing after someone in the dark jungle. "Pamela, I need your help," he said.

She didn't answer but she did stand up. He led her back to the cockpit, where he opened the first-aid kit again, removed a wrapped gauze pad and opened it.

He motioned for her to get as close to the pilot as she could. "I need you to press this hard against that cut. Can you do that, Pamela?"

"I'm not touching blood."

He'd been just about to get to that. He pulled a pair of gloves out of the first-aid kit and handed them to Pamela. She hesitated and then put them on.

"Okay," he said. "Put pressure on and don't stop until I come back."

He shone his flashlight ahead of him. At the back of the small plane, Elle was kneeling next to the elderly couple. Her hair was still dark, cut shorter than it had been in college when she'd worn it past her shoulders. He could see her slender neck, her collarbone.

Elle had always been slim and in good shape. She'd been a good athlete, too. The bar where she'd worked had fielded a volleyball team that played on Sunday afternoons, and he'd loved watching her. So graceful yet she could jam the ball down an opponent's throat.

Now she had one arm out, patting the shoulder of Mrs. Hardy, who was talking a mile a minute. She had her other arm tucked into her side.

When she heard him moving down the aisle, she stepped aside.

The elderly woman stared at him. "My husband says it doesn't hurt, but he can't move. Please help him. You have to help him. We're on our fiftieth anniversary trip. He's—"

"I'm going to do everything I can," Brody said. He looked at the woman's cheek. She had a cut that was bleeding, but it didn't look deep. "But here's what I need from you. I want you to stand up and move to the other side of the plane. I'm going to need your spot."

The woman shut up now that she had some direction. She got out of her seat and stood next to Elle. That's when he realized that Elle also had blood on her face. And her eyes held the look of someone in pain.

He reached for her.

She jerked back.

"You're bleeding," he said.

"It's nothing. Help the others first."

He gave the cut on her forehead another look. Head wounds always bled a lot, and this one was no exception. But it appeared to have stopped bleeding. Still, there could be glass in it. He took a quick glance at her very brown eyes. Pupils were the same size.

"Him first," she said.

"Okay. But I'm going to look at that arm, too."

She nodded.

He stepped into the seat that Mrs. Hardy had vacated. It was awkward, but he got a good hold of the debris and shoved it away from her husband. He put a hand on the man's back, assuring him. "Don't move just yet," Brody said. He ran his hand down the man's spine. "Are you in pain?"

"No. Damn thing didn't hit me hard, thank goodness."

"Okay. Then try to sit back." The man had been very
lucky. He was at an age when it became difficult to re-
cover from severe injuries. When the man was upright,
Brody took his pulse and used the flashlight to check
his pupils. Both okay.

Brody stepped back. It was quite frankly amazing
that everyone on board had survived the crash. He'd
seen enough aircraft-crash-scene victims over the
years to know that there were common injuries caused
by the pressure of rapid descent. Vertebrae compres-
sion. Or a ring fracture at the base of the skull caused
by force traveling through the spinal column. Sometimes even internal injuries caused by the jerk of the lap
belt. Lower-limb injuries were common as legs flailed
around and struck things, so Angus's fractured tibia
didn't surprise him.

He'd set the leg as best he could. Unfortunately, however, what might be a relatively minor injury in a fully
equipped operating room became potentially life threatening when there were nonsterile conditions and delayed treatment. And the humidity in this part of the
world was a virtual breeding ground of bacteria.

He turned, only to realize that Elle had returned to
the cockpit. She was talking to Angus, obviously trying to comfort him.

It was difficult to tell how badly the captain was hurt.
Angus definitely needed the most immediate treatment,
and there wasn't any room in the cockpit area to do that.

Elle saw him start back down the aisle and met him
halfway. "What do you think?" she asked.

"On the plus side, I think Mr. and Mrs. Hardy are

fine. They're probably going to be stiff and sore as the night wears on. The biggest risk for Pamela is to keep her from running off into the rain forest. You, I'd like to see that shoulder."

"I'm fine," she said.

He shook his head. When she'd moved out of the way earlier so that he could get to Mr. Hardy, he'd seen enough to realize that it wasn't her arm that was injured, but rather her shoulder. "Elle, please don't be stubborn about this. It's just wasting time. I'm going to need help with Angus and you're the only logical person to do it. I need you to have two arms and hands that are working."

It was the right approach. She clearly didn't want to impede the others receiving medical care.

She put her flashlight down and moved so that she stood in front of him. They were just inches apart and he was reminded of how nicely her head used to fit under his chin. He took a deep breath, put his hand on her shoulder joint and probed gently. "You dislocated your shoulder," he said.

"My seat belt broke," she said. "I got tossed out and hit the back of another seat with my shoulder."

"When you hit it, your humerus popped out of the shoulder socket. I can pop it back into place, but it's going to hurt. Maybe a lot."

She nodded. "Just get it over with."

Chapter Three

He stretched out her arm, raised it above her head and, at exactly the right spot, used the heel of his hand to pop the joint back into place.

She let out a hiss of air. He'd seen big, tough guys yelp when they experienced the same thing. "Okay?" he asked.

"Lovely," she managed.

He almost smiled. "I think it's possible that the captain has some internal injuries that we'll have to watch for. He probably hit the dash pretty hard. I'll bandage his head after I set the copilot's leg. Unfortunately for Angus, we don't have any ice and it's going to be difficult to keep the swelling down. His leg really needs stitches, but I didn't see any needles or thread in the first-aid kit. Same issue with Captain Ramano. I'd like to stitch up his head wound."

"I have a sewing kit," Elle said. "It's just a small one. I think it was a giveaway at a conference I attended a couple years ago and I toss it in my carry-on when I travel, just in case."

It was better than nothing. The needles wouldn't be nearly as sharp as what he was used to, but he could make them work. He could sterilize the needle and the thread with one of the antiseptic wipes in the first-aid kit. Not great but better than leaving a gaping wound. "Please get it," he said.

She found her bag in the rubble and dug through it, pulling out a tiny plastic box with three needles and six small coils of thread in it. She handed it to him.

"What else do you need me to do?" she asked.

The Elle he remembered had turned a little green when he discussed the surgeries he was observing in medical school. "There's going to be blood," he said.

"I'll be okay," she said, swallowing hard.

He studied her. So familiar. Yet so different. It was hard to get his head around it, so he did what was simple. He pushed it to the back of his mind. There were wounded. That's where his energies needed to be.

"Okay. Clear some space in the aisles. It's the only place where there will be room to work. I really need something to…" He let his voice trail off. He saw something that would work. In Mr. Hardy's seat pocket, there were several newspapers. Brody grabbed one and handed it to Elle. "Once the space is clear, lay this down on the floor."

He was going to need something to sop up the blood, especially if he got unlucky and the sharp edges of bone cut a vein or an artery.

"If I only had a scalpel, I'd be in good shape," he said, under his breath.

Mrs. Hardy pointed to one of the large suitcases that had spilled out of the cabinet. "I've got a knife in with my makeup. Never gets caught by airline security."

Brody figured security had seen it but just decided they didn't want to have the twenty-minute conversation with Mrs. Hardy about why she had to fly with a knife. He opened the suitcase. Mrs. Hardy's makeup was in the zipper pocket. He was surprised when he saw the lovely pearl-handled instrument, tucked in beside lipsticks and powders. He'd expected something like a butter knife or at best a little pocketknife. No. Mrs. Hardy was *packin'*. Fully unfolded, the knife had at least a three-inch blade. The woman could have done some serious damage with it.

Brody looked from the knife to Mrs. Hardy and then back again. "And I had to give up my four ounces of shaving cream," he said.

Mrs. Hardy smiled. "There are advantages to being an old woman."

Brody tested the point against the palm of his hand. It was very sharp and would make a difference. "Thank you," he said, and started for the cockpit.

When Brody got there, Angus had his head back and his eyes were closed. Captain Ramano also had his eyes shut. Pamela was wide-awake and looking pretty agitated.

She was still dutifully pressing down on the pilot's head wound. "How is he?" Brody asked.

"I don't know. I'm not the doctor," she said crossly.

"You're doing fine," Brody assured her. "The bleeding looks as if it has stopped. You can go back to your seat."

He'd assist Captain Ramano once he finished with Angus. He tapped the young man on the shoulder. Angus opened his eyes.

"So it wasn't a dream?" Angus said.

Brody shook his head. "Wish it was, my friend. Once we get that leg set, you'll feel better. I promise."

He helped Angus up out of his seat. There was so

little room that as careful as they were, at one point Angus brushed his injured leg against something and let out a yelp as if he were an injured dog.

The young man leaned heavily on Brody as they carefully maneuvered back to the main cabin area, where Brody helped him lie down. Angus wasn't a big guy, but he filled the small center aisle, and right now he looked as if he was about ready to pass out. His pant leg was still rolled up and Brody got his first really good look at the leg. It was already starting to swell. Brody untied the man's shoe and took it off.

It was going to get worse before it got better. This was frontier medicine and he didn't even have any rot-gut whiskey to give to Angus.

Elle took a spot on one side, Brody on the other, each of them shoehorned in the seating area. Both were on their knees.

She could see the pain on Angus's face and she looked up at Brody. "He's lucky you were on this plane," she said.

He didn't answer her.

When Brody didn't answer, Elle realized that the young man she'd loved was gone. Instead, there was a stranger, who didn't feel the need to be particularly polite to her.

The Brody Donovan she remembered was always polite. She'd met him during his first year of med school. Had known he was supersmart after an hour of conversation, not because he told her he was—he just was. She'd enjoyed it when he and his friends came into the little bar where she'd been cocktailing. And when he asked her out, it had been flattering.

She'd declined. Men like Brody Donovan were out

of her league. But he hadn't given up. Finally, she'd agreed, thinking it might be a nice holiday romance, and to her great surprise, and great joy, it had worked. They had clicked.

Loved the same movies, enjoyed the same food, laughed at the same things. She hadn't been a bit surprised when she learned that he'd been an Eagle Scout in middle school and the senior class president in high school. When he casually mentioned that his father was a novelist, she'd rather belatedly put together that Larry Donovan, hottest thriller writer around, was Brody's dad. Learning that his mother was a scientist who worked off and on for NASA didn't even make her blink an eye.

Brody was special.

When he graduated from med school with honors and had been accepted into his first choice for a residency program, everybody had assumed that he was rightfully on his way.

Everybody loved Brody. And she had, too. Which had made leaving him the hardest thing she'd ever had to do.

Brody opened the sewing kit, threaded a needle with a piece of dark blue thread and set it down on the spread newspaper.

He opened a couple packages of antiseptic wipes, then handed her a pair of gloves and slipped a pair onto his own hands. "Angus, I'm going to move your bone back into position. To do that, I'm going to make a very small incision, but given that I don't have anything to numb the pain, it's going to hurt. I need you to keep the leg as still as you possibly can. Can you do that for me?"

Brody's voice was calm, reassuring.

Angus nodded.

"Elle, wipe that blood away," Brody said, his voice still calm.

She took the antiseptic wipe and as gently as possible, tried to clean around the wound so that Brody could see what he was doing. Her stomach was jumping.

"After that, I'll be ready to stitch up the wound and bandage it. You'll be on the road to recovery. How's that sound, Angus?" Brody asked.

He got a nod from the man.

"Okay," Brody said, his voice soft. He wiped the knife off, using two more antiseptic pads.

With confidence that she could only imagine, he made a small incision on Angus's leg. The young co-pilot jerked and moaned but kept his leg fairly still.

Then, using his hands, Brody pressed on the protruding bone and eased it back inside the leg. He was concentrating fiercely and she knew that he was trying to align the two sections of snapped bone so that healing could begin.

"It's going fine," he said, smiling at Angus.

The young man nodded and closed his eyes.

She'd always assumed that Dr. Donovan would have a good bedside manner. So confident, so smart. So calm.

Once Brody seemed satisfied with the position of the bone, he looked up at her. "Wipe off the needle and the thread with the antiseptic wipes."

She did as instructed and then handed him the needle.

"Thank you," he said automatically. "I need you to gently press the edges of the wound together while I stitch it up." That part seemed to go relatively well. The stitches closing up the incision were a nice straight line.

When he got to the torn jagged edges of skin where the bone had poked through, they weren't quite as pretty.

Still, Brody looked satisfied when he put the needle back down on the newspaper. The wound was closed and the bleeding had stopped. He opened the tube of antibacterial cream and spread a liberal amount over the whole area. Then it was a bandage and some tightly wrapped gauze.

Brody took off his gloves and dropped them on the newspaper, then patted Angus's shoulder. "All done."

"Thank you," the young man whispered.

Elle didn't need a medical degree to know that she'd just witnessed something amazing.

"Now what?" she asked.

"I need to find something to immobilize the leg, to give the bones a chance to knit together."

His gaze settled on Mrs. Hardy's dark suitcase. It was still open from when he'd gone looking for the knife. The suitcase was a roller, with a nice sturdy handle. He ran a hand down the back of the suitcase before he looked up at Mrs. Hardy, who had been watching the entire process with Angus. "I might be able to use this," he said.

"Take what you need out of it," Mrs. Hardy said.

"It's not quite that easy," he said. "I hate to do this, but I'm going to need to tear the bag apart. I can use the two rods that connect to the handle."

Mrs. Hardy shrugged as if to say that she and her husband had survived a plane crash and she didn't intend to sweat the small stuff.

Brody used Mrs. Hardy's knife to cut through the fabric, exposing the rods. Elle wasn't an expert, but they looked perfect. At least twenty inches long with a plate that attached them at the bottom. There were screws that connected the plate to the wheel assembly and another set of screws that fixed the rods to the handle.

Elle leaned toward the young pilot. "Angus," she said softly, "do you have any tools on board, like a screwdriver?"

"No, I don't think so."

Brody was already using the end of the knife to turn the screws. It was slow going, but he was making progress. Finally, the rods were loose. He looked up. "I need some strips of cloth."

"I've got T-shirts in my bag, young man," Mr. Hardy said. He pointed to a small bag that matched Mrs. Hardy's. It had somehow ended up near the front of the plane.

Brody opened the suitcase and pulled out several white T-shirts. He cut one into strips and used two more to wrap around the metal rods.

Then he put the padded rods in place, one of each side of Angus's leg. The metal plate at the end of the rods fit underneath Angus's foot.

Then Brody efficiently used the strips of T-shirt to tie everything tight. When he finally sat back to inspect his work, Elle could tell that he was pleased. He patted Angus's shoulder. "We're going to help you get up. You can take a seat in that last row so that you can keep your leg extended straight."

It was awkward, but between the two of them, they managed to get Angus up from the floor and onto a seat. There were beads of sweat running down the young man's face by the time they were finished.

"Thanks, Doc," he said.

"You're welcome," Brody said, smiling.

"I'm worried about Captain Ramano," Angus said. "I don't think he's doing so good."

"Don't worry," Brody assured him. "I'm going to check him next. First I'm going to elevate your leg a little. Just stay still." He grabbed several magazines that were lying around, stacked them and slid them under Angus's foot. Then he pulled a small foil-wrapped package of ibuprofen out of the first-aid kit. "Take a couple of these. It will help with the discomfort."

Elle reached for her backpack and pulled out a bottle of water that she'd bought at the airport after she got through security. She handed it to Angus.

Angus braced himself up on one elbow and took a big drink.

"Better save some of that for later," Brody cautioned.

The passengers all looked at each other. They heard the unspoken warning. *We may be here awhile and we don't want to run out of water.*

Pamela stepped forward. "Someone needs to be in charge of supplies. I'll do it."

Everyone was looking at Brody. He'd become the leader of the group, whether he wanted the post or not. "That's a good idea, Pamela," he said. "I suggest everybody throw in what you've got in your bags and we'll take an inventory. Just in case," he added.

Rather optimistically, Elle thought. She'd been living in this part of the world for several years. Planes didn't frequently crash in the jungle, but when they did, sometimes it took weeks to find the wreckage.

"I'm going to stitch up Captain Ramano's head wound," Brody said.

Elle swallowed hard. She'd gotten a look at that cut. "Do you need help?" she forced herself to ask.

Brody shook his head. "I'll manage," he said. "Do you think you could clean up Mrs. Hardy's cut on her face?"

She was getting the better end of the deal. "Of course."

"If there's any glass, leave it and I'll remove it," he said.

Elle didn't see any glass or anything else in Mrs. Hardy's cut. She cleaned it with an antiseptic wipe, smeared antibiotic cream on it and covered it with a small bandage. She could handle this kind of first aid. There was always some kid at the school getting a scraped knee or a skinned elbow.

She was almost done when Mrs. Hardy turned her head to look at her. "Do you and Dr. Donovan know each other?"

"Uh...why do you ask?"

"Well, I don't mean to be a meddling old lady, but I heard what he said. He didn't sound very happy to see you. And you looked very surprised to see him."

"We knew each other a long time ago. It's been thirteen years since we saw each other."

"Did you work together?"

"No. We were..." Friends. Lovers. For a minute, she considered lying about it. But she'd stopped running from the truth some time ago. "We were engaged," she said. "And I broke off the engagement."

"Gracious."

Indeed. "I'd appreciate it if you could keep that information to yourself," Elle said. "We've got our hands full here and I don't want it to be a distraction."

Mrs. Hardy nodded. "It's not easy to be young," she said.

She had been young and probably immature. But she'd made the right decision. For Brody.

Who was returning from the cockpit. "How's Captain Ramano?" she asked.

"Conscious. I got his head wound cleaned up and stitched. I suspect he has a concussion and I'm still worried that there may be some internal injuries."

She looked around. The others were huddled around Angus, quietly conversing. "If you're right and he has internal injuries, he might not survive the night," she said.

"I'll watch him," Brody said. "These just aren't great conditions to have to cut someone open and try to stop internal bleeding."

"You would do that?" she asked.

"I'll do what I have to do," Brody said simply. "Right now I think we need to concentrate on that," he said, pointing to a hole in the roof of the plane. It was almost as if the hard impact had ripped apart a seam.

But it hadn't ripped neatly—the area around the hole was a jagged mess of metal. "We need to get that covered, but first, I'd like to use the hole to take a look around outside. I need something to stand on."

"There are some boxes in the closet at the front, the one where the flight crew hangs their jackets," Elle said.

"An empty box won't work," he said.

"They're not empty," Elle said.

He walked toward the closet, kicking additional debris out of his way as he went. He opened the closet door and, sure enough, there were two boxes. He picked one up. It was heavy. "What the heck is in here? Cement?"

"Books," Elle said.

He carried a box and set it down under the hole.

The floor was wet and more water was dripping in. He got the second box. "I hope you don't mind if they get wet," he muttered.

"Under the circumstances, I think I can get past it," she said, her tone dry.

"People can get past a lot," he said to no one in particular. He stood on the boxes and carefully stuck his head outside. Rain pelted his face and shoulders. It was very dark and the moist smell of wet foliage was almost overwhelming. He raised his arm and shone his flashlight out into the distance.

Trees. And more trees. He pivoted, carefully moving his feet so as to not lose his balance on the stacked boxes. Every direction was the same. When he brought the light in closer, he could see where the plane had knocked through some trees, breaking off branches before it had come to rest on the floor of the jungle. The trees, big and leafy, towered over the plane, probably some seventy to eighty feet in the air.

Angus had been right. It was going to be very difficult for rescuers to find the plane.

ELLE REALIZED SHE'D been holding her breath while Brody was surveying the outside. When he pulled his torso and head back inside, she gulped in a big lungful of air.

"Well?" she asked.

For a minute, she thought he was going to tell her to look for herself. Then he let out a soft sigh, as if in acceptance that he was going to have to talk to her, regardless of how distasteful it might be.

"I don't think we're in any immediate danger," he said. "The plane appears to be on a flat surface. It's hard to see much, but I'm fairly confident of that. I think we need to sit tight tonight. I suspect they'll suspend any search until daylight."

She looked at her watch. Daylight was ten hours away. "We should probably cover this hole," she said. "No need to advertise that there's fresh meat in the jungle," she said, attempting to insert a hint of levity into her tone.

He didn't smile. "I agree. If nothing else, we need to keep the mosquitoes out as best we can."

He was right. She'd had a malaria vaccine, but there wasn't one for dengue fever or several of the other diseases that mosquitoes carried. "There are some blankets in the front cabinet."

"I saw that, but let's see if we can find something else. We should reserve the blankets for warmth."

She started looking around. The plane was small with few hidden cracks or crannies. Behind the last row of seats was a built-in cupboard for passenger luggage with a double door. Both doors had come open during the crash and the few pieces of luggage inside had spilled out. On the shelf above the open space was… something. Whatever it was, it was covered in dust. Rather gingerly, she reached for a corner and pulled it toward her. With it halfway out, she realized what it was. She held it up for Brody and the others to see. "Look. A parachute."

"I think it's a little too late for that, dear," Mrs. Hardy said, humor in her tone.

Elle smiled at the woman. She didn't miss the odd look in Brody's eye. He was probably thinking that she was pretty good at bailing out.

"This makes no sense," Elle said. "This is not the kind of plane you'd jump from."

Brody nodded. "You're right. It looks as if it got stuffed in here and somebody forgot about it. Regardless, it's a good find and quite frankly, we're due some luck."

Elle pulled the parachute out, spreading the nylon canopy as best she could in the small space. "I think this is a job for Mrs. Hardy's knife."

It took Elle several minutes to slice a section of the fabric that would cover the hole. When she was done, she looked up. That had been the easy part. Now she was going to have to go outside, climb on top of the plane and place it over the hole. She was worried about the jagged pieces of metal piercing the nylon, but she couldn't do much about that right now. Also, she'd have to find something heavy enough to lay over it to keep it in place. Maybe a few branches from some trees or even some heavy palm leaves. She could use Mrs. Hardy's knife to cut them off. "I'll go outside and put it over the hole."

"You're not going outside and climbing on top of this plane," Brody said, his tone adamant, as if it were the dumbest thing he'd heard today.

"Getting the hole covered is important," she reminded him.

"Cover it from the inside."

"I need tape and nails for that," she said. "I haven't come across any of that."

"There's some bandage tape in the first-aid kit. That should be strong enough to hold it."

"Shouldn't we save that, just in case?"

"It was a new roll," he said. "If you use some, we

should still be okay." He walked toward her, first-aid kit in hand.

"How's the shoulder?" he asked.

"Fine. Good as new," she said.

"Okay. I want to clean up your head wound."

She let out a huff of air. "Fine."

He opened the first-aid kit and motioned for her to have a seat. Holding a flashlight in one hand and alcohol sponges in the other, he quickly cleaned and disinfected the wound. She tried to hold very still.

Brody Donovan had always had nice hands. Gentle. Yet strong.

There were no rings on any fingers. Was it even possible that he'd never married? Married and divorced? She doubted that. Once Brody made a promise, he'd keep it.

Unlike her.

"The cut is about an inch long but not too deep. I'm going to cover it. If you can keep it from getting infected, it will heal and probably won't even leave a scar."

She wasn't worried about a scar. She knew that small imperfections like that hardly mattered. "It will give me character," she said, trying to make light of the situation.

"You have a tan," Brody said, surprise in his voice.

She felt her whole body heat up. He used to tease her that her fair skin would never tan. On the other hand, she'd called him *Goldenboy*. He'd always been perpetually tanned from all his outdoor activities. That, combined with his light brown hair, which was naturally streaked with some lighter blond, and he looked as if he'd stepped out of a California tourism advertisement.

And while his hair was shorter than it had been in med school, he still looked very much the same. What had he been doing for the past thirteen years? And what had led him to be on a small charter plane in Brazil?

She had a thousand questions and no right to ask any of them.

Chapter Four

They found a total of four blankets. Brody gave one to the Hardys and one to Elle, who immediately offered to share with Pamela. The third he used to cover up Captain Ramano, who had finally gotten out of his seat and moved back into the main cabin area with the rest of them. The fourth went on top of Angus, who was restless with pain.

For himself, Brody pulled an extra shirt out of his bag and put it on. He was too wired to sleep and the jungle was anything but quiet at night. Even though Elle had done a good job covering the hole in the roof of the plane, all kinds of sounds still floated in.

He'd thought he'd be listening to the sound of surf outside his bedroom window tonight. Instead, he was listening to who knows what. The only given was that it likely wanted to eat him.

At the crack of dawn, he was going to build a fire. That would make it easier for a search plane to locate them. He hoped the winds were light; otherwise the smoke would dissipate too fast. They did have one other weapon in their arsenal. Angus had said that there were some emergency flares. So, if a plane got close, they'd send up one of those.

Pamela snored, so around three in the morning, Elle threw back her portion of the blanket and walked over to sit in a seat on the other side of the cabin. It wasn't as if she could go far. The plane was not that big.

Brody watched her. She ignored him even though he was pretty sure she knew he was awake.

Which, for some crazy reason, rattled his chain. "So, what's with the books?" he asked.

It took her so long to answer he began to think that she wouldn't. No skin off his back.

"I teach English at a girls' school. These were extra books that we received. A priest that I know has a brother who is a teacher in Fortaleza at a very poor school. I offered to share the books with him."

"Couldn't you have shipped them?"

"Of course. But I was headed this direction anyway and I've gotten to know him, too, over the past couple of years. I was going to stay overnight with him and his wife before going on."

Before going on? "Where's your final destination?"

"Back to the States," she said, finally look at him.

"Really?" He paused. "For good?"

She shrugged. "I don't know. Things are…complicated."

He waited, hoping she'd tell him more. But she stayed quiet and his mind went about six directions.

Complicated because she was leaving a man? Leaving a family? Complicated because she no longer had a job? Complicated because she was on the run from the government? Complicated because she was part of the witness-protection program? Each thought was becoming more and more bizarre. He needed to stop.

They didn't owe each other any explanations. They

were strangers who, a very long time ago, had had a moment.

A moment that had lasted two years.

A moment that had ended so fast that his head had whirled for months.

It had been thirteen years since he saw her. They'd met two years before that. He'd been in the middle of his second year of med school. She'd been a waitress in a little bar where the med students hung out. She'd been beautiful and articulate and very sexy in her short black skirt and white shirt. And she'd seemed to enjoy their brief conversations as he tried to devise ways to stretch out ordering a beer.

It had taken him six weeks and four invitations before she'd agreed to go out with him.

He'd relentlessly pursued her and pretty soon, they'd been spending all their free time together. On Christmas Eve, almost exactly two years after their first date, he'd asked her to marry him. When she'd said yes, he'd known it would be the best Christmas ever. They'd planned an early June wedding. In February, she'd bought a dress, which she refused to show him, saying it was bad luck. In March, they'd created a small guest list of close friends and family, which grew exponentially bigger when his parents had added their friends and extended family. As the list grew bigger and bigger, he'd noticed Elle's nervousness increase.

Don't be concerned about the expense, he'd told her. While it might have been traditional that the bride's parents paid for the wedding, he knew that Elle's mother was divorced. He suspected resources were limited. He'd encouraged her to add more guests from her side of the family, but she'd simply smiled and said that there was no one else.

They'd registered for wedding gifts, spending time he didn't have selecting china patterns and silverware. But he'd been happy enough to go without sleep. Nothing mattered except marrying Elle.

In the middle of April, eight weeks before the wedding, the invitations had gone in the mail and he'd arranged for Ethan and Mack to get fitted for tuxes.

On May 10, he'd walked out to get the mail, never anticipating that his life was about to change, that nothing would ever be the same, that nothing would ever be quite right again.

He'd seen the letter and had recognized the handwriting. Under a warm spring sun, wearing his pajama pants and his favorite Notre Dame sweatshirt, he'd opened the letter, thinking she'd probably sent him a funny card.

He'd read it twice. Nothing funny about it.

It had been full of apology. Full of a bunch of junk about how he'd be better off without her.

He'd run back into the house and frantically dialed the phone. She hadn't answered. He'd jumped in his car and gone to her apartment. Again, no answer. He'd found the landlord and given him a hundred bucks to open the door. Her clothes and personal things were gone.

He'd gone to Elle's workplace, but nobody had talked to her. Her boss, a man younger than Brody, seemed more concerned about how he was going to fill her shifts than that she was missing. He'd turned to her family only to realize, rather belatedly, that he didn't even have her mother's number.

With the help of his family's attorney, he tracked

down Elle's mother in a small town in central Utah. It had been a horribly awkward conversation. He'd said his name, expecting some sign of recognition. But there had been none. And it had quickly become apparent that Elle and her mother were not close when her mother had finally said that she hadn't heard from her daughter in months.

She'd also said she didn't understand why her daughter always had to be difficult.

The Elle he had known hadn't been difficult, but he was rapidly coming to the conclusion that he likely hadn't really known Elle.

The attorney had gotten the name of the stepdad through the divorce papers that were filed with the county. Even though Elle had never talked about her stepfather, Brody had contacted the man, who was living in Kentucky. Brody had left a message on the phone for the man, didn't get a call back for days, and finally when he followed up again, the man had said he wouldn't bother to open the door if Elle Vollman came knocking.

He'd called the police. They'd read the letter and looked at him with sad eyes and said there didn't appear to be much they could do.

He'd thought about hiring a private investigator. After all, people couldn't just disappear. He got as far as dialing the number one day. What stopped him was knowing that Elle hadn't disappeared. No. She'd left. Packed her bags and left.

Pride kept him from chasing after her.

But it had not kept him from holding his breath every damn day in anticipation of going to the mailbox. It had not kept him from being neurotic about making sure that his phone was charged.

After about a year, he'd stopped expecting her to make contact. At three years, he even got into the habit of not looking at his mail for weeks at a time.

At five years, he'd been able to think about it and not get sick. And within the last couple of years, he'd actually thought he was over it.

Now he knew he was wrong about that.

"Do you still keep in contact with Ethan and Mack?" she asked.

His friends had liked Elle. Had said that she was a good match for him. They weren't generally so wrong. "I do. They're both getting married this summer. In just a few weeks, actually."

She pulled back in surprise. "No way."

"Yes. Ethan is marrying Chandler McCann, Mack's little sister. They reunited at the cabin last fall when somebody was trying to kill Chandler. Ethan wasn't having any of it. And Mack met Hope Minnow when he had a couple free weeks between leaving naval intelligence and starting a new job. Her dad is a television preacher and he and his family had been receiving some anonymous threats. Turned out there were a bunch of snakes in that crowd."

"Hope Minnow," Elle repeated. "Oh, yeah. I remember. I read an article about her in *People*. I suspect most men only looked at the pictures."

"Gorgeous and nice. Same for Chandler. My friends both got lucky."

She sat quietly for a long time with her eyes closed and he thought that she'd maybe fallen asleep. She surprised him when she turned to him. "Did you ever marry, Brody?"

He shook his head. "You?" he asked, and cleared his throat because his damn voice squeaked.

"No," she whispered.

He closed his own eyes. *Ask her why. Ask her why she left you.* The voices in his head were hammering to be let out.

He kept his mouth shut. He'd survived a plane crash. He wasn't sure he could survive hearing her say that she just hadn't loved him enough.

He listened to her even breathing and pretty soon, he was confident that she was asleep.

Only then did he relax enough to drift off and catch a few hours of badly needed rest.

WHEN ELLE WOKE UP, she was sweating. The interior of the plane was warm. She looked around. Pamela and the Hardys were still sleeping. Angus was in his spot, his leg stretched out, his shoulders twitching in restless sleep. Captain Ramano was… Yikes, he was staring at her. When their eyes met, the captain quickly lowered his gaze. The previous night he'd been almost uncommunicative and she'd wondered if he wasn't in shock.

"How do you feel?" she whispered.

"My head hurts," he said. His voice was low, rusty from little use.

She smiled. "I'll bet it does. I'm sure help will come today. Do you remember what happened?" she asked gently.

He shrugged, then winced when that evidently hurt. "We started losing power in our engines. I did the best I could to get us down. It sure as hell wasn't *my* fault."

She wasn't imagining the emphasis on the one word. Who said something like that unless there was someone else that deserved the blame?

Had the plane been tampered with? Did he suspect that? Who would do something like that?

A chill ran down her spine. She knew someone who likely had the means to do something like that. Someone who hated her. Someone who would do most anything to make sure that she never reached the United States.

T. K. Jamas.

He was evil but was he crazy? Would he bring down a plane with innocent people on board just to harm her?

She had to know. "I'm not sure I understand what you mean by that," she said, her voice still a whisper. She didn't want anyone to overhear. "Whose fault is it?"

He stared at her. "How would I know?" he asked.

It wasn't an answer. And despite his head injury, she wanted to shake it out of him. "But the way you said…" She stopped. Brody stood in the doorway of the plane, his frame backlit by a streak of early-morning sunshine that had managed to make its way to the jungle floor. It caught the shine of his hair, the width of his shoulders.

He'd changed clothes. Instead of the cargo shorts he'd worn last night, he'd changed into jeans and a T-shirt. He had boots on his feet instead of sandals, and his jeans were tucked into the boots. It wasn't a great fashion statement but a good idea in the jungle where there were poisonous things crawling everywhere.

"Good call on the boots," she said, turning away from Captain Ramano.

"I threw them in at the last minute," he said, shaking his head. "I always loved hiking in Colorado and knew there were some mountains fairly close to my destination."

Elle wished she'd thought to bring boots. She had the loafers she was wearing and a pair of water shoes. At least she had on pants and a long-sleeved shirt over her cami. Her skin was mostly covered, which could be helpful in the jungle.

Brody walked over to Captain Ramano and looked at his eyes. Then he took his pulse and checked the bandage on his head wound. "I think you may have a slight concussion," he said. "Don't move around any more than you have to."

"I guess it was our lucky day that we had a physician on the plane," Captain Ramano said.

Brody shook his head. "It was our lucky day that you managed to land the plane without it being scattered around the jungle floor. We're going to get out of here. All of us."

Pamela stretched and then stood up. Her hair was going every direction. "They better find us today. We could starve. We have very little water and almost no food."

Mr. and Mrs. Hardy looked at each other. Brody shook his head. "We aren't going to starve. We may get a little hungry, but nobody has ever died from that. We'll have to be careful with our water."

Elle knew exactly how much water they had. And it wasn't enough. They would make it through today, but by tomorrow, they would need more. There was the bottle that Angus had drunk out of. The Hardys both had water bottles and Captain Ramano had had a large thermos of water wedged under his seat. Pamela had a sports drink.

Fortunately, water was generally readily available in the jungle. Unfortunately, it wasn't safe to drink. Unless it was boiled.

She watched Brody inspect the assortment that Pamela had gathered the night before. Four breakfast bars, a sack of chips, a can of mixed nuts, beef jerky, cheese popcorn and twelve tea bags.

"Who had the tea bags?" he asked.

Mrs. Hardy raised her hand. "A good cup of tea always makes me feel a little more civilized."

Elle didn't know about that. T. K. Jamas always drank tea. The first thing she'd noticed about the man was that he always had a cup of tea. He'd arrive at the school, cup in hand.

It made her sick to think that on more than one occasion she'd brewed him a fresh cup.

Brody smiled. "My mother always travels with tea bags. Says she can get through anything with a cup of tea."

"Smart woman," Mrs. Hardy said.

"Very. Anybody allergic to nuts?" Brody asked.

Everyone shook their heads.

"Okay," he said, "then I recommend we take a couple breakfast bars and some nuts, divide them up and save the remainder for later."

Pamela split two breakfast bars into seven equal pieces. It didn't take very long to distribute the portion, along with a handful of nuts, to each person. It took even less time for everyone to consume the meager breakfast. Still, Elle knew they were lucky to have something. It was supposed to be a short flight and she hadn't thought to pack any treats. However, she'd been able to contribute the breakfast bars because they'd been at the bottom of her backpack from a school excursion she'd had the prior week.

Brody made a special point to make sure that Angus ate and that he took some more ibuprofen for his pain.

"I'm going to get a fire going," Brody said.

"How are you going to manage that?" Pamela asked crossly.

Brody smiled congenially, choosing to ignore the testiness of Pamela's inquiry. "I was a Boy Scout. I know how to create friction and generate a spark."

Captain Ramano reached into his pocket. He pulled out two matchbooks, tossing one in Brody's direction. "This might make it easier."

Elle, who had wanted to shake the man five minutes ago, now wanted to hug him. The ability to make fire could be the difference in them surviving.

"Lots easier," Brody said, opening up the flap to show a half-full matchbook. "Someone will see our smoke and help will come."

There was no reaction from the group. Either they were afraid to jinx it by saying anything or they just didn't want to burst the good doctor's bubble.

Brody walked back outside. Pamela worked on the knots in her hair and Mrs. Hardy helped Mr. Hardy change his shirt.

Elle smeared some bug repellant from one of the two small tubes in her backpack on her bare ankles, her hands and neck before following Brody outside. She wanted to see the area in the light of day.

There were parts of the Amazon that you dared not venture into without a sharp machete because the massive undergrowth made walking almost impossible. In other parts, the undergrowth was almost nonexistent because of the thick canopy of trees that blocked any sunlight from hitting the jungle floor.

Where they had landed was sort of a hybrid of the two. There were trees of varying heights. Palms with big leaves, some just a few feet taller than her, some stretching another ten to twelve feet. There were kapok trees, one of the few she was familiar with because they grew so extensively in the Amazon. With a relatively skinny trunk, the tree could grow hundreds of feet. There were plants, big and bright green, some with beautiful flowers, ranging from knee-high to above their heads. In the spots where there weren't plants, the floor of the jungle was a tangle of wet dirt and short, mossy-looking grass.

It was in one long stretch of dirt and grass that Captain Ramano had managed to land the plane. It was a flat-out miracle. She stole a look at Brody's face and thought that he was thinking the same thing.

"You might want to put some of this on," she said, offering him the tube.

He looked at it. "Nice," he said.

"Yeah. I only threw a couple small tubes in my backpack. I thought I was going to be out of the jungle by tomorrow. If we don't have some on, the bugs will eat us alive."

He carefully put a little dab in his hand and smeared it on his exposed skin. She watched him rub his neck, watched the smooth motion of the hand that had tickled her in fun, stroked her in passion.

She looked away.

From the corner of her eye, she watched him approach a midsize kapok tree that had fallen, likely some time ago. It had probably been hit by lightning. There were long branches at the end that extended wide on the ground. Working methodically, he started snapping off the twigs from the branches and building a large pile. After watching him for several minutes, she started doing the same. When he saw that she had the hang of it, he moved on to picking up larger limbs.

It was tedious work and she could see the sweat on his face and wetting the back of his shirt.

They didn't stop until they had a pile of logs and an even bigger pile of twigs. Using a big stick, he drew a circle, maybe three feet wide, and started to dig out the dirt, making a small circular trench.

"I don't want to tell you what to do," Elle said, her tone hesitant. "But if you build the fire there, it's going to be difficult to protect the fire from the rain that will inevitably fall. If you move over there, under those heavy palms, it might be better."

Brody walked over to the area she'd indicated. "It's drier over here," he said.

She nodded.

He looked at her rather oddly. "If you have a better idea than I do, Elle, speak up. We can't afford to make any mistakes out here."

She shrugged, feeling uncomfortable. It was just that in her experience, Brody Donovan didn't make mistakes. He always seemed to have the right answer, know the right thing to do, make the right choice.

He drew another circle and started digging his two-inch-deep trench. Then he arranged four of the logs, end to end, in a pyramid style, and filled the bottom of the pyramid in with the smaller twigs.

He struck a match and, very carefully protecting

it from the wind, held it in the center of the pyramid. After just a second, she could tell that the twigs had caught fire.

Tears came to her eyes and they had nothing to do with the smoke in the air.

And she was reminded of a Tom Hanks movie that she'd seen years ago. He'd been the lone survivor of a plane crash on some island, and she could vividly recall the scene where he successfully managed to get a fire going.

Fire sustained life.

And right now that felt really good.

"Thank you," she said. "This makes a difference," she said. "Somebody will find us," she added, somehow wanting him to know that she believed his earlier statement.

BRODY HEARD THE hopefulness in Elle's voice. He had learned the value of hope in the cold, mountainous terrain of Afghanistan. And the power of fire. He could have gotten a fire started without the matches, but they were definitely a plus. He counted them. Fourteen left. They would have to be careful to keep the fire going in the event that it took some time for rescuers to come.

But he wasn't going to dwell on that. He turned when his peripheral vision caught Captain Ramano in the doorway of the plane. The man stepped onto the jungle floor and studied the nose of the small plane. It was pretty much trashed, having taken a beating when they'd first skimmed the trees.

The majority of the fuselage remained intact—if anyone wasn't overly concerned about a two-foot hole in the roof. It was hard to tell if Captain Ramano was concerned or not. He barely looked at the rest of the plane before he wandered off in the jungle to take a leak.

That didn't make sense. Granted, the man had taken a jolt to the head and no doubt had a slight concussion. But even so, it was his plane.

Brody had dealt with a lot of aviators in the air force, and his friend Ethan had been a helicopter pilot in the army. Fliers were normally take-charge types.

They felt very responsible for their planes and for the individuals aboard. Brody knew that if Ethan had been flying a plane that had encountered mechanical problems, he would have been all over the wreckage, trying to figure out what had happened.

It was almost as if Captain Ramano was trying not to look at it. Which seemed odd. But one thing Brody had learned in recent years, in war-torn countries where no one escaped unscathed, was that everybody coped in his or her own way.

When the man returned to the plane, it was more of the same. He glanced at the fire, at Elle, and finally at Brody. Then he went back inside without a word.

Brody could see the questions in Elle's pretty eyes, but he ignored them. If Captain Ramano was out of the game, so be it. The plane wasn't going to fly again. His skills as a pilot were of no use to them.

Almost as soon as Captain Ramano went inside, Mr. and Mrs. Hardy came outside. Mrs. Hardy had raided her suitcase and come up with something sparkly that she spread on the ground. Then she pulled up a log near the fire that Brody had built, and both she and Mr.

Hardy leaned back, him with a book, her with a deck of cards, as if the jungle had been a scheduled stop.

As if anyone regularly picnicked in a place where poisonous frogs, tarantulas and jaguars lingered nearby.

Chapter Five

Brody wanted to order the Hardys back inside, where they would have less chance of being bitten or stung by something that could seriously compromise their well-being. But he didn't say anything. If they could pretend that everything was *just fine,* then more power to them.

Elle offered the Hardys some bug repellant. Mr. Hardy took some and put it on his wife. Then Mrs. Hardy reciprocated. It was sweet.

Five minutes later, Mrs. Hardy was jawing on Mr. Hardy for breathing too loud.

Hell, maybe he ought to thank Elle from saving him from marriage. She had found a big walking stick and she was using it to poke around at various plants. She was smart to be careful. Everything in the jungle sort of blended in, and grabbing hold of a snake was guaranteed to make a bad day even worse. He watched her for about five minutes before he approached. "What are you doing?"

"The husband of the couple that I worked for in Peru was a scientist, and one of his hobbies was studying plant life in the jungle. He loved to talk about plants, to show the pictures that he would take on his jungle trips. I learned a few things while I was there. The berries on this evergreen tree are allspice. They're edible. On the other hand, this is a curare plant. Very poisonous."

He was impressed. He knew next to nothing about jungle fauna. Her knowledge might come in very handy.

"I'm not as worried about our food supply as I am our water," Elle said. "We barely have enough to last a day. But fortunately, there are multiple ways to access water in the jungle. Come here." She motioned him over to a plant with long green-and-white leaves and a brightly colored flower in the middle. It was literally growing out of the trunk of a tree. "This species is a bromeliad. The leaves overlap and when it rains, water is captured in the little pockets at the base of the flower."

He thought about what he had with him that they could use to gather water. "Probably some of us have small plastic bags in our luggage that had our liquids in them. Maybe we could use that."

"Good idea. Once it rains, which it undoubtedly will, we'll capture the water then. The other thing we can do is get water from those bamboo trees," she said, pointing off to her left, where there was a whole stand of tall, skinny bamboo plants. "It takes some patience but it's relatively easy. All we have to do is bend the bamboo stick, somehow tie it down, and cut it at the bottom. The water inside the bamboo will drain out."

"And we can drink that?"

"Yes. Probably even without boiling it. We might also find water in a nearby stream. That could be dangerous to drink if we don't boil it first. That's why I'm so darn happy to see the fire."

He studied her. He wasn't surprised at her knowledge. It was one of the things that he'd always really appreciated about Elle. She knew a little about a whole lot of things. How to make a good Hollandaise sauce. How to grow orchids in pots on their small patio. How to build a model airplane. How to dance the tango. His mother had once described her as very eclectic and she'd meant it as a compliment.

Elle had always dismissed her knowledge, saying that she knew a bunch of really useless things that were good for starting a conversation at a party but for little else. *I'm just a cocktail waitress,* she used to say.

"Should we boil all the water we gather just in case since we have a fire going?" Brody asked.

"I think so. Better safe than sorry."

"Perhaps Mrs. Hardy will want to brew herself a cup of hot tea?"

"How are your parents, Brody?" Elle asked, evidently remembering his earlier comment about his mother and tea.

"Good. Dad is still writing. Mom has cut back on her consulting and is doing quite a bit of volunteer work at their local hospital." He paused. "How's your mom?"

Elle looked startled, as if she hadn't expected the question. "I don't know. I haven't talked to her since shortly after I left the States."

She had not just walked away from him. She'd walked away from her family, too. What the hell?

"It's sort of pretty, isn't it?" she asked, changing topics quickly. "I mean, if we were here sightseeing, we'd think that."

They would. The plant and flower colors were vibrant and he'd probably already seen ten different types of birds. When he first came out of the plane earlier, there'd been a couple monkeys in the trees, cackling. Probably laughing their asses off at them.

He saw motion out of the corner of his eye and realized that Mr. and Mrs. Hardy were already gathering up their things and heading back inside. He waited a few minutes and followed them. They'd started some kind of domino game with Pamela. Brody knelt down next to Angus. The young man was awake and definitely running a low-grade temp. The first-aid kit had not contained a thermometer, so Brody couldn't get a true reading. A low temp could be a reaction to the injury—the body giving a shout-out that hey, all is not right. Or it could mean something much worse. If that was the case, the young man needed to be in a fully equipped hospital where they could pump some antibiotics into him.

It was infuriating. He'd saved the young man's leg and he could still lose him to infection.

Captain Ramano was sitting in one of the seats, his head back, his eyes closed. His breathing was steady. Brody didn't wake him.

He stepped outside the plane, expecting to see Elle.

But there was no one there.

His heart started to beat very fast. Maybe she'd stepped away to go to the bathroom. He waited.

He didn't hear or see anything.

"Elle," he called.

No response.

"Elle!" This time he really yelled.

He heard rustling off to his left. She appeared. "What?" she asked, her tone anxious.

Relief flooded his body. And that irritated the hell out of him. "I couldn't see you," he said, sounding very much like a petulant six-year-old. "I don't want to have to go chasing after you in the jungle."

"I wanted a better view," she said. "I didn't go far. I just walked up that hill," she said, pointing to a rise about two hundred yards out. "I would not expect you to chase after me, Brody."

Oh, really? He should just let her die in the jungle? "I tried that once," he said. "You know, the chasing, and it didn't work out so well for me."

Her heard her quick inhale and knew that his verbal punch had landed. Maybe not a knockout, but it had been a solid left hook. It should have made him happier.

Unfortunately, it made him feel like scum.

And it made him feel even worse when she didn't come back with something but rather just took the punch. As if she deserved it.

"Well?" he asked, after a very awkward moment of silence. "Were you able to see anything?"

To her credit, she didn't march off and refuse to talk to him. Instead, she stood her ground. "Not really," she said. "It's not high enough. We probably need to get at least that high," she said, pointing to her right. Off in the distance, he couldn't tell how far, was higher ground. Having grown up in the Colorado mountains, in Crow Hollow, Brody couldn't call it a mountain. At best, a small foothill. But she was right. It would probably give them a good view in every direction.

Getting there would be a bitch. Walking in the jungle wasn't like walking on the treadmill at the gym.

"What do you think?" she asked.

"About what?"

"About next steps," she pushed.

Even though he'd known better than to hope for a rescue plane last night, he'd still spent the night listening for engine sounds. He'd been doing the same this morning. Unfortunately, he'd heard nothing like that. He was just about to give her some glib reassurance, but he saw the look in her eyes. The message in them was clear. *Be real, Brody.*

"I don't know what to think," he said. "If Angus's distress call went through, somebody should be out looking for us. I know the Amazon is huge, but they don't have to search all of it. How tough is it to identify the potential area where the plane crashed? They hear the call, they look at their radar, and somebody ought to be smart enough to figure out where our particular blip fell off the screen."

"Maybe the distress call never went through?"

"Even so, air-traffic control should have been tracking us. I assume there is some regular communication between them and a pilot. When Captain Ramano didn't answer, that should have made somebody sit up straighter in their chair. Even if that didn't happen, somebody surely noticed when our plane didn't land as expected. It's been light for several hours. What's taking them so long?"

"I guess that gets back to the sheer magnitude of the jungle. Even with some idea of where we are, it's probably like looking for the needle in the proverbial haystack."

He nodded. "Then we have to hope for the best."

"So we wait?" she asked.

"For now," he said. "But I think we should start to gather and boil water. Just in case."

"What are we going to boil it in?"

"I think we can use the first-aid kit. It's probably twelve inches by eight inches and several inches deep. I'm going to build a grate to go over the open fire."

"I'll gather up things that we can use to collect the water in," she said.

He nodded. It was good to have someone else in the group to count on. Pamela didn't seem all that steady. Mr. and Mrs. Hardy were too elderly and Angus was out of the race. Captain Ramano was the unknown. So far, he'd been distant, not even intellectually curious about their predicament. The one good thing was that he wasn't complaining about pain anywhere except his head, which was a good sign that he'd managed to escape internal injuries.

If Brody and Elle could remain civil to each other, they had a chance of making it out of here. So far, she'd shown amazing strength. She'd been calm, resilient and had come up with good solutions.

Of the two of them, he'd been the bigger ass.

It wasn't something to be terribly proud of.

TWO HOURS LATER, Elle sat inside the plane, looking out one of the small windows. The rain had come, forcing them all inside.

Just as it dampened the earth, it seemed to dampen everyone's spirits. No one was talking. Not even Mrs. Hardy.

And the silence gave Elle plenty of opportunity to think.

She'd been so stupid earlier when she asked about his parents. But she'd really liked Mr. and Mrs. Donovan. They were super nice to her and always made her feel welcome in their home. They were so smart, so successful, yet they treated her as an equal.

She'd honestly been curious about them, but she'd never have asked if she'd thought that that would prompt

Brody to ask about her mother. Brody had never met her mom. She didn't figure he lost much sleep thinking about it.

If he'd been startled by her announcement that she hadn't spoken to her mother for thirteen years, he'd hidden it well. For only a second, she'd again debated lying and saying something innocuous, such as she's fine. But the truth had popped out.

She was done lying and especially done with lying to Brody Donovan. She didn't have any reason to tell him the whole ugly truth; nothing would be gained by that. But she wasn't going to compound her errors and continue her lies.

When they had been dating, Elle was able to explain away Catherine Rivers's absence from her life. Whenever Brody had asked about her family, she'd made up some crazy excuse about her mom living in Utah and not liking to fly.

She had no idea whether her mother liked to fly. They'd never discussed it during their brief telephone conversations that occurred two or three times a year, whenever Elle forced herself to dial the damn phone and endure the stilted, forced exchange that passed as mother-daughter bonding.

After they became engaged, Brody had insisted that he needed to meet her mother, to officially ask for permission to marry Elle. He said that he did not want their first meeting to be at the wedding.

How could she tell Brody that she hadn't planned on inviting Catherine to the wedding? It would have spurred all kinds of questions that she didn't want to answer, didn't plan on ever answering.

Elle had tried to convince him that it wasn't necessary to ask permission, that she'd talked to her mom and the woman was on board. But Brody had worked like crazy to arrange a couple days off and had purchased two round-trip tickets from Boston to Salt Lake City. She'd left the country four days before the trip was to occur.

And to this day, had very little contact with Catherine.

The conversation about parents had left her shaken. After Brody had gone back inside the plane, she'd had to do something to expel the anxiety that had flooded her system with the mention of her mother.

Sure, she'd wanted a better view, but what she'd really needed was a little space, a little time to compartmentalize her thoughts about Catherine. She'd practically run up the small hill and, once there, had stood at the rise, her breath coming hard. By the time he'd come back outside and had been yelling for her, she was back in control.

So he didn't want to have to chase after her.

She didn't want him to. Had never wanted that. Had hoped he wouldn't and had made it as difficult as she could if he actually tried.

She'd had to. She hadn't been sure that she was strong enough to walk away a second time.

Now, as they all huddled in the aircraft and listened to the afternoon rain hit the outside of the plane, she covertly watched Brody. He was looking out one of the small windows. She knew he was worried about the fire.

She thought it would likely be okay. He'd built a grate out of bamboo that traversed the circumference of the fire circle and then had hung the wire hanger of the first-aid kit over one of the long bamboo sticks. The first-aid kit swung freely over the fire and they'd successfully managed to boil a small amount of water and saved it in one of the empty water bottles.

He'd also constructed, over the fire, a crude-looking tepee that was about four feet high at the apex. He'd covered the sides with thick palm leaves, giving the fire even more protection.

Mrs. Hardy had looked at it on one of her trips outside and proclaimed him a genius. Elle knew that there were more matches and it would be possible to start another fire. It dawned on her that Brody was already preparing for the worst—for the likelihood that it might be many days before they were found.

The downpour lasted about forty minutes. When it was over, Elle put on her water shoes. She didn't intend to go wading through any standing water, but the ground would be damp and she wanted to keep her loafers as dry as possible. She motioned to Pamela and then to Mrs. Hardy, who had earlier insisted that she was able to help collect water.

They followed her outside, as did Brody. She showed them how to gather water from the plants. Once Elle explained that they needed to gather water so that it could be boiled, Pamela had run back to the plane and come out again minutes later, holding what appeared to be a ball of tissue paper. She'd peeled back the paper to reveal a brightly colored coffee cup.

"I bought this in Brasília for my nephew. We can use it to collect water."

"It's beautiful," Elle said. "But we need to be careful to keep dirty and clean utensils separate. Let's make sure that no water goes into that cup that hasn't been boiled. Then we can all drink from it. We'll gather the water in these plastic bags."

"We can also use my coffeepot," Mrs. Hardy said.

Brody, Elle, and Pamela had immediately stopped what they were doing. "You have a coffeepot in your suitcase?" Elle asked.

"Never travel without it. It's just a little four-cupper."

Brody shook his head. "Mrs. Hardy, you don't happen to have a spare plane in your luggage, do you?"

"Why, no, I don't," she said. "But I may put it on the list for the next trip."

The other three exchanged looks. Elle knew what she was thinking and suspected the others were tracking. She hoped Mrs. Hardy got to take another trip. She hoped they all did.

"It's good to know we have another vessel to use," Elle said. "We'll use it to brew tea."

"Now you're talking," Mrs. Hardy said, and got busy gathering water. With multiple trips to the first-aid kit with their baggies, Pamela and Mrs. Hardy were able to fill the container with water in less than forty minutes. While they did that, Elle gathered edible berries in a basket that she fashioned out of one of Mr. Hardy's long-sleeved shirts. She found several coconuts, as well.

"It's a tropical feast tonight," she said, bringing her stash back to the group.

Mrs. Hardy smiled. Pamela rolled her eyes, but she did give the coconuts an appreciative glance. Elle looked for Mrs. Hardy's knife to cut the coconuts and realized that Brody was using it to notch out a couple long sticks. Elle wasn't sure what he was doing until she saw him use the sticks to hook the handle of the first-aid kit after the water had boiled for ten minutes.

Mrs. Hardy was right. He was pretty damn smart. If someone had tried to grab the handle, it would have been so hot that they'd have likely jerked back and risked dumping all the freshly boiled water.

"Whatcha got?" he asked, catching her eye.

"Coconuts. Young ones that will have more milk. Mature ones that will have good meat inside."

At her school, Father Taquero used a hammer and a nail to drill a hole through the coconut so that the sweet milk would drain out. She didn't have a nail or a hammer, but she did have sharp eyebrow tweezers and a flat piece of wood to hit them with.

She got her tools and they worked as intended. She held the coconut over Pamela's cup and the watery milk drained out. She held it up toward Pamela. "You first. You're the one who had the cup."

Pamela took a tentative sip. She pulled back. "That's good," she said.

"And full of things that are good for you," Elle said. "You know people have survived a very long time with just coconuts."

"I hope we don't have to do that," Pamela said, her voice low. "Can I ask you something?" she added.

"Of course."

"You knew Dr. Donovan before this, didn't you?"

Had Mrs. Hardy said something? She didn't think so. Unfortunately, Pamela had definitely heard Brody's first comment, too. "I did," she admitted. "We knew each other many years ago but haven't seen each other for more than a decade."

"I think you were more than casual friends."

Had Brody said something? "Why?" Elle asked.

"Because of the way he looks at you when you're not looking."

And damn her needy self, because she wanted to know more. "I'm sure it's nothing," she said, dismissing the comment and turning away before Pamela could see the warmth flood her face.

Chapter Six

By evening, Mrs. Hardy's internal battery had evidently recharged and she was talking like crazy, telling a very long story about some friends who'd been on a cruise ship that had mechanical trouble and the deplorable conditions that they'd had to endure until help came some five days later. At one point, when she was providing intimate details of one woman's conversation with the ship's purser, she said, "Well, you know Delores."

Pamela stood up suddenly. "No. No, I don't know Delores and I don't know any of these other stupid people that you're talking about and even more important, I don't care. Just please shut up."

Mrs. Hardy's already wrinkled face crumpled and her eyes filled with tears.

Mr. Hardy shot an evil stare at Pamela but didn't say anything. He just patted his wife's hand.

"Bitch," Captain Ramano said, almost under his breath.

Pamela turned on him. "This is your fault," she yelled. "You and your shoddy little plane's fault."

Elle sucked in a breath, waiting for Captain Ramano to reveal exactly whose fault it really was. But the man simply leaned his head back and closed his eyes.

"You don't know what you're talking about, lady," Angus said, anxious to protect his friend. "You're alive because of Captain Ramano."

Pamela whirled toward him. "We never should have been flying in that storm. I'm going to sue everyone involved. Every single person."

Elle stood up. "Listen," she said. "We're all under a lot of stress. It's easy to say or do things that probably aren't in our best interest right now. We can't let the situation get to us. We need each other. And we're going to have to work at getting along in order to survive this."

Pamela muttered something and Elle stared at her. Finally, Pamela waved a hand. "Fine," she said. "I'm sorry," she added to no one in particular.

For the moment, the tension appeared abated. Elle had done a good job, Brody thought, but it was only a matter of time before frustration mounted again. As the hours dragged on, even the most levelheaded would react to the strain.

He'd been so confident that they would be rescued today. Probably had been blindly optimistic in his approach. This was no *Field of Dreams*. He could build all the fires he wanted and still they might not come.

They were going to have to do more than simply wait. And for the past hour, an idea had been kicking around in his head. He would go for help. It was really the only answer.

He walked outside to add more wood to the fire. Between him and Elle, they had gathered enough wood during the day to keep the fire going for days. Food would be gone within a day, but thanks to Elle's help, there would be water. Maybe not a lot but certainly enough to sustain life. Plus there was fruit, thanks to

Elle helping them identify what they could and could not eat.

They couldn't wait forever for someone to find the wreckage. He'd been a Boy Scout. Hell, a damn Eagle Scout. He knew how to tell directions by the sun and how to mark a trail so that he could lead someone back for the others.

He would leave at first light.

He heard a noise behind him. It was Elle. She came up and stood next to him at the fire. That surprised him. For most of the day, unless there was a need to communicate, they'd kept their distance from each other. Now neither of them said anything for a minute. Finally, she turned to him.

"I'm going to go for help," she said.

No. That had been his line. "That's crazy," he said.

Her spine straightened. "Pardon me," she said, her tone icy.

Was he doomed to always say the wrong thing around her? Maybe it was because she raised emotion in him that interfered with what was usually a consistent ability to moderate his comments and actions. "If anyone is going to go for help, it's going to be me," he said.

"Why?"

Because you're a girl clearly wasn't the right answer. It wasn't because he considered women to be the weaker sex. He was pretty sure that the women he served with were smarter and worked harder than most of his male counterparts. And physically, Elle was clearly in good shape and could probably handle the terrain.

But the jungle was full of danger. From all venues. Poisonous plants. Carnivorous animals. And when he'd been researching the area prior to his trip, he learned that the jungle was still home to a number of humans who might not necessarily be friendly.

Elle could be injured, attacked, even killed.

He would never forgive himself.

"Because I already made the decision that I'm going," he said, knowing it was a lame excuse.

"You don't know the jungle. I do."

"You're needed here. You're the voice of reason. You can keep everybody calmed down."

"There are injured here. You're the only one who has the skills to treat them."

"I can't do anything else for either Angus or Captain Ramano. And I'm afraid that time is not Angus's friend. I'm confident that he's developing an infection. Every hour he goes without an antibiotic is an hour closer to losing that leg or even his life. I have to go and I have to go soon."

"What's your plan?" she asked.

He shrugged. "Walk until I find help."

"Which direction?" she prodded.

"North. We're south of the Amazon River. If I can get there, we have a good likelihood that there will be someone who can help us."

"It's too far. It would take you weeks to walk that distance."

She was probably right. But it had seemed like the best option. "Then I guess I'll head south, back toward Brasília."

She shook her head. "We flew for about twenty minutes before we crashed. I asked Angus how fast we were flying and he said about 250 knots or roughly 300 miles per hour. Our destination was north, at about a thirty-degree angle. I think we're roughly 130 miles north and just a little east of Brasília. If I'm right, that means we're less than a two-day walk to Mantau. It's a small village, due east, and I have a friend there who can help us. That's why I'm the one who is leaving at first light."

Her math made sense. Her confidence was admirable.

And her stubbornness was damn irritating. "But—"

"Brody," she said, her voice softer. "You have always wanted to take care of things for everybody else. I suspect that makes you a great doctor. You care. But you don't have to shoulder this burden alone. I can do it."

He stared at her. So beautiful in the firelight. So determined to convince him that she was right. He could not let her go by herself. There was really only one solution.

It didn't appeal to him as a particularly great one. "We'll go together," he said.

She stared at him.

And he thought for a moment that she might back down, that the idea of traipsing through the jungle, just the two of them, was enough to make her rethink her strategy. Thus far, they'd managed to coexist. But he could feel the energy swirling just below the surface and thought it was unlikely that she was oblivious of it. Like hot lava bubbling up through the cracks, there were buried emotions waiting to spew out, to scratch and rip at old scars that had taken forever to heal.

"Do you think that's wise?" she asked finally.

"Hell, no," he said.

He thought he caught a flicker of hurt in her pretty eyes but he couldn't be sure. Maybe it was just the reflection of the fire.

"We'll leave at first light," she said.

"Fine," he replied, gritting his teeth.

She turned and walked away without another word. He stood by the fire and listened to the sounds of the jungle. There were chirps and caws and the subtle rustle of leaves. And it was not a stretch to imagine that there were eyes watching him.

After several minutes he went back inside the plane. It was becoming an oppressively small space and the smell of damp air and human fear and frustration permeated it.

Mrs. Hardy was digging around in her ruined suitcase. She pulled out an envelope. When she opened the flap, there were dozens of snapshots inside.

"What are those?" Pamela asked, evidently trying to make amends.

"Pictures of my grandchildren," Mrs. Hardy said. "I have seven of them. Ages three to seventeen." She handed a photo to Pamela. "That's all of us last Christmas."

"Very nice," Pamela said.

"Do you have children?" Mrs. Hardy asked.

Pamela frowned. "I have a very important job and I work sixty hours a week. I don't have time for children."

"Of course," Mrs. Hardy said, nodding. "How about you, Captain Ramano? Any children or grandchildren?"

"Two sons," the man said. "Both married in the last couple of years but no grandchildren yet. You and Mr. Hardy are very fortunate."

Given that the captain had been mostly uncommunicative, Brody was surprised that he'd tacked on the last sentiment. He prepared himself for the inevitable question given that Mrs. Hardy seemed determined to work her way around the small space. *No wife, no children.*

Four words. That's all he had to say. Didn't have to offer up any excuses, as Pamela had felt inclined to do. Certainly wasn't going to admit that on more than one occasion he'd thought about how different his life might be if he and Elle had gotten married. They might have a houseful of kids by now.

That would be nice. He'd been an only child growing up and had wished for siblings. Maybe that was why Ethan and Mack had been so important. Brothers. Just not the same bloodline.

Mrs. Hardy turned to Elle. "What about you, dear? Do you have children?"

He thought Elle hesitated just a moment too long. Then she offered up a sad smile. "I do. Mia. She's eleven."

Brody could feel the blood rush to his head. She had a child?

She'd said she never married.

Yet she'd loved some man enough to carry his child.

"Do you have a picture of her?" Mrs. Hardy asked.

His head was buzzing so loud that he didn't hear Elle's response. But she pulled her phone out of her backpack and turned it on. Within seconds she was handing it to Mrs. Hardy.

"Oh, she's lovely," Mrs. Hardy said.

"Thank you," Elle said. "She's very sweet."

Mrs. Hardy gave the phone to her husband, who nodded appropriately and then, at Mrs. Hardy's urging, handed the phone to Pamela.

And Brody had to practically sit on his damn hands to keep from reaching out. Why the hell did he care? She had a child. What difference did it make?

He didn't know. But it did.

Eleven? She certainly hadn't wasted any time.

"Almost a teenager," Pamela said, when she looked at the phone. "They say those are the toughest years."

Elle smiled and her eyes filled with tears. "She can hardly wait to be thirteen. It's all she talks about. She's frustrated that she has to be twelve first."

Pamela handed the phone to Captain Ramano. He looked at it, then at Elle. "She go to that school you teach at?" he asked.

It was odd but Brody thought Elle's chin jerked up, as if the question had surprised her. She nodded. "Yes, she does."

Brody couldn't stand another minute. He got up, opened the plane door and walked outside into the dark night.

Had she not loved the father enough to marry him? Had she left him, too?

Had he not wanted her or the child?

Idiot.

Hell. His thoughts were bouncing around, making his head ache. He walked over and stood next to the fire that he'd fed all day and would feed again several times during the night.

The smoke burned his eyes.

Off in the distance, he heard the howl of something wild. He felt a bit like making the same noise.

He'd spent years missing her like crazy and she'd been humming along, living life to the fullest. Meeting a guy. Having his baby.

Suddenly it was May 10 and he was standing by the mailbox in his bare feet all over again. The pain was intense.

When she told him that she'd never married, he'd told

himself it didn't matter one way or the other. He was over her. Had been over her for a long time.

Even though he'd been assigned to a military post in the Middle East for long stretches, he'd also been stateside a number of times over the years. Colleagues and family friends had fixed him up. The women had been nice.

He'd even slept with a couple of them.

He was over her.

But that didn't stop him from knowing that there was a big difference between having a physical relationship with somebody, which was really just biology, and having the connection of a child.

She might not have married but she'd committed herself in an even more important way. To someone else.

His gut hurt and it wasn't from eating fresh coconut.

When the hell was he going to stop being stupid over Elle Vollman?

Chapter Seven

Elle thought she was the first one awake the next morning. The inside of the plane was dark. She turned on her flashlight. She could see the Hardys. Mr. Hardy had his head on Mrs. Hardy's shoulder. Elle could hear Pamela and Captain Ramano. They were both snoring. She turned in her seat so that she could see Angus. His eyes were closed but his breathing seemed shallow. He'd thrown off his blanket and it appeared he was sweating.

Brody was likely right. Angus was on the decline.

She flashed her light in the seat where Brody had slept the previous night. Empty.

He'd beaten her up. Even though she'd been asleep before he came back inside the plane the night before.

She guessed it wasn't her business if he was tired today. It was too bad they didn't have any coffee for Mrs. Hardy's pot. It was really too bad that they didn't have any electricity to plug it in. It was really, really too bad that she couldn't have her favorite barista at the local coffee shop whip up a nonfat latte with a shot of hazelnut.

"One little cup of coffee," she whispered, as she pulled on socks. "That's all I'm asking for." She slipped her shoes on. "And maybe a cherry-walnut scone.

Warm," she added because if she was going to dream, she might as well dream big.

"That sounds lovely, dear," Mrs. Hardy whispered back in the dark. "Don't forget the butter. And I do love a bit of cream in my coffee."

Elle flashed her light in the older woman's direction. "I didn't realize you were awake," she said.

"Just for a few minutes. I'm worried about you and Dr. Donovan. Don't you think you can just wait for someone to rescue us? I mean, we have some food and water, thanks to you. Do you really have to go traipsing off in the jungle?"

Elle knew their grip on survival was tenuous at best. And to sit back and wait wasn't her nature. Plus, she had this crazy feeling that danger was close. Didn't know where the danger was coming from, but her gut was telling her that time was of the essence.

She'd tried to push away her crazy thoughts that somehow T. K. Jamas was responsible for the crash and that he wouldn't rest until he knew that he'd succeeded in keeping her from testifying. When Captain Ramano had asked whether Mia attended the school where she taught, it had startled her. She didn't recall ever telling Captain Ramano that she was a teacher. How did he know? It had been the middle of the night when she explained to Brody about the books and her teaching position. Captain Ramano had been sleeping. She supposed it was possible that he'd simply been pretending to be asleep and had been listening to everything around him, but she didn't think so.

How had he known about her school? Why had he known that?

Surely, he could not have been in cahoots with T. K.

Jamas. No pilot would deliberately crash his own plane? Unless he was desperate.

And T. K. Jamas made people desperate. In a corner, getting poked with a sharp stick kind of desperate.

And evidently he also made them tongue-tied. If Captain Ramano knew why his plane had suddenly developed mechanical trouble, he wasn't talking.

Going for help was the only answer. And if that meant that she had to endure another couple days of Brody's snide remarks, so be it. She deserved them. She deserved worse.

"We'll be fine," she said. "By tomorrow night, we should be able to make contact with my friend and send help to you."

"At least if you get injured, Dr. Donovan will be able to take care of you," Mrs. Hardy said.

She wasn't so sure. If she tripped and fell, he'd likely be inclined to just leave her in the jungle to die. The Hippocratic oath *might* save her—he was always a stickler for playing by the rules.

There weren't really any rules in the jungle. While she brushed her hair, she amused herself with thinking about jungle rules. Rule number 1: Run fast when being chased by a lion. Rule number 2: Never sit on anything that moves. Rule number 3: Avoid alligators at all cost.

She could go on and on, but while it was a fun little mind game, these were very real threats. She could only hope that she and Brody had good luck.

She was determined that he wasn't going to regret her insistence to come along. She opened her backpack and checked the contents. Once she'd decided to walk for help, she'd examined the contents of her small carry-on bag. She had very little with her because she'd been intending to purchase something to wear once she got back to the States. Her wardrobe needs at her small school were pretty basic, just pants and a shirt. Certainly not appropriate for a meeting with government officials.

Although she suspected what she wore was of considerable less importance to them than what she was going to say.

Human trafficking.

Young girls sold into a dank underworld of sick, twisted souls who used and abused them until they finally put them out of their misery and killed them.

Big business. And she'd trusted the person who was at the top of the pyramid. Had inadvertently helped him find innocent girls to prey upon. That still made her sick.

But he would pay. Her testimony would ensure that. She could still recall the excitement in the agent's voice when she'd told him why she was calling and what she knew.

Evidently, T. K. Jamas had been on their radar screen for years, but they had no hard evidence to charge and convict him.

Until now.

She just had to find her way out of the jungle first.

Last night, after she'd verified that she hadn't packed any socks, she immediately went to Pamela and explained what she needed. The woman had opened her suitcase and there were two pairs, besides the pair on her feet. She'd given both to Elle. "Take whatever you need. Just find somebody who can help us," she'd said.

Elle had assured her that they would and had finished packing her backpack. She kept it light, adding a change of clothing, her flashlight and her cell phone, just in case. She had kept one of the tubes of bug repellant and left the other with Mrs. Hardy to dole out as needed to those they were leaving behind.

Initially, Elle had assumed that she and Brody would take some water with them but leave the food behind. Mrs. Hardy had claimed that she wouldn't be able to sleep knowing that Elle and Brody were doing the difficult work of traipsing through the jungle without food. Finally, Elle had agreed that she and Brody would take one breakfast bar and some nuts along with enough water to get them to their first campsite. She'd added that to her backpack. Then, at Mrs. Hardy's insistence, she'd added the coffeepot. It made sense. They would need something to boil water in.

Mrs. Hardy had also assured her that she and Pamela would take care of getting more water from the bamboo stalks. Elle knew she couldn't count on Angus to do much—he had to keep his leg immobilized. And Captain Ramano mostly slept. He did wake up long enough to say that he'd watch over the fire. They left one of the matchbooks with him just in case it was extinguished by rain and needed to be rebuilt.

If her calculations were correct, and if their walk through the jungle went well, they could be in Mantau by tomorrow night, sitting at Leo Arroul's table. And there was no doubt that Leo would help. She'd first met the man almost five years before, even before coming to Brazil. He was a friend of friends, originally from Canada, but had been living in Brazil for years when they'd ended up at the same dinner party in Peru. He'd told her about Father Taquero and his school for girls and years later, when she'd been looking for someplace to settle down, someplace where she could make a difference, she'd thought of the school.

Leo had made his money in the stock market and after his wife of twenty-two years had left him for her personal trainer, he'd left his job, left his country, and for the last ten years, had dedicated his life to helping purify water systems in the jungle. He was a person who knew how to get things done.

She heard a noise behind her and turned. Brody was coming back inside the plane, dressed in the same jeans as yesterday with a different long-sleeved shirt. He had on his boots again, with his pant legs tucked it. He had his duffel bag over one shoulder.

She waited for him to say good morning. He didn't.

She pointed to the many red fabric scraps that were tied up and down on the bag's strap. "Nice decoration."

He shrugged. "My favorite red shirt. It makes sense to mark a trail."

Of course it did. But he'd said it as if he was looking for an argument.

It was going to be a long couple of days.

He opened his bag. Inside was his water bottle, some clothing and the remains of the parachute. "What are you bringing that for?" she asked. It had to weigh several pounds, and over many miles, that added up to a whole lot of strain on a shoulder.

"I'm hoping I can find two trees, tie an end up to each one, and make a hammock."

It was a good idea. Sleeping outside in the jungle was a horrifying thought, and having to sleep on the ground in the jungle took it up a notch. She'd put the remaining newspaper in her backpack along with a blanket, figuring that she'd put the newspaper on the ground, wrap the blanket around her as tight as possible and sleep sitting up. It wasn't perfect but it was the best she'd been able to come up with.

"You may want to take a blanket, too," she said.

He shook his head. "That would only leave them with two for five people. I'll be fine. Let's go. We're going to need to find more water along the way."

"We will," she said. "Look for ants. Trails of them. They can lead you to a water source."

He stared at her. "You're certainly full of jungle folklore."

Was he trying to pick a fight? "I've lived in Brazil for several years. I do know a couple things. If you can stand the idea of taking advice from me, you might actually learn a couple things."

He stared at her and she could hear him suck in a deep breath. "I've learned, Elle. Trust me on this one. You taught me several important life lessons."

And he would never forgive her. "This is a mistake," she said. "I'm going by myself." She turned on her heel.

"No," he said. He moved fast and got in front of her. "Look, I'm sorry. Let's just get going. We can do this. I can do this."

Above the ringing in her ears, she could hear the squawk of birds and the squeal of nearby monkeys. "Fine," she said, her teeth jammed together so tight she was surprised she didn't crack one.

Brody nodded, looking relieved. "I've got Mrs. Hardy's knife and a few basic medical supplies. And I have one of the small plastic bags for the matches. Above all else, we need to try to keep them dry."

He zipped his duffel and slung the strap over his head

so that the strap crossed his torso and the bag rested at his hip. It left both of his hands free.

"Here's the bug stuff," she said. "We'll take one tube with us and leave the other one for the rest of the group." She walked toward the plane and picked up the two walking sticks that she'd hunted for earlier. She handed the taller one to him.

"Thank you," he mumbled. He pointed at the cut on her forehead. She'd taken off the bandage before she went to sleep. "Did you put more antibiotic ointment on that?"

"No. It's healing."

"Yeah. But you need to be careful." He opened his bag and pulled out a tube of the ointment. Then he put a dab on the end of his finger and smeared it over the cut. Then he got out a fresh bandage and put it on.

Damn him. It was hard to be mad at somebody who was hell-bent on taking care of you. Even if he didn't like you.

THEY SAID THEIR goodbyes to those remaining behind. Mrs. Hardy hugged her hard and Mr. Hardy patted her shoulder. Pamela voiced the collective concern. "Don't get lost."

"We won't," she promised, praying it was true. Following the sun was rudimentary at best, especially in a jungle where walking in a straight line was virtually impossible.

"Which direction are you going?" Captain Ramano asked.

"Toward…Brasília," she said.

Brody looked at her oddly, but thankfully he didn't

say anything until they were safely away from the plane. "Change of plans?" he asked.

"No."

They walked another hundred yards before he spoke again. "So why lie to Captain Ramano?"

She couldn't tell him the truth. The whole truth. "His attitude since the crash has been bothering me."

Brody nodded. "I thought maybe it was just me."

"No. Not you. Let's get walking."

They walked steadily for an hour, him in the lead, her following three steps behind. His legs were longer and she knew that he was moderating his stride so that she could keep up. Every hundred yards or so, he stopped to tie a rag onto a bush or a small tree. As she'd suspected, there was no such thing as following the trail in a straight line. There was no trail and the random nature of the plant life had them weaving back and forth. That was really the only choice. While they had Mrs. Hardy's knife, and that was certainly better than nothing, it was no match against the dense growth. That called for a machete. Every time they angled their path, she watched him lift his face and judge the direction by the morning sun that at times, was barely visible through the thick canopy of trees. She'd told him to head due east and he was doing his very best.

It was warm and getting warmer. Sweat trickled down her back and between her breasts, making her camisole damp and the cotton shirt that covered it stick to her skin. Her loafers were damp from the wet ground. Her socks were still mostly dry, but she knew that was only temporary. It was a foregone conclusion that they would get caught in one of the many rain showers that occurred on a daily basis or that they'd have to cross a body of water at some point.

That scared her the most. The idea of moving through water that might be filled with snakes and all kinds of other dangerous things was so frightening that it was all she could think about.

There were birds everywhere, squawking and swooping, their colors brilliant against the deep green foliage. She could name a few. There were the scarlet macaws, so easily recognized with their red bodies and stripes of yellow and blue on their tail feathers. The black oropendola with its bright yellow beak and tail feathers. She'd heard its raspy call before she'd seen it.

There were so many more that she'd probably seen before but couldn't name and many that she was probably seeing for the first time. Bird enthusiasts flocked to the Amazon to see the many species.

She should probably be more appreciative.

It was hard to remember that when she had to swat at something that grazed her chin. Even with the repellent on, the bugs found her. They were everywhere. All a nuisance. Most harmless. Some likely more dangerous.

After another half hour, Brody stopped. He turned, wiping his forehead with his sleeve. "Doing okay?" he asked.

Her legs hurt, she had sweat in places that polite women didn't talk about, and she was still thinking about the coffee that she hadn't had. "Dandy," she said. "You?"

"About the same. I think we're still pretty much on course."

"I think so, too." She pulled her water bottle out of her backpack and took a drink, careful not to overindulge. "I'm guessing that even with all the twists and turns, we're still doing a twelve- or thirteen-minute mile."

"I'd say so. That's good," he added.

Once again, he was being positive, trying to keep her focused on what was going well. It was his nature. He'd been like that in med school. Even when he was bone tired and he still had three hours of homework to do, he'd been able to find something positive in the situation. If they went to a restaurant and the food was bad, he'd focus in on the drinks that were good. If they went to a movie that was bad, the popcorn and soda were just what he'd been craving. He wasn't stupid about it—and he wasn't over-the-top with it—but he simply chose to try to find something positive in every experience.

She often wondered what he'd found positive in her leaving.

"Ready?" he asked.

She put away her water bottle. "As ever," she said.

And things went pretty well for the next half hour until Brody stopped so fast that she literally ran into his back.

He turned fast, grabbed Elle's arms and steadied her, keeping her from bouncing backward and him from tumbling into what looked to be a fifty-foot-deep ravine.

"Oh, hell," Elle said, looking around him.

Indeed. The gorge was impressive—deep and stretching as far as he could see in both directions. Going around it wasn't an option.

"What do you think?" he asked.

"I'm not sure that going down is going to be any easier than going up," she said. "But we have to get across. And," she added, putting her hand up to shade her eyes from the stream of sun that managed to sneak through the canopy of trees, "that may be water." She pointed deep into the ravine.

Brody looked. The plant growth was heavy in the bottom and he couldn't be sure. It would be wonderful if it was water. They'd both been careful with their supply, but they needed more.

"I'll go first," Brody said.

He got about ten feet and looked back. Elle had shifted over at least three feet and was taking her first step.

"Is that a better path?" he asked.

"No. About the same."

"I'd prefer it if you'd stay behind me."

"That's what I was trying to avoid," she said. "Just keep going and don't worry about me."

Right. As if that was going to happen. He knew what she was doing. She was afraid that she was going to slip and if she did, she'd tumble into him and they both might end up rolling down the damn hill. But if she slipped now, she'd roll past him and he wouldn't have a chance in hell of catching her.

"Stay behind me," he said. "In the same path."

She looked as if she wanted to argue.

"Please," he said.

She rolled her eyes but then stepped diagonally, once again lining up with him.

"Thank you," he said. It was slow going and he knew that if he and Elle were both not in good shape, they would simply have not been able to do it.

By the time they got to the flat portion of the ravine, they were both panting. If it had been that much work getting down, going up would be a real bitch. "Well, that was fun," he said, not expecting an answer. But Elle had been right. He could hear water. He walked twenty feet to his right and, sure enough, behind a big, sprawling palm tree, water was trickling over a shelf of rock that jutted out from the canyon wall.

He turned to tell her. She was half bent over, her hands on her thighs, absolutely motionless.

"Elle," he said.

"Yes," she responded, her voice small.

"What's wrong?" he asked, taking big steps toward her.

"Stop," she said. "Don't come any closer. Snake."

Chapter Eight

He looked. Sure enough. Winding through the long grass, its color blending in with nature so that it was difficult to immediately discern, was a snake, almost six feet long, with slightly pink skin that was heavily dotted with brown squares.

"I think it's a bushmaster," she said.

Brody really wished he'd read his guidebook a little more closely. He tried to visualize the chapter on deadly threats. Yes. Bushmaster had been in there. Definitely poisonous.

Normally not a snake to attack, it would when provoked.

Elle had clearly provoked it by almost stepping on it. It wound around, near her feet, its head less than six inches away from her ankles.

Pamela's socks were going to be of little assistance.

"Don't move," he said.

"Can't," she whispered.

If she got bit, he would not be able to save her. The venom would travel through her bloodstream and within minutes would begin to paralyze vital organs.

He would lose her again.

Once again, a machete would have really come in

handy. Or a rope that he could swing from a tree and she could catch it and be whisked away from danger.

Here, we have to use what we have.

How many times had he heard that from his commanding officer these past several years? Even when he did surgery at a fully equipped base camp, it wasn't like a North American operating room in a multimillion-dollar surgical suite. And those times when he'd had to go even closer to the front line, to administer aid to the most critically wounded, he'd performed miracles with even less.

What did he have? Mrs. Hardy's knife. And steady hands. A surgeon's hands. Used to making very accurate, precise incisions. Used to the feel of resistant flesh. Spurting blood from severed arteries was an everyday occurrence.

He pulled the knife from his pocket. Unfolded the blade.

He took another step forward, wishing for some of the steadiness to seep into his legs.

"No closer," Elle whispered. "Go. One of us has to get out of here."

Did she really think that he would just walk away, leave her at the mercy of the snake who might or might not get bored and slink away at some point? Assuming Elle could stay absolutely motionless for some prolonged period of time.

Still four feet away from Elle and the snake, he stepped sideways. Then again. One more step. He was at a ninety-degree angle. Then a cautious step toward Elle. Toward the snake.

One more.

Less than three feet separated him from Elle and the

snake that now had stopped moving. Did that mean it was getting ready to strike? Damn it. He knew next to nothing about snakes.

He did, however, know something about human anatomy. And the weight of organs. And how much force it took to cut through that organ with a supersharp instrument.

By his best comparative guess, he figured the snake weighed between five and ten pounds. And Mrs. Hardy's knife was sharp but not razor sharp.

"Stay still," he said. "No matter what until I cut the snake. Then step back fast."

"Okay," she said, her voice stronger now, as if she'd managed to overcome her initial fear.

He took another step forward, close enough now that he could reach the snake. And in one smooth, fast movement, he raised his arm, squatted, and made a clean slice through the snake, separating the upper one-third of its body from the lower two-thirds.

And there was blood and twitching and slithering that seemed to go on forever. Of course, by that time, he and Elle were a safe six feet away.

He circled around the still-moving carcass and wrapped an arm around Elle, who looked as if she was about to fall down. He pulled her in close to his body. She was shaking.

"It's okay," he said. "We're both fine. The snake is dead."

"I can't look," she said.

He pulled her in tighter. "You don't have to," he said, his mouth close to her ear.

"I guess it's just another average day in the jungle," she said, her face still against his chest.

He smiled and, without thinking, bent his head and kissed her forehead. She stilled. Then raised her face.

"Brody," she whispered.

She was so beautiful. And he could not help himself.

He bent his head and kissed her. And it was if the thirteen years apart had never happened. This was Elle. He knew her lips. Knew the feel of her teeth against his tongue. Knew the little sounds she made.

And he might have kissed her forever if the wild screech of a low-flying bird had not had them jumping back from each other.

"Oh," Elle said, her fingers touching her lips.

Hell. Now his legs felt really weak. He tried to summon the memory that it hadn't been thirteen days or weeks or even months since he'd seen this woman. Years. Thirteen years. More than a decade. They were different people than they'd been back then. It didn't make one whit of difference how familiar her mouth felt.

"I shouldn't have done that," he said.

"It's fine," she said, dismissing it with a wave of her hand. "Adrenaline."

Well, that certainly sounded better than *lust*. He stared at her.

"It was just a kiss, Brody. Let's forget it. We need to find that water," she said.

It hadn't been just a kiss. It had been a startling hot rush and his body was still humming.

But Elle was acting as if it had been nothing, meant nothing.

He turned and started walking. And by the time they found the stream ten minutes later, his pulse had slowed down and was once again beating pretty normally. The water was running off a ledge of rock that extended from the ravine wall. Brody looked up and tried to trace the flow. "Hard to tell where the source is."

"Which means it may or may not be fresh water," Elle said.

"Which means that finding it is good but we need to boil it before we drink it. I have a couple empty bottles in my bag," he said. "We'll gather it now and boil it tonight when we make camp."

She nodded and held out her hand for a container. "Maybe we should finish off our bottles of water so that they're empty, too. We can collect more then."

He shook his head. "We've got a long walk ahead of us. Let's combine our good water in one bottle and share that. That will give us one more empty."

It took them just a few minutes to hold their bottles under the running stream. Then they crossed the narrow bottom of the ravine and started the hard climb up the steep hill. They were about a third of the way up when it started to rain.

There was no gentle ramp-up to the storm. No little drizzle that turned into a light shower. It was immediate and it was a full-blown drenching. It was as if the damn sky had opened up.

Elle could not even see Brody through the driving rain. She didn't know what to do and had a momentary feeling of panic. She was just getting it under control when she felt a hand on her shoulder.

"Hang on," he said.

He pulled her under a big tree with full foliage. It didn't protect them totally, but it cut the impact of the driving rain. "Wow, that came up fast," Brody said, wiping his streaming face with the back of his forearm.

"It's always like that here. One minute, nothing. The next, a monsoon. We're lucky," she added. "June is the end of our rainy season. If this was March, this ground might be flooded. The Amazon River floods every year."

"I'd rather walk it than swim it."

"Definitely. There are piranhas and anacondas and all kinds of nasty things in the river."

"Not to mention the crocodiles," he added.

The conversation had her glancing down, looking for more snakes. It was hard to see, but nothing popped out at her right away. "I imagine it's going to take me a while to forget the sight of a bushmaster wrapping itself around my feet."

"You handled it like a champ," he said.

"I was this close to wetting my pants," she said.

Which reminded him that neither one of them had gone to the bathroom all day. "Do I need to turn my back?"

"No. I think I'm sweating out all my excess water."

He was, too. Which was not good. "How long will this last?"

"Probably not that long. Maybe a half hour. It feels good, but our clothes are going to be damp now, which isn't going to be very comfortable."

He turned to look at her and his gaze settled on her. Her shirt was wet and clinging to her. He could see her full breasts through the thin cotton shirt. Could see the outline of her nipples. She was not wearing a bra.

Hell. One little kiss had made him smolder for hours. This was likely to cause a full-blown implosion.

If somebody took his vitals right now, his temperature would be off the charts. His blood pressure would be screaming stroke.

"I think comfort was ten miles back," he said, his voice husky.

He'd meant it as a casual comment but realized immediately, when she crossed her arms over her chest, that she'd picked up on the double entendre.

"Brody?" she asked.

"What?" he responded innocently. He stuck out his tongue and tried to catch a few rain drops, hoping to let the awkward moment pass.

It worked. "You look ridiculous," she said. She cupped her hands and held them out from her body. It was raining hard, but still she captured a ridiculously small amount, barely enough to lick off her palms.

"Oh, yeah. Your method is *much* better."

She ignored him. "How do you think they're doing back at the plane?" she asked.

"I think they have shelter and access to water and food. They'll be okay."

"I hope so."

He could hear the uncertainty. "We're going to be okay, too, Elle," he said, suddenly desperately wanting to assure her. "We kept up a good pace today. If we can do the same tomorrow and if your calculations were correct, we should be having a drink with your friend by tomorrow night."

"It's a lot of ifs. And you forgot some. If one of us doesn't twist an ankle. If we don't get sick from bad water. If some native doesn't get mad that we're walking across his family's sacred graveyard, we should be okay."

"Family's sacred graveyard," he repeated, one corner of his mouth lifted.

"You know what I mean," she said, waving her hand.

"I do. I'm just giving you a hard time. Yeah, there's lots of obstacles. But we're tougher."

She let out a loud sigh and was quiet for several minutes. Finally, she pushed her hair back from her face and gave him a smile. "Okay. I think I'm over my pity party. I just needed to get that out of the way."

He stared at her. "You have been incredibly brave, Elle, from the beginning. You're entitled to have a few nagging doubts. It doesn't make you weak."

She looked off into the distance. "If anyone would have told me that I was going to be in a plane crash and have to walk my way out of the Amazon, I'd have laughed at them."

"What if they'd told you that you were going to have to do it with me?"

It took her a full minute to shift her gaze. When she did, her eyes were bright. "I'd have said that it would never happen because whatever direction I walked, Brody Donovan would go the opposite way. Anything to keep some space between the two of us."

"That's not true," he said. Maybe at one time he'd have thought that but not now. Not after seeing Elle in action, not after realizing that she was more than equal to the task. Not after realizing that he…that he still… thought a lot of her.

Chicken.

Maybe. But he wasn't ready to go further than that. Thirteen years ago he'd been dealt a blow, one that might not have been fatal to his other organs but had certainly damaged his heart.

"Brody, you have every reason in the world to hate me."

She'd always had this uncanny ability to read his thoughts. She was on the right track but a little off course. "I never hated you, Elle," he said, his voice cracking on her name. There had been so many emotions following her leaving, but hate hadn't been one of them. He'd loved her too much. "The way you did it was wrong," he said.

"You're right," she said. "I took the coward's way out."

That surprised him. He expected her to have a thousand reasons why that had been the only way she could have done it. "I tried to find you," he admitted. "I talked to your mother, to your stepfather."

Her head whipped his direction. "What did they tell you?"

"Not much. Your mother said that she hadn't spoken to you for months. She didn't recognize my name. I thought that was odd given that we were supposed to be married in just weeks and that we were supposed to be visiting her in days."

Elle blinked rapidly but didn't say anything. That made Brody crazy. He wanted to demand to know the truth. Why hadn't she told her mother about him? Why hadn't she been honest about her relationship with her mother?

When it was apparent that she wasn't going to offer up any explanation, he went on. "Your stepfather said he hadn't heard from you and didn't expect to."

"Hoped," she said.

"What?"

"Hoped he didn't hear from me. Never mind. It would have been difficult to find me. I moved around a lot," she said. "Especially in those first years."

He couldn't imagine not keeping in contact with his parents. Even when he was in Afghanistan and Iraq, he'd stayed in touch through email and regular telephone calls.

She'd been too busy *moving around*. But she'd stayed long enough in one place to get pregnant, to have another man's child. "What happened to your daughter's father?" he asked.

She looked startled, as if that hadn't been the question she'd been expecting. "He's…dead," she said.

He was a bad person because even that didn't make him hate the man any less. Elle had loved him enough to have his child. "I'm sorry," he managed.

She didn't say anything until finally she lifted her pretty chin. "So is her mother."

What? And Brody's thoughts might have been a little sluggish from general dehydration, but it still clicked into place. "She's adopted? Your daughter is adopted?"

"Yes," she whispered. "Mia is a student at the school where I teach. Her parents were killed in a bus accident several years ago and she'd been living in an orphanage since that time. I adopted her about a year ago."

"Mia," he repeated. "Did you know her parents?"

She shook her head. "No. Mia has a few pictures of them. They seemed like a happy family. She has lost a lot. But she's very, very brave."

It seemed sort of an odd way to describe a child. "She's not afraid of snakes?" he asked.

She smiled. "I'm not sure about that. Look, the rain has stopped. We need to get going."

Secrets. Half-truths. Elle was a master at them.

She shut people out.

Because a heart could only take so much, especially a damaged one, he turned and started walking.

Chapter Nine

By four in the afternoon, Elle felt as if she didn't have the strength or the energy to put one foot in front of the other. But she kept moving, knowing that Brody had to be as weary. When it was impossible to go around foliage, he'd had the extra burden of using Mrs. Hardy's knife to saw through dense palms and other plant life. It was painstakingly slow and she grew agitated, knowing that nightfall was edging closer every minute.

The heat was sweltering and her clothes were sticking to her. She could smell herself and it wasn't pretty. It was some disgusting combination of sweat and the bug repellant that she'd reapplied after the rain stopped. Her hair felt heavy and even though she tried to push it away from her face, pieces clung to her neck.

Her shoulders and arms ached because, after the snake incident, she taken to swinging her sturdy walking stick in front of her every time there was a patch of long grass or undergrowth to walk through. Unfortunately, that had meant a lot of swinging.

She had a raging headache. Probably because she was dehydrated and probably because she was still whirling from Brody's statement that he'd talked to both her mother and stepfather.

She'd called her mother a month after she was in Peru. Hadn't told her where she was living. Her mother hadn't mentioned that she'd spoken to Brody. Hadn't mentioned that a fiancé she didn't know about had called.

She would have been surprised if her mother had been chatty with Brody. Catherine Rivers wasn't going to talk about something that had happened all those years ago. Talking about it would make it real, and that was something that she was never going to admit.

Same for Earl Rivers, the man who had been her stepfather for three years.

She hadn't really thought it through that Brody might attempt to contact her family. The idea that he'd spoken to her mother was hard to get her head around, and the idea that he'd had to lower himself to have a conversation with Earl Rivers was so distasteful that she had to swallow hard to keep her empty stomach from jumping.

"We'll need to make camp soon," Brody said. "The sun will set shortly after five."

She was grateful for the interruption. Thinking about Rivers wasn't going to help her headache go away.

"If I stop walking, there is a distinct possibility that I may never start again," Elle said.

She felt compelled to say something because it was the first thing Brody had said to her since they resumed walking after the rain. She'd been shaken when he mentioned talking to her mother and stepfather. Then when he abruptly switched the topic to Mia, she'd been so startled that she blurted out information. Not that it was difficult to talk about the little girl who had become so important to her over the past year. Mia was a delight. Beautiful. Funny. Polite. Brave, as she'd said.

Thank goodness for the last trait. If not for Mia's bravery, Elle might never have realized the truth about T. K. Jamas. And once Elle had discovered the truth, nothing would have stopped her from testifying against Jamas, not even when the man had threatened to kill both her and Mia.

With Father Taquero's help, she'd safely hidden Mia away. Nobody was going to find her until Elle could get her out of the country.

And while intellectually she knew that Brody was absolutely no threat to Mia, when he'd started asking questions, Elle shut down. Mia's safety was too important. She couldn't let something slip to Brody that might compromise her little girl's safety. Elle knew all too well what it was like to be young and vulnerable and to be in the care of adults that were careless about a child's safety. She knew all too well that sometimes a child's pleas for protection could go ignored.

But she needed to not dwell on that right now. Every bit of her energy had to be focused on putting one foot in front of the other before her legs cramped up from overuse and lack of water.

A half hour later, she saw a possibility. "Brody, what about this?" she said, pointing to a small rise. There were a couple palm trees close together that might work for tying up the parachute-turned-hammock. Also a couple small plants, but otherwise the little hill was clear of foliage.

Brody studied the space and nodded. "Looks good to me."

Good. Well, not exactly. Off and on throughout the day, she'd thought about spending the night in the jungle, and the concept hadn't improved with time or distance. The two nights that she'd slept in the plane were bad enough. She'd heard the howl of wild animals, and even the knowledge that the plane would be an effective deterrent had not made her feel much better.

Tonight, she and Brody would be vulnerable, and that scared the heck out of her. But she wasn't going to admit that. She knew enough to avoid being near a water source. That would attract all kinds of animals. And they needed to be somewhere that offered some protection if it decided to rain again.

"Let's gather wood on our way," Brody said.

Definitely. She intended to keep the fire burning all night. That would also be a useful deterrent to unwanted visitors. She reached down to pick up a log and realized when her hand was just inches away that there was a hairy spider, three times the size of her thumbnail, staring at her.

She jumped back.

And she must have squealed because Brody whirled.

"It's okay," she said, holding up a shaking hand. "Spider. Big enough that it probably eats small children for breakfast."

"One of those," he said, nodding solemnly. He started walking again.

She held her breath as she walked by the log, as if that would somehow protect her. After that, she viewed each piece of wood critically before poking it with her stick. Then she pounded one end on the ground, to dislodge any stubborn bugs or spiders, before picking it up.

It took a while, but by the time they reached the top of the hill, she had an armload of wood that looked as if it would burn. Night was fast approaching and Brody quickly made his circle and stacked the wood for a fire.

It caught with the first match. He carefully put the book of matches back in the small plastic bag and back in his shirt pocket.

She helped him unfold the parachute and string it between two trees. They tied it tight using the suspension lines. There was the section missing that Elle had cut out that first night, but that was at the very end. Brody would simply have to be careful or his feet would fall through.

"Get in," Brody said, surprising her. "Test it."

She supposed she could. She sat her rear down and swung her legs up, then lay back, one arm folded underneath her head. She raised her other hand and motioned with her finger. "Waiter, can you bring me another rum smoothie?"

Brody laughed, and it sounded so much like the old Brody laugh that she couldn't help laughing along with him. It was contagious and pretty soon, the two of them were whooping it up like a bunch of hyenas.

It probably lasted less than a minute, but the absolute joy that flooded her system was a welcome relief from the strain of the past two days. "That felt good," she admitted.

"It did." He stared down at her, his gaze intense.

Was he remembering all the times they had laughed together? Like when they read the *New Yorker* magazine together and came across a joke that cracked them up. Or when they used to lie in bed for hours on his rare free day with a pile of DVDs of the latest comedies? Watching. Laughing. Making love in between.

She swung her feet over the side of the hammock, sat up, then stood quickly. "We should probably boil water. Before it's totally dark."

They used Mrs. Hardy's small coffeepot. They'd collected three bottles' worth from the stream, and that
meant that they had to boil six batches. It was a tedious
process because they had to wait for each batch to cool
before they could pour it back into plastic bottles. There
was very little to do besides stare at the fire.

"Tell me about your school," Brody said after some
time.

"We have about a hundred students, both boys and
girls, all between the ages of ten and thirteen. Some
from families that might be middle-class. Most from
poor families and they receive assistance from the
church. I teach English and they're all eager to learn.
These are children who realize that education is their
way out of poverty, to have a better life."

"Sounds like rewarding work. You're making a difference in those kids' lives."

She felt warm and she didn't think it was due to the
fire. "I hope so."

When the last batch was cooling, Brody pulled a tea
bag out of his duffel bag and held it up for Elle to see.
"Join me for a cup of tea?" he said, as if they'd just happened to meet each other at the corner bistro.

"Love to," she said.

He dropped the tea bag into the glass pot and after
a minute or so, poured the still-warm liquid into one
of their plastic water bottles. They took turns sipping
tea out of the bottle while they split their one breakfast
bar and slowly chewed it and a handful of nuts. There
was something so civilized about drinking tea that it
was almost possible to forget that they were in the middle of nowhere, surrounded by wild, poisonous things.

Although the mosquitoes were doing their best to

remind them that it was their jungle first. "We're going to get eaten alive," Elle said, swatting at one on her sleeve. She pulled the mosquito repellent out of her backpack. "Better put a little more of this on for the night."

They both put it on the faces and necks.

"We should get some sleep," he said.

She opened her backpack and pulled out the newspaper and the blanket. She found a spot between the fire and Brody's hammock and put the papers on the ground.

"What are you doing?" he asked.

"I'm going to sit on the papers and wrap myself up in the blanket. Then I'm going to sleep."

He shook his head. "The hammock is for you."

She pulled back in surprise. "No. You carried it all day. You should get the benefit of sleeping in it."

"Don't be ridiculous," he said. "I'm not going to take the hammock while you're on the ground."

"Why not?" she challenged, knowing it was a stupid thing to fight about, but she couldn't help herself.

The fire gave off enough light that she could see him roll his eyes. "Take the hammock, Elle."

She couldn't let it go. "But what about you?"

He waved a hand. "Don't worry about me. I was a Boy Scout. I know how to sleep on the ground."

She shook her head. "It's not a matter of being tough enough. There are poisonous creepy crawlers in the jungle. If there's a way for you to sleep off the ground, you need to do it."

"Creepy crawlers," he repeated.

"Too numerous to mention," she said. "The hammock was a good idea. It's yours."

"Nope."

"Rock, paper, scissors?" she asked sarcastically.

"Nope," he repeated.

They were getting nowhere. "Oh, for goodness' sake. Then we'll share it."

He shook his head. "Hammocks aren't exactly meant for two people, Elle," he said.

"Well, we're going to have to figure out a way to make it work. You get in first."

He blew out a long breath, sat down in it and stretched out. "Okay. It should hold both of us. Get in."

His tone was exasperated, not at all tender, yet it made it remember how he used to get in bed before she did on really cold nights and warm up the sheets because she absolutely hated to climb into a cold bed. *Time to get in, darling.* That's what he would say.

She sat on the edge of the hammock and tried to lie down, her back to his back. However, the weight distribution was all wrong and the hammock would have turned over on itself and likely ripped off the trees if he hadn't moved pretty quickly and somehow vaulted out of the hammock into a standing position.

"That's not going to work," he said, looking down at her.

She realized that if any animals were watching them, they were giving them quite a show. *Look, see, the human circus has come to town.*

Feet to head wouldn't work because of the missing section of parachute. The only position that would really work was him spooning her.

He must have come to the same realization. Or maybe he'd known it all along. "It's not too late," he said.

"Don't be ridiculous," she said, throwing his earlier

words back at him. She got out of the hammock and motioned for him to get back in.

He did.

Then like an Amazonian princess, with her chin held high, she got into her bed, her back to his front.

The only logical place for his right arm was under her head, and for his left, resting lightly on her hip.

She pretended that it didn't even bother her that she could feel him everywhere. His thighs against her thighs. His chest against her back. His breath against her neck.

His groin against her rear.

The Amazonian princess wanted to squirm.

But she held herself rigidly still. Like royalty.

"Everything okay?" he asked, a hint of challenge in his voice.

"It's fine. Just pull the blanket up and let's get some sleep. Please."

He did as instructed. The blanket came up to their necks, but he evidently didn't want to leave their heads exposed. He hooked an arm around his bag and pulled it close. Then he opened it, pulled out his extra shirt, and carefully zipped his bag back up. He draped the shirt over their heads and part of their faces, leaving their mouths and noses free but relatively nothing else uncovered.

She'd thought she couldn't possibly sleep. But within minutes, she felt the overpowering need for rest consume her body. And she let go.

And didn't wake up until she heard the bone-chilling cry of an animal, or several animals, off in the distance. Angry, threatening sounds. She stiffened.

"It's okay," he murmured, his voice close to her ear,

his voice sleepy. "Sound carries at night. They aren't that close."

She realized that at some point in the night, instead of rigidly trying to keep a thin line of demarcation between the two of them, she'd slipped into his embrace. She waited for him to realize it, to stiffen, to pull away.

Instead, he tucked her in tighter.

And in the middle of a dark Amazon rain forest, a tear leaked out of her eye because of all she had given up.

THE NEXT TIME she woke up, she was all alone in the hammock. It was light out and Brody was standing by the fire, his back to her. The angle was right that she could see he had his arms folded over his chest and was deep in thought.

She didn't want to intrude. She'd given up the right to his thoughts many years before.

He turned, as if he had somehow sensed she was awake. He stared at her. "Good morning," he said, his voice rusty.

"Good morning."

"There's tea," he said.

"Thank you." She reached over the side of the hammock, grabbed the end of her walking stick that she'd placed there the night before, and tapped and swished it around on the ground, giving the vermin in the area fair warning that she was about to get up.

Brody watched her and she could see a slight smile at the corner of his mouth.

Great. She was amusing.

When she got close enough, he handed her the tea bottle and she took a drink. The liquid was still warm and she thought it might have been the best cup of tea that she'd ever had.

The breakfast bar and nuts were gone, but with any luck, they'd find bananas and berries that would sustain them for the journey. By tonight, if her calculations were correct, they'd be sitting around Leo's table.

As if he could read her thoughts, Brody turned to her. "Tell me about your friend that we're looking for."

"His name is Leo Arroul. I've known him for more than ten years. We regularly keep in touch online and see each other every couple of years. He's very smart, maybe not as smart as you, but smart."

"I'm not that smart," he said.

"Right. Anyway, he had a big corporate job at one time but now he works on developing clean water systems."

"Is he married?"

It was an odd question. It took her a minute to realize that Brody was fishing, that what he really wanted to know was whether there was something more than friendship between her and Leo. "Not anymore. Divorced some time ago. We've never had that kind of relationship." She dug the toe of her loafer into the dew-covered dirt. "I haven't had that kind of relationship with anybody," she said. "I didn't leave you for someone else," she added, suddenly believing it was very important for him to know that.

There was a long moment of silence before he turned to her. His eyes were bright. "Why did you leave, Elle? What was so wrong that you had to run away, three weeks before our wedding?" His voice sounded strangled.

She could not say a word.

"You know, my mother had to return all the gifts that people had already sent. Everyone said how badly they felt for me. *Poor Brody. Left at the altar.* That's what they said. People pitied me, Elle. I hated that."

"I'm sorry," she whispered. "I…I didn't think," she admitted. She'd acted. Not necessarily on impulse. No, it had been too important for that. But once she'd decided, she'd acted fast, scared that she wasn't strong enough.

Strong enough to leave him.

"That's it. That's your whole explanation. *I didn't think.*"

She shook her head. "Does it really matter, Brody? What's done is done. I'm sorry I hurt you. I'm sorry I didn't handle it better. Happy?" She knew she sounded angry and antagonistic when in truth she was simply heartsick.

"Happy?" he repeated incredulously. He didn't say anything for a long minute. Finally, he spoke. "Yep. Happy as a duck in water. Now let's go."

Chapter Ten

Brody set an aggressive pace and, to her credit, Elle kept up. However, two hours into their morning, their pace slowed considerably. The tree and plant growth was substantially heavier, making it impossible to easily skirt around obstacles. There was no choice but to go through it, and Mrs. Hardy's knife wasn't really up to the task.

Sweat ran down his back from the exertion of sawing through plants. His shoulders hurt and he had a four-inch rip in his shirt where the sharp end of a plant had collided with his arm. Fortunately, he'd jerked back in time to avoid a deep cut in his skin.

"If the rest of the way is like this, we aren't going to make your friend's house by nightfall."

She nodded, her hands on her hips. Her breath was labored from the difficulty of getting through the thick growth.

"We just have to keep going," she said. "Every step is one step closer."

He appreciated her optimism, but it was likely they might have to spend another night in the jungle.

Another night in the hammock with Elle.

Great. Probably add another couple years to how long it would take to get over her this time.

He put his head down and concentrated on putting one foot in front of the other. But five minutes later, he stopped. And listened.

Over the years, his senses had become finely attuned to the sounds of helicopters bringing wounded to the base medical camp. He could be in a dead sleep and somehow, he would wake up.

"What?" Elle asked, scanning the bushes and trees, probably thinking he'd seen something dangerous.

He almost didn't want to tell her, didn't want to get her hopes up. "Helicopter. Do you hear it?"

She stood very still and looked up. A minute later, she grinned. "I do. Oh, God. I do."

Brody stopped to unzip his bag. "I'm going to grab the parachute. It's the brightest thing we have. Maybe they will be able to see it from the air. There's no place to land, but at least they'll see us and know we're here."

When she didn't answer, he looked up and realized that she'd run ahead, probably trying to get to a spot where they could see her.

Brody's heart was thumping in his chest. He'd been confident that he and Elle had the stamina and the will to make it out of the jungle. But stamina and will could get sidelined fast by a bite from a poisonous spider or a broken ankle or any number of things that could happen on a stroll through the jungle. The helicopter coming was a great relief.

It would mean saying goodbye to Elle again.

He tried to push away the despair that settled over him. She'd probably be terribly relieved. She hadn't spoken to him in over two hours after he'd verbally beaten her over the head this morning.

The helicopter was closer. Off to the left, above the tree line. Then he saw it. Dipping and swaying, avoiding the trees, obviously looking for something on the ground.

Looking for them. He started to run, hoping to catch up with Elle.

And, then, through a thin slit in the thick canopy of trees, he saw something incredible happen.

The helicopter stopped weaving and hovered and its side door opened. A man appeared.

Then Brody saw the big gun.

And it took him just a second to realize that the man was shooting.

At Elle.

SHE RAN INTO Brody hard enough that it knocked the wind out of her. Then he was yanking on her arm, dragging her behind one of the bigger trees in the deep foliage.

"What the hell?" he said.

If he expected an answer, he was out of luck. That man in the helicopter had been *shooting* at her. No one had ever shot at her before.

They could hear the helicopter hovering above, close enough that it was stirring the air and leaves were whirling. But what Brody had been bemoaning just minutes earlier was now saving their bacon. They were safely hidden and there was no place to land.

T. K. Jamas. It had to be him. He had the resources

to organize a private rescue effort and he had much to lose if she testified against him.

It was quite frankly almost impossible to get her head around the idea that the man had seen her, lifted his gun and started shooting. By some miracle, the first shot had landed at her feet. Whether it had been the fault of the pilot or the shooter, she was grateful. It had given her a chance to run and the next three shots had missed as well.

"I'm so sorry," she said. "This is all because of me."

He stared at her, emotion flashing in his eyes. "Talk fast, Elle," he said. "What the hell do you mean?"

"It's a very long story. I'm on my way back to the States to testify against a man who at one time I trusted very much. I discovered that he was leading a human-trafficking ring and that most of his victims were eleven- and twelve-year-old girls. I think he may be determined that I don't ever get a chance to tell my story."

"His name," Brody said, his tone insistent.

"T. K. Jamas. He's Peruvian but has lived in Brazil for many years."

Brody looked as if he had a hundred other questions but, to his credit, he didn't ask them. When they heard the sound of the helicopter fading, he grabbed her hand. "Let's go," he said. "We need to get away from here. If you're right, that helicopter is going to look for the closest space where they can land safely and then pursue us on foot."

She hadn't thought she could get any more terrified.

"I dropped my bag and the parachute when I saw that man shooting at you. Stay here while I get it," he said.

She managed a nod.

While Brody was gone, the monkeys in the trees chattered at her, mad that she was in their space, mad that she'd brought the noisy beast with the rotating blades to their home.

Brody was the one who had a right to be furious. When he came back, she put her hand on his arm. "We need to separate. You keep going east. I'm going to head north."

"But you said that your friend would help you."

"I'm not going to lead Jamas to Leo's door," she said, shaking her head. "It's bad enough that I've dragged you into my troubles. You need to get away. I don't think there's any way they could have seen you. You need to keep going, find Leo, and he'll help you."

"Stop talking," Brody said.

"What?"

"I said, stop talking. If you're only going to talk nonsense, then I don't want to hear anything."

Nonsense. She was trying to save his life. "Listen to me," she said. "I think it's possible that Jamas was responsible for the crash."

"What?"

"Captain Ramano seemed mad at me and made odd comments that made me think that he thought I was responsible for the crash. He also knew about the school where I teach. Maybe Jamas paid Captain Ramano to crash the plane?"

Brody shook his head. "That doesn't make sense. It's a bad business proposition. Ramano was as likely to die as anyone else in a plane crash."

Elle tried to think. "All I know is that Captain Ramano acted oddly toward me."

"Not good enough," Brody said. He grabbed her hand. "Let's go."

She took about ten steps before stopping. "What if Jamas was somehow responsible for the crash and he wanted to verify that everyone had died? What if he found the plane? He's a horrible man. He may have killed everyone."

Brody put his hands in the air. "I hope to hell you're wrong, but right now we can't think about that. We need to focus our energies on safely getting out of this jungle without anybody else shooting at us. We're close to Mantau and to your friend Leo. We have to keep going. There's no other choice."

"But—"

"We're not separating," he said. "End of discussion. Is there any reason to think that Jamas knows that you would seek help from Leo?"

She thought. Had she ever mentioned Leo to Jamas? She didn't think so. "No. But he knows the jungle well. He knows that Mantau is the closest village. He might suspect that I'm headed that way. He might also think, however, that I'm headed toward a river. That's always the fastest way to travel in the jungle."

"Okay, then we stay on course. We're going to need to pick up the pace even more and if we hear the helicopter, make sure we stay out of sight."

She put her hand on his arm. "I'm sorry. I feel as if I'm destined to keep telling you that and I'm sure you aren't all that impressed with my apologies, but I am truly sorry."

He shook his head. "Elle, let's just focus on the here and now. I think that's about the best I can do. It sounds

as if you're trying to do a very good thing. You're trying to make a monster pay for his crimes. You don't
have to apologize."

For that, she added silently. But he was right. Now
wasn't the time. They were literally running for their
lives.

Two hours later, hot, exhausted and filthy, Elle almost welcomed the afternoon rain that hit with a vengeance. But Brody didn't stop. Twice, they'd heard the
helicopter and it had hovered over the thick canopy of
trees, but still Brody had pushed ahead. He'd stopped
marking the trail with the red strips of cloth. It would
make it more difficult to find their way back to the
plane but more difficult for Jamas to track them, as well.

She stepped over a rotting log and her foot slipped
on the long wet grass. She went down.

Strong hands picked her up. "Are you hurt?" Brody
asked, his voice close to her ear. Water ran down his
face.

"My knee," she said. "Went down hard on it. It'll
be fine."

He knelt in front her, pulled her pants out of her dirty
socks, and lifted up the wet material. With practiced
hands, he felt around her leg, her knee. His skin was
warm against her cold, wet legs.

"It looks okay," he said. "Can you walk?" He stood
up.

"Were you going to carry me?" she asked, trying to
put a little levity into a very grim situation.

"I'll do what I have to do," he said.

It was the same thing he'd said when faced with the
possibility of operating on Captain Ramano when there
was concern about internal injuries.

Brody Donovan was that kind of guy. He'd do what he needed to do to get the job done.

"I can walk," she said. "We have to be very close, maybe less than an hour from Mantau. As I recall, there are several trails that lead from the village into the jungle. The jungle provides many of the raw materials that the villagers use to survive and to eke out small livings. Once we hit one of those trails, we're going to start to see people. We'll need to be careful."

"Why?"

"Jamas has a lot of money. I suspect that he's already sent someone this direction, waving a handful of money, probably more than these people make in six months, asking for information about me. There's no way that they wouldn't turn us in for that kind of money."

She could see the frustration on his face. Understood it.

"So we *are* going to need to split up," she said. "I'll stay back in the jungle while you go into town. Find Leo and come back for me."

"No. I'm not leaving you," he said.

"You have to. It's the safest way. For you. For both of us."

He looked as if he wanted to argue. Then he evidently changed his mind and before she realized what was happening, he was kissing her, his mouth hard, insistent.

They were filthy, in the middle of a steaming-hot jungle, with bad men chasing them, and she forgot it all. She was lost in the wonder of his kiss. The total abandon of caution.

She opened her mouth and welcomed his tongue.

She pressed her body against his. Every curve fit, every touch burned.

"Oh, Brody," she said when he finally lifted his head.

"Elle," he whispered. "you have been amazing these last two days. So strong. So wise. I can't imagine anyone who might have handled it better."

She felt warm. There had been a time when praise like that from Brody would have meant everything to her. But now it was too late. Too much time had passed. They were different people.

She felt him lift her shirt and put the palm of his hand on her back. With his index finger, he traced her spine.

It didn't feel different. It felt dazzlingly familiar.

He kissed her for a very long time. Finally, he lifted his head. "You keep apologizing but I'm the one who should be sorry," he said. "I've been an ass toward you. I had thirteen years to get over being mad. I don't know what got into me. I saw you and suddenly I was twenty-five again and all those old feelings came rushing back at me. It wasn't fair to you. You had a right to end it."

"I may have had a right, but I did it badly."

"You were young."

He was right. Just twenty-one. "It was a long time ago," she said.

Could he forgive her? Could she forgive herself?

He held her. Tight. And she rested her head against his shoulder. "You should go," she said finally. "You need to get into the village and back again before it gets dark."

"I don't want to leave you," he said. "Not with those men looking for you."

"I'll be safe," she said. "I'll stay hidden."

He kissed her again. More tenderly this time, more

sensuously. He slid his hand from her back to her stomach, then up, until the pad of his thumb brushed across her nipple.

The sensation shot to her core and she wanted him with an intensity that she had not felt in many, many years. Thirteen years.

She arched her back. He raised her shirt, exposing her breast to the warm air, holding the weight of it in his hand.

"So pretty," he murmured. His kisses traveled down her neck.

And when he took her breast in his mouth, her legs would have crumpled had he not been supporting her. "I smell," she protested weakly.

"Wonderful," he said.

She could feel him, his erection straining at his pants, pushing at her. She wanted him desperately.

But there was no time. "Brody," she said, stepping away. She pulled down her shirt. "You have to go."

He shook his head, as if to clear it. "I know, damn it. I know," he added, his tone rueful. He looked in her eyes. "I'll find your friend and we'll be back. And you damn well better be here."

BRODY CHANGED INTO his last clean shirt before he walked into Mantau. Elle was right in that the men in the helicopter probably hadn't seen him. But if they had come upon the plane wreckage and talked to the other survivors, then they knew that Elle was not alone.

He carried his water bottle in one hand and his walking stick in the other. He had Mrs. Hardy's knife in his pocket.

He and Elle had discussed whether he should take the

knife or leave it with her. In the end, she'd won, insisting that she intended to stay hidden, that she wouldn't need the knife, while he still had an hour's worth of jungle to navigate and the knife might be absolutely necessary.

He encountered his first person less than thirty minutes from where he'd left Elle in the jungle. He was a thin, dark-skinned man, wearing a big straw hat and carrying a small shovel.

The man paid no attention to him and Brody let out a sigh of relief. Another fifteen minutes later, there were two women, both with tan blouses, long dark skirts and sandals. They carried baskets. They rested their gaze on him and he nodded politely in their direction but didn't break stride.

It was frightening and exhilarating at the same time to finally see other humans. It had been almost seventy hours since the plane crashed and more than once in that time, when he'd been surrounded by trees and plants, with no trail in sight, he'd doubted that this would be the eventual outcome.

He wanted to run up to them and demand to know whether they knew Leo Arroul, but he waited. Elle had been right about almost everything so far. If she believed that people might be looking for American strangers, then he didn't intend to raise their curiosity more than absolute necessary.

The village of Mantau was less than fifteen minutes down the dirt road that would only have been wide enough for one American car. But there were no cars. There were people pulling three-wheeled carts, but that was the extent of the moving vehicles.

There were probably twenty-five small square bamboo huts, all on risers so that their front doors were at least six steps up. All had thatch roofs. Most had a porch of some kind and he was close enough that on one, he could see an old woman using a brick fireplace to cook a fish with its head still on.

He kept walking. On a street in roughly the middle of town, there were two stands akin to the hot-dog vendor he loved in New York, without the hot dogs or wheels on their stands. On the right was a young woman who had raw fish and baked bread on her counter. Next to her was a much older man selling fresh fruit, vegetables and something that resembled hard brown sugar.

Jungle commerce.

He reached into his pocket and fingered a real. He had exchanged dollars for the Brazilian currency at the bank before boarding the plane in Miami. Before leaving the plane with Elle, he'd made sure he had the money with him. Everywhere in the world, money talked.

And right now he wanted the young woman to feel chatty.

He admired her bread and selected a long, flat loaf that would be easy to carry. She wrapped it in tan paper that she secured with a piece of string.

"Obrigado," he said. Thank you was about the extent of his Portuguese. She smiled and put the money in her skirt pocket.

"Do you speak English?" he asked.

She shrugged. "Some," she said with a heavy accent.

He took a deep breath. "I am looking for an old friend. His name is Leo Arroul. Do you know him?"

Chapter Eleven

She smiled wider this time and he noticed that one of her eyeteeth was missing. She raised her arm and pointed to a building at the end of the street, on the left side. "Leo," she said. "Good man."

He could feel his heart start to race in his chest. But he contained his energy, much like before he did a very complex surgery. *"Obrigado,"* he repeated.

He turned and caught the stare of the man selling the fruit. A frisson of unease settled between his shoulder blades, but he ignored it. He walked at the same pace that he had used when entering the village. It took him ninety-three steps to reach Leo's front door.

He knocked and waited. The door opened and there was an older man, maybe close to sixty, wearing wrinkled cotton pants and a matching shirt. He was completely bald. He had friendly brown eyes.

"Are you Leo Arroul?" Brody asked.

The man nodded.

Brody looked over the man's shoulder. There was no one else inside the small one-room house. "My name is Brody Donovan. I am a friend of Elle Vollman. She needs your help."

Leo pulled him inside and offered him something to drink. Brody drank the water and then filled up his water bottle, intending to take it back for Elle. He quickly told Leo about the plane crash, the walk through the jungle, the helicopter and the men shooting at Elle.

When he said the name T. K. Jamas, Leo's eyebrows shot up.

"Do you know him?" Brody asked.

"I have met him," Leo said. "He can be quite charming. I wish I'd known that Elle was involved with him. I'd have warned her."

Brody started to argue that Elle wasn't *involved* with Jamas but then realized it wasn't important. What was important was getting back to Elle and getting her safely to the United States.

"Elle believes that he's involved in human trafficking."

Leo did not look surprised. His next statement, however, took Brody off guard. "Jamas has a home somewhere near here. I'm not exactly sure where. I've never been interested enough to find out. I believe it belonged to his father and Jamas is only there occasionally."

"I don't think Elle had any idea that he had any connections to this area. She would never have come this direction."

"Well, then, I'm glad she didn't know. I can help you. But how did you find me?" Leo asked.

"I asked the young woman who was selling bread, just down the street."

"Did anyone hear you?" Leo asked.

"I think the man behind the other stand might have."

Leo nodded and stood up. "Then we must hurry. We might not have much time."

"What?" Brody demanded.

"His name is Paulo and let's just say he's easily influenced by others. And most easily influenced by money. If it's known that Jamas will pay for information about Elle, then Paulo would be in line for the money."

"I never said her name."

"You wouldn't have to. You are American. Elle is American. I am perceived to be American, even though I am really Canadian. That would be enough."

"Let's go. It could take an hour to get back."

Leo grabbed a large black backpack off a hook near the door. He filled it with mangoes and bananas from the bowl on his table. Then he opened a container on the table and pulled out something wrapped in white paper. Finally, he opened the door of a freestanding cupboard and retrieved several items that Brody couldn't clearly see and added them to the backpack. The last thing he did was sling the strap of a machete over one shoulder.

They did not walk past the fruit stand on their way out of town. Leo turned the opposite direction. Brody took a fast look down the street before they left and he did not see Paulo at his stand.

And while he knew there could be many explanations for the man's absence, Brody could not shake the fear that Paulo was contacting Jamas. Money talked, after all.

Leo led him out of the village and around the small collection of houses. Brody's strides were long, his pace fast.

"Slow down," Leo said, barely moving his mouth. "We're out for a stroll. Two old friends."

Brody forced himself to slow down, to appear relaxed. He glanced at the birds in the trees, at the brilliantly colored flowers that bloomed everywhere.

He watched to see if anyone was following them or taking a particular interest in them but saw nothing that concerned him. It would be okay. He and Elle would be okay.

"Perhaps it's best that we don't tell Elle that I've seen Jamas in Mantau before," Leo said.

Brody shook his head. "We need to tell her. She needs to know everything."

Leo shrugged. "Maybe you're right. Forewarned is forearmed."

When they finally passed a bend in the road that protected them from view of the village, Leo turned to him. "Are you a runner?" the man asked.

Brody nodded.

Leo started off jogging and quickly picked up the pace. "I gained forty pounds after my wife left me," he said. "Then I realized an early death from heart disease wasn't going to hurt her and I started running."

Whatever the reason, Brody was grateful. He would soon be back with Elle.

ELLE HATED THE JUNGLE. She'd come to that conclusion about six minutes after she'd watched Brody walk away. It was noisy and damp and too green.

She was tired and she desperately wanted to sit down, but she was scared to—something would bite her on her butt, it would swell up, Brody would have to administer first aid, and he'd see the cellulite that hadn't been there thirteen years ago.

While it was hard to know exactly how much cellulite might be there, it was not a stretch of the imagination to imagine that there must be some. After all, her legs were not those of a twenty-one-year-old college student who went to the gym every day and cocktailed most nights. Her arms? Well, she saw some jiggle the other day. Her neck. She didn't even want to talk about that.

You're thirty-four, not sixty-four, she told herself. If sixty was the new forty, then thirty-four was the new fourteen. Great. If she slept with Brody, it'd be illegal.

If she slept with Brody. She repeated the words in her head and let them simmer there, in her half-baked brain. Wasn't that presumptuous of her? She was jumping way down the track. Sure, he'd had a physical reaction to her. But maybe that was just because he'd been busy and hadn't had sex for thirteen years?

Who was she kidding? Of course he'd had sex. She had, after all. At least once every two years, that's what she'd told Father Taquero when the two of them were sipping bad wine in the back of the church late one Saturday afternoon.

He'd assured her that was barely worth a Hail Mary.

Even so, after he'd left to get ready for evening mass, she'd added a couple of Our Fathers just to hedge her bets.

The men had been decent guys that she'd met either through her work or through friends. But none of them had been Brody.

And so even the ones who had called several times afterward, she'd politely turned down. And in the past year she hadn't even dated because she'd had Mia, the absolute sweetest little eleven-year-old.

And as Father Taquero was fond of saying, God willing and if the creek don't rise, she and Mia would soon be safe in the United States and they would build a new life together.

But first she needed to get out of the jungle.

Which brought her thoughts full circle to where they'd started when her mind had contemplated cellulite on her rear end. She looked at her watch. Brody had been gone for almost forty minutes. Time enough for him to reach the village and inquire about Leo.

Please, please, let Leo be home. There were times when he was in the depths of the jungle, teaching natives about the importance of clean water and how to test their water using his little strips.

It would be dark in a half hour and that would make it very difficult for Brody to find her. He'd said that he wouldn't mark the trail, but rather he'd find her through several prominent landmarks. But landmarks easily got out of focus when the sun went down.

She saw a sudden burst of white birds, as if they'd been scared up from a tree. She looked. Was that bush moving? Did she hear something?"

There were sounds from her left.

She whirled.

Only to turn back quickly.

Brody and Leo emerged from the jungle. She didn't think she'd ever seen a more welcome sight. And without thinking, she ran toward them and it seemed the most natural thing in the world to get caught up in Brody's strong arms.

"You made it," she murmured, her mouth against his neck.

"Of course," he said, his voice soft. "I wasn't going to leave you out here in the jungle."

His touch felt warm and safe and she didn't want to pull away. But she forced herself to.

"Leo," she said. "I can't begin to tell you how wonderful it is to see you." She stepped close to her friend and gave him a hug.

"It's always wonderful, Elle, but knowing just a little of what you've been through in the last three days, it's better than usual. I am grateful that we found you. Brody was confident, but I was getting concerned that it would soon be too dark."

"We have to tell the authorities about the crash," Elle said.

"Of course," Leo replied. "I've been thinking about that on the way here. Brody told me about your trouble with Jamas. You know he's a very evil man?"

"I do now," Elle replied. "Did Brody tell you about the man in the helicopter?"

"Yes."

"I'm confident that was Jamas's doing. I didn't want to drag you into this, Leo, but I didn't have any choice."

The man waved a hand. "Nonsense. Of course you should have come to me. But we'll need to be very careful. Jamas's family has a home in this area. As I told Brody, I'm not exactly sure where but I've heard it is north of Mantau, near where our small river merges into the Amazon."

Elle shook her head. "You've got to be kidding me. Of all places."

Leo did another hand wave. That was clearly his favorite gesture. "I don't believe he's here very often. But in any event, it would be best if you and Brody could keep a low profile until we can safely move you out of the country."

Brody stepped forward. "How do we do that and lead the authorities to the crash?"

"There is someone I trust in the local government. I'll tell him that I received an anonymous tip about the crash. You indicated that you marked the trail up until a few hours ago. If I give them the approximate location and the trail is marked, they should be able to find the wreckage."

"Will they believe you?"

"I think so. Because of my work with the natives, I often get information that people in more official positions cannot easily obtain. I use my discretion about which information I pass on."

Elle stepped forward and gave her friend another quick hug. "I kept telling Brody that you would help us. Thank you so much."

"You're quite welcome. And while I'd love to invite you back to my home for a meal and some rest, I don't think that's a good idea. Brody may have been overheard asking about me. I don't want to take the chance that Jamas will be watching my house and see the two of you."

A meal and rest, even if the rest was on a wooden floor, sounded heavenly, but she knew that Leo was right. She would handle another night in the jungle. "I understand," she said.

"I have someplace you can go," Leo said. "A house. Outside the village, in a very private area. I...I have a... friend. A special friend. She lives in Costa Rica with her husband and grown children. While that's a substantial distance, her husband is a very powerful businessman, so when she is able to visit, we still must be very discreet."

Elle was happy for her friend. He'd been terribly hurt when his wife left him so many years before. And the offer of shelter for the night sounded heavenly. But she could not afford to make any mistakes. "Are you sure it will be safe?"

"I am. Fortunately, we're already halfway there. It shouldn't take us more than another forty-five minutes to walk there, but it's going to be dark soon and forty-five minutes in the jungle at night is a long time."

"We can do it," Brody said. "We've been a good team so far, right, Elle?"

His comment was bittersweet. They had almost been a team. A real team. The ultimate team.

A lifetime ago.

"We can do it," she said, keeping her eyes focused on her friend. She was afraid to look at Brody. Afraid that he might see the longing on her face, might realize the truth that she'd regretted leaving him from almost the minute she left.

"Let's go, then," Leo said, taking the lead.

Elle followed with Brody taking up the rear. Mindful that Jamas might have people looking for them in the jungle, they did not talk on the way but tried to move quietly through the heavy growth. Twenty minutes into the trip, they did have to turn on their flashlights. Leo had his own and Brody carried theirs. Both men were careful to keep the light down, to have it shine only a few feet ahead of them. Twice they did have to resort to clearing the path. Fortunately, Leo's machete was much more effective than Mrs. Hardy's knife. It was also noisier and while Elle knew it was difficult for sound to carry through the heavy jungle, she was still worried. She'd brought danger to Brody and now Leo was involved, too.

Just as Elle was thinking that she was going to fall over from fatigue, the little house seemed to suddenly pop out of the jungle in front of them. Leo flashed his light up, allowing her a minute to inspect it. It was on stilts, with bamboo walls and a thatch roof. It was almost frightening how well it blended it with the surrounding area.

They climbed the steps and Leo opened the door. The inside was one big room. There was a small table and two chairs to the right. On the far wall was a large fireplace. That surprised her. Most of the homes in the jungle villages did not have indoor fireplaces for fear of highly flammable materials catching fire. There were two large tanks of water. That didn't surprise her. After all, water was Leo's business. There were several buckets, stacked upside down, next to the tanks.

And there was a bed, stripped bare of any blankets or sheets, but they appeared to be in the plastic container that sat on the bed. There were two other clear plastic containers on the floor and they contained dishes and silverware and pots and pans.

"The water that is inside is safe to drink and to wash in. There are towels in with the sheets."

Elle figured that was the nicest way Leo could say, *Hey, you two could benefit from a bath.* She could easily get past the gentle criticism.

"I'd suggest that you don't use the fireplace. No need to attract attention to this location. I brought a few things that don't require cooking." Leo opened his backpack and pulled out wrapped cheese, some mangoes and bananas, and a jar of peanut butter.

Elle smiled when she saw that. Leo had been having peanut butter shipped to him for years.

Her friend caught her eye and tipped the jar in her direction. "Brody bought some bread in the village. You won't starve," Leo said. "There's some wine, too." He pulled out a glass bottle with a cork stopper. "Although I suspect you're more in the mood for water."

"How long will we need to stay here?" Brody asked.

"Tomorrow morning I'll report the location of the wreckage. At the same time, I'll arrange for a flight out of the country. You won't be able to go commercial. If Jamas knows you're alive, and we have to assume he does, he surely has connections that will allow him to monitor airline-ticket purchases. I know a few pilots that I trust. It's a matter of getting in contact with them and seeing who is willing and available to help. I'll try to be back by noon with a plan. The faster we can get you out of Brazil, the better."

Brody stepped forward. "Leo, I don't think we can thank you enough."

Leo waved his hand. "Elle would do it for me. I suggest you stay inside as much as possible over the next eighteen hours. Eat, rest, replenish your fluids. That's your job."

Elle kissed her friend on the cheek. "Thank you. You are literally saving our lives."

"Happy to do it. I'll be happier, however, when you're safely away from here. Jamas will be relentless in his search to find you."

"Who knows about this place?" Brody asked.

Leo shrugged. "I don't make a habit of telling too many people about it. However, the jungle is not nearly as isolated as many think. Even if you never see them, there are many natives. They watch and listen and see and know more than you might think. I've never been bothered by them because I'm pretty well-known in this area for my work in developing safe water systems. There's no lock on the door, but no one has ever taken the few things that I keep here."

It made her feel a bit like a goldfish in a glass bowl to think that there might be people outside the small hut. Watching. Waiting.

It was as if Brody was reading her mind when he asked, "How will they know that we're not intruders, that we have your permission to be here?"

Leo smiled. "I imagine several of the natives saw us on our journey here. I know, we didn't see them but trust me, they were there. Word will pass that I led you here." He pushed open the narrow door. "Good night. Don't worry."

Brody moved quickly, catching Leo before the door could shut. "One more thing, Leo," he said.

"Of course."

It was subtle but Elle was pretty sure that Brody used his body to edge Leo out the door. Whatever it was that Brody wanted to tell Leo, he didn't want Elle to hear. Which under normal circumstances might make her curious or even mildly irritated, but quite frankly, she was so tired and so emotionally exhausted that she didn't really care.

Whatever it was, it didn't take long because Brody was back inside the hut in just a few minutes. "Sorry," he said, "I was hedging our bets."

"Huh?"

He smiled. "I'll tell you later. I think he's a good man. I'm glad you have friends like that, Elle."

She nodded. "While I haven't known him as long, he's sort of my Ethan and Mack. Someone I trust implicitly. Someone I can count on."

Brody nodded. "There have been times in the last twenty years, when Ethan, Mack and I were all in different corners of the world, that we wouldn't see each other or even talk for months at a time. But that never mattered. We knew that we were still there for each other. No matter what."

"What would they say now if they could see you?" Elle asked.

Brody smiled. "Probably something like, *Hey, you smell. Hit the shower.*"

Elle walked over and opened the plastic tote that was sitting on the end of the bed. There were sheets, a thin blanket, two towels, two washcloths, as well as a bar of soap. "I'm grateful for everything—the food, the shelter, the water. But I'm really grateful for the soap. I feel as if the bug spray is three layers deep on me."

"Go ahead and get cleaned up. I can wait outside."

Elle shook her head. Maybe it was Leo's comment about the natives hearing and seeing everything, but she was suddenly very nervous about either one of them being outside. They would ultimately have to go out to take care of basic hygiene needs, but that should be the limit.

"We both want to clean up. We're adults, Brody. You turn your back, I'll turn mine."

He didn't say anything. Just calmly walked over to the water tanks, picked up a bucket and filled it halffull. Then he repeated the actions with a second bucket. He brought her one of the buckets and set it down at her feet. In return, she handed him a washcloth and towel.

He took it without a word and returned to the other side of the room.

He pivoted on his feet so that his back was toward her. Then he started to take off his shirt.

And she watched.

He finished with his buttons and slipped the shirt off one shoulder, then the other. His back was still smooth, still tan, still masculine with finely sculpted muscle. He did have a heck of a bruise, however. It was various shades of purple, and she realized that he'd probably gotten it when the plane had crashed and the ceiling had fallen in on him.

He'd never said anything, never complained.

He unzipped his pants, started to pull them down.

Gracious, as Mrs. Hardy was prone to saying.

She turned, almost kicking over her bucket of water in the process. What the heck was wrong with her? They were dirty. They needed to wash. It was a simple human need.

The problem was, she was struggling with a much more complex human need. Ever since Brody had kissed her, she'd been imagining what it would be like if it was something more. Ever since she'd felt his erection, so tight, so perfect, she had been wanting him with a vengeance.

But she wasn't going to do one thing about it. She and Brody had had their day a long time ago. It had been a one-act play and the theater had been closed for a lot of years.

She unbuttoned her own shirt and let it drop to the floor. Then she pulled off the cami with its built-in bra. The cotton material was practically sticking to her skin. She stood naked to the waist, happy to let the warm air inside the hut wash across her bare skin. She dipped her cloth into the water, scrubbed some soap across it, and wiped down her arms, her breasts, her stomach.

She heard two soft thuds and a swoosh and figured that Brody had kicked off his boots and stepped out of his pants. Was he totally naked?

She wanted to look. She desperately wanted to peek, to take a memory of his body back with her.

Her hands were shaking and the hut seemed warmer. She unbuttoned her pants, pulled down the zipper, stepped out of them. She pulled her bright blue panties down, too. She dipped her cloth in the water and soaped it up again.

And realized that Brody didn't have any soap. There had only been one bar.

"There's soap," she said. "I can share."

Chapter Twelve

"Okay," he said, his voice sounding rusty.

She started to turn, only to stop quickly. No looking, she told herself. She again faced the wall. And took three steps back. With each step, she could feel her body responding to Brody's naked nearness. Her skin felt more sensitive, the fine hair on her arms felt alive.

She reached her right arm back. She was holding the soap in a death grip. "Here," she said.

He reached back and brushed the back of his hand across her bare buttock.

She sucked in a breath.

Neither of them moved. She couldn't even breathe.

Until finally she felt the faint stirring of air as Brody moved his body. His hand connected with hers. She released her fingers, letting the soap shift to his hand.

She heard the soap hit the floor. Brody still had her hand. He was turning her, pulling her close.

"Brody?" she whispered, her eyes on his handsome face.

His gaze was steady. "A lot of years have gone by, Elle. I don't see much sense in wasting another day."

And then he bent his head, pulled her tight into his wet, naked body and kissed her.

For a very long time.

Making her forget that she was in the middle of a South American jungle. Making her forget all about T. K. Jamas. Making her forget everything except the fact that she loved kissing Brody Donovan.

She wrapped her arms around his neck and settled in. She felt his desire. So hard. So needy.

She felt alive.

"Brody?" she said, her voice soft.

"Yes, Elle."

"I'm glad there was only one bar of soap."

"I'll never look at soap the same way again," Brody agreed. He took a step back, separating their bodies.

He stared at her, his eyes lingering on her breasts, her hips, her legs. "You're beautiful," he said.

"I'm thirty-four," Elle protested. "I don't have the body of a twenty-one-year-old cocktail waitress anymore."

"It's even more amazing now," Brody said. He reached for the cloth that Elle held in her hand. "Let me," he said. Then he dipped the cloth in the water and gently ran it down the length of Elle's right arm. Then he bent his head and kissed the soft skin inside her elbow.

She drew in a deep breath. Held it.

He repeated the action with her left arm, spending time gently massaging her hand. Then it was a kiss on each finger.

He dipped the cloth again and this time he started at the collarbone and worked his way down the gentle slope of her right breast, using the cloth to softly rub the pink nipple.

"Ohhh." Elle sighed.

He licked the spot his cloth had just cleaned. Used his tongue to pull her nipple inside his mouth, to suck on it.

"Brody," she said, her voice sounding thin.

"Don't hurry me, Elle," he said softly. "I intend to take my time."

And he did. He washed her with long strokes, followed by quick licks and soft kisses. Her ribs. Her stomach. Her legs. Her feet.

"Spread your legs," he said, kneeling in front of her.

He cleaned her and then tasted her.

She squirmed and he held her tight.

"Oh, my," she said. And minutes later, when her first orgasm hit hard, she knew she would have fallen if he'd not had a good hold. When it was over, she bent her knees and he let her sink down onto the floor, boneless, satisfied.

He sat down next to her and wrapped an arm around her, pulling her close. "Okay?" he asked.

"That was amazing," she said. "I can't breathe," she added.

"Yes, you can. You're talking. That means you're breathing."

She let her head loll against his shoulder. "Just because you're a doctor doesn't mean you know everything."

"I know what I'm going to be doing for the next hour," he said.

She lifted her head. "And what's that?" she asked, her tone teasing.

"I'll tell you what. You make the bed while I finish getting cleaned up, now that I've got some soap. And then I'll show you."

She smiled. "Making the bed in normal situations

might be a real mood killer, but I think I'd do most anything for a real bed right now."

He helped her stand up and, in the process, let his body slide against her, let her feel how much he wanted her.

She wrapped her arms around his neck and pulled him even closer. "Make it fast," she whispered.

"Don't you worry, darling. Just get those sheets on."

ELLE VOLLMAN HAD always been a wonderful lover. Imaginative. Demanding. Tender. Playful. And when she stretched her slim body out next to his, he felt an almost overpowering need. He wanted to be inside her, to know the great joy of having her come apart in his arms.

"Nice job with the sheets," he said.

They were simple cotton, wrinkled from having been folded tight in the plastic container, but they were clean and felt heavenly. "I'm never leaving this bed," she said.

"Sounds good to me," he replied, smiling. The real world seemed very far away.

"Brody," she said.

"Yes."

"Make love to me."

And he did. And it was everything he remembered and more. A myriad of contradictions. Hard kisses and soft touches. Hot skin and cool sheets. Yielding muscle and driving force.

When he was inside her, seated deep, she wrapped her legs around him and rocked up. He hissed through his teeth. She did it again and again until he shifted and his strokes became long and sure.

And he felt her need spike. She exploded around him and he threw back his head and poured himself into her.

HE LAY ON his side, one arm under Elle's head, the other stroking her naked body. She was on her back, her eyes closed.

The sex had been amazingly good. Perfect.

But now they needed to talk. "I suppose it's a little late to ask," he said, "but are you on any birth control?"

She didn't open her eyes. She did, however, shake her head.

Well, okay. He waited, to see if she would initiate more conversation. She had a child. She had taken deliberate and specific action to be a parent to Mia. That had to mean that she was open to the idea of children.

What would it mean if Elle was pregnant with his child?

He would want to marry her. For sure. But was he destined to repeat his mistakes of thirteen years before? Would she leave him again?

His stomach was rolling and it had nothing to do with being hungry. He was borrowing trouble. There was no reason to believe that Elle was pregnant from one hugely fantastic bout of sex. People had sex all the time without conceiving.

He was going to stop worrying about it. And he was going to stop thinking about whether it meant as much to Elle as it had meant to him.

"Are you hungry?" he asked, determined that he could steer the conversation into some normalcy.

Now she opened her eyes. "A little."

He got out of bed and pulled on clean shorts from his bag. He cut slices of cheese and bread and mango, put them on a plastic plate that he found in one of the bins and brought it over to the bed. Then he filled their empty water bottles with water from the dispenser and brought those, as well as the bottle of wine, back to the bed.

She was sitting up, with the faded cotton sheet pulled up almost to her neck. Her cheeks were pink and the worry that had been ever present in her eyes for the past three days was gone.

"A feast," she said, smiling.

"I never thought I'd look so fondly upon a mango," Brody agreed.

"When I get back to the States, I'm going to have a bacon cheeseburger. And fries. Lot of fries," Elle added.

That sounded good. "I'm going for the desserts," he said. "Chocolate cake. Maybe cherry pie with vanilla ice cream."

She frowned at him. "And you, a respected member of the medical community," she said, her tone deliberately shocked. "Have you seen the latest research on saturated fats?"

He shrugged and helped himself to a piece of cheese. "I don't care. After I have dessert, I'm going to have a steak with a baked potato and lots of sour cream."

"Now you're talking," she said, layering cheese and mango on her slice of bread.

They ate in silence for several minutes. After Elle drank her entire bottle of water, she picked up the wine bottle. "Cheers," she said. She uncorked the wine, drank and passed the bottle to him. He took a sip. It made the back corners of his mouth tighten up in response.

"This tastes remarkably similar to something that Ethan, Mack and I made in college with a bottle of grain alcohol and blackberry brandy."

She smiled. "You'll certainly have a story to tell your friends when you get back to the States. You mentioned that they're both getting married soon, right? You'll go to the weddings?"

"Yes, it's a double wedding at the McCann cabin. Mack and Hope were initially reluctant to go along with Chandler's suggestion because they didn't want to horn in on her big day, but she was insistent. Said that nothing would make her happier than sharing a wedding day with her brother."

"I'm sure it'll be wonderful," Elle said. "Have you, Mack and Ethan seen much of each other in the last couple of years?"

"We'd go for long stretches of time without seeing each other but always kept in contact with texts and phone calls. Ethan was in the army, Mack in the navy and I just retired from the air force."

Her eyes widened and she sat up straighter. The sheet slipped and he worked hard to keep his gaze eye level.

"I never pictured you in the air force," she said.

"After my residency, I worked in Boston for a couple years but I was restless. I thought about going back to Colorado, but I decided that I'd try something very different." How could he tell her that he'd always dreamed that they'd go back to Colorado together, that he simply hadn't been able to make the trip without her?

Some things were probably better left unsaid.

"I enlisted and have had several deployments to Iraq and Afghanistan during the last eight years. Fortunately or unfortunately, depending on your perspective and which end of the scalpel you're at, war presents opportunities for advancements in medicine. Dollars become available for research, and new techniques and treatments are developed. That has certainly been the case as we've tried to better respond to bodies damaged by roadside bombers."

She shook her head. "I'm so sorry. The carnage you've seen is probably staggering."

"Of course. But I also had the opportunity to witness true heroics. So many very brave soldiers. Some of whom are going home without arms or legs. Then, of course, there's the traumatic brain injuries. But still, they're determined to have a life, even if it's going to be a very different life from the one they had once anticipated."

"Thank you for your service," she said.

She didn't say it because it was the politically correct thing to say. He could tell she meant it. And it felt good that she was proud of him. He ate a slice of bread, not sure how to tell her that her opinion mattered.

"How about you?" he asked instead. "I know that you're teaching now but what did you do before that?"

She picked at the hem of the sheet and looked toward her feet. "I lived in Paris for a few years and worked at odd jobs. I make a mean latte," she added, looking up. "Then I moved to Peru and worked as a nanny. The husband and wife were both high up in the government and they had three children. While I was working for them, I finally finished college." She made eye contact. "Took me long enough, I know. I imagine you never thought it would happen."

He shrugged. Elle was one of the smartest people he'd ever met. He'd never even considered that she wasn't smart enough to go to college. He'd figured she just wasn't interested.

"Anyway, after the youngest started school, I moved

to Brazil and started working at the school, teaching English. I loved it."

"And that's where you met Jamas?"

"Yes," she whispered. "He was a great benefactor to our school and to several others. I had no idea that he used his access to our students to pick out his next victims."

"How did you find out?"

"Mia told me. I'm not sure why he targeted Mia. Perhaps because she's such a beautiful girl. Perhaps because I'd adopted her and maybe he was trying to hurt me. What I learned from the authorities recently is that they believe he tries to make it look as if the girl is a runaway with fake notes and other clues."

"Bastard," Brody said.

"Absolutely. He played on the emotions of these young girls. He had several women working for him. Why they would do this, I have no idea, but they would make contact with these young girls, giving them small gifts at first to earn their confidence. You have to understand, these are very poor children with many needs and wants. Once they accepted, they were of course warned to tell no one, that they and their families would be in trouble for accepting the gifts. That's nonsense, of course, but adolescent girls don't understand that."

"Of course not," he said. "Oldest trick in the book."

"Once their confidence was earned, the women would use some excuse to get the children into their vehicle and they were taken somewhere. Based on what I now know, they would be sold within hours and moved out of the country, never to be heard from again."

"You said that Jamas made a mistake with Mia."

"Yes. Evidently several different women tried to

entice Mia into accepting gifts, but she would accept nothing. Maybe Jamas became intrigued by the challenge. Once he told me that he fancied himself a collector of all things rare and beautiful. At the time, I thought he was talking about art," she admitted.

"For whatever the reason, he was obsessed with Mia," she went on, determined to forgive herself for not realizing sooner that Jamas was a monster. "He made contact himself, figuring that Mia would trust him because he was a frequent visitor at the school. He made a mistake, though. The gift he gave her was a fashionable fragrance, one that all the girls saw advertised in the magazines that they devoured. When Mia saw that, she realized it was the same thing that she'd seen in her friend's backpack, just a week before the friend had suddenly run away from the orphanage."

"She associated the fragrance with her friend's absence?"

"She knew her friend would never have run away, because there was a family that had expressed interest in adopting her. Mia was very grateful to have been adopted. She knew that this girl also wanted to be adopted more than anything. Mia connected the fragrance and the girl's unexpected leaving and came to me. Thank God she trusted me enough to tell me."

"What did you do?"

"I had to be sure. I arranged a party at the school, a fund-raiser, and invited all the donors from previous events. Jamas was on that list. He came and I made sure there was an opportunity for him to talk with Mia. He gave her another gift, a signed photo of a popular band in Brazil."

"Something that most adolescent girls would see as valuable."

"Exactly. When he gave her the gift, he told her that he had something even more special that he wanted to show her and that his sister would pick her up from school on Monday of the following week. I wanted to confront Jamas but I knew that it would be a mistake. I didn't know who I could trust. He's a very powerful man with ties to the local police and government. I conferred with Father Taquero and at his suggestion, I contacted the FBI. At that time, I thought these were kidnapping cases. Let's just say that my inquiry sparked quite a bit of notice. Within hours, I had talked to several people from different agencies. I didn't realize it but Jamas was a known figure to many, but no one had been able to personally connect him to any crimes. He had made a big mistake in approaching Mia directly."

"What happened next?"

She hesitated and he got scared. "What happened, Elle?"

"I had been assured that only a very tight circle of people were aware that I had contacted authorities. But the next night, I was attacked on my way to see Father Taquero. Two men were pulling me into a waiting car when Father Taquero and his dog, his very big dog, came around the corner. One of the men got bit and the other tried to shoot the dog. But by that time, we had attracted some attention and the men drove away."

Brody felt a chill run down the length of his body. Elle had been manhandled by goons and likely would have been killed. Lost to him forever. He had never been a particularly violent man, but he was filled with the urge to kill those responsible for hurting her.

She must have sensed his emotion because she didn't wait for him to ask the next question. "With Father Taquero's help, I arranged for Mia to go to a safe place that same night. No one will be able to find her, I'm confident of that. The story I told you about taking books to a teacher in Fortaleza was partially true. There are books in those boxes. There is a teacher at the school that I know. But the reason I was going there was that I had contacted the one person that I believed I could trust, told him that I thought he had a leak, and he had promised that he would meet me in Fortaleza and arrange safe passage for both Mia and me back to the United States."

"So when our plane didn't land, the person you were supposed to meet should have immediately sensed that something might be wrong."

"Yes. That's why when I heard the helicopter, I was so excited. I figured that he had come for me. But he would never have shot at me. Mia and I are his key witnesses."

"What's his name?"

"Flynn O'Brien."

Brody smiled at her. "I imagine he's not Irish."

"I suspect he is, based on the accent I heard when I talked to him. I don't really care. What's important to me is that he can safely get Mia and me back to the United States." She yawned, covering her mouth with the back of her hand.

He smiled at her and gathered up the plastic plates and the wine bottle. "You need some rest," he said.

She nodded and slipped down in the bed. "This could all be over tomorrow," she said.

He didn't want his time with Elle to be over. But he

wasn't sure if he was ready to tell her that yet. First he needed to understand why she'd left so many years before. "Elle," he said.

There was no answer. Her breathing was steady and deep.

He settled in next to her, pulling her in tight to his body. He could wait. He could do most anything as long as Elle was in his arms.

Chapter Thirteen

Elle woke up feeling warm and comfortable and, oddly enough, content. That was not an emotion that she was generally up close and personal with. She'd spent a lifetime searching, looking for the thing that was going to make her feel whole, make her feel as if she'd truly left her childhood behind.

Contentment might be an elusive emotion, but right now it filled her, surrounded her, even led her to do something that she might normally not do. She turned in Brody's arms. He was awake.

"Make love to me," she said.

His eyes widened. "Well, hell," he said.

"Huh?"

"I want the last fifteen minutes back, because I spent them thinking about how I was going to convince you to let me do just that. You're easy."

"But still worth it," she countered as his lips traced her collarbone.

He lifted his head. "That, darling, is not even worthy of discussion."

An hour later, they lay in bed, him on his back, her on her side, nestled close. She was stroking his bare stomach. "We should get up," she said. "Leo said he'd be here by noon. But if he comes early, I don't want him walking into this."

Brody didn't answer. He was staring at the ceiling.

"Penny for your thoughts," she teased.

He shifted so that he could look her in the eye. His face was very serious. "Why did you leave?"

She'd expected the question. How could he not ask it? How could she not answer it now, after all this.

"The first night that you came into the bar, I noticed you. I wasn't even waiting on your table and still I noticed you. You have this way of bringing light into a room, making everything around you brighter, making everything look better. I know it sounds crazy but I could *feel* you in the room."

"You never said a word to me."

"Of course not. But I watched you. And then when you came back and I was your waitress, I thought, *Wow, he's as nice as he looks.* You were polite and funny and I heard you tell your friend to clean up his act after he let loose an F-bomb in front of me. And you left very generous tips."

"I was trying to get your attention."

"You had it. And when you asked me out, I couldn't believe it. And I meant it when I said no. But you were persistent and…it was probably wrong but I wanted what you were offering, I wanted a chance to be *that* girl. The girl with the incredible boyfriend that everybody admired and respected. Even if it couldn't last."

"But—"

She held up a finger, stopping him. "You amazed me. So well educated, so confident, so emotionally whole. I would lie in bed at night and think, how does one get to be Brody Donovan? Then when we visited your pa ents over the holidays and I saw how perfect they were, it made sense to me. You were destined to be perfect. Destined that everything you did or touched for the first twenty-five years of your life would be golden."

"You left because I had a good life?" he asked, unable to keep the disbelief out of his tone. "Because I had nice parents?"

"No. Of course not. I left because I saw how different we were. How different we would always be."

She saw the look on his face and knew that he was never going to understand unless she told him the truth, the whole truth. "Brody, I grew up in a series of trailer parks."

"It's no crime to be poor, Elle."

"You're right." She swallowed hard. "When I was twelve, I was molested by my stepfather. He touched me. Made me…touch him. Do things to him."

She could see the shock, the revulsion, on his face. "Rivers?" he asked.

"Yes."

"I hope the bastard spent time in jail," he said.

"No charges were pressed even though it happened many times. I told my mother and she didn't believe me. She said that if I told anyone else, we would all be in big trouble."

"How could she say that?"

"I don't know. At twelve, I didn't understand how wrong it was for her to respond that way. I did know that I hated what Rivers was doing to me. I lived in constant fear that my bedroom door was going to open. I stopped sleeping, I was failing school."

"What happened?" he asked, his voice subdued.

"A teacher contacted a social worker, who called

my mother. I don't think my mother ever admitted to the social worker what was happening, because Rivers was never arrested. But it evidently scared my mother enough that she decided that she and I were leaving. That night we packed the car while Rivers was working second shift at the factory. I was so grateful that I didn't ask many questions. It was only years later that I realized that we left because my mother was afraid that she was going to be arrested because she'd allowed it to happen."

"I'm…so sorry," he said.

She could see the distress on his face. She put a hand on his cheek. "It's okay. It's over. It's been over for a long time."

He didn't respond. Probably because he knew her words were empty. Things like that were never really over.

"We moved to Utah. To another trailer park. My mother said she wasn't angry with me, but I knew she was. She blamed me."

"You know that's ridiculous?" he said.

"I do now. At twelve, I figured she was right. She and Rivers got divorced and my mother never remarried. I think that somehow she blames me for that, too. That she's had to spend her life alone because of me."

"Just because a person is an adult, it doesn't mean she has mature thinking skills," he said.

"Very true. It was a difficult environment to live in. I quit school when I was sixteen and left home."

She stopped and looked at him expectantly.

"That was probably a really scary thing to do," he said.

She waved a hand impatiently. "Brody, I never graduated from high school. You were already in med school, about to graduate at the top of your class, and you were engaged to a high-school dropout. I always made a joke about not being ready for college. It had nothing to do with being ready. I couldn't enroll because I didn't meet the minimum entry requirements."

"I wouldn't have cared," he said. "I would have helped you."

She shook her head sadly. "I wanted to tell you. When you asked me to marry you, I told myself that I deserved you and all the happiness that you'd brought into my life. But then you started interviewing for positions. A couple of the hospitals invited us to dinner. And I realized that in the world that you were entering, people would make judgments about you based on their impressions of me."

"You made a wonderful impression. Everyone loved you."

"I have a criminal background, Brody. I was arrested six days after I turned eighteen. I spent thirty-two days in jail."

He swallowed hard, probably because he wasn't totally unaware of what young girls on the street did to earn money for food and shelter. "For what?"

"I vandalized a man's car. I was working at a bar. Those are the only jobs a young girl without a high-school diploma can get. This guy kept coming on to me. Wouldn't take no for an answer. One night, after he'd put his hand up my skirt, I went a little crazy. I took bottles and bottles of alcohol and broke them open inside his vehicle. The interior of his Audi was a mess of broken glass and liquor."

"He deserved it, Elle. He was a jerk. And it makes

sense. You had a history of abuse. It was no wonder that you reacted that way to unwanted advances."

She shrugged. "There were too many things. At some point, at some time, it was all going to come out that Dr. Brody Donovan was married to a high-school dropout with a criminal record. I could not be the first not-perfect thing in your life. I could not let the man who never made a mistake make a real whopper. I just couldn't."

BRODY WAS STUNNED. Speechless. She'd left to protect him.

He stood up and walked around the small room. He felt as if there was energy bubbling up in his body and that the top of his head would blow off if he couldn't expel some of it. His heart was pounding in his chest.

The thirteen-year-old mystery was solved. She hadn't left because she didn't love him enough; she'd left because she loved him too much.

It had never seemed more important to say the right words. He stopped walking and faced her. Her face was pale and streaks of fresh tears ran down her cheeks.

She was beautiful.

"Elle, I am not perfect. And I'm sorry that you ever felt that you needed to be perfect for me. I don't expect that, I don't want that."

"But—"

He held up a hand to silence her. "Please, let me finish," he said. "You are very smart and probably the most courageous and giving woman I've ever met. You survived something that no child should have to survive. How you managed that, I'll never know but it tells me that you can survive anything." He shook his head at her. "You do realize that you were on your own at an age where I still needed my mother to iron my shirts. I'm the one who's not worthy."

"Don't be ridiculous," she said.

"You say that to me a lot. I don't care if I'm ridiculous. Not as long as you're there to witness it. You're an amazing woman, Elle. I thought that thirteen years ago and I still think it today. I love you, Elle."

She launched herself into his arms. "Oh, Brody. What did I ever do to deserve you?"

"We deserve each other. We're perfect for each other."

He kissed her, his tongue in her mouth, his body holding her tight. And then he backed her up until the back of her knees touched the end of the bed. He gently pushed her backward and when she collapsed, he followed her down onto Leo's wrinkled sheets. And he made sweet love to her.

WHEN ELLE WOKE UP, she could feel the jungle heat seeping into the small hut. Brody was cutting slices of mango, arranging them on a tray with hunks of cheese and bread.

"Hungry?" he said, turning toward her.

"Yes. I'm still having thoughts of cheeseburgers and fries," she said.

He shrugged. "I'm sorry. That's what they're having in the hut next door. You, unfortunately, landed in the fruit, cheese, bread and peanut butter hut."

"Better than the Brussels sprouts and eggnog hut."

"For sure." He handed her a piece of bread with peanut butter. "Once we land in the States, I'll take you for a cheeseburger and fries. Maybe a chocolate shake if you're really nice."

They'd talked a lot about what had brought them to this place but not much of what was next. As horrible as the trek through the jungle had been, these last hours had been an almost miraculous interlude, something that she had never anticipated, never even hoped for, because it just wasn't going to happen.

But it had. And it would soon be over. "What are your plans when you get back to the States?" she asked.

"I have a job waiting for me in San Diego. I'm joining a group of orthopedists. I hope that I never see another bombing victim." He ate a piece of cheese. "What about you?"

"I need to find a place for Mia and me to live. Then get her enrolled in a school. Then find a job." She smiled. "I guess I have about a thousand things to do, all equally important."

He stared at her and she felt herself get even warmer. His gaze was intense. "San Diego has really great weather—good for a kid who is used to a warm climate with lots of sunshine. I mean, you wouldn't want to go to Seattle or Buffalo or someplace like that."

His tone was challenging. "I wasn't thinking Seattle or Buffalo," she said.

"San Diego has the ocean, too. And a great zoo. I'm sure there are some wonderful schools for Mia and probably lots of jobs for teachers."

What the heck was he saying? Did he want her to come to San Diego? Did he want her and Mia to be with him?

"I guess there's more to San Diego than I realized," she said. "Maybe I should check it out."

"I wish you would," he said, his voice cracking at

the end. He cleared his throat. "You and Mia could stay with me. While you're looking," he added.

Baby steps. He was acting as if they should take a few baby steps after they'd run the 100-yard dash in less than five seconds. But he was right. The sweaty jungle sex, even if it had been spectacular, had been serendipitous. Living together, making a life together—that required careful planning, careful consideration.

It was enough to know that he wanted to see her again, to meet Mia. It was enough to know that somehow he'd found a way to forgive her for all the hurts she'd inflicted upon him so long ago.

It might take a little longer for her to forgive herself. She'd never considered that Brody would question that she hadn't loved him. She'd been so wrapped up in doubting that she was good enough that she hadn't even considered that he might question his own worth.

It said something that Brody, so confident, so smart, so damn together, had come a little undone. And that something gave her the confidence to say what definitely needed to be said.

"I'm sorry for what I did thirteen years ago, Brody. It was selfish and inconsiderate and I don't blame you for being very angry with me."

He shook his head. "Everything happens for a reason, Elle. We were together and then we were apart and now we've found each other again. All of that happened for a reason."

"It's almost noon. Leo should be here shortly," she said. "I'm going to step outside," she said, "and take care of some things. Fortunately, it appears that I am fully rehydrated."

"Be careful," he said.

"I won't go far," she promised. While she hated to do it, she slathered on mosquito repellant. Even a short time outside warranted some protection.

When she opened the door, the oppressive humidity and heat of the jungle hit her hard. She climbed down the steps and walked twenty feet into the trees. She looked around before squatting and taking care of business. She was pulling up her pants when she heard a noise off to her left. She advanced toward the edge of the tree line cautiously.

There was a man, heavily armed, approaching the hut.

Leo was not with him.

She had no idea whether he was friend or foe. All she knew was if he was the enemy, she was not going to let him surprise Brody.

There was really only one alternative.

"Hello," she said, her tone as confident as she could manage under the circumstances. "May I help you?"

BRODY HEARD THE three quick knocks followed by a sharp, separate knock. He picked up Mrs. Hardy's knife and carefully opened the door. He saw the man first, then Elle, and his heart rate shot up.

"It's okay," she said, reaching out for him. "Friend of Leo's. We met up outside." She turned back to the men. "This is Brody Donovan. Brody, meet Bob."

The dark-skinned man nodded and murmured hello in a very thick accent.

Brody would bet his last nickel that his real name wasn't really Bob.

"We have to go," the man said. "Leo has arranged transport and will meet us at a small airfield about ten miles from here."

Brody looked at Elle. Ten miles in the jungle was a long way. "We're walking?"

"Only for the first mile. We'll take river transportation for most of the trip, finishing up with a half-mile walk."

"You have a boat?" Elle asked.

Bob shook his head. "This particular river is too shallow for motorized craft. We have a sturdy raft." His voice was deep. "I brought you a few things to wear."

The things included drab-colored shirts and pants, much like Brody had seen people in the village wearing. There were hats for both of them.

"It is better if others do not realize that there is a woman with us," Bob said.

"No problem," Elle said. She pulled on new clothes. The pants were too big, but she rolled them at the waist. She put on the hat, tucking her short hair up inside the band.

Brody knew that up close, her fine features would never pass for a man's, but perhaps from a distance, others might be fooled. He pulled on his own new clothes and put his hat on.

"You don't exactly look as if you're out for a pleasure ride on the river," Brody said, his eyes on the guns that the man wore strapped across his chest.

Bob pulled out another big shirt from his bag. He pulled it on. "I have someone loading the raft right now with freshly picked fruit. We are going to look like three farmers, taking our crop to market."

Brody smiled at Elle. It could work. It had to work. "Do you know if Leo reported the plane wreck?"

"Yes. I suspect help is already on its way to your friends."

They walked single file, Bob in front, followed by Elle, then Brody. Brody smelled the river before he saw the narrow stretch of muddy water. It was twelve, maybe fifteen feet wide. There were dead fish floating near the shore. "Glad we boiled the water," he said to Elle, under his breath.

"That's why the work that Leo does is so important. Look," she said, nodding toward the river. "I think that's our ride."

It was a flat bamboo raft, maybe eight feet wide and twelve feet long. There were crates of fruit on both sides, keeping it balanced.

"What do you think?" Brody asked.

"I can't think. I'm too busy trying to walk like a guy," Elle whispered.

Brody smiled. Even in the grimmest of situations, Elle could make him laugh.

They got on the boat. He turned to help Elle but dropped his hand. He probably wouldn't help another guy.

There were four long poles, attached to the raft by thick rope. Bob untied and distributed three of them. He motioned for Elle to join him on his side and Brody took the other side.

It took Brody a couple minutes to get the swing of sticking his pole in the water, deep enough that he could touch the bottom, and then pushing off.

"On the count of three," Bob said, when it became apparent that both Brody and Elle needed a little direction. Fortunately, the river had a slight current that was flowing the same direction they were trying to go.

They got the hang of it pretty quickly and were making good progress. While it was hard work, it was still infinitely easier than fighting their way through the thick jungle. About ten minutes into their trip, Brody glanced over at Elle. It didn't matter if she was dressed in rags and swaggering around like a sailor—she was simply the most beautiful, sexiest woman he had ever met.

The past eighteen hours had been amazing. And she'd seemed receptive to the idea of staying with him in San Diego while she looked for housing. If he had his way, she wouldn't need to find a house. She and Mia could move in with him. They could find a good school for Mia and if his condo wasn't big enough, they could look—

He heard the bullet right before he saw Bob crumple to his knees. Brody lunged for Elle, grabbed her around the waist, pulled her down to the deck and lay on top of her. He could hear bullets hit the water, the raft, the crates of fruit.

He lifted his head.

Bob had been hit in the upper thigh. His pants were already soaked with blood. Still, he'd ripped his shirt open to get to his gun and he was firing toward shore, trying to protect them. Brody felt a bullet skim past his ear, so close that had he not bent his head at the last minute, he'd have caught the round in his head.

"Stay down," he said. He needed to help Bob. He got up but stayed low, crouching behind the crates of fruit.

Too late he realized that the threat was coming from both sides.

"Drop the weapon. Or we will kill her."

Chapter Fourteen

The accent was heavy, the cadence fast, but Brody understood. He also had excellent peripheral vision and he could see the two men who had waded out from the opposite shore of where the attack had originated. They both had their guns pointed at Elle.

The taller one boarded the small raft, causing it to sway in the shallow water. The other man, younger and shorter, maybe not much over five feet, grabbed the tie rope on the raft, keeping them from moving with the current. He started to pull them to shore.

The tall one yanked on Elle's arm, pulling her up. She stumbled to her feet. Her face was white.

Brody fought the urge to lunge and tear the man's arm off at its socket. *You were always so smart.* That's what Elle had told him. He needed to be smart now.

"You have caused us a great deal of trouble," said the man holding Elle's arm. He shook her hard enough that her head jerked back.

Was this Jamas? Now that he was closer, Brody could see that the man was older than he'd first thought. His patchy beard was gray. Brody guessed him to be in his sixties.

Elle had said that Jamas was in his early forties.

"Who are you?" Elle asked.

"Shut up or I will kill you where you stand."

Not Jamas for sure. Someone who worked for him, then. Who else wanted Elle dead?

If T. K. Jamas was not with the group, they would need to take Elle to him. The man was bluffing. He didn't intend to kill Elle.

Patch, as Brody dubbed him, waved his arm in the air and three other men emerged from the heavy tree line. One of them was swaying and Brody could see beads of sweat running down his face. He had his left forearm pressed against his abdomen, but Brody could still see the growing ring of fresh blood. Bob had landed a shot.

Five all together. One injured, but still the odds were not in their favor, because these men were all heavily armed and all he had was Mrs. Hardy's knife in his pocket.

"Who are your friends, Elle?" Patch asked.

She glanced impersonally in Brody's direction. "He told me his name is Brody. Our plane crashed. He was the only passenger in good enough shape to walk for help."

She was trying to help him. The hell with that. Except that her plan was good. If they knew there was a personal connection between the two of them, they would use it against them.

It was a risk, however. Would they realize that she was lying? Did they know that the two of them had spent the night together at Leo's?

Brody waited, his breaths so shallow that he was surprised he stayed conscious.

Patch shrugged. "You have bad luck," he said to

Brody. Then he ignored him and moved on to Bob. "Who is this man, Elle?"

"I don't know his name. My friend Leo hired him to take us upriver."

Brody understood what she was doing. The men had been waiting for them. That wasn't happenstance. Somehow they'd known that they were going to be on the river. That meant that information had leaked into the wrong hands. Into Jamas's hands. She no doubt was figuring that these guys had to know something about Leo.

The man looked satisfied.

She'd played it right.

But Brody realized it didn't matter when the short man still in the river started chattering in what Brody assumed was Portuguese. By the look on Bob's face, it wasn't good news for the rest of them. Patch nodded and the short man raised his gun and pointed it at Brody.

His finger was on the trigger.

"Wait. I'm a doctor. I can help him." Brody pointed to the man holding his gut.

Patch held up his free hand, stopping the shooter. "How do I know that you are telling the truth?" he asked Brody.

He was going to follow Elle's lead and give them as much of the truth as he could. "My name is Dr. Brody Donovan. I've been a physician for over ten years and I'm a board-certified orthopedic surgeon."

He saw the man's eyes change and a speculative look settle in them. It gave Brody the courage to keep going.

"I can help your man," Brody said. "He's got a bullet in his gut. It may have nicked his spleen or some other organ. I need to examine him, but I can't do it here." He wasn't sure how much English the man understood, but he made sure his tone was authoritative, as if he was used to being in charge, giving orders.

Patch seemed to make his decision quickly. He pointed at Elle and Brody and said something in Portuguese to the short man, who shrugged and switched his gun to Bob.

"You have been exceedingly helpful, but your time is up," Patch said.

Had the information leaked through Bob? By the look on Bob's face, Brody didn't think so. Everything about him, from the blazing hate in his dark eyes to the tenseness of his stance, screamed that he wanted to rip Patch's head off.

"I wouldn't help you. I've never helped you," Bob said.

Patch chuckled. "You're very stupid, you know." He nodded at the shorter man, giving permission for him to shoot.

"No," Brody said quickly. He had to take the chance. This man had risked his life to help him and Elle. "I don't know what your issue is with her, but as far as I'm concerned, everybody goes. Or I don't go."

There was some dialogue between Patch and the short man, with the short man furiously shaking his head. But Patch was clearly in charge, because finally he held up a hand, stopping the conversation. "If he makes one wrong move," he said, looking at Bob, "I will shoot him."

Bob showed no reaction to that, but Brody could see Elle's chest rise and fall with the deep breath that she took. It wasn't a huge victory, but somehow all of them were going to make it off the raft.

"It's time to go," Patch said. "The boss is not a patient man." He looked at Elle. "And you have made him angrier than I have seen him in a long time."

The other men spoke quietly to one another, nodding frequently, leaving Brody to speculate that when Jamas was irritated about something, it wasn't good for anyone.

Patch stepped closer to Brody. "I do not trust doctors. They live in their fancy houses and they do not care that they make many mistakes." His tone was challenging.

Brody didn't think backing down was in his best interest. The man was a bully, and bullies thrived on intimidation. "I haven't lived in a fancy house for a long time and I don't make very many mistakes," he said.

Patch shrugged, as if he couldn't care less. "Just know this, my new friend. If either of the injured men dies, it proves you are not a good doctor and of no use to me. You will be next."

Brody knew that he'd be lucky if both men didn't bleed to death before they got someplace where he could render treatment. A walk through the jungle was a death sentence for all of them.

He looked at Bob. "I need to stop the bleeding," he said.

Patch looked at his watch. "Two minutes."

Brody moved quickly. A quick look at Bob's leg told him everything he needed to know. The bullet had entered in the front thigh and gone through, leaving a slightly larger, more irregularly shaped exit wound.

Brody took off his shirt, scrunched it to make a rope and then wrapped it tight around Bob's thigh, just inches above the wound. It would slow or stop the bleeding. It was the best he could do.

The man was pale and his face was drawn in pain, but he did not cry out or complain. He breathing was steady.

Brody took a quick look at the other injured man. He was in worse shape. He was very pale and his breathing was short and fast. There was lots of blood on his shirt. "We need to put pressure on his wound," he said.

Patch released Elle's arm long enough to rip at the big shirt she was wearing. Buttons flew. "Use this," he said.

Elle hurriedly took the shirt off and tossed it to Brody. Brody got off the raft, which was now at the shore. He took a quick look at the man's wound and then quickly wrapped the shirt around his torso and tied it tight.

It would be a miracle if the man didn't die before they got to wherever they were going.

"Neither of these men can walk," he said. "We need to help them."

Patch pointed at his two healthy men that they should assist the man who'd been gut-shot. He let go of Elle's arm and pushed her toward Bob. "Help your friend," he said.

Brody and Elle each took a side, with Bob sandwiched between them. "Lean on me," Brody said. "Use Elle for balance."

The short man led the group, machete in hand. Then the gut-shot man with his two helpers. Then Brody, Bob and Elle. Finally, Patch brought up the rear. He walked with his gun pointed at Elle's back.

Fortunately, they didn't have to walk far. They went less than a quarter of a mile before they came upon a clearing and a waiting helicopter with a pilot in the seat. Still, Brody knew that for those carrying the injured, it was far enough to be carrying extra weight, and for the injured, it probably felt as if it had been a ten-mile-long death march.

They were loaded into the helicopter and Brody immediately went to work assessing Jamas's man. Now that he was closer to him, he could see that he was probably no more than twenty although his young face and body already showed signs of wear and tear.

He untied the makeshift tourniquet and peeled back the man's bloody shirt. He gently turned him to look at his back. No exit wound. The good news was that he wasn't bleeding out from the back. The bad news was that a single bullet could do a lot of damage to multiple organs. If he didn't open him up and retrieve the bullet, the kid was going to die for sure. If nothing else, the infection would kill him. "What's your name?" Brody asked.

"André," the man whispered through his crooked teeth.

"Okay, André," Brody said. "You're going to make it. Just hang on." He couldn't do much for him while they were on the helicopter. Brody looked up at Patch. "How long is the flight?"

"Not long. Fifteen minutes."

ELLE WAS SICK at the idea of coming face-to-face with T. K. Jamas. But she was not going to come apart now. Not when Brody had been so amazing. He'd been just seconds away from his own death when he saw the one card that he held that made him different.

And for whatever reason, it had been the right card.

She'd felt the physical reaction the man had when Brody said he was an orthopedic surgeon. The energy had run through his body, down his arm and into his hand that had been still tightly clamped around her arm.

The only logical explanation was that someone in Jamas's camp was injured or sick and needed health care. Physicians were certainly available in Brazil—there were many fine ones. There had to be some reason that the person wasn't seeking help from a more traditional source.

Maybe Jamas was dying. She could only hope.

It wasn't long before the helicopter landed in an open space and the group was hurried into a one-story wood frame house that seemed to literally grow from the exterior of the mountain. It had dark green siding and a green roof.

Once she was inside, she could see that the inside was much plusher than the exterior. It was larger than it appeared from the outside and she realized that it must extend deep into the hillside, safe from prying eyes from above.

They were led to a large room in the center of the house. It had a gleaming hardwood floor and beautiful rugs. There were oil paintings on all four walls, and lovely chandeliers hung from the ceiling. They were electric, which told her that there were likely generators pumping electricity into the house. Even Jamas was not powerful enough to have had electricity run into the jungle. Well, maybe he was powerful enough, but given the exterior and how it blended into the surrounding area, she doubted he wanted to draw that much attention to this property.

Oh, God. Was this where he brought the young girls?

Jamas was sitting on the brown leather couch in the middle of the room. He was holding a cup and she suspected it was tea. On more than one occasion when he'd visited the school, before she realized he was a monster, she'd brewed him a cup.

He did not get up when they entered. He did not look ill. If he didn't require a doctor, then who?

The man who had done the talking at the river grabbed her arm and yanked her to the front. She was going to have a hell of a bruise.

That was going to be the least of her injuries given the look in Jamas's eyes, and she felt the fear that she'd managed to keep at bay rocket up.

He wasn't a man who took risks.

But he'd given instructions to bring her to him alive. Which told her that he was confident that whatever he had planned for her, she would never testify against him.

She remembered what she'd learned when she contacted the authorities. It was believed that Jamas had been involved in human trafficking for years. The girls were whisked out of the country and sold to the highest bidder, to be at his mercy. To be used, abused.

She would rather be dead.

But first she needed to do what she could to insure that Brody and Bob were able to escape. Brody was certainly holding up his end of the bargain. He'd kept everyone alive so far. She had attempted to catch his eye once or twice before realizing that he was deliberately not looking at her or appearing to be too interested.

Jamas looked at the man holding her arm. He spoke in Portuguese. The only part that Elle really caught was the man's name. Felipe.

They were talking and assessing Brody. Brody met their stare. She heard Felipe say Brody's full name, then something else, and finally *orthopedic surgeon*.

Jamas got off the couch and walked toward Brody. He carried his tea with him. "I have resources, Dr. Donovan, that will tell me very quickly whether you're lying or not."

Brody shrugged. "I'm not lying. Brody Donovan. Grew up in Colorado. Went to medical school at Harvard in Boston. Did my residency at Mass General. For the last eight years, I've been in the air force, working as an orthopedic surgeon in Iraq and Afghanistan."

Elle could almost feel the energy radiating off Jamas. He was excited about something. It was eerily similar to Felipe's reaction.

"Felipe tells me that he's given you a challenge. You get to live awhile longer if you can save these two men."

"That's my understanding, but my chances are getting worse by the minute," Brody said. "These men need treatment. Now. I need a place to work."

Jamas smiled. "There is a clinic in the basement that I believe will suit your needs. And a nurse who can assist. But first things first." He walked back to the couch but did not sit. He stood in front of Elle.

"I want to know where Mia is," he said.

"I don't know," she replied.

He gently set his teacup down on the table. Then he hit her so hard across the face that she would have fallen down if Felipe had not still had his hand clenched around her arm.

"I will ask you one more time," he said, his tone insincerely polite. "Where can I find Mia?"

She shook her head.

He punched her in the stomach. Air burst out of her lungs and she bent double.

"I can see we are getting nowhere," he said. He walked over to a side table, pressed a button and spoke in Portuguese.

Less than a minute later, a woman entered the room. Probably in her late thirties, with very dark hair pulled back into a low ponytail, she wore white pants and a white shirt and Elle assumed she was the nurse that Jamas had mentioned. She carried a small white box.

She opened the lid, withdrew a syringe and took a step closer. She did not make eye contact with Elle.

"Hey," Brody said, his tone agitated. "Sounds as if you two have some history, but quite frankly, I could probably use a couple pair of hands in the operating room. Can she help?" he asked, pointing to Elle.

Jamas shook his head. "I'm sorry, Dr. Donovan. But I have other plans for Elle." He motioned for the nurse.

Elle tried to wrench her arm away, but Felipe held her tight. She felt the poke and a hot burn in her arm muscle. Then she didn't feel anything at all.

BRODY WAS GOING to kill Jamas. He was going to rip him apart, limb by limb. And then he was going to take Mrs. Hardy's knife and disembowel him. He wanted him conscious for that.

Then he was going to do the same to every other one of his little army, too, starting with Felipe.

Jamas had hit her hard enough to crack a cheekbone or loosen some teeth. And the punch to the stomach had been brutal.

The man was an animal.

When Brody realized that Jamas intended to drug

Elle, he'd almost blown it. Had hoped that Jamas would buy that he might need an extra pair of hands patching the men up. But either Jamas didn't care or his hatred of Elle ran so deep that nothing would sway him from his original purpose.

Only the knowledge that what Jamas seemed to really want was Mia's location kept him from ripping that syringe out of the nurse's hand. The drug might be something that would make Elle sleep or even make her ill, but Brody didn't think that Jamas intended to kill her.

Not yet.

Whatever the drug had been, it had knocked her out fast. Her knees had buckled and Felipe had half carried, half dragged her from the room. They'd gone to the right. After that, he'd lost the sound of the footsteps.

He was worried sick about her. Even if the medication didn't kill her, depending on what it was, it could still to do significant damage to internal organs, to a person's mind.

"Maria, can you show the doctor and his patients to the clinic?" Jamas asked the question as if he were a genteel host offering an opportunity to peruse the flower garden.

Maria nodded and put away her syringe.

Jamas motioned for two of his men to assist André, whom to this point Jamas had not even acknowledged. How the man inspired loyalty, Brody had no idea.

The interplay between Jamas and Felipe was odd. Jamas was clearly the boss and Felipe the employee. Felipe's attitude had been appropriately deferential, yet there'd been a subtext that Brody couldn't quite figure out.

And right now he needed to focus on other things.

Brody motioned for Bob to drape an arm across his shoulder. Brody glanced at the leg. The tourniquet had been very effective in stopping the flow of blood, which meant that Bob had hit the lottery and managed to avoid any severed arteries or veins.

All they needed was for a few other things to start going their way and maybe they could escape from this hellhole in one piece.

Maria walked quickly, leading the group down a hallway. At the end, she opened a door and started down some steps.

Great. He was going to get to do surgery in the basement.

He'd done it in worse places.

But when Maria flipped the light on, Brody almost stumbled. It was amazing. In the middle of the Amazon jungle, tucked into a remote hillside, Jamas had built himself a modern clinic. It was well lit, with an exam table, a glass-fronted cabinet full of medications and two shelves stocked with medical supplies. There were boxes of gloves and a stack of what appeared to be pale blue lab coats wrapped in plastic.

Maria motioned for the men to put André on the table. They did as instructed, then took spots on either side of the door, as if prepared for the prisoners to make a break for it.

Brody settled Bob in the chair. "I'll be with you as quick as I can," he said.

He walked over and studied the medications in the cabinet. Many, many analgesics, used for treating pain. Both over-the-counter and narcotics. Hydrocodone. Oxycodone. Several different types of antibiotics. For the first time in what seemed forever, Brody felt a ray of hopefulness. In these surroundings, with these medications, he should be able to save both Bob and André.

It was his first test. Both Felipe and Jamas seemed to want some proof of his capabilities. Jamas had pounced on his qualifications and Brody had no doubt that the man was upstairs, somehow checking out his credentials. That's why he'd told him the truth. For some reason, his medical skills were important. Jamas didn't look ill. Neither did Felipe or the other men.

But Brody was willing to bet that somebody in this house was. That was the only possible explanation.

Maria washed her hands in the small sink in the corner of the room and pulled on blue surgical gloves and a lab coat that came to her knees. Then she selected instruments from the cupboard and placed them on a tray. He watched her. It appeared that she knew what she was doing.

"Maria, do you speak English?"

"No talking," instructed one of the men in a heavy accent.

Brody threw him a glance. "A doctor needs to be able to quickly and efficiently communicate with his nurse, especially when I'm digging bullets out of people. I need to know what she understands."

The man frowned but he nodded at Maria.

"I have been a nurse for over twenty years," she said. "I worked in a small hospital near Salvador for most of that time. I have delivered babies, cut off legs and held people's hearts in my hand."

"Okay, then." He repeated the same routine as Maria, washing his hands, gloving and gowning up. Then he selected some local anesthesia from the cabinet and drew up a syringe.

"André," he said. "I'm going to remove the bullet. You'll be awake while I do it, but this will numb the area."

The young man nodded, looked up at the ceiling, and made the sign of the cross.

Brody would take whatever help he could get.

Chapter Fifteen

Elle woke up with the worst headache that she'd ever had in her life. It took effort to open her eyes. She was lying on a wooden floor in a totally empty room. She raised her hand to feel the side of her jaw and it felt as if her arm weighed a hundred pounds.

She'd been drugged. She remembered the nurse poking her and then it had been lights out.

She patted her jaw. It was tender.

Her stomach hurt, too.

But what was worse was a horrifying realization to know that Felipe, who dragged her into this room, had had his hands on her body and she'd been totally unable to protest in any way. It made her empty stomach cramp up.

She had no idea where she was or how long she'd been out. She looked at the walls. Real wood, not the thin bamboo that most huts were made of. The ceiling wasn't hatch—it was wood, like the floor. So she was likely still inside Jamas's house.

There were no windows in the room and only one door. She got up off the floor and tried to turn the handle. Locked. From the outside.

Jamas was holding her prisoner. Why the heck hadn't

he just killed her? Then there would be no question that she'd never testify against him.

He'd have to kill Brody and Bob, too. The irony was heartbreaking. She'd left Brody thirteen years ago so that he would have the kind of life that she wanted him to have. Now she'd led him into terrible danger.

And she hadn't even had the courage to tell him that she loved him. That she'd always loved him.

He would try to save her. But he wouldn't be any match for Jamas. Brody had a conscience and there were things that he would not and could not do. Jamas had no conscience and the sky was the limit on what he was willing to do, what he was willing to subject his victims to.

She heard a noise outside the door. Locks flipping. The handle turned. And then Jamas walked in. He wore a clean silk shirt and pants and sunglasses, which made no sense at all. He carried a cup of tea and she suspected it was fresh because she could see steam coming off the cup.

"Well, well. The little stool pigeon is awake," he said. "How nice."

He didn't sound as if he thought it was really nice. She said nothing.

"What? No questions? No conversation? You disappoint me, Elle. You were always the life of the party."

"Where am I?" she asked.

He smiled. "Why, you're a guest at my home, of course."

"Do you lock all your guests in?" she asked, unable to keep her hatred below the surface.

Again the smile. "Only the troublesome ones. And you, Elle, have caused me a fair amount of trouble. But that's behind us. Now I am going to make a good profit on you. Maybe I'll donate a pittance of it to that stupid little school that you work at. Would you like that, knowing that you helped the helpless? You'll be a true martyr, Elle, because where you're going, your life is going to be hell. Maybe worse than hell."

She felt a chill settle in her body.

He came close and he raised his free hand. She braced herself for another hit across the face. Instead he gripped her chin hard. "Captain Ramano was a fool. He was supposed to take off and land in short order so that I could remove you from the plane. Fortunately for me, I didn't trust that he would follow directions and I made sure that his plane wouldn't fly for long. I was confident that no one would survive the plane crash. But I had to be sure. We were looking for the plane when we saw you. I'm suddenly very glad that Felipe is not a great shot. I must admit. I was very angry at first, especially when we couldn't find you afterward. And poor Felipe was worried that it might prove to be his last mistake. That even his trusted service to my father for all those years would not be enough to save him. But then he redeemed himself by finding not only you, but the good doctor as well."

"I'm so sorry to hear that you're ill," she said, her tone dripping with sarcasm. She was not going to let this man know that he intimidated her. He would revel in the knowledge. Plus, maybe it would encourage him to say why he needed Brody.

He tightened his grip. "Sassy. I'll have to make sure I include that in your information. Many men will pay extra for the chance to teach a feisty woman to be submissive."

The idea of it made her sick, but she didn't flinch. "Whatever," she said.

He smiled. "Are you even curious about how we found you?"

It had to have been through Leo. Her friend would have died before he'd willingly revealed their location, so she could only assume that Jamas had somehow forced the information from him. "I'm not sure it matters," she said.

Now he laughed. "True." He released her chin and walked toward the door. "You'll be happy to know that I let your little friend Leo live. I thought about killing him, but unfortunately, he's well-known and favored by the natives. Don't need that kind of trouble. He does need to hire better help. Bob's housekeeper has been on my payroll for years. You see, he also does some security work for the government and I like to keep my eye on what he's doing."

Leo would be sick at the thought that he'd led Jamas to Elle. He would never forgive himself.

"In addition to dusting and sweeping," Jamas continued, "she monitors the tracking software on Bob's computer that allows her to see every file, every message, every keystroke actually. Wonderfully helpful, really. When she relayed the information about your need to be accompanied up the river, she had no idea that she was giving me the best present ever. It was a brilliant stroke of good luck."

By now, Leo probably knew they had not reached their destination. She remembered what Leo had said about there being eyes in the jungle. She supposed it was possible that there could have been natives in hiding, watching everything that occurred at the river. If that information somehow got to Leo, he'd know that she and Brody were in Jamas's clutches.

He would call the authorities, perhaps both local and in the States. He would have no other choice. She did not have much faith that the local police would be of much assistance. Jamas likely made large contributions that insured that they looked the other way. If Leo could get the attention of someone in the United States, it was unlikely that they could respond in time to save them.

It was a very bad situation.

"Nothing to say now?" Jamas taunted her, his hand on the door.

"Yes," she said. "Go to hell."

Jamas snorted. "That's where you'll be. You'll be wishing you were dead. You know, if you'd just tell me where Mia is hiding, perhaps I could be persuaded to find a buyer who is a bit more compassionate."

She pressed her lips together.

"This is tiresome," he said, his tone angry. "Just wait, pigeon. Spend the little time you have reflecting upon why it's never a good idea to cross T. K. Jamas."

He left, closing the door behind him with a solid thud. She heard the locks slip shut.

She sank down onto the cold floor and drew her legs up tight. She had desperately wanted to ask about Brody, to know what was going on with him.

I love you, Brody. She willed him to hear her silent message.

MARIA PROVED TO be a very competent assistant and in less than twenty minutes, Brody had removed a bullet from André, repaired the damage to his liver and sewn up his gut. André's injuries were out of his normal scope, but he was happy enough with the results when he was finished.

The men standing at the doorway proved to be helpful when they assisted in transferring their comrade onto a cot. André was pale but alert. He gripped Brody's hand and nodded his thanks.

"You'll be okay," Brody said. It was not the first time in his life that he'd performed surgery on an enemy. That happened during war, too.

When it was Bob's turn, Brody thought he'd see significant muscle and tissue damage because the bullet had traveled all the way through the thigh. It was about what he'd expected and not all that different from many of the injuries he'd been treating for years. Brody made the repairs and sutured both the entry and exit wounds.

Bob would need months of physical therapy to regain the strength and motion in his leg. But for both men, the most immediate worry was infection. However, Jamas's selection of antibiotics was quite extensive, likely because even a scratch in the jungle could be problematic without an effective antibiotic. Maria selected one off the shelf. Brody examined the choice, agreed with it and picked up the first syringe.

Delivering the drugs intravenously was the best way to get a strong antibiotic into them quickly.

"These men need to rest," he said.

"We have another cot in the room next door," Maria said. She motioned for the men standing by the door to move André's cot to the other room. When they returned, they linked arms and carried Bob out of the room. When they were out of earshot, Brody took his chance.

"You're a good nurse, Maria. What are you doing here, working for Jamas?"

The woman looked over her shoulders, as if to make sure that she would not be overheard. "It's not a terribly complicated explanation," she said, her tone sad. "Jamas pays three times what I could make working somewhere else. My sister and her husband were killed in a car accident two years ago. My mother is raising their four children. My financial contribution is very helpful. Plus I am able to go see the children once a month."

"Those are good reasons, but you have to know this isn't right. He's going to kill us, isn't he? You've seen it before."

Maria did not answer.

Brody took a chance. "Will you help us? Show us a way out?"

The woman met his look, her brown eyes flat. She'd sold her soul a long time ago. "I will not help or hamper any escape efforts. That's the best I can do."

Brody heard returning footsteps. "Why does Jamas need a full-time nurse?" he asked quickly.

"You'll see," Maria said cryptically.

When the men returned, Brody was on one side of the room and Maria was on the other, tidying up the supplies.

"Now what?" Brody asked.

"So far so good," Felipe said, entering the room. With a motion of his hand, he dismissed the other two men. "Come with me, Doctor."

Felipe pointed him toward the stairs and Brody went. Instead of taking him back to the big room where they'd first met Jamas, Felipe led him down a hallway. He unlocked a door and motioned for Brody to enter. There was a single bed and a dresser with a lamp.

"You will wait in here," Felipe said. Then he left.

Brody heard the door lock engage and knew that Felipe had used a key to lock him in. He sat down on the bed. The mattress was firm and the bedding looked new. Evidently Jamas didn't entertain in this room often.

But for some reason, he'd given it to Brody. And even Felipe seemed to have a slightly different attitude toward Brody than he had initially. Certainly not deferential but there was perhaps a reluctant respect. Whatever it was, he intended to use it to his advantage.

Now it was a waiting game. How long would it take for Jamas to tip his hand?

He had to find some way to insure Elle's safety, some way to convince Jamas that Elle was necessary, without tipping his own hand that Elle mattered.

It was like walking on a tightrope over a swamp filled with alligators. One wrong move and he'd be toast.

He could not fail Elle.

Hang on. Just hang on, Elle. Be strong. Don't let the bastard win.

His bag was in the corner of the room, on the chair. No doubt someone had searched it by now. There was nothing in there to see. He had Mrs. Hardy's knife in his pocket still. He fought the desire to reach in, to touch it, to feel the sharp point. But he didn't. He would be surprised if the room was not monitored. Probably for sound and there could even be a camera. He wasn't taking any chances.

Jamas wouldn't be happy if he knew that his men were sloppy. They had taken Bob's gun and roughly searched him for other weapons, but they hadn't done the same for Elle and him.

He still had his matches in his shirt pocket and one

other ace up his sleeve. He could feel the slight weight of the pen flare guns around the waistband of his pants. Before leaving camp that first morning, he'd grabbed the plastic bag that contained the three pen flares and thrown it into his bag.

Pen flares were easy to use. Simply screw the flare onto the end of the cylinder, aim high, pull back on the trigger and let it go. The flare could usually go a couple hundred feet in the air. But it only burned for seconds, maybe six or seven. That was why flares were generally only an effective tool if your rescuer was already in the general vicinity and you were attempting to help him pinpoint your location.

He had dropped the bag of flares on top of his clean shirts and started to zip his bag but stopped. Something that he'd learned about flares probably twenty-five years ago from some Scout leader suddenly had popped in his head. *Always be ready.* He remembered the man telling the troop that people sometimes wore flares around their necks on a lanyard, just so they would be available fast.

Brody sure as hell hadn't wanted to be in the position of searching in his bag when an opportunity of rescue suddenly presented itself. He also hadn't wanted to take the chance on losing the flares if he somehow got separated from his bag.

So he'd taken an extra two minutes and used the needles and thread from Elle's sewing kit and stitched the plastic bag to the inside of his waistband.

Of course, that effort would likely be for naught if Leo had not been able to act upon his final instructions. Had Jamas already killed the man?

If Leo was somehow still alive, would he remember

what Brody had told him outside the small jungle hut before Leo left him and Elle for the night? If he remembered, would he act upon it or would he be too scared to go up against Jamas?

If he acted upon the instructions, Brody had no doubt of the response on the other end. His friends would want to help. But with no communication systems available, coordinating the plan was going to difficult if not impossible.

Tell them this, Leo. Exactly this. Come at the Witching Hour.

The man had looked at him oddly, but he'd nodded. Brody had not wanted to tell him anything else. While he knew that Elle trusted Leo and the man had been very helpful so far, he hadn't felt inclined to give him more information.

Ethan and Mack would know the Witching Hour.

Of course, even if they came, there was no guarantee that they would be close enough to see a flare and more importantly, that he and Elle would be in position to take advantage of a rescue effort.

Brody forced himself to breathe. One obstacle at a time. That's what he needed to deal with. So far they'd managed to all stay alive.

If it was a chess game, the next move was Jamas's.

Chapter Sixteen

He realized he wasn't going to have to wait long, because he heard footsteps coming down the hall. The lock flipped. Jamas and Felipe entered. Jamas had a cup in one hand. He was close enough that Brody could smell the scent of the strong black tea. They did not close the door. "Come with us," they said.

Brody stood up. Jamas led the way, with Brody following and Felipe trailing behind. They walked down yet another hallway. Brody was starting to get a feel for the house. It was oddly shaped, but then again, it was more cave than structure, given that it was mostly underground. The living room where they'd first met was in the center of the house and then there were multiple hallways, like spokes of a bicycle wheel, leading off from it. So far he'd been down the hallway that led to the clinic in the basement and now this one. He suspected that meant that wherever they were keeping Elle, it was down one of the other two remaining halls.

Jamas went to the very end, the last door. He knocked.

"Come in."

It was a woman's voice. Not Elle's.

Jamas opened the door. An attractive woman, probably in her late sixties, sat in a chair, reading a book. She wore a blue robe and had a blanket over her legs. She looked up and smiled but did not speak.

Jamas kissed her on both cheeks. "My mother," Jamas said, his voice proud.

Brody nodded. Did she have any idea that her son was a horrible man?

"Evening, Rita," Felipe said. "You're looking well."

The woman smiled. "Thank you, Felipe. You've always been an accomplished fibber."

Brody wasn't sure, but he thought Felipe was blushing. Was this part of the odd relationship that existed between Jamas and Felipe? Did Felipe have some kind of thing going with Jamas's mother?

"This is Dr. Donovan," Jamas said. "He is here to help you."

Well, that solved that part of the mystery. She was the patient. Brody saw the wheelchair in the corner of the room.

"My mother has had arthritis for many years. She is in constant pain and it has robbed her of her strength and her enjoyment of life. Doctors have said that her condition has resulted in the loss of much of the cartilage in her knees and they should be replaced. She is no longer able to walk on her own, and even taking care of her own basic needs is becoming more difficult. Maria is very helpful with that, but Mother does not like having to depend on her."

"There are many good hospitals in Brazil," Brody said. "Knee replacements are a common surgery."

Jamas shook his head. "She will not go. Her husband of forty-five years, my father, died three years ago at a hospital. He went in for a routine operation to remove his gallbladder and he was dead within twenty-four hours."

Now Felipe's comment about doctors and their mistakes made sense. "But surely…"

"She will not go," Jamas repeated. "And I will not make her. But if she could have the surgery here, in her own home, that would be different."

He could do it. But even with Jamas's connections, it would likely take days before he could secure the right implants. The idea of being in Jamas's home, of Elle being in Jamas's sights for that long, was repulsive.

Almost as if he'd been reading Brody's mind, Jamas spoke again. "We have already purchased the necessary medical supplies. I have three types of knees from three different manufacturers. I had thought at one time that Maria might be able to do the surgery, but she lacks the confidence, which makes me not confident."

"There are risks to any surgery," Brody said. "With knees, there can be infection or blood clots that result in cardiac arrest or stroke."

"You need to keep my mother safe," Jamas said. "I checked you out, Donovan. You're exactly who and what you say you are."

It was time to play the final card. "I'd do the best I could. And Maria is very helpful. But I am used to having two nurses with me in the operating room. I need another pair of hands."

Jamas looked at Felipe. The older man shrugged, then said, "Peitro can help. He does not mind blood."

"Are his hands delicate and small? I need someone with small hands because I'll be working in a very tight space." It was pretty much bull that he was feeding them, but they were so focused on moving forward with the surgery that they didn't seem to realize it.

Jamas and Felipe spoke in Portuguese. After several minutes, Jamas nodded. "Earlier you asked if Elle could assist you. We will allow that."

Brody shook his head. "I only asked for her because I didn't see anybody else. I'm not crazy about the idea of working with her. Based on what I've seen so far, she's the reason I'm in this mess."

Jamas smiled. "I understand your hard feelings, but Elle will assist you."

Brody ran his hand through his hair. "Listen, I'll do the damn surgery and I'll do a good job. Your mother will be dancing in a week. But I want a little something in return. I quite frankly don't care what happens to the woman. Can we agree that you'll let me go, once you know that your mother is okay, of course? I won't tell anybody that I was ever here and you'll never hear from me again."

The two men exchanged a look. Finally, Jamas spoke. "Yes. That seems fair. You will be free to go."

It was an empty promise. Brody knew that he and the rest of the group would be killed just as soon as Jamas didn't need them anymore.

"Thank you," Brody said, hoping that he sounded genuine. Maybe Jamas didn't even think it was odd that Brody could so easily walk away from Elle without a backward glance. It was the world he lived in, where sacrifice and caring for others was simply not done.

"You will do the surgery now," Jamas said.

The sooner Brody could see Elle, the better. But he wasn't ready to make a move. If help was coming, they hadn't yet had enough time to get into place. "Has your mother eaten recently?"

"She had lunch several hours ago."

"It's dangerous to do surgery when someone has eaten, especially an older person. Only liquids from here on out and we do the surgery at eleven o'clock tonight. Before that, I will want to talk to Maria and I suppose Elle, too, about what I need from them. And we should all eat a meal. I don't want anyone passing out from hunger or dehydration during surgery."

Jamas nodded. He had probably been wanting his mother to have this surgery for years. Being delayed for a few hours, for what appeared to be a good reason, was not raising any concerns.

"Felipe will escort you back to your room."

On the way out, Brody turned toward the man. "I'd like to go back to the clinic. I want to check on the patients."

"Maria is watching them."

"I'd still like to take a look. Also, if you've got three different types of knees, I'd like to take a look at them now and identify the one I'll be working with. That will allow me to better explain the process to Elle and Maria."

Felipe motioned for him to walk down the hallway that led to the basement. When they got downstairs, Brody opened the door. Maria was indeed with the patients.

"How are they?"

"Both doing well," she said.

Good. Bob was going to have to be well enough to travel soon because they weren't leaving without him. "Thank you," Brody said.

He and Felipe went into the room with the exam table. Felipe pointed him toward the cabinet in the corner. Brody opened it and examined the contents.

Jamas hadn't been exaggerating. There were three major brands of prostheses to choose from. Brody picked one that he was most familiar with. He opened the package and examined the tibial component, then the femoral.

He left the box out and shut the cabinet doors. "So, how long have you been in love with Rita Jamas?"

He heard Felipe suck in a deep breath. "Shut up."

"Did you work for her husband?" Brody pressed.

He saw a range of emotions pass over the man's face. Brody wasn't worried about him responding physically. He needed Brody whole, with his hands in working order. Brody waited for him to turn away, to ignore the question. But Felipe didn't.

Maybe because no one had ever asked and he wanted to explain himself, perhaps especially to someone that he intended to kill very shortly so his secrets were guaranteed to be safe. "For twenty-five years," he said. "I respected him. He was not only my employer, he was my friend."

"And somewhere along the way, you fell in love with his wife."

Felipe held up finger. "And never once acted upon it until the man was dead, even when he was unable to leave his bed for the last two years of his life. Never once. I would not do that to him and Rita is too much of a lady."

"You hate seeing her in pain."

"It has become much worse this last year. She rarely leaves her room."

"What were you going to do if I hadn't fallen in your lap?"

Felipe smiled, showing yellowed teeth. "That's an interesting way of putting it. I had other options. I had already identified the top orthopedic surgeons in Brazil."

The plan was pretty obvious. "She wasn't going to them, but you were going to make sure that one of them came to her."

"People will generally do what you want, especially when you have a gun pointed at their wife or their child."

Brody doubted that Felipe would have lost a minute of sleep over it. Not if it helped Rita Jamas. While the plan was twisted, the devotion was admirable. And Brody was counting on it working in his favor later.

"Come," Felipe instructed. "It is time for you to return to your room. Maria and Elle will join you. You can eat and discuss and then perhaps all get some rest. I want all of you very fresh. Now you understand why it is important to me that this operation go very well. If it does not, you will all pay. Immediately."

"Understood," Brody said. "I'll keep up my end of the bargain if you'll keep up yours. I get to walk away and not look back."

"Of course," Felipe said quickly.

Brody could hardly wait to see Elle, to know that she was okay. He wanted to run down the hall, but he forced himself to walk alongside Felipe and to wait patiently while the man unlocked the door to his room. He nodded his thanks and sat down on his bed, as if he didn't have a care in the world.

Felipe left, shutting and locking the door behind him. It was eighteen minutes before he heard footsteps coming down the hall. The door was unlocked, then opened.

And there was Elle. Looking beautiful.

The side of her face was slightly swollen where Jamas had hit her. But she looked alert and otherwise unharmed.

Her eyes lit up when she saw him, but she didn't cry out or make any other motion.

Felipe stood behind her. "Dr. Donovan needs your assistance. You will provide it to him."

"Assistance with what?" she asked.

"With surgery," Brody interjected. "A double knee replacement."

"Dr. Donovan will explain to you what needs to be done," Felipe said.

"Do I have a choice?" she asked.

Before Felipe could answer, Brody stepped forward. "Look, I don't either, so I'd appreciate it if we could just make the best of this. You got me into this mess. You could at least try to be helpful now."

She let out a sigh. "I guess I did. Fine. What do I need to do?"

"I'll walk you through the process now," he said. "Before the actual surgery, I'll show you the instruments and explain what I'll need from you."

She nodded.

"I've arranged for us to have some food. We can talk while we eat."

She walked into the room.

"Do you have any paper?" Brody asked Felipe. "It's easier if I can draw pictures to explain the process."

"I will make sure some is delivered along with your food." Felipe stepped back, closed the door and locked it.

Brody got in front of Elle and deliberately rolled

his eyes, trying to tell her that they were likely being watched. She must have understood because she made no move to touch him. She sat on the chair, near the dresser. He sat on the bed.

They said nothing to each other.

It was another five minutes before Maria joined them, carrying a tray of sandwiches. There was also cut-up fruit, several different kinds mixed together, and cookies. It looked delicious. Jamas lived well.

Felipe was behind her. His hands were free. There was a second man, whom Brody recognized from the river, carrying a card table and one chair. He unfolded the table and motioned for Maria to take the chair. Elle pulled her chair up to the table. Brody sat back down on the bed.

The three of them ate. Brody watched Elle chew, still concerned about her jaw and the blow she'd taken. But she seemed to be doing okay.

Once they were finished, Brody pushed the plates to the side. Then for the purposes of Maria and Elle and whoever else was likely monitoring the room, Brody went through the surgery process with painstaking detail. He made a big deal of identifying when he would need both Maria's and Elle's help at the same time just in case Jamas suddenly got the idea that Elle's presence wasn't necessary.

He picked up the pencil and drew a picture of a kneecap and pointed out where he'd be cutting damaged bone and the process of inserting the implants. He turned his head toward Elle. "Since you've never done this, let me shade that so you can see it better," he said.

He made a big deal of shading and erasing, then shading some more. Maria leaned back in her chair and picked up her half-eaten cookie. *I will not help or hamper.* It appeared she was living up to her end of the bargain.

He quickly wrote, "I have a plan. Tonight." He pushed it toward Elle. Saw that she read it. Pulled it back. "That's still not quite right," he said. "Guess I'm not an artist." He erased the note, then drew over it just to make sure that his words couldn't be seen later. "This is better," he said, giving her another look.

"I think I have it," she said. "I can do it."

He knew what she meant.

Plan was really stretching it. It was more of a shot in the dark.

There was no need to tell her that.

He folded his drawings and left them on the table. It was only minutes later that the door opened and Felipe entered. He motioned for Maria to leave the room. "Come with me," he said to Elle.

She got up and left without a backward glance at Brody. The door closed and he heard the turn of the lock. He lay back on the bed and closed his eyes. But he could not rest. Energy was churning within him. His timing was going to have to be perfect. He would only have one chance.

AT EXACTLY ELEVEN o'clock, Brody heard his door lock flip. When the door opened, it was Felipe. "Let's go," he said.

They walked the length of the hall and then down the stairs. Felipe led him into the same room where he'd worked earlier. Elle and Maria were already there. So was Jamas and his mother. The room had been cleaned and Brody suspected that Maria had done it. Instruments were laid out. He inspected them. Again, this had to be Maria's work and she'd done a good job.

Brody motioned for Jamas to assist his mother in getting up on the exam table that was about to be turned into an operating table once again. The woman seemed frightened to death.

He looked the woman in the eye. "I want to assure you that I'm an experienced orthopedic surgeon and that this is going to go really well. You'll be taking a walk down the hall on your new knees by tomorrow."

"I am not afraid. I am tired of living with the pain."

"I understand. You're going to be awake for the surgery, but you're not going to feel a thing. I'm going to give you a mild sedative and then a regional anesthetic. It's called an epidural. It will numb everything from the waist down. Do you understand?"

She nodded, then shifted her eyes toward Felipe. He smiled at her.

"After the surgery," Brody continued, "we'll control your pain. Do you have any questions for me?"

The woman shook her head. "I am grateful for your help."

He wanted everybody grateful and happy and very celebratory. So far, Jamas had not played into his plan. He was going to have to improvise. "When this is over, we'll all have a drink."

"I have a glass of wine every day," she whispered, as if she was confiding some big secret.

"Good for you. I was thinking more along the lines of that tea your son was drinking earlier. It smelled delicious. My mother used to drink tea that smelled just like that."

The woman looked at her son. "T.K. has always loved

his tea. His father and I were coffee drinkers. I'm sure he'd be happy to share a cup."

Brody hoped so.

He walked over to the sink and scrubbed his hands and arms. Then he pulled on gloves. He motioned for Elle and Maria to follow the same routine.

"Ready, ladies?" he asked.

THE SURGERY WENT WELL. Damaged bone and cartilage were cut away and the implants set in place, to insure that the kneecap would move fluidly and without pain. Elle held up well, and he made sure to give her small tasks to do during the surgery. Felipe and Jamas stood quietly near the wall and did not interfere.

Maria anticipated what he would need. It almost made him angry. She was a very talented nurse. Yet she was squandering her gift on the likes of Jamas. It made no sense to him, but then again, he wasn't responsible for the financial welfare of four children.

After closing the surgical site, he stepped back. He took off his gloves and reached for Rita's hand.

"We're done," he said.

She nodded, still slightly under the effects of the medication he'd given her.

"Everything looks good," he said. He turned to look at Felipe and Jamas. "She did very well. I don't expect any complications. We'll need to watch her carefully for the next several hours. She may suffer some limited nausea from the anesthetic."

"Maria can watch her."

No, that wouldn't work. "If you prefer. She can be moved to her own room where she'll be more comfortable. She will need to be monitored for blood clots," Brody added, trying to give them something to consider.

Felipe and Jamas spoke in Portuguese. Brody was really getting a little tired of them doing that.

Their conversation was short. "Maria can clean up in here. Felipe will go with you to my mother's room," Jamas said. "I will return Elle to her room and join you later."

Brody wished he could think of an excuse to keep Elle with him, but there just wasn't anything that wasn't going to create suspicion and put his entire plan at risk.

"I'd appreciate a cup of that tea that we talked about earlier. I don't want to get sleepy."

Jamas shrugged. "I don't see why not. I think you've earned a cup, Doctor."

Chapter Seventeen

Elle and Jamas did not speak as he walked her down the hallway. She was so anxious that she felt as if she was going to jump out of her own skin.

Brody had told her that he had a plan.

Throughout the surgery, she'd been waiting for some sign, but there hadn't been anything unusual. At least not that she could see. He'd been calm, very methodical in his approach, giving direction to both her and Maria in a very gentle tone.

He'd been kind to Rita Jamas. That hadn't surprised her. Brody would not take out his feelings about Jamas or Felipe on Rita. He wasn't that type of man.

When the operation was over, she'd desperately wanted to say something to him and tell him how absolutely wonderful he'd been. She'd wanted to tell him that she loved him. She'd wanted to tell him goodbye. Because whatever his plan had been, it didn't appear to have worked out the way he'd intended.

"You'd have made a fine nurse, Elle," Jamas said, unlocking her door.

She didn't acknowledge the comment. She just walked into the empty room and stood against the far wall.

"Tell me where Mia is," he said, his voice quiet. "Make this easier on yourself."

She kept her lips pressed together.

Jamas waited.

He walked closer. Raised his hand. Slapped her across the face hard. Her head hit the wall.

"You're a fool, Elle," he said, his voice hard. "Your buyer will be here in just a few hours. Compared to him, I'm a pussycat. I'm going to get enjoyment in the future thinking about you, Elle. Imagining your life, if you want to call it that."

He turned and left the room and she heard the door lock.

She swallowed hard, afraid that she would throw up. He'd hit her on the same side as before. The already tender skin throbbed.

Time was running out.

BRODY GOT RITA settled in her bed. "I'm going to give her a little something for the pain," he said. He dumped two pills out of the bottle that he'd carried from the clinic. There was a carafe of water and a glass on her bedside table. He poured her a glass and helped her take her pills.

Felipe stood next to the bed, holding Rita's hand.

"I'll talk to Maria about the exercises she should do to aid her recovery," Brody said. "Before I leave in the morning." He had to keep acting as if he still believed that they were going to let him walk out once it got light outside.

Felipe did not respond. Brody wondered if it was possible that the man actually felt somewhat bad that Brody had held up his end of the bargain while Jamas and Felipe had no intention of holding up theirs. Did he have a conscience? Or had that slowly eroded away as he'd done one bad thing after another over the years?

After about ten minutes, the door opened. Jamas came in, carrying a tray. On it were three cups. He set down the tray and handed one cup to Felipe. "Coffee for you," he said. He handed the other cup to Brody. "And tea for you. Black tea with orange and a hint of clove," he said. "One of my favorites."

Then Jamas took the other chair, as if they were old friends visiting. "How is my mother?" he asked, before taking a sip out of his own cup.

"I think she's doing okay," Brody said, letting a little concern sneak into his voice.

Jamas sat up in his chair. "What's wrong?"

"I gave her a mild sedative before administering the epidural. Her breathing appears to be a bit labored now and she's not waking up as I'd hoped. I've seen this before with patients who are very sensitive to pain medication. It might be helpful if you talked to her. Patients can hear far into states of unconsciousness. Tell her something she'd be really interested in. Something that will stimulate her."

Jamas got up and stood next to Felipe. On the topic of Rita Jamas's health, the two men were united. They cared very deeply for her.

"Mama, it's T.K.," he said, his voice soft. "I planned our trip, you know, the one to the beach. I got us a lovely villa and they tell me the sunsets are…"

Brody tuned him out. He casually reached into the pocket of the blue lab coat that he still wore and then reached for his cup. In the process, he passed his hand over Jamas's cup.

After several minutes, he stood up and joined the men at the bed. Rita Jamas was still sleeping. It was no wonder given the medication that Brody had given her. It wouldn't hurt her, but the woman wasn't likely to be waking up for some time.

"She's not waking up," Jamas said, his tone concerned.

Brody used a stethoscope to check her lungs. "It's okay. She's breathing better," he said. "I think that worked."

Jamas nodded and backed away from the bed. He took his seat. "My mother has always loved the ocean," he said. "I do not think she would have been able to make the trip this year. But now I am confident that she will."

"There are no bad times at the beach," Brody said. He took a sip of tea and sighed in appreciation. He leaned his head back and closed his eyes.

Ten minutes later, he sensed movement next to him. He opened them just a slit.

Jamas had his hand on his abdomen, and his face had a pinched look. He said something to Felipe in Portuguese and made a quick exit out of the room.

Brody didn't need an interpreter. He knew where Jamas was headed. Where he'd be for the next thirty minutes.

Brody pulled the thermometer out of his pocket. "I'm going to check her vital signs," he said.

Felipe stepped back. Brody took Rita's temperature. Then reached into the pocket of his lab coat to pull out the stethoscope that he'd stuffed there.

He put his fingers around Mrs. Hardy's knife and

turned fast. In one smooth movement, he had it up against Felipe's throat.

"Be quiet," he said. "Or I'll kill you first and her second."

"No," Felipe pleaded, likely more for Rita than himself.

"Lie on the floor," Brody instructed.

When the man did, Brody placed his boot in the middle of his back. Then he took the sheet off the bed, sliced it into strips, and used it to tie the man's hands together. He yanked Felipe to his feet and walked him over to the chair. "Sit down," Brody said. He tied his feet together, then he took his longest strip and tied Felipe into the chair itself.

Cotton bedsheets were not the strongest material, but he'd been an Eagle Scout and knew how to tie a knot that wouldn't slip.

Finally, he took a small strip and gagged the man.

The last thing he did was remove the ring of keys from Felipe's belt.

He took a final look at Rita. "Good luck with the recovery, Rita." He hoped she'd soon be getting lots of exercise visiting her son in prison.

He opened the door a crack. He had not seen any of Jamas's other men all night and he hoped that they were safely away from the property. He ran down the hallway, knife in hand.

While he didn't know exactly which room was Elle's, he was confident he knew the hallway. He didn't think it was the hallway that led to the basement and the clinic, or the hallway that led to Rita's room. That left two. He decided that it wasn't going to be the one leading to the kitchen—too much foot traffic would go by.

He chose the remaining one and knocked on the last door on the right side. "Elle," he whispered.

No answer. He debated whether he should unlock the door, but what if it was someone else's room? It could be Maria's.

He crossed the hallway. Knocked softly.

"Elle?"

"Yes."

He was so relieved he almost dropped the keys. Now he just needed to find the right one.

It was the fourth key he tried.

He swung the door open and there was Elle. He gathered her up in his arms and pulled her tight. "Thank you, God," he said. "I was so afraid that I'd never hold you again."

She kissed him. "I love you, Brody Donovan. I've never stopped loving you." She took a breath. "I was afraid that I'd never get to tell you that. I. Love. You."

He kissed her nose. "I love you more."

"Where's Jamas and Felipe?"

"Felipe is all tied up and Jamas, well, he's out of commission, I hope. I was able to put some medication in his tea that is a very effective relaxant when used appropriately but when taken in a large dose causes bad stomach cramping and all the things that go along with that. I bought us a little time, but we have to go now."

He grabbed her hand, pulled her out into the hallway and looked at his watch. Seven minutes to two. The Witching Hour was approaching. It was something Mack McCann had thought of all those summers ago at Crow Hollow. *We'll meet at the Witching Hour.* It was code that only Ethan, Mack and Brody knew. Mack had said that most people would think the Witching Hour was midnight, so by making it two hours later, they could fool everybody.

He only needed to fool one very evil man.

"We have to get Bob," Brody said.

"Of course."

They ran down the hallway to the clinic, then down the stairs. Both men were sleeping. Brody put his hand over Bob's mouth and woke him up. The man's eyes opened.

Brody smiled and put a finger up to his lips. "We're getting out of here. Lean on us."

Bob nodded and swung his legs over the side of the cot. He could put a little weight on his leg, but it was slow going up the stairs. Brody looked at his watch. Less than two minutes remained.

Elle looked at Brody. "This is going to be hard. But we can do it. We have to."

"Honey, it's possible we might not have to walk out of the jungle. There could be a ride coming."

"What? Who?"

"Ethan and Mack. I gave Leo their numbers and told him to contact them immediately if something happened to us. He was to tell them to come at the Witching Hour, which is upon us. I was confident that with Leo's connections he could discover the location of the house. Of course," he said, not wanting to get her hopes up too high, "Leo may already be dead."

"He isn't. Jamas told me that he let him live."

Brody could feel his heart beat faster. He'd done all this on a wing and a prayer and it looked as if it might possibly happen.

"And I don't think Jamas ever found the plane. They were looking for it when they saw me in the jungle. I'm

sure everyone is still okay and probably has been rescued by now."

"We're next," he said optimistically.

They moved as quickly and as quietly as they could,
with Bob between him and Elle. When they got to the
front door, Brody reached for the handle. He whirled
when he heard a noise behind him.

It was Maria. Still in her white uniform. Her hair
was down and she looked younger.

"Stop," she said.

"Maria," Brody said, his tone soft. "You said that
you would neither help nor hamper."

"I know. I'm breaking my word." She pointed to the
door. "There's an alarm. If you open that door, it's going
to blare. You need to enter the code."

She walked over and punched in a number, then
opened the door. There was no noise.

"You helped Rita," Maria said. "Besides all the other
reasons I stay, I stay for her, to help her. And tonight,
you gave her back her life, her independence. I kept
watching you, sure that you were going to do something
to harm her, to send her into cardiac arrest or something to create a disturbance. I had told Jamas not to
let you operate, but he was so desperate for her to have
the surgery that he insisted, saying that I should signal
the minute I saw you do something questionable. But
you did everything perfectly. And you were so kind to
her. Thank you for that."

He grabbed Maria and hugged her. "Come with us."

She shook her head. "My home is here."

He hugged her again. "If you ever come to the States,
look me up. Brody Donovan. San Diego, California. I'll
hire you in a minute."

"Goodbye, Dr. Donovan," she said.

They left and Brody heard the door close behind them. Thirty steps later, they were in the trees, hidden by the trees.

"Okay?" he said, grabbing Elle's hand.

Okay? No. She was scared to death. It was dark, so terribly dark. But her heart felt lighter than it had in years. Brody loved her. Again. Still. It didn't matter which.

"I'm good," she said. Nothing was as frightening as being in Jamas's house, knowing that he intended to sell her to some monster. "What's next?"

"We wait."

"How long?"

"Not long, honey. If they're coming, it should be any minute."

"What if they don't?" she forced herself to ask. It was the middle of the night, and they were in a dark jungle, with no idea of what direction to go, with an injured man. Danger was everywhere.

"We're going to have to try to get as far away as we can. Jamas isn't going to be in the bathroom forever. He's going to check on his mother, see Felipe, and all hell is going to break loose.

"How are they going to find us?"

"I got another plan. I need my hand back for just a second."

She heard rustling. "What are you doing?"

"Getting ready," he said. "Bob, you hanging in there? How's the leg?"

"Grateful to still have it," he said. "Thank you."

"No pro—" Brody stopped midword.

Helicopter. He could hear it.

Closer now.

He pulled the trigger of the first pen flare, sending it up. It burned bright. Was it high enough? Damn these trees.

He sent up the second one.

Yes, the helicopter was closer.

He sent up the third and final flare and was practically blinded by the searchlight that hit him in the face.

"They came," he said. "I knew they would."

ETHAN MOORE LANDED the helicopter with a light touch. Mack McCann, gun strapped across his torso, had the side door open and put a hand out to help Elle. Bob was next and finally Brody.

Brody hugged Mack and gave a thumbs-up to Ethan. "Go," he yelled, knowing that neither man could hear him over the noise.

They understood. And the helicopter started to lift off.

Brody took one last look. He pointed to get Elle's attention. The front door was open and Jamas was standing in the doorway, holding his pants up with one hand. There was a look of pure astonishment on his face.

Brody grabbed Elle and kissed her soundly.

"We getting married," he said, enunciating carefully, to make sure she got it. "I can't wait to meet Mia."

Epilogue

It was a sunny, warm June day in the Colorado mountains. Crow Hollow was normally a quiet place, but today there was activity everywhere.

A triple wedding caused that kind of commotion.

At two in the afternoon, Ethan Moore married Chandler McCann. Then Hope Minnow became Mack McCann's wife. And finally, at a little after two-thirty in the afternoon, with a dark-eyed, dark-haired eleven-year-old serving as maid of honor, Elle Vollman *finally* married Brody Donovan.

* * * * *

Snow, sleigh bells and a hint of seduction

Find your perfect Christmas reads at
millsandboon.co.uk/Christmas

MILLS & BOON®

Why shop at millsandboon.co.uk?

Each year, thousands of romance readers find their perfect read at millsandboon.co.uk. That's because we're passionate about bringing you the very best romantic fiction. Here are some of the advantages of shopping at www.millsandboon.co.uk:

* **Get new books first**—you'll be able to buy your favourite books one month before they hit the shops

* **Get exclusive discounts**—you'll also be able to buy our specially created monthly collections, with up to 50% off the RRP

* **Find your favourite authors**—latest news, interviews and new releases for all your favourite authors and series on our website, plus ideas for what to try next

* **Join in**—once you've bought your favourite books, don't forget to register with us to rate, review and join in the discussions

Visit **www.millsandboon.co.uk**
for all this and more today!